The Last American

The Last American

Steven Burgauer

Northwest Publishing, Inc.
Salt Lake City, Utah

The Last American

For information address: Northwest Publishing, Inc.
6906 South 300 West, Salt Lake City, Utah 84047
WC 3.12.96 /ASJ

PRINTING HISTORY
First Printing 1996

ISBN: 0-7610-0438-6

NPI books are published by Northwest Publishing, Incorporated,
6906 South 300 West, Salt Lake City, Utah 84047.
The name "NPI" and the "NPI" logo are trademarks belonging to
Northwest Publishing, Incorporated.

PRINTED IN THE UNITED STATES OF AMERICA.
10 9 8 7 6 5 4 3 2

To Opa Siggy,
who knew enough to get his family out
in time when it really mattered.

One
Traitor

Fall 2398
The East China Sea

Even as the moon blinked in and out from behind the bank of threatening clouds, the dark-haired saboteur crept stealthily along the gunnels lining the rolling deck of the sleek ship. He was not a big man, and he wore a close-fitting wet suit beneath his poncho to protect his scrawny body from the elements. A six-inch-long, stainless steel diver's knife hung from a sheath at his webbed belt. On his back he shouldered a leather rucksack, and in his sweaty palms he gripped a long-range locator equipped with a waterproof, magnetic casing. As the frigate *Intrepid* lurched from side to side in the developing storm, the cloaked figure hugged the wave-splashed deck searching for precisely the right spot to slap the cold, platinum-colored device onto the ship's steel bulwarks. Not only would the locator's radio-signal broadcast the vessel's precise longitude and latitude to the enemy's global positioning satellite twenty-three thousand miles up, by blanketing the area with resonating emissions, it would also render useless much of the fleet's advanced-warning radar.

Camouflaged by the ebony shadows of the forwardmost lifeboat, the Lieutenant could barely make out the running lights of the lead missile-boat in the distance off the *Intrepid*'s starboard bow. Plying the choppy waters in their wake lay the battle cruisers, the airchop carriers, and the rest of the fleet. Overhead, the eye-in-the-sky ramjets maintained their vigilant watch over the strike-zone, their sensors scanning the coastline for any hint of enemy activity. Every five seconds they would complete a sweep, their ultra-sensitive monitors programmed to pick up any telltale heat plumes or heightened radio traffic or ominous troop movements. Together with dozens of other naval and airforce units spread out along the coast, the U.S. flotilla was moving to enforce the President's blockade of the Chinese mainland. By interrupting the flow of essential matériel out of certain key harbors dotting the eastern seaboard, the President hoped to finally bring Overlord Ling Tsui to heel, a project which was long overdue. Considering how, ever since his father's horrible death thirty years ago, Overlord Ling had been engaged in a desperate, nonstop battle to consolidate his power over his forebear's empire, now that he had decisively snuffed out the last of the opposition forces, Ling was hellbent on reasserting Chinese hegemony over the Pacific—a goal President McIntyre was determined to thwart.

As the saboteur paused to let the uncooperative moon slide behind yet another cloud, his stoney face was resolute.

Surely, after all the terrible wrongs he had perpetrated, he should have felt some remorse, but he did not. To the contrary, he seemed unfazed that his treasonous act would soon cost the lives of so many of his countrymen; that before the night was over, thousands of American sailors would be resting lifelessly on the bottom of the bay; that what he was doing might change the course of the war. Yet, instead of being filled with guilt, he was filled with pride. Thus far, he had executed his heinous plan with military precision: Not only had he already stuffed his rucksack full with several days' worth of provisions he had stolen from the galley and with an inflatable life raft he had taken from the emergency rescue kit, after slitting the throat of the ship's signal officer, he had disabled the *Intrepid*'s comm as well. The traitor knew that once he activated the enigmatic locator its 30 megahertz radio beacon would allow the wing of Chinese airchops lying in wait off the Asian coast to hone in on and sink the unprepared American fleet. By then, if everything had gone according to plan, he would be overboard in his inflatable dinghy, paddling for his life.

Crouching now in the shadows, he imagined what the high-speed attack of the squadron of enemy airchops would be like, how the killing machines would hug the water as they approached, how their short, stubby wings would glisten in the rain, how their overhead rotors would slice effortlessly through the night air. Armed with dozens of Phalanx armor-piercing projectiles, each possessing multiple honing capabilities, these highly-maneuverable, flying war-wagons would leave behind nothing but twisted metal and charred bones as they bushwhacked the unsuspecting contingent of American ships. Of course, it wouldn't be as one-sided as all that. After all, every single one of the American battle cruisers was equipped with auto-tracking deckguns which were quite effective at taking out airchops, not to mention robotic gatling guns capable of knocking down any Phalanx projectiles they picked up on radar, yet the technological enhancements the Chinese had developed for their warbirds made them nearly invincible. Their exhausts cooled by lightweight, superconducting magnets affixed to their tails and their bodies built from stealthy alloys, the incoming airchops would be cold to infrared and transparent to radar. Though a thick swarm of stealthy airchops advancing from a single direction would show up easily on radar as a black hole in the sky, in small scattered groups of two or three, the warbirds would be able to approach to within several hundred yards of the fleet without being detected—and then only visually.

When the bow of the *Intrepid* was suddenly bathed in the glow of a searchlight, the turncoat put the upcoming attack out of his mind, instinctively pressing himself flat against the slippery deck. Though he had rehearsed this particular maneuver in his head a dozen times before, he had nearly forgotten that with tensions between their two countries so high, Captain Daniels would order a sweep of the fo'c'sle every three minutes. Another lapse of memory like this one would surely cost him his life.

As he lay there immobilized on the cold metal waiting for the powerful beam to swing past, the traitor snickered, knowing full well that even if he were to be apprehended at this late date, it wouldn't change the outcome of today's events one little bit—the fleet would still be sunk and his debt to Overlord Ling would still be paid. Indeed, considering the many nefarious acts he had committed these past one and a half years, it might even have been a relief of sorts if he was to be arrested now and thrown in the brig. Not only had he polluted his body with all manner of debilitating narcotics, but by stealing the secret code book from his grandfather's safe, the Lieutenant had jeopardized the old man's political legacy and sold out his own country in a single despicable stroke of cowardice.

As the counterclockwise sweep of the searchlight swung swiftly away from the poncho-clad man, he got back into a crouch and slid silently forward towards the bow of the frigate, his body advancing over the deck like a sure-footed panther. He hadn't covered more than a couple of meters, however, when his cat-like eyes spied the glint of an automatic weapon in the spackled moonlight ahead of him. Although the fowling piece measured barely 14 inches overall, he immediately recognized it as a mini-Uzi, the standard weapon of issue for American servicemen, a "little monster" in sailor jargon. Unaware that the bridge had posted a sentry on the forecastle, the Lieutenant had practically stumbled over the poor fellow in his haste.

"Who goes there?" the beefy sailor asked in a startled tone, holding tight to his safety-tether as a rush of waves crashed against the hull of the *Intrepid*, rocking her from left to right. Dressed as he was, it was difficult to make out his features, but the man had a pair of nightvision goggles perched on his forehead.

Though the saboteur moved slowly out into the open from the shadows where he had been hiding, he didn't utter a single word to his fellow officer. Yet, in spite of his outward silence, the Lieutenant had already made up his mind what he had to do. Edging nearer to the sentry in a nonthreatening, almost chummy kind of way so as not to spook the man, the Lieutenant smiled and extended his fingers out in front of him as if he meant to shake his hand.

"Oh, it's you, Lieutenant," the watchman acknowledged, issuing a sigh of relief as he recognized the cloaked figure standing before him. "Pardon my surprise, but I didn't remember seeing your name on the duty roster. Are you on duty tonight?"

Still silent, the Lieutenant moved a step closer to the newcomer, his eyes fixed on the barrel of the man's gun. When held in the hands of an experienced marksman, a mini-Uzi was an awesome killing machine.

"What's that you've got there?" the night-watchman asked, pointing with the muzzle of his Uzi at the frisbee-sized locator clenched in the Lieutenant's hand.

Knowing full well that even the most ill-informed crewmember would immediately recognize the device he was holding for what it was, the Lieutenant hurriedly slid his palm around the edge of the apparatus until his fingers made contact with the cold, metal switch on the rim of the housing. All his efforts, all his planning, all his treachery would be for naught if the locator were confiscated from him before being activated. Silently clicking the switch into the "on" position, he instantly felt the reassuring throb of the machine as it began pulsing out its deadly message to the anxiously waiting wing of enemy airchops.

"I say again," the guard repeated, lowering his stubby weapon towards the Lieutenant in a menacing fashion, "what have you there?"

Realizing that he had no choice now but to take the sentry out, the saboteur flung the magnetized locator towards the bulkhead on his right even as he lurched his scrawny body adroitly to the left. Pivoting to one side, he swept his right foot between the guard's two ankles, knocking the unprepared man to the ground. As the sentry's weapon clanked noisily against the deck, the saboteur popped his stainless steel blade from its holster at his belt and drove the razor sharp cutting tool deep into the man's gut. Twisting it viciously inside the sailor's abdomen, the assailant grunted with satisfaction as his adversary's blood spurted from the lethal wound, filling his hand with warm spillage.

Keenly aware that it would only be a matter of minutes

now before the Overlord's airchops locked onto the locator's radio beacon and commenced their attack, the Lieutenant vaulted over the side of the ship, descending hand-over-hand down the cable towards the churning sea below. Even though his progress was burdened by the weight of the rucksack strapped to his back, he couldn't afford to jettison it—what was inside was his only hope for escape!

By the time the klaxon sounded from the battle-deck, signaling that one of the bridge crew had a visual on the lead airchop, the Lieutenant was already hunkered down in the inflatable dinghy he had been carrying with him, paddling like mad to put some distance between himself and the *Intrepid* before it was hit. On the horizon, he could see a menacing blotch swelling ever larger against the sky as the vanguard pair of assault-airchops approached the flotilla at high speed.

"Battle stations! Battle stations!" the P.A. system barked, sending legions of sailors scurrying to their posts on Captain Daniels' command. But with the ship's comm smashed and the signal-officer not responding to his beeper, the Captain could not put into service any of the standard methods for warning the other boats of the mortal danger which lay just ahead of them in the night. Nevertheless, Daniels had a responsibility, and if anything separated a Captain from a member of his crew, it was his ingenuity, his ability to improvise, his aptitude for turning a hopeless situation into a fighting chance for life. Understanding how critically vital the next few minutes might be, Daniels settled on the unusual tactic of using his boat as a decoy to lure the airchops away from the main battle group. Thinking that perhaps the *Intrepid* could outrun them, he gave the order to engage the foils.

The *Intrepid* was a frigate, a vessel uniquely suited for advance scouting. When its hydrofoil wings were extended and its diesel turbines throttled up to full power, it was capable of scooting across the surface at speeds approaching that of an airchop. Unlike a double-hulled destroyer, however, it was not heavily-armored nor was it able to withstand a direct hit from a weapon as lethal as a Phalanx. Still, he had to try.

"They were just sitting there waiting for us!" Captain Daniels rasped, his teeth clenched and his jaw set. Even as he ordered the *Intrepid* through a series of high-speed, zig-zag maneuvers intended to foil the attacker's air-to-ship missiles from locking-on to her, his face looked grim as he calculated the odds. Though much of the *Intrepid*'s hull was constructed from high-tech polymers specifically designed to avoid detection by a magnetically-honing torpedo, many of the bulkheads and most of the deck were still made of metal. It couldn't be helped: steel was strong, it didn't burn, and it was eminently cheap. Nervously rapping his fingers against the nav-console as the frigate swerved frantically from side to side, he instinctively ducked when a squadron of enemy airchops roared overhead at low altitude.

Even though the traitorous truth was self-evident, Daniels quizzed his helmsman rhetorically. "How could they have known our position?" Off the starboard bow, the lead missile-boat could be seen launching its first set of countermeasures against the intruders. "And why didn't the signal officer pick them up on his scope?"

The helmsman replied with a shrug.

Turning to the sailor standing directly behind him, a sailor who had been his personal aide since his first days at Annapolis, the Captain ordered, "Ensign, I want you to go down to the signal officer's quarters right away. Find out what the *hell* is happening down there!"

"Aye, aye," the Ensign answered bravely. As he scurried away, vacating his usual spot at the Captain's side, the

Ensign gathered from the worried look on his mentor's face that this would be the very last order his Captain would ever give him. There would be no opportunity for final farewells; if the ship and its crew were to be saved, they would each have to carry out their duties without flinching.

Desperate now, yet hoping to gain the attention of the fleet without needlessly drawing enemy fire, Captain Daniels ordered a megaflare launched into the moonlit shroud. Though this offensive weapon would have limited useful-ness against the attacking airchops, the baseball-sized globe filled with lyddite-gel would unquestionably serve to focus the flotilla'a eyes on the sky in a way no other means at his disposal possibly could. Upon being hurled into the air, the megaflare would shatter into a thousand fluorescent frag-ments, illuminating not only the battleground, but blinding a few unlucky airchop pilots in the process as well.

Within moments of the globe being lofted skyward, the night was as bright as noon. But much to the Captain's chagrin, two of the incoming airchops immediately broke formation and turned to confront the newly illuminated frigate. From the battle-deck of the *Intrepid*, machine-gun fire pounded into the sky, strafing one of the stubby-winged fighters and driving it flaming into the sea. Yet even as the rat-a-tat of gunfire filled his ears and the downing of the airchop sparked a ray of hope in his heart, Daniels sensed the effort would prove futile. Indeed, as the second airchop closed in on their position, he spied the telltale flash of ignition as the fighter dropped a Phalanx torpedo from its metal undercarriage and into the black water below. Driven by the airchop's engines, a magneto-powered electronic can-non gave the 205mm self-propelled shell its initial pulse. But unlike a conventional torpedo, the Phalanx could lift itself out of the sea once again if its target was skimming the surface on hydrofoil wings as the *Intrepid* was.

As the helmsman swung the wheel hard to port to avoid the inevitable collision, Daniels shouted into the P.A., "Deploy primary countermeasures! I repeat, deploy primary countermeasures!"

Although the Captain mouthed the authoritative sounding words into the mike, he suspected that launching a battery of c.m.'s would prove to be an empty gesture. By now the jet-propelled torpedo would have already locked onto the composite hull of his ship, and even with the *Intrepid*'s great speed, he figured she couldn't outrun a Phalanx at this close of a range. Praying that death would come quickly, that his men would not be made to suffer, that he had bought enough time for the fleet to retaliate, Daniels girded his loins for the unavoidable impact.

"Cap'n," the gunner's mate reported, "Sparky confirms 'pedo lock."

"Aye," the Captain acknowledged calmly. "Drop secondary countermeasures. Helmsman, sound the alarm. Prepare to be hit! I repeat, sound the alarm. Prepare to be hit!"

Grabbing the rail as the craft lurched to the left for perhaps the last time, the Captain ticked off the seconds until the next report. Though the fate of his own ship was sealed, launching the megaflare had had its intended effect. Within moments of it reaching its apogee, the battle cruisers had begun their counterattack, launching a wave of nuclear tipped missiles against strategic targets on the Chinese mainland and catapulting their own wing of airchops into the fray.

"Sorry, sir, radar shows secondary c.m.'s didn't take," the reconn officer reported stoically. "Sparky says 'pedo has reacquired signal."

"How long?" Daniels asked, knowing it was over.

"Eight. Maybe ten. Seconds."

"Give the order," the Captain snapped even as the

helmsman took the boat through yet another set of high-speed zig-zags.

"Yes, sir," the reconn officer nodded as he punched the button on the P.A. "All hands on deck! Abandon ship! I repeat: By Captain's order, all hands on deck! Abandon..."

As the Phalanx projectile slammed into the *Intrepid*'s hull with the force of a one megaton bomb, the reconn officer's announcement was interrupted by a blinding flash and a deafening detonation. Only moments passed before all evidence of the ship ever having been there had disappeared beneath the waves.

Regrettably, the tragedy didn't end with just the sinking of that one swiftly moving frigate. As the long night wore on, and as wave after wave of Chinese warbirds swooped down upon the flotilla from the muddy sky, the carnage became a travesty. It wasn't so much that the American Navymen were stupid or even that they had been taken by surprise, it was more that they had sorely underestimated the Chinese firepower. In sum total, an attack force of twenty-eight hundred airchops was mounted against the U.S. blockade, more than in any other sea battle to date. And though the U.S. forces had initially been caught off guard by the offensive, as the situation deteriorated overnight, they actually became progressively more adept at knocking the enemy warbirds from the sky. Indeed, the airchop losses were so horrendous that at one point, just before dawn, it looked as if the Americans might repel the onslaught. But it wasn't to be. By the time the sun had risen above the horizon that morning, it was clear that the bulk of the U.S. fleet had been pounded into oblivion, totally decimated by the attack.

Though some of the sailors had managed to jump clear of their ships into the seething water only to be eventually eaten by sharks, most of them died at their posts. Thousands of American lives were lost that night, and all because of one arrogant, self-serving traitor.

Having had a headstart, the Lieutenant was able to survive the attack, but just barely. By the time he washed up on shore—his arms locked around a hunk of wood just buoyant enough to keep him afloat, his dinghy long ago punctured by a stray bullet—he had endured so many days at sea that he was free of the blue-devil addiction which had led him down this destructive path to begin with. Unfortunately, he would never be able to shake off his addiction to money so easily. In the Lieutenant, Overlord Ling had bought himself a faithful, if not cunning, servant for life.

Part I

Two
Camp Na-Cha-Tan

Sixteen Months Earlier
Northern Wisconsin

Although the two young men had been hiking in silence for nearly an hour, the paucity of words which passed between them was not to be taken as a sign that they were angry with one another or that they had had a nasty argument. To the contrary, their lack of conversation was more out of respect to the wonderful weather than to anything else. Though a sign, perhaps, of contentment or of pleasure, their silence was certainly not born out of apathy or irritation. Each fellow knew, even without vocalizing the sentiment, that it was simply much too good of a day to risk ruining it with mere words or idle chatter. The sun, the temperature, the clouds, the breeze—all were just right. And so, seemingly without a care in the world, the two young men glided along the narrow trail without exchanging a word.

The taller fellow led the way through the forest, his unruly mop of brown hair shifting with each step he took. Not unlike a great many youths his age, Samuel Matthews had broad shoulders, narrow hips, and a pair of long muscular legs peeking out from beneath his khaki-colored Scout shorts. Behind him, struggling to keep up, was his best friend Siegfried Tonnelli, though he preferred for his buddies to call him Ziggy. Whereas Sam was tall and lanky, Ziggy was short and squat. And where Sam was clearly of northern European stock, Ziggy's roots were obviously from somewhere in the Mediterranean—Sicily if his stories were to be believed.

After all the rain they had endured these past three days, this morning's cool, crisp air was a welcome change. Nevertheless, as they set out upon the trail following breakfast, Sam had calmly pointed out to his exuberant friend how unwise it was for them to get their hopes up too soon for a hot, dry summer. Invariably, spring in northern Wisconsin came much too late, and invariably, it lingered into June far too long. All too often, the onset of summer was a cold and muddy affair punctuated, at best, by only one or two splendid days like today.

Keeping the weather's unpredictability in mind, Sam and Ziggy had pestered Camp Director Tovas over pancakes this morning to give the entire camp staff a few hours' leave. Though they didn't have to remind their boss how hard they all had been working these past three days, they did have to make the point that it would be a crime if he forced the staff to stay at it on a day such as this one. To use Ziggy's words, there would be mutiny for sure. But despite the threat,

Director Tovas would not be intimidated. With a long list of work projects yet to be completed, and with opening day less than two weeks away, he needed everyone at their posts. In fact, he issued a threat of his own, suggesting that if they didn't like their current work assignments, they could always clean latrines instead. But not to be outdone, Sam and Ziggy raised the ante, recruiting three other staffmen to help in their enterprise. After chipping away at Tovas for another fifteen minutes, he finally relented.

Flush with success, Ziggy bounded out of the messhall with a hoot and a holler, racing halfway up the trail ahead of Sam before Tovas shouted after them both to be sure and be back before noon. As was so often the case with Ziggy, his natural enthusiasm for life had to be tempered with a dose of reality: with so much work yet to be done, Director Tovas couldn't afford to give them more than the morning off. Still, that was time enough for the two boys to explore an area of Na-Cha-Tan they had never visited before, an area Tovas had told them about just three evenings ago as they made their way around the lake to their cabin that first night.

The drive up from the city to the North Woods had taken seven hours, and Sam, for one, had fallen asleep long ago, his body lulled into unconsciousness by the drone of the gcar's tires against the pavement. Yet, the instant Camp Director Tovas' gcar began the torturous trip down the gravel road into camp, bumping and lurching with each pothole it struck, Sam was jerked awake just in time to swallow that first breath of pristine air. Though it was already dusk when they arrived, he could still see the silhouette of the primeval forest glowing in the evening sun. Letting his imagination get the better of him, Sam fantasized that he saw the Lord's reflection in the still waters of Lake Na-Cha-Tan. If indeed there was a God, after seeing what man had done to his cities—the squalor, the crime, the desperation—surely, He would have given up on them by now and ventured out into the wilderness instead. Surely, Na-Cha-Tan was the sort of place only a God could build, and surely, having gone to this much trouble, He would have chosen to dwell here until the end of His days.

"Heh, boys, heads up," Tovas had yelped in his tinny voice as the gcar sputtered to a halt before their shuttered cabin. Not many vehicles circa 2397 could long stand the punishment of these prehistoric roads, and inasmuch as Director Tovas' gcar wasn't quite a prize to begin with, it sounded perilously close to gasping its last breath as he turned the motor off.

To someone accustomed to the creature comforts of a modern, middle-class Farmington home, the cabin which now confronted them might have appeared dreadful, even boorish. But to *these* boys, their two-room, wood-frame haunt for the summer was heaven on earth. Nestled by the lake in a stand of virgin pine, their secluded hideaway afforded them a measure of privacy uncommon in their century.

To begin with, the structure was elevated off the ground on a stack of cinder-blocks. This unusual arrangement made sense for two very good reasons: Not only did being propped up off the soil discourage animals from hibernating inside during the winter months, it also prevented the building itself from washing out and rolling over during the spring melt.

The place had six windows, each dressed with a colonial-style wood shutter, plus a tattered screen door which, riding on a spring-loaded cylinder, slammed automatically shut with a bang each time someone crossed the threshold. Inside, it was furnished spartanly with nothing more than an aged oak desk, a deteriorating table lamp, four lumpy cots, and two time-worn clothes cabinets. The interior walls were splattered not only with graffiti, they were also punctuated here and there with holes and with other abuses they had suffered in the long course of the dwelling's many years of service to the camp.

Yet despite these obvious shortcomings, the four Scouts had eagerly bounced out of Tovas' gcar that night and begun unloading their gear. Along with Sam and Ziggy, the passengers included Sam's older brother Lester and their overweight friend Jim Carr, nicknamed Gcar, to reflect his awesome size.

"We're here!" Tovas had announced. It was clear from his expression that he was equally as excited as his charges to have finally arrived. Unfolding himself from the driver's seat and stretching his long arms and spindly legs in the cool evening breeze, Tovas twisted his face into a look of disgust and surprise as the first mosquito of the season got him through his shirt. To hear him curse one would have thought he had never been bitten before, and to watch the tall man squirm with discomfort was a comical sight indeed.

It was a curious fact of nature that the very first mosquito prick of the season had to be on the back, directly between the victim's shoulder blades, at the one spot where it was physically impossible for even the longest arm to reach. And make no mistake about it, Director Tovas had long arms! He stood well over six feet tall, had thinning black hair, and a stupid-looking moustache. His slenderness bordered on gaunt. His friends addressed him as "Stovepipe," a reference Sam didn't quite understand, but applied nonetheless.

Stovepipe hadn't been alone, however, in suffering the indignity of being bitten. Within moments, the entire group was swamped by a horde of blood-thirsty mosquitoes—Na-Cha-Tan bombers in the campers' lexicon. By summer's end the bites of these two-winged irritants wouldn't faze them a bit, but that night—before their bodies had had a chance to build up an immunity to the bothersome toxin of these winged warriors—the itches accompanying the first wallops were excruciating.

"Home again," Sam had murmured happily as he did his best to ignore the buzzing invaders. There was something about Na-Cha-Tan which made each return especially satisfying. As he stood there reveling in his freedom, he tried to put his finger on just what that something was. A spell, perhaps? A bit of black magic left behind by some tribal medicine man? Or was it something less mystical, something more tangible? Perhaps the incongruity of discovering a clump of paper-birch in amongst a stand of towering pines? The rustle of the wind coursing through the quaking aspens? The unchanging hue of the spring-fed lake? The sandy hills echoing with the sounds of laughing scouts?

"Home again," Sam repeated. Only this time, as the setting sun flashed patches of brilliant orange against the pale blue sky, there was more reverence in his voice. "Land's-sakes but the lake looks inviting tonight."

Nodding his head as he frantically searched the ground beneath his feet for a twig long enough to reach the mosquito bite lodged in the center of his back, Stovepipe said, "Listen, Sam, if you think *this* lake is pretty, when I give you some time off later in the week, you should pay a visit to our very own bog!" Scratching furiously at the swelling between his shoulder blades, he added, "The bog is on the shores of a spot called Muskrat Lake, only about an hour's walk from the East Camp messhall." As Stovepipe proceeded to give them directions on how to get to Muskrat Lake, the look of relief on his face suggested that, for the time being anyway, he had finally scratched the welt long enough to dull the itch.

With Stovepipe's hastily drawn map in hand, Sam and Ziggy had set out this morning after breakfast hiking south along the shore of Lake Na-Cha-Tan, and then onto an obscure trail which veered due east for several miles before winding its way south again. Trekking up one hill and down the next, they greedily drank in the panorama and hungrily gulped down the sweet smelling air as they passed first through the Dust Bowl and then across Grasshopper Valley, two landmarks aptly named for what was found there in abundance.

Grasshopper Valley was one of those enormous pockets scooped out of the bedrock by some primordial glacier as it swept down from Canada and across the state of Wisconsin during the last ice age. The mammoth depression was easily six football fields in length and no less than one in width. By the time August arrived, the valley would be teeming with tens of thousands of flitting green grasshoppers as they spent the dying days of summer jumping from one blade of prairie grass to the next in a field of gold which would by then stand waist high. But this early in June, the valley was just a muddy hole, and had there been an alternate route around it, they would have avoided the soggy vale at all costs. Instead, they tromped across the swampy mess as quickly as they could, spending the better part of the next ten minutes scraping mounds of mud off their hiking boots.

After completing the arduous climb out the opposite end of Grasshopper Valley and after rounding a huge bend which turned them west once more, the trail led them into a series of precipitous switchbacks which descended into another depression known to the loggers as Little Grass-hopper Valley. It was at this point that the tenor of the day changed abruptly.

They had come about halfway down the steep incline when Sam stopped dead in his tracks, cupping his hand behind his ear and peering off into the distance as if something were there. Following him close behind, Ziggy unintentionally slammed into his buddy's rear, a grunt issuing from his mouth with the impact.

"What is it?" the shorter boy asked, embarrassed by the collision.

"I don't know," Sam replied, a look of deep concern on his face. "I thought I heard a strange noise."

"What do you mean 'strange'?" Tonnelli asked.

"I don't know—mechanical sounding maybe."

"What, like an engine?" Ziggy questioned, twisting his face into a frown. For some reason, his swarthy skin seemed paler than usual.

"Yea," Sam mumbled, "something like that."

"Forget about it," Ziggy chided. "What you heard was probably a chain-saw. There are dozens of logging roads crisscrossing all through these woods and what you heard was probably some paper company out cutting pulpwood."

Waiting a moment to see if the unusual swishing noise started up again, Sam confessed, "You must be right, only it didn't sound like a chain-saw. It had more of a high-pitched whine to it."

"Whine?" Ziggy teased disrespectfully. "Now you're beginning to sound like our good buddy Fat Jim. Gcar is always imagining boogey-men and such."

Breaking into laughter over the antics of their heavyset chum, the two of them set off again along the trail, only this time there was a little less deliberation in their step than there had been before. They hadn't gone far, however, when Sam stopped short for the second time, throwing his arm out in front of his friend as if it were a roadblock. "There! Do you hear it now?" he asked, the pitch in his voice rising.

"Sure do," Ziggy acknowledged, cocking his head in that direction and assuming the pose of a bird dog. "It's coming from that clearing up ahead."

Brimming with curiosity, Sam and his sidekick raced

through the forest and down the remaining switchbacks to the open area just below them. Bursting into Little Grass-hopper Valley just in time to be pelted in the face with clumps of mud and sod, they were witness to a great machine lifting off the ground in a rush of swirling air. Only, blinded by the flying debris, they couldn't make out the markings on its tail. Nevertheless, there was no denying that what had taken off in front of them as they broke into the clearing was a military style airchop!

Three
Mogen David

"Land's-sakes!" Sam exclaimed, brushing the wet dirt from his clothes. "What in the world was that thing doing out here?"

"Beats me," Ziggy replied, following the path of the craft with his eyes. "But I'll bet we weren't supposed to see it."

By this time, the airchop had lifted at least a thousand feet into the air and was moving away from them at high speed. It was headed north—towards Ontario.

"We've got to tell Tovas," Sam insisted.

"Tell him what?" Ziggy countered, shrugging his shoulders and rolling his hands palm up in a questioning manner. "That we saw a UFO? He'll laugh us both right out of camp. Anyhow, it was probably just some cadet from the National

Guard base over at Tomahawk showing his girlfriend one of their hot new airchops; the two of them probably got horny and decided to set down here to do something about it."

"Get serious, this is camp property for heaven's sake! Maybe we ought to try and find some evidence to prove that it was here," Sam suggested soberly. "Hurry, let's check it out."

Though his heart wasn't in it, Ziggy reluctantly tailed behind Sam as the taller boy edged into the clearing to the approximate spot where the airchop had been parked. Except for a couple of depressions in the mud carved out by the wheels, the area was clean.

"Curious," Sam commented, stooping down to examine the landing site. Pulling out the tiny note pad he always carried with him in his pocket, he said, "Lookie, here, Ziggy. Footprints!"

Joining Sam where he was kneeling pencil in hand, Ziggy crouched down alongside his friend to inspect the impressions of several boot marks in the sandy soil. One imprint was particularly clear, and Sam hastily made a sketch on his pad of the diamond-shaped cross-hatching which ran the full length of the sole. Though it wasn't complete, in the center of the sole was a pattern which resembled that of a six-pointed star.

"What do we do now?" Ziggy petitioned, looking nervously about as if they had broken a law.

"I say we show this to Tovas."

"And get some poor soldier in trouble for screwing his girlfriend on his day off? Forget it, Sam. Let's just finish our hike and get back to camp before we miss lunch."

Though he harbored his doubts about this course of action, Sam nodded his head in agreement and permitted Ziggy to lead the way across Little Grasshopper Valley and up the slope on the far side of the hollow. If Stovepipe's crude map was even close to scale, it couldn't be more than a few hundred yards to their destination.

As the two young men climbed the rutted path back into the dense woods, Sam reckoned that not only should he inform Director Tovas of what they had seen, the military authorities should be notified as well. But before he could decide on just who would be the right person to tell, his heart stopped pumping again as he and Ziggy heard two men's voices echoing out from the forest ahead of them. Thinking that they were on to something big now, Sam and Ziggy sprinted silently to within earshot of the pair. Without exchanging a word, they crept closer and closer, but before they could even hear what was being said, Ziggy carelessly stepped on a dry branch, breaking it in two with his boot.

As if on cue, the two unknown figures grew hushed, and while Sam and Ziggy debated whether to freeze or whether to flee, one of the men shouted in their direction, "Who goes there?"

Instantly recognizing the voice as that of his brother, Sam swore under his breath, "Damn! It's Lester!"

"What's *he* doing way out here?" Ziggy blurted incredulously. "And who the hell is that with him?"

"Let's find out," Sam retorted, leading the way.

"Yoah," Sam shouted back. "That you, Lester?"

"Little brother, you scared the shit out of me," Lester exclaimed as he and his swarthy companion approached. "What are you doing, sneaking around the woods like that?"

"I might ask you the very same thing," Sam shot back defiantly. Though the two brothers tolerated one another well enough, they were not particularly close. Ziggy, for one, didn't like Lester at all, referring to him constantly as a velcroid, a lowlife who was always trying to stick close to anyone of importance.

"I heard Tovas' story about Muskrat Lake same as you," Lester returned, his mind racing to come up with a plausible explanation. "Only me and Abe got a little bit earlier start than you two slowpokes."

"Did you hear that thing?" Sam cross-examined, wiping his still dirty face clean with a handkerchief.

"Yeah," Lester stuttered, looking nervously over his shoulder at his cohort. "Sounded like a truck or something. Me and Abe didn't actually see it."

"That wasn't no truck," Ziggy interjected passionately. "We saw it—it looked like one of those newfangled airchops."

"Out *here*?" Lester squawked, turning white at the revelation. "Not possible."

"Why don't you introduce us to your friend?" Sam requested, changing the flow of their conversation. Even as he spoke he gestured towards the good-looking man standing alongside his brother on the trail.

"My apologies. This is Abe Levinson. From Israel."

"Oh, yes," Sam acknowledged, extending his hand in welcome. "I had heard you would be joining us for the summer," he added, reviewing in his mind what little he had already been told about the outsider.

Abe was a personable and pleasant-looking 18 year-old from the Kingdom of Israel. He had been late arriving in camp because the suborb out of Damascus had been delayed by yet another of the frequent uprisings in that Israeli province. That he had found his way to Na-Cha-Tan at all was purely Lester's doing. Lester had taken his last semester of school in Israel as part of a foreign exchange program organized by their grandfather, the senior Senator from the state of Missouri and the chairman of the Senate's powerful Military Oversight Committee. And with his grandfather's help, Lester had even arranged for Abe to obtain a work visa for the summer. Abe would function both as the camp's Rabbi—conducting Friday evening services for the many campers of the Jewish faith—and as Na-Cha-Tan's assistant Nature Director. At the end of the summer, he would be remaining here in the U.S. for a semester with a reciprocating foreign exchange family. As for Lester, at summer's end, *he* would be attending the Naval Academy at Alameda, again courtesy of their grandfather. Though the one year program at Alameda was not nearly as prestigious as the topflight school at Annapolis, it was the best the Senator could do for Lester given his grades.

Although Sam found it peculiar that Abe and Lester should have been able to make it all the way out here in advance of him and Ziggy, he put his questions aside for the moment, trying instead to get better acquainted with the newcomer. It was a little bit awkward at first, made even more so by Abe's tenuous hold on the English language, but while the four young men resumed what remained of their journey towards Muskrat Lake, he worked on it as best he could. Although Abe was well-versed in the textbook version of English, as so many teachers and parents are often quick to point out to the children, the spoken tongue is rife with idioms, incomprehensible expressions which made Abe's job of communicating just that much harder. Still, getting to know one another was an interesting study in contrasts. While somewhat similar in temperament and in intellect, Sam soon discovered that their philosophies on life were diametrically opposed.

To Abe, who had his hot, dry, and sandy homeland as his only point of reference, the shaded coolness of the climax forest they were hiking through was unimaginable. Not only was the towering height of the statuesque oaks beyond his comprehension, the grandeur of the unspoiled wilderness astonished him. Much to Sam's delight, Abe "oohed" and "aahed" at the scenery time and time again as they continued along the path to the base of the next hill.

There, the trail all of a sudden turned rather soggy. Although there was no visible signs of running water, it was as if the ground had become mysteriously waterlogged by an underground spring or a hidden brook. Not that it mattered a great deal to any of them—it was after all a bright and sunny day—but before long their socks and their footgear were sopping wet. Though he and the others pressed on, Sam suspected that an hour's hike back to camp in damp boots would be no pleasure tour.

After another twenty yards, though, the wet path broke into a clearing where it abruptly ended altogether. Yet, instead of being disappointed by this turn of events, the four men were elated. Much to their amazement, they found themselves standing at the perimeter of a spongy bog which ringed a small but nearly circular lake along its entire circumference. Not only that, the bog itself was ringed by a forest of blue-spruce so virgin, so untouched by human hands, that Sam openly wondered whether they were as near to Camp Na-Cha-Tan as he instinctively knew they were. It was hard to believe that the crushing weight of civilization had somehow avoided brushing against this little corner of the world. After all, with a billion and a half Americans crowding the once empty continent, there were precious few places where one could go and be left alone with his thoughts.

"Muskrat Lake!" Sam clamored, wriggling his toes inside his damp socks. "Stovepipe was right after all!"

Even as he spoke, Abe knelt down to study this span of vegetation, this thing called a bog. It was a tightly-woven mass of floating grasses, colorful pitcher plants, and assorted reeds. This buoyant stretch of greenery, which measured perhaps forty yards from the fringe of the forest to the edge of the water, was thick enough to support their weight, yet it bounced and undulated eerily as they advanced cautiously across it, their feet getting wetter with each step. As they pushed forward, they could "feel" the lake pulsating beneath their feet.

Being a naturalist by trade, Abe was eager to explore this newly-discovered playground, but Sam was quick to restrain the foreigner's enthusiasm. While crossing the wet, tangled surface might have admittedly been seen as fun, there was a certain element of danger here as well. Already they were sinking up to their ankles in water seeping to the surface between the reeds. Like thin ice on a half-frozen lake, a man could break through the delicate skin of the bog at any time, perhaps drowning himself in the process. Indeed, when Abe's boot suddenly punched through the mat, the Israeli came to an abrupt halt, backing off from the rim a few feet. Hands in his pockets, Abe stood there fidgeting; he had wanted so badly to dip his hands into that water, to scoop out a mouthful, to taste its virgin blueness. It disappointed him no end to have to stop well short of the basin's edge with nothing but wet feet to show for his trouble.

Equally impressed by this wondrous creation of Mother Nature, Sam marveled at a sight he was unlikely to soon forget. The color of Muskrat Lake was unlike that of any pond or any sea or any lake he had ever encountered in his eighteen years. It was of such a peculiar, oxidized shade of copper-blue, Sam imagined that God might have mixed up just one batch before tossing it in here and throwing away the recipe.

Intoxicated by the day, the four men withdrew to a log wedged in a dry spot near the forest's edge, yet still within clear view of the lake. Sitting down on the makeshift bench to absorb the beauty of the morning directly into their bloodstreams, they allowed its images to become indelibly etched upon their brains.

After a spell, Abe broke the silence. "Why do they call

you Samson?" he inquired, his dark curious eyes flashing. "Where I come from, Samson is considered somewhat of a biblical hero."

"Where *we* come from, he is also considered a passionate lover," Ziggy injected, winking at Sam before his friend could object. It was a standing joke between them that Sam had a girl in every port.

Abe grunted, mentally filing that explanation away for future reference, yet the troubled look remained on his face. "English is so strange to me," he pointed out. "Your words have double, sometimes even triple meanings. And sometimes, their meanings are even contradictory."

"For instance?" Ziggy questioned, unsure what Abe was driving at. Though the son of an immigrant himself, Ziggy was uneasy about outsiders. Americans were funny that way.

"Well, for example, I once overheard a fellow say, 'I will run to the store for some groceries' but he didn't actually run, he *drove*," Abe declared in a deadpan voice. "When someone is all wet, they are wrong, yet when someone has taken a *bath*, it means they have been wiped out financially."

"Yes, I'm beginning to see your point," Sam admitted as he picked at the mud on the bottom of his boot with a twig.

Not to be sidetracked, Abe continued with his questions, "Dating an awful looking girl is bad, yet having an awful lot of money is good; a hot dog is made from a cow or perhaps a hog, but certainly not from a canine, and a *ham*burger has no pork in it at all; a messhall is usually tidy, not messy; and being gay does not mean you are funny. How can a fly or a spider be used to bug a room? And how can a cock describe both a rooster and a…?"

"Whoa, ole buddy, slow down," Sam interrupted before Abe could veer too far off in the wrong direction. "Let me try to explain. According to my grandpa Nate—and he's a pretty smart guy—English is a language of conquest and of immigration."

As Lester chuckled his disrespect for their grandfather in the background, Ziggy groaned sarcastically, "This, I gotta hear."

"Yes, please explain," Abe interceded, "because I am confused by your many strange sayings."

"At one time," Sam elaborated, "the British Empire encircled the globe, assimilating not only your Palestine, but our America as well. From each of these vanquished lands came words which entered the conqueror's tongue, words like shalom and squash and khaki. In its turn, America received hordes of worthy immigrants, each of whom brought their *own* words to the table, words like kaputt and bimbooker and tortan. So, hamburger comes not from ham but from Hamburg, a city in Germany, and messhall comes not from the sense of being untidy, but rather from the word 'mass' which in Medieval days meant feast. And as you have already figured out, hardly any of these imported words obey the traditional spelling or pronunciation rules of the underlying language. English is what we call a hodgepodge."

"Dare I ask?" Lester challenged, shocked by his brother's scholarly tone.

Not wanting to risk being made fun of, Sam didn't mouth the words of his grandfather out loud. Nonetheless, they rang in his ears as if Nate had explained it to him yesterday. "Hodgepodge comes from the French word 'hocher', meaning to shake, plus the English word for 'pot'. That is, a hodgepodge is a stew blended with many different ingredients all shaken and cooked together in the same pot."

"Let's just say English is like Hungarian goulash—a mixture."

"Samson, I must say," Abe complimented, "you are a very smart chap. But you know, America herself confuses me. She seems so willing to cater to everyone, and yet, in actuality, she seems to cater to *no* one."

"Now it's *your* turn to explain," Ziggy insisted, wondering whether Abe wasn't suddenly being too critical of the Tonnelli's adopted land.

"And so I shall," Abe agreed, "for I have given this subject much thought. America has debased herself by granting every tiny little splinter group, every inconsequential sect, every angry mother who corrals two others who agree with her, every single person, the unfettered right to assemble and the unrestrained right to speak their minds just as I am doing right now. And with each of these factions demanding that this or that injustice be corrected, these valuable franchises which you fought so hard to obtain have been needlessly squandered and diluted to such a degree that *no* one in your country has the right to say *any*thing for fear of offending *some*one. There are no universal truths if every trifle is given voice."

"Eloquently put and perhaps even correct," Sam declared uneasily. It startled him how well this strange man with the swarthy skin spoke proper English and how deflated it made him feel whenever the Israeli uttered one of his simple truisms; much to Sam's annoyance Abe spoke volumes in just a few sentences.

"Thank you for the compliment," Abe responded nonchalantly, "but I am not finished yet with what I have to say. There is one more thing about America I just cannot understand. In an overzealous attempt to save everything from baby seals to spotted owls to unborn fetuses to broken-down termite-infested homes to terminally-ill people, you have indeed saved *nothing*! To be sure..."

"Don't you think you are being just a tad bit hard on us here?" Ziggy cross-examined in a tone approaching anger. As he spoke, the squat Sicilian got to his feet and with a menacing grimace on his face, began circling the log where the others were still seated.

"Am I?" Abe snapped back, the muscles in his arm rippling as if he were preparing to defend himself against an attack. "Just look at how the insurrection among the Amerind population is being handled by your Congress!"

Equally tired of the foreigner's criticism by now, Sam rebutted. "And your system is *better*? Isn't the Kingdom of Israel a—how do you say it—a socialist theocracy? See, Ziggy," Sam remarked, turning to his friend, "I learned something in civics class after all."

"Yes, it is a socialist theocracy," Abe shot back defensively. "What of it?"

"How can you stand to live in a country where the government decides which apartment you may rent, where you are forbidden to choose your own vocation, where bigbrotherism limits how much you can earn and how much you can spend? I dare say…"

"My dear and oh so passionate Sam," Abe interrupted in a holier-than-thou fashion, "your critique of our system is incorrect and your faultfinding, much too harsh. It is true that certain of our freedoms are circumscribed, that we shoulder certain societal burdens, but we suffer no tyranny as you imply—the Kingdom of Israel is not a dictatorship, it is a monarchy. Your capitalism, on the other hand, is cruel—especially to the less able. The Jewish people are humanists; *we* believe in God!"

By invoking the Almighty, Abe had promptly taken the moral high ground, a stance which irritated both Sam and Ziggy no end. For his part, Lester couldn't have cared less one way or the other about the whole debate.

"Land's-sakes, what does *God* have to do with it?" Sam demanded angrily, jumping to his feet and taking on a defiant look.

"Hear, hear," Ziggy agreed, hovering nearby. "Don't forget: the competitive forces of capitalism assure the consumer freedom of choice for products and for services."

"And low prices too," Abe mocked. "Yes, yes, I have heard it all before, but let me make one thing perfectly clear: the *only* thing which your sacred competition assures is that there will be winners...and that there will be losers."

By now it was abundantly clear that Sam was out of his element. Not only was he academically unprepared for such a discussion, he was ill-equipped to debate the merits of capitalism versus socialism with the likes of Abe. Like Ziggy, Sam believed blindly in a system without ever having taken the time to study its philosophical underpinnings. Standing there mute, Sam reckoned that it was about time he learned *how* to think, not *what* to think, only today wasn't the day for such deep thought—the sky overhead was too blue and the moist summer air around them too fresh.

"So tell me, Abe, how are the girls in Israel?" he inquired, laboring to change the subject to something more pedestrian.

"They are loose in their connections, if that is what you mean," Abe answered sincerely. He too was relieved to tackle a less controversial topic.

Swallowing a chuckle, Sam calmly replied, "Yes, that's more or less what I was interested in, but perhaps I should rephrase my question. What I meant to say was: How do you feel about the girls in your country?"

"With my hands, same as you," Abe volunteered with a straight face.

Much to Abe's consternation, his reply was greeted with a howl of laughter, and when he tried to extricate himself from the faux pas, he only dug himself in deeper.

Deciding that he liked Abe despite their differences, Sam came to the Israeli's rescue, gently explaining to him the humor in what he had just said and intervening on his behalf before there could be any further unintended revelations regarding the man's sexual practices. Though it wasn't long before they set back on the trail towards camp with lunch on their minds, each promising to be more judicious in their word choices in the future, Sam had not forgotten about the mysterious airchop he had seen in Little Grasshopper Valley, nor about the unusual bootprint he had spied in the mud. At his first opportunity, he was going to post a letter to his grandfather in Washington at the Senate Office Building. Though it would take somewhat longer to get there that way, the old man much preferred handwritten mail over the electronic variety.

"Whew, that was a close call," Lester remarked to Abe once the two of them were out of earshot following lunch. Everyone was supposed to wait for Stovepipe outside the messhall until he could hand out this afternoon's work assignments.

"A little too close for my taste," Abe replied with a brooding look on his face. "Do you think Sam and Ziggy suspect anything?"

"Perhaps, but once camp gets going, they'll forget about the whole thing," Lester assured, wiping his miserable excuse for a moustache with the back of his hand.

"Are you positive?" Abe countered. "We have a lot at stake here. I say we take them both out."

"Are you *crazy*?" Lester yelped, looking around to see if anyone had heard him. "Sam's my brother, for heaven's sake!"

"I'll slit both their throats," Abe calmly replied. "No one will even know."

"You're even more screwed up than I was led to believe. No, Abe, that won't be necessary."

"Do you even know what you are doing? I don't relish

the idea of being teamed up with a numbskull."

"I'll admit, this is all a little new to me," Lester granted, reddening in the face at the affront, "but I'm following the procedures I was given."

"Which were what?"

"Which were to verify the shipments as they arrived in from the south, hide them temporarily in the forest, then hand them off to the Amerind pilots who come in from across the border to pick them up. As I told you when we first met, I make a percentage off each load."

"I know why I am involved in this, but why are you?" Abe questioned, his eyes darting nervously about to see if anyone was listening in on their conversation. "Besides the money, what is in this for Lester Matthews?"

"The thrill," Lester answered, suppressing a devious smirk.

"Of what? Being caught? Being tossed in front of a firing squad?"

"I suppose. But it's more than that."

"What then?"

"The chance that I might do something dastardly enough to ruin my grandfather's good name and his reputation."

Abe shook his head disapprovingly. "You are as crazy as I am," the Israeli announced. For an instant, he debated whether to press the issue further or to let it drop. Deciding that nothing would be gained by pointing out how, in the process of besmirching his grandfather's name, he would be destroying his own, Abe clamped his mouth shut and lost himself in his own private deliberations. He was confident that, sooner or later, he would get a chance to use his blade. That, more than anything else, accounted for his wicked smile.

Four
Revenge

Next Day
Two-Story Brownstone, District of Columbia

"Though we have been able to halt much of the flow of heavy munitions across the border, it's the little stuff—the ammo, the ignitors, the timing fuses—which concern us the most now," the liaison officer summarized to his civilian counterpart. Unlike the man in the gray business suit seated across the room from him, liaison officer Jenkins was dressed in full military uniform. Separating the two of them was a coffee table stacked high with manila folders and important looking documents.

"What are you saying exactly?" the well-dressed administrator from Internal Intelligence asked, frustrated by the

young officer's reluctance to give him a straight answer.
Though Director Jonathan Harper was a trim, good-looking
fellow about 35 years old, his mild manners obscured how
dangerous an adversary he could be in a fight. His topnotch
hand-to-hand combat skills were legend. Director Harper
was an awesome opponent, and Jenkins knew his reputation for uncontrollable outbursts. Rumor had it that, in a fit
of anger, Director Harper had strangled his predecessor to
death with his own two bare hands. Even if it wasn't true,
Jenkins wasn't taking any chances.

"What I am trying to say, sir, is that as recently as
yesterday we apprehended an airchop stuffed to overflowing with contraband as it was making its final approach into
Thunder Bay. The airchop was spotted by one of our patrols
as it came across Lake Superior from somewhere in northern Wisconsin," Jenkins reported in a professional tone.
"We've got the pilot in custody even as we speak, but so far
he hasn't given us a thing."

"This is intolerable!" Director Harper exploded, rising
from his chair. "The Amerinds have been fomenting trouble
all up and down the frontier, and the Canadians are furious!
They are blaming us because the weapons seem to be
coming into Canada from across our border. Apparently, they
have reports of there being transshipment points all over the
northern tier—in Wisconsin, in Minnesota, and in Upper
Michigan. Ontario has even threatened to throw up a fence
and double patrols if we don't get the situation under
control. You have *got* to get that pilot to spill his guts!"

"The only lead we have so far is a clump of mud which
we found hanging from the airchop's landing gear," Jenkins
revealed knowingly, his hand sliding to the sidearm slung
from his thick leather belt. It was a double-action 9mm
Ruger, and if Harper came too close for comfort or if he
started acting too aggressively, Jenkins was prepared to use

his piece to defend himself.

"Mud?!" Harper exploded again, drawing to within inches of Officer Jenkins' face. "Hell! What good is a clump of mud to our investigation?"

"With today's technology, spectral analysis of a surface mud is almost as reliable as a gene-print," Jenkins explained patiently, his fingers coiled around the hilt of his gun. "We have a complete satellite spectrogram of every square inch of U.S. soil on disk. If this mud originated in the continental United States, we should be able to pinpoint its origin within two, maybe three, days."

"Pinpoint?" Harper cross-examined excitedly as Jenkins' hand relaxed. "How close?"

"One, maybe two, miles."

"That's outstanding! Just outstanding!" the Intelligence man asserted, strutting about the formal sitting room. The brownstone they were meeting in was a safehouse operated under the auspices of the Military Oversight Committee, and it was one of the few places Director Harper could really be at ease. Like so many big cities, Washington was a miserable and dangerous place to work. The air was foul and the street people as likely to shoot you as rob you. A stromberg vest was the order of the day if one wanted to survive the more than occasssional stray bullet, and the sidewalks were so thick with bimbookers and slugs, one could hardly pass unmolested.

"The Senator should be told," Jenkins suggested cautiously as Director Harper circled the room behind him. Not being able to see the other man's face made Officer Jenkins understandably nervous.

"I know, I know."

"Well?"

"Well what?"

"Are you going to tell him?" Jenkins probed, twisting

around in his straight-backed chair to face Harper. "Or should I?"

"I believe it's my responsibility to do it," Director Harper observed, his keen mind racing. "But I won't open my mouth until you have the location nailed down more precisely," he added, throwing the burden of proof back into Jenkins' lap. "We must be sure of ourselves before we act."

Nodding his head as if he understood perfectly, Jenkins volunteered, "Oh, by the way, before I forget, there *is* one other thing."

"Yes?" Harper petitioned, growing weary of Officer Jenkins' habit of revealing key bits of information one sentence at a time.

"The Mossad informs us that one of their people has gone AWOL."

"I see," Harper replied even though he didn't. "And why should that concern me? People go over the wall there all the time."

"Near as we can tell, the operative entered this country traveling on a work visa issued as part of a foreign exchange program."

"What damn fool issued him a work visa, for God's sakes?" Harper demanded, the pitch in his voice rising. Even as he spoke, the Director rapped his powerful fist against the coffee table, upsetting a stack of file folders in the process.

Watching helplessly as his carefully arranged stack of papers were strewn to the floor, Jenkins' eyes narrowed. Though he looked as if he were about to boil over with anger, he said nothing.

"Who issued the work visa?" Harper repeated vehemently, not even bothering to apologize for the mess he had made.

"Well...sir..." Jenkins stuttered.

"Who, damnit?"

"If you must know...the visa was authorized by Senator Matthews."

"Oh, my lord," Harper exclaimed as he bolted for the door. "The old fool! Call me as soon as you have a fix on that mud," he clamored as he dashed down the hallway at a run. Moments later, he was out the front door and into the street.

Same Day
Central China
The gaunt man was escorted along the inlaid brick sidewalk by two hulking officers of the Royal Guard. After his long tenure in prison, he was stooped and hunched over, which—for a man of his considerable height—made for a rather curious sight. Even in his prime, Silas Whetstone had never been a particularly attractive man: like Ichabod Crane incarnate, he had hollow cheeks, long thin fingers, spindly legs, and a gawky stride. At this point in his life, with his prime well behind him, all that remained of the onetime president was his anger, an anger which dated back to his scandal-ridden term in office. Three decades ago, he had been convicted of treason and remanded to jail for his role in the assassination of then President Chester Nolan. Though it was a life sentence—capital punishment having been eliminated by the Laborites centuries ago—given the present overcrowding in the Federal penitentiary system, and given Whetstone's advanced age, the current Commander-in-Chief, President McIntyre, had seen fit to pardon him. This unlikely turn of events was tantamount to a second lease on life.

No sooner had Whetstone been released from the lockup than a courier had arrived at his apartment with a personal message inviting him to come join Overlord Ling for a parley at the Emperor's Imperial Palace outside Beijing. Whetstone had been surprised, and even a little intimidated, by the overture. Considering how much bad blood had passed between himself and Overlord Ling's father Mao, on the surface it would seem they had little to talk about. Even so, the terms of the meeting were very inviting, and he had decided at the last minute to accept Ling's offer. The way Whetstone saw it, this might be his only opportunity to get back at the man he held responsible for landing him in jail—Nate Matthews. After all, if it hadn't been for the Senator's damning testimony, plus that of the late General Felix Wenger, Silas Whetstone might never have been sent down the river to begin with.

As the vengeful man reflected back upon the chain of events which led up to him being here in China today, the two soldiers of the Royal Guard escorted him first through a sumptuous garden and past an oddly-shaped pool brimming with colorful koi, then down a long hall lined with life-like statues of Chinese warriors outfitted in full battle regalia. From there he was deposited in an enormous sitting room lined with expensive tapestries and bamboo-backed chairs. A banner emblazoned with the likeness of a humongous grasshopper framed the wall behind him. Seeing the giant insect gripping the rampart like a bloodsucking parasite, Whetstone was reminded of the biowarfare extortion scheme Mao had attempted to pull off during Whetstone's brief tenure as president, the same brief tenure which saw Hawaii make its initial attempt at seceding from the Union, and which saw him make the mistake of trusting General Felix Wenger with his darkest and innermost secrets.

It had been nearly three decades since Ling had elevated himself to the status of Overlord, and in all that time Whetstone hadn't seen so much as a photograph of the reclusive Chinaman; the intervening years had not been particularly good to him either. Thinking back upon it now, Whetstone remembered Ling from when he was China's ambassador to the United States; in those days, Overlord Mao's number one son had been pudgy like a giant Buddha with a pair of fat hands, a bulging belly, and a tiny slit of a mouth. Seeing his slender frame today, it was obvious to Whetstone that the man had aged considerably, his most prominent feature now being the long whiskers of his flowing fu-manchu moustache. His younger brother Chang, on the other hand, looked not a day older than when Whetstone had first met him years ago. Still immobile like a statue, Chang had a sloping forehead, a set of bulging arms, and a barrel-shaped chest. While Whetstone had wasted away the better part of his life rotting in a prison cell, the brothers Tsui had spent the past thirty years putting down one insurrection after another in a slow uphill battle to hold their father's empire together. It was ironic that the same Nate Matthews who had sent Whetstone to the penitentiary had also been the one responsible for putting an end to their father's life. That Ling and Whetstone should now choose to join forces could only be considered a bad omen for America—and an even worse one for Senator Matthews!

"I am so glad you consented to meet with me," Ling opened, offering the bent and broken Whetstone a chair. "It is no secret that my father and you were once great enemies."

"Was it not Confucius who once said 'the enemy of my enemy is my friend'?" Whetstone intoned, softening the potential for animosity between them.

"I understand your meaning and I appreciate what you are saying," Ling complimented, "though I believe the author of your truism was not Kong Fuzi."

"Kong Fuzi?"

"Yes, like so many of your Euro-based conceits," Ling remarked contemptuously, "Kong Fuzi's name was Latinized by Jesuit missionaries in the seventeenth century."

"Que sera, sera; what will be, will be," Whetstone

recited in a deranged voice. Such topics bored him no end.

"It has occurred to me that—like myself—perhaps you have a score to settle with Senator Matthews," Ling volunteered as a compressed snicker escaped from his brother Chang's pursed lips.

"I have no score to settle," Whetstone objected with feigned sincerity. "I have now paid my debt to society."

"You are so modest, Mister Whetstone," Ling observed snidely, his fu-manchu twitching nervously, "but with so few years remaining in your life, I can hardly believe you are willing to go to your maker unfulfilled. I know that if I had been the one who had sat for thirty years in a prison cell, the first thing I would have thought of every morning when I awoke, and the last thing I would have thought of every night before dropping off to sleep, would have been the manner of my revenge."

Smiling widely as Ling finally pushed the right button, Whetstone declared, "What do you have in mind?"

"Matthews must be made to pay," Ling asserted darkly, "not only for murdering my father, but also for embarrassing our nation in the eyes of the world. Chang and I have put a plan into motion to accomplish this, but we need your help to complete it successfully."

"I'm listening," the gaunt man assured, suddenly interested in what the Overlord had to say.

"For some time now we have been supplying rebel factions in Canada with sufficient arms to support an insurrection against their oppressive white masters. The politics of the uprising don't concern us much, only that the Amerinds now appear ready and willing to overthrow both the Canadian and the U.S. governments, if necessary, in order to carve a homeland for themselves out of North America. We have recruited dozens of collaborators in this enterprise, but the identity of one of our *newest* enlistees might be of interest to you," Ling offered, dangling the bait in front of the former president's eyes.

"Who?" Whetstone pounced, hooked by Ling's story. "Who have you recruited?"

"Lester Matthews," Ling reported, pumping up his chest proudly.

"You have got to be kidding! Are you talking about the elder of Nate Matthews two grandsons?"

"One and the same."

"Of what possible good is he to you?" Whetstone objected. "He's just a boy; barely twenty if memory serves."

"Twenty-one, actually."

"But why him? Why not the other boy? Sam is even younger and presumably, even *more* susceptible to manipulation."

"Lester is a natural. Though the records have been expunged, he has previous arrests for petty larceny and for home invasion. Not only that, Lester is to enter the Naval Academy at Alameda in the fall; we hope to use him to gather intelligence for us once he has his commission. Already he has been helping us move light arms north to the Amerinds in Ontario."

"Well, that's quite an accomplishment," Whetstone congratulated sincerely. "So what do you need *my* help for?"

"Our sources tell us there is a book; a book filled with fail-safe passwords and encrypted codes, a book which originated with your nemesis General Wenger and which subsequently became the property of Senator Matthews when the good general died. We want that book," Overlord Ling asserted, "and we want you to help us get it."

"So *that's* who has had the book all these many years!" Whetstone exclaimed. "I should have known that Matthews would end up with it. I underestimated you, Ling."

"If I were you, I wouldn't make the mistake of ever

letting that happen again," Ling responded ominously. "Am I to assume, then, that I have your cooperation?"

"Yes. By all means."

Five
Mess Call

The next morning, Sam slept right through both the blare of the bugler sounding reveille and the dinging of his own wake-up alarm. In fact, it was not until Ziggy slammed the rickety cabin door shut behind him on the way out, that Sam even stirred. Then, when he leapt from his bunk half awake, he smacked his head hard against the dresser, a stunt which brought forth a round of good-natured jibes from his departing cabinmate. Nearly knocked senseless by the impact, Sam fell back down on his cot rubbing his head and nursing his bruised ego. While Ziggy and the others raced up the hill to the messhall for breakfast, Sam dragged himself up again, this time staggering groggily to the wash basin. Sickened by the stench of last night's tacos belching from his breath, he opened up the spigot and plunged his face into the ice-cold water. The shock therapy worked, and he was immediately alert. Furiously brushing his teeth until he was satisfied that he no longer reeked of hot sauce, Sam rushed across camp to join the rest of the staff already in the dining hall eagerly shoveling down the first meal of the day.

As he made his way up the steep steps of the trail in the direction of the messhall, Sam's insides warmed at the sight of the indescribably perfect dawn. The hue of the sky and the color of the lake were so closely matched that no mortal could possibly tell where one ended and the other began. At the start of such a day Sam had no trouble imagining himself rowing a boat to the far end of the lake, then paddling it off into the morning sky, jettisoning everything worldly in the process. And if things went just right…

Without warning, the harsh screech of a hawk echoed across the forest, jolting him back to reality. As he came out of his coma, Sam found himself at the door of the ponderous structure. Na-Cha-Tan's messhall was a page torn carefully from a history few individuals remembered. It dated to an era when robust opportunists still roamed the wilderness seeking furs and precious gems. To appreciate its nobility, all he had to do was close his eyes and take a step back into time.

In the first place, the building was huge. Carving out a rectangle 80 feet wide and 120 feet long, the hangar-sized edifice was like a glimpse into the past, a past filled with daring men and fearsome creatures. To begin with, the architecture was of a sort found nowadays only in yellowed books and tattered magazines. The walls, for instance, were constructed in a log-cabin style with mortar forced between each successive layer of ancient timbers. This technique not only cemented the logs in place, it also kept all but the tiniest of animals from invading the warmth within.

Vaulting skyward from each of the two longest walls, an

immense, asphalt-shingled roof soared to a peak some fifty feet above the dining hall's creaky, hardwood floor, a floor which had been polished smooth over the years by the footfalls of thousands of eager Scouts. And like all of the buildings at Na-Cha-Tan, the messhall was raised off the ground upon a dozen or more concrete supports.

Stone steps serviced the main entrance, even as a grand fireplace majestically filled the opposite wall. The mouth of the hearth was so tall that an average-sized man could comfortably stand upright within it, and it was so wide that that same man could readily lay his bunk across its breadth with plenty of room leftover for his night table and his clothes dresser. Unlike the puny fireplaces found in a typical Farmington home, entire unsplit logs could rest easily on the grate of this giant hearth. And once these monster logs were set ablaze, approaching to within a half-dozen feet or less of the inferno meant being scorched. Although the chimney probably hadn't been cleaned in a generation or more, it was of no consequence—to a true outdoorsman, the everpresent aroma of fires past was delicious.

This morning, though, it wasn't the faint odor of the fireplace which drew Sam along the sandy path towards the messhall, it was the exquisite smell of bacon, eggs, and pancakes cooking on the grill. Yet another long day of hard work lay ahead of them, and a hearty breakfast was just what the doctor ordered. Hungrily bounding up the dining hall's craggy steps, Sam flung open the screen door and there—hanging just in front of him exactly as he remembered it—was the ancient canoe.

Built eons ago by the aboriginal Americans who had inhabited these dense north woods well before the Euros had arrived, the rustic, birch-bark canoe now hung over the center of the messhall on thick wire cords. Though the remarkably well-preserved canoe would have fetched a high price from most any museum in the country, the camp had refused to part with it despite several good offers. The canoe symbolized the spirit and the lore of a past now irretrievably lost, and if it were ever to be sold, the soul of Na-Cha-Tan would undoubtedly have been emasculated.

As a Tenderfoot, Sam had been told the story so often he could now recite it almost by heart. The first white explorer to enter the area was Jean Nicolet in the 1630's. Nicolet encountered an Indian Chief of a Nation calling themselves the Wisconsin, or the "gathering of the rivers" in their language. Unlike the Beothuk tribes to the east who spread red ochre on their bodies (hence the Euro term "red-skin") the local Wisconsin tribe—the Na-Cha-Tan or "birch forest warriors"—used a multitude of pigments to emblazon their torsos. Until they were driven out by white settlers two hundred years later, the Na-Cha-Tan fished and hunted all through these tranquil forests. Unfortunately for those who came after, the Na-Cha-Tan left behind few traces of their presence, the canoe being one of the most precious. Legend had it that the last Na-Cha-Tan chief built this superb canoe to transport the remains of his lifeless squaw to her final resting ground on the eastern shores of this very same lake after she was slain by a berserk settler.

Mindful of the somber legend, Sam dipped his head in reverence as he passed beneath the ancient craft on his way to join his buddies who were busily devouring their second plateful of pancakes and eggs. As usual, fat-Jim was muttering bitterly about having to start work so early; everyone else was arguing energetically about the proper way to set up a wall-tent.

During their two-week stay at camp, the Scouts lived in one of eight tent cities which dotted the vast area bordered on one side by the lake, and on the other side by the main logging road. Barely wide enough to accommodate a single vehicle, the main logging road wound its way through the forest in a grand semi-circle from the lake's south end to its northernmost shore. Each of these tent villages were self-contained units configured to accommodate up to fifty Scouts in four patrol sites of twelve boys apiece. In keeping with the camp's tradition of paying tribute to the country's native inhabitants, each village took its name from one of the vanquished Amerind tribes which once used to populate the area. Ironically, some of these very same tribes were now involved in the current clamor for an Amerind homeland in North America.

The boys slept, two-by-two, under the cover of spacious wall-tents elevated off the ground on sturdy wooden platforms. Although these open-air canvas tenements had neither a sewn-in floor nor a mosquito netting to protect their occupants against the sometimes vicious Na-Cha-Tan bombers, these sleeping arrangements were actually quite comfortable, and only under the most adverse of weather conditions would the adventuresome tenants not remain warm and dry in their khaki-colored apartments.

That a wall-tent even remained erect was a fortunate blend of several of Newton's Laws, plus a measure of good luck. The assembly began with the placement of two, 6-foot long wooden poles, poles which, because of their vertical orientation, were generally referred to as the "uprights." Each upright was capped by a thick metal shank which extended perhaps five inches beyond the tip of the pole, and which was essential to holding the entire framework together.

To complete the scaffolding over which the bulky canvas tent was to be hung, a third pole was required. This 7-foot long "ridge-pole" had holes drilled through each of its ends, holes broad enough to accept the metal shanks protruding from the tops of the two uprights. Together, the three poles formed a skeleton which vaguely resembled an upside-down U.

Once the framework was pieced together, the tent was then draped over it in such a fashion that the shanks stuck, not only through the holes in the ridge-pole, but also through the center grommets of the canvas. Subsequently, the whole affair was hoisted onto the wooden platform and held there while ropes were extended from the side grommets of the tent, drawn taut, and tied off to a series of wooden stakes pounded in the ground parallel to the supporting platform.

With a little practice, an energetic, well-organized crew of four could complete the whole process of leveling a platform and securing the canvas to its moorings in about 15 minutes. However, when multiplied by several hundred such tents camp-wide, the magnitude of the job was staggering, and if the weather didn't cooperate, they ran a real risk of not being equipped to house the boys by the time they arrived. Moreover, setting up tents wasn't the only job that had to be accomplished before camp could open—not by a long measure! Hidden deep within the pocket of Stovepipe's trousers was a two page list of work projects which still had to be done as the staff struggled to ready both themselves and Na-Cha-Tan for that moment when the first campers would arrive in the West camp field late next week. As was so often the case with enterprises of this sort, over the course of that struggle, a bond would be nurtured between counselors, a bond which would remain with them for the rest of their lives. There was, of course, the inevitable comradery which accompanied hard work and a job well done, but there was more to it than that. Now, as they worked their way through the remainder of the training program, the staffmen shared a commonality of purpose. Believing they could surmount any obstacle, beat any odds, a "can do" attitude now fired their imagination in strange and unusual ways. And as the pace of the work projects hastened in anticipation of opening day and as the training sessions carried on late into the night, it was this esprit de corps which would see them through it to the end.

One blue-sky day after another would be spent painting buildings, waterproofing rowboats, repairing fences, patching latrines, anchoring the boat docks, and moving supplies into the quartermaster. One starlit night after the next would be spent fidgeting in the messhall while Stovepipe did his best to school them in the camp's safety and first-aid procedures.

Although some of their nightly lessons—like how to correctly use an axe and a knife, or how to properly treat a burn or a rash—were redundant and even boring to the "seasoned" staffmen like Sam and Ziggy, other exercises— like how to administer CPR or how to rescue a drowning swimmer—were critical considering the large stable of tenderfoots on this year's crew. And even though the staff was supposed to have been well-versed in these maneuvers as a prerequisite before ever having been hired, with so many young lives at stake, Stovepipe was determined to leave nothing to chance. It was his job to see to it that by the time the staff escorted the hordes of incoming Scouts and their voluminous gear from the parking lot in the West Camp field, along the logging road, and out to their "home" in the woods, they would be doing so with the confidence of being well-prepared. *That*, after all, *was* the Scout motto.

But there was more to being a good Scout than merely just being prepared. There was also that little matter about keeping oneself physically strong, mentally awake, and morally straight. And therein lay the conundrum. Sam had seen something out there in Little Grasshopper Valley that day and he was unsure whether to tell Stovepipe about it or not. Sam had already dispatched a handwritten note to his grandfather about the incident along with the sketch he had made of the bootprint, but with Stovepipe it was another matter altogether. Stovepipe was at once Sam's boss and his friend, and yet their difference in years was enough that Sam sometimes found it difficult to confide in him. Still, after lunch that day he tried.

"Stovepipe, there is something I've been meaning to talk to you about," Sam began, wiping the sweat from his brow. All morning long they had been hard at work in the villages setting up tents and now they were relaxing for a bit under the shade of a tree, each of them with a glassful of lemonade.

"Good," Stovepipe said. "There's something on my mind as well. And since I'm the boss, I get to go first. What do you make of our new camp nurse?"

Sam couldn't help but smile at the question.

Even though serious accidents were rare, given Na-Cha-Tan's immense size and the diversity of its terrain, and given the sheer numbers of kids that it tried to serve each summer, the camp had to have a full-time nurse on call to deal with its many hazards. With the everpresent opportunity for emergencies to arise unexpectedly, and with the nearest medic facility being some twenty minutes away by gcar, the situation practically shouted that prompt attention be given to any injuries right on the spot. Only, in Stovepipe's opinion the resident nurse left a little something to be desired.

The truth be known, Miss Loddy was not quite what the staff would have conjured up if they had been asked to describe the perfect medic. Though she was admittedly single—thereby fulfilling one of the items on their wish list (the others being that she be young, well-built, and friendly)—she was in fact, a cranky, hard-of-hearing, relic of a woman with several irritating habits. Not only did she regularly mispronounce the names of her patients, she frequently misdiagnosed their ailments as well. But what really got Stovepipe's goad was how she bungled *his* name. No matter how hard he tried to convince her that his name was Al Tovas, Miss Loddy continued to address him as that "nice Mister Alomas." And whenever he would take the time to correct her, she would just smile knowingly at him, nod, and reply, "Whatever you say, Mister Alomas."

All this and more went through Sam's head as he contemplated how best to answer Stovepipe's question, and when he did answer, it was with a wisecrack.

"How's that, Mister Alomas?" Sam croaked using his best imitation of an old woman's voice. "Speak up, son," he added, cupping one hand behind his ear as if he were hard of hearing. "Speak up, I say."

"Enough already," Stovepipe barked irritably, "I get the message. Now what's on *your* mind?"

"Two things, actually."

"I don't have all day," Stovepipe said, knocking his head back and downing his glass of lemonade in two gulps. With each passing day, summer had been showing itself with more and more potency. Along with the heat and hard work had come thirst.

"About the canoe race," Sam stammered, not sure of the best way to phrase the question. He valued Stovepipe's friendship highly and didn't want to make it sound as if this were a demand or that he was taking advantage of their friendship.

"I'm not going," Stovepipe replied flatly. "Too much paperwork to get done before opening day." Even as he spoke, Stovepipe cracked the knuckles of his long fingers with a disconcerting pop.

"That's a shame," Sam sympathized, moving a few steps higher on the slope. Because Stovepipe was so tall, Sam always had to stand uphill from him just to look him in the eye. "It promises to be fun, you know—what with the dance afterwards and all."

"Can't be helped. Now what's on your mind already?"

"May we borrow your gcar for the weekend?" Sam asked, hoping Stovepipe would not be angered by the request and say yes.

"Who's 'we'?" Stovepipe answered, obviously a little cross by the solicitation.

"Me and Lester and Ziggy and Jim."

"Who's gonna drive? I don't much relish the idea of your brother behind the wheel of my gcar."

"If you don't trust Lester to drive, then lend the gcar to Ziggy," Sam suggested, tugging at his glass of lemonade and swirling the melting ice cubes around on the inside. By now, drops of condensation had beaded up on the outside of the glass on account of the humidity. "Ziggy has a license, you know."

"Let me think about it a day or two, will you? What else is troubling you, Sam?"

"I saw something the other day, something very strange, something you should know about."

"You're not going to tell me about that fracas in the shower house, are you? 'Cause I already know all about the damn mess that was made with the shaving cream."

"No, that wasn't it," Sam snapped impatiently, pawing the ground with the toe of his boot. "Now, boss, would you please just listen to me for a moment?"

"Sorry, old buddy. Tell me: what did you see?"

"An airchop."

"Yeah? So? I see them all the time. There's a National guard base over in Tomahawk."

"No, I mean on the ground. Here in Na-Cha-Tan," Sam clarified, lowering his voice so as not to be overheard. "In Little Grasshopper."

"Are you looney?" Stovepipe roared, straightening himself up to his full height. "What in the…"

"Let me explain."

Pulling Stovepipe aside, Sam proceeded to tell him everything that had happened that day on their hike to Muskrat Lake, including his meeting up with Lester and Abe out on the trail. When he was done, Stovepipe's mouth was agape. After some hesitation, however, he said, "Sam, for now anyway, let's just keep this between ourselves, shall we? We don't want to alarm anyone unnecessarily. Colonel Beck will be up here shortly with his troop and maybe we can talk to him about what you saw and straighten this whole thing out."

Nodding his head with approval as he walked over towards the messhall to get himself another glass of lemonade, Sam bellowed, "Agreed. But don't forget now, we need your gcar for the canoe race."

Though Stovepipe waved him off with a grin, Sam wasn't satisfied with waiting until Colonel Beck arrived to get an answer. He had it in his mind to get himself to an info-terminal at his first opportunity. Though there were none in camp, he might find one at Jack's. Sam had to see for himself whether he could bring up a public domain file showing pictures of military aircraft; maybe one of the airchops would look familiar.

Six
Harper

"Director Jonathan Harper here to see Senator Matthews," the stern-faced man from Internal Intelligence announced as he stepped across the threshold of the unpretentious outer office and introduced himself to the tough-looking, male receptionist seated behind the oversized desk.

"Yes, he's expecting you," Nate's secretary indicated, bidding the handsome, well-proportioned fellow to enter. "Do come in."

Following the unsmiling clerk from the simple vestibule into the Senator's much plusher private suite, Director Harper placed the map tube he had been carting under his arm on the countertop of the wet bar. Like a brass rail snatched from a bygone era when having a drink was considered a gentlemanly way of conducting business, the handmade bar was a first-rate piece of workmanship. Running along the entire length of the room's south wall, it said something about the character of the man who occupied this office. In the center of the suite were several easy chairs, and standing against the opposite wall was an oversized video screen suitable for watching a visicast or for viewing a fiche.

Although he and the Senator had worked closely together for six or seven years now—Harper as the youngest Director of Internal Intelligence and Matthews as the oldest Chairman of the Senate's Military Oversight Committee—the two men had never gotten along as well in private as their public image suggested. Harper was brash and undisciplined; Matthews seasoned and cautious. Harper was prone to violence; Matthews abhorred it. Still, this meeting couldn't be avoided, and at least at the outset, the Senator felt he held the upper hand.

"Jonathan, so good to see you," Matthews opened, extending his right hand even as he clutched at his weatherbeaten cane with his left. In his prime, Nate had been an impressive specimen of a man: tall; with intelligent gray eyes; light, almost blond hair; an athletic, but not rock hard build; and the faintest hint of a cleft in the center of his strong, but proud chin. Now, though, as his years wound down to a precious few, he looked like a man who was up to fighting, at most, one more great battle. Nate didn't know it yet, but he was about to be engaged in the fight of a lifetime—the preservation of his name.

Seeing the crotchety old man standing there looking so enfeebled, Harper sensed that he could take immediate charge of the conversation. Like any sharp competitor, Director Harper kept a dossier on all his political adversaries; therefore, he knew everything there was to know about

Nate's medical problems. He was aware, for instance, that the Senator had an inoperable cancer, one of the few remaining cancers for which an algorithm had not yet been discovered to regenerate the damaged tissue. Interestingly enough, in the course of gathering this intelligence, Harper had also learned that for as long as records had been kept, *every* Matthews had suffered from an early demise. In his own devious way, it had occurred to the Director that perhaps he could somehow use this devastating knowledge to his own advantage against the Senator.

"It is good to see you too," Harper echoed, accepting Nate's offer of an outstretched hand. "Why don't we sit? You look as though you're about ready to topple over," he suggested none too tactfully.

"Don't take that tone with me, boy!" the Senator exploded, rapping his cane against the floor. "I'm perfectly capable of deciding when to stand and when to sit."

"Of course you are, Senator. I meant nothing by it," Director Harper intoned apologetically. "I was just trying to be polite."

"Condescending perhaps, arrogant perhaps, but certainly not polite," Nate shot back disagreeably.

"I didn't come here today intending to spend our short time together arguing," Harper softened as he went around to the back of the bar to pour himself a drink. Though Harper had no present way of knowing it, Nate's secret wall safe was built into the brickwork directly behind him. "A tortan for you, sir?"

"No, I don't touch the stuff anymore, but knock yourself out, Jonathan." Even as he spoke, Nate shoved Sam's curious missive deeper into his pocket. Though he enjoyed hearing from the boy, it bothered him that his grandson had spotted an airchop so close to Na-Cha-Tan. That there might be nefarious goings-on there only reaffirmed his decision to ask an old and a dear friend to keep an eye out for the lad. "As you said, Director, we're both busy men, so do tell me what this is all about."

"So I shall," Harper agreed as he reached for the sturdy map tube he had brought with him to the meeting. Popping the plastic cap off one end of the tube with his thumb, Harper shook the brown cylindrical carton until several tightly coiled parchments came sliding out onto the bar. Unrolling the maps on the countertop with one hand even as he placed a heavy drinking glass on each corner with the other, he cleared his throat to begin his explanation.

The glossy sheets were a little over two feet in length and just under that in width; that is, they were the customary size for a standard quadrangle map published by the U.S. Orbital Survey. They were similar to the sort Nate had used years ago for compass training during his brief stint as a Boy Scout. He could see from the legend at the bottom that they were of the so-called 7.5 minute series where one map-inch represented 2000 ground-feet, the minute designation coming from the fact that sixty arc minutes comprised a degree of latitude or longitude. Although a single map covered about 55 square miles, it was still detailed enough that individual houses showed on it as black squares or rectangles. Surface features were either in brown, green, or blue, depending on their type, and contour lines squiggled across the paper revealing every 40-foot change in elevation. A red circle had been drawn on the uppermost sheet with a grease pencil.

"Several days ago," Harper began as he sucked on his drink, "one of my people commandeered an airchop trying to land near Thunder Bay."

"Canada?" Nate interrupted hoarsely.

"Yes, Senator, Canada. May I go on?" he inquired in a disrespectful tone.

"By all means," Nate shot back, thinking of the enigmatic letter he had just received from Sam.

"The airchop was loaded to the gills with arms intended to resupply the Amerind stronghold just north of there—Stingers, manual firebombs, megaflares, the whole shooting match," Harper described as Nate nodded his head. "Using a new, but highly reliable soil-sampling technique, my forensics team was able to locate its point of origin," Harper asserted, gesturing to the red circle drawn on the map. "According to my people, at some point in her travels that day, the airchop apparently landed here where it was undoubtedly loaded with the weapons she was carrying when we picked her up."

"You managed to come up with all this on the basis of a *soil* sample?" Matthews questioned, a look of incredulity plastered across his face.

"Officer Jenkins did, yes."

"Was the mud off the pilot's boot?" Matthews wondered out loud, remembering the sketch Sam had sent him along with his note. There had been something hauntingly familiar about the insignia on the bottom of that boot, but so far he had been unable to identify it.

"No, the mud was off the craft itself."

"I see. And what do you intend to do with this information?" Nate asked, fixing his bifocals in place so that he could study the map in detail. All the names and places were printed in tiny one-point type.

"It is absolutely essential that we put some of our people on the ground there," Director Harper reasoned as Nate scrutinized the topographic sheet. "We have to see whether we can stop these shipments at their source."

"I agree," Nate replied without looking up. "And who do you have in mind for this job?"

"That's really none of your concern now is it Senator?"

Harper declared sharply.

"Geez!" Nate exclaimed, rearing his head back in horror as he tore his glasses from his face. "Do you know where this place *is*?"

"In Wisconsin, sir," Harper allowed, enjoying his moment of sway.

"I can *see* that, you buffoon!" Nate bellowed, slamming his cane against the bar with a resounding crash. "This is Camp Na-Cha-Tan! You see, it says so right here," he exclaimed, pointing to the words with his index finger.

"What of it?" Harper returned nonchalantly, though he already knew the significance of the answer.

"Both of my grandsons work there as counselors," Matthews reported anxiously.

"So we've been told," Harper acknowledged arrogantly. "Perhaps one of them would be willing to be our eyes on the ground."

"Absolutely not! I won't hear of it!" Nate interjected vehemently. "To the contrary, I want one of *your* people assigned to watch over *them*! Especially the younger one—Sam."

Even as the Senator expressed his shock and indignation at Harper's suggestion that one of the boys act as his spy, he was glad for having had the foresight to call in Miss Loddy to keep an eye on his favorite grandson. She was a retired Army nurse Nate had once met at the Bethesda Naval Hospital. For a short time, years ago, they had been lovers, and now, she was probably the one person in the whole world he could trust to always tell him the truth. Not only that, she was familiar with eavesdropping devices and could be counted on to be discreet.

"Why is Sam the only one you seem concerned with?" the Director questioned in a curious tone. He was caught off-guard by how callously the octogenarian apparently felt towards his other grandchild.

"Lester isn't worth the trouble; he's much too much like his father."

"That doesn't make any sense to me, I thought you had arranged for Lester to attend the Naval Academy this coming fall?"

"Only to keep him off the streets," Nate pointed out coldly. "Maybe they'll teach him some discipline. Lord knows, he needs it."

"Senator, I hate to bring this up, but there is one other small matter we should discuss before we get too far afield. And let me give you fair warning before I start: this may turn out to be a bit of an embarrassment for you."

"That would suit you just fine, wouldn't it Mister Director?"

"Not in the least," the Intelligence man countered innocently. "But tell me, Senator, what do you know about a chap named Abe Levinson?"

"Isn't that Lester's friend from Israel?" Nate asked, scratching his head to see if he could remember anything in particular about the man.

"Yes, we already know he is from Israel. What *else* can you tell me about him?"

"Not a thing! Geez, Harper," Matthews exclaimed in a perturbed tone. "What is this all about? Na-Cha-Tan needed a Rabbi for the summer, and Lester said the boy wanted to visit the States. I don't see a problem here. Is there one?" he asked nervously.

"We think this Levinson fellow is Mossad. Not only that, we think he may be involved in these shipments of arms to the Amerinds," Harper explained, pausing for effect. "I wonder, Senator: If you had such a low opinion of Lester's judgment, how is it that you could have been so foolish as to issue a work visa to a complete stranger? I take it you didn't even bother to order a background check on this Hebe?" It was less a question than an indictment.

"Oh, my Lord, what have I done?" the ancient man groaned, sinking into the closest chair. He could feel his heart pounding inside his chest.

"You see our dilemma."

"Well then, you must protect Sam from this renegade at all costs! It is imperative you put someone in there to keep track of him and see that he doesn't get hurt."

"It is already in the works," Harper revealed, "but you of all people should know how this business operates. Tit-for-tat and all that."

"You mean to hang me out to dry on this one don't you?"

"There *are* other ways."

"Name your price," Nate urged resolutely.

"We protect your precious Sam, but only if you agree to do something for *us*."

"What do you want from me, you bastard?"

"Now, now, Senator, such anger, and I thought we were such good friends," Harper suggested in a condescending tone.

"You bloodsucker," Nate declared, his face turning red. "What do you want?"

"Like I said, I'll find a way to protect your precious grandson, but when the Military Oversight Committee meets next month to discuss my department's budget for the coming year, I want to read in the newspaper that you have recommended a 25 percent increase in our appropriations."

"That's blackmail."

"No...that is your grandson's life. Without it, he's on his own."

"I'll do it," Nate relented quickly, afraid that this nefarious Mossad agent had already found a way to compromise his favorite grandson. Though Nate could certainly count on Miss Loddy to provide him with regular reports, she was far too old to actually protect Sam from harm. What was needed here was someone younger, someone better trained.

"I'll do it," Nate repeated in a whisper. "But understand me in no uncertain terms—you had better put someone good on this. And one more thing, Harper, I want to meet the man personally."

"Consider it done," the Director said as he rolled up his maps and rose to leave. "It has been a pleasure doing business with you, Senator. And oh, by the way," he added in his characteristic fashion, "I understand that President McIntyre pardoned your old friend Silas Whetstone."

"What of it?" Nate grumbled, impatient for the disagreeable man to leave.

"He's been to see Ling you know."

"No, I did *not* know."

"I'd watch my backside if I were you," Harper warned.

"I assume that for a 25 percent increase in your department's budget you can watch my backside *for* me."

"That's assuming a lot," Harper replied in an intimidating tone as he paused on the way out the door. "But don't worry, I'm already one step ahead of you."

"I want to know Whetstone's every move."

Nodding his head in agreement, Director Harper left as abruptly as he had arrived. As the door swung shut behind him, the old man cradled his face in his hands. For Senator Nate Matthews, life had suddenly gotten much more difficult.

Seven
Sindy

Psychologists commonly refer to the phenomenon as "transference," though head-doctors often find it preferable to label it a condition rather than a phenomenon. That is, when the object of one's hatred cannot be held accountable for his transgressions, the aggrieved party tends to redirect his foul passion against someone or something else. In the textbook case, a man detests his job and hates his boss, but rather than quitting or telling his boss off, he beats his wife up instead. In another typical situation, a man loathes his social-climbing sibling, so one day when his brother isn't looking, he kicks the crap out of his brother's dog as a proxy for his contempt. Both are examples of transference, and the truth be known, Silas Whetsone suffered from this condition in a big way. Though he hated Felix Wenger to no end for his role in sending him to prison, the good general had committed the unspeakable atrocity of dying of old age before Whetstone could be released from his cell to even the score. As a consequence, Flix's protégé, Nate Matthews, had now become the target of Whetstone's fury.

The trip to see Overlord Ling had been therapeutic in the sense that afterwards, Silas could begin to see just the faintest glimmer of a light at the end of his long desperate tunnel. Ling had agreed to keep feeding arms north to the Amerinds using Lester as one of his many conduits, and in return Whetstone had agreed to further ensnare the Matthews' boy in an expanded round of treasonous activities. While a public disclosure of Lester's support to the rebels' cause would probably have been a big enough embarrassment to cause the Senator to step down, it wasn't enough of a black mark against the Senator personally to satisfy Whetstone's craving for revenge. His plans for damaging Nate's reputation didn't end with merely implicating Lester as a middleman; there was still the little matter of Flix's black code-book. To get it, to get Lester to steal it for him, Lester would have to be manipulated like a puppet on a string. And what better way to accomplish that than with the services of a woman?

As Whetstone sat there in his poorly-lit apartment reflecting on what he was going to say to her when she arrived, there was a sharp knock at his door. A grim smile consumed his face.

"Come in, young lady," he urged from the darkened corner of his bare room. After thirty years of being confined to a drab and gloomy cell, Whetstone would never again be able to stand the bright light of day. Even the shimmering reading lamps of his dingy flat made his eyes water. Nowadays, he preferred to sit alone with the shades drawn and the visicast set droning quietly in the background.

Of the many simple pleasures he had been denied while in the slammer, probably none had been more difficult to endure than his inability to cope sexually. As a younger man, he had taken out his carnal perversions on his wife, on his daughter Nikki, and on any other vulnerable women he had encountered in the course of his long, sick climb to the top. These wayward, even bestial, feelings had been bottled up for so long now he wasn't even sure any potency remained.

"Is that you Mister Whetstone?" the scantily-clad bimbooker murmured in her husky voice as she pushed the door open a crack. She wore a tight leather skirt which hardly covered her buttocks plus a red tube-top which barely held her generous breasts in place. Women of her persuasion operated in that drugged nether world somewhere between self-preservation and self-destruction. Though she made a half-hearted attempt to hide them, her white arms revealed the tracks of the intravenous injections which kept her going each day; the jitters in her step revealed the debilitating effects of her hardcore blue-devil addiction. Yet despite her apparent shortcomings, she was not a stupid woman, and in her handbag she carried a Smith & Wesson 9mm with a 15-shot clip, an unsheathed six-inch steel blade, and a set of brass knuckles. Though she was barely twenty years-old, she had been around the block long enough to know how to defend herself against the predators she so often frequented.

"Yes, please come in," he urged, motioning her to a chair next to his. Whetstone was an ugly caricature of a man, and a tiny gasp escaped from her lips as she got a good look at him.

"You find me unattractive?" he challenged, studying

the outline of her body in the murky light. Seeing her lovely head of blond hair and her big breasts pressing against the narrow band of material holding the two round orbs in place, he was reminded of his own daughter. Flix had shot his Nikki dead the day after she gunned down President Nolan, and although Nolan's assassination had paved the way for Whetstone to assume the presidency, he had never been able to come to grips with losing his only child. Someone had to pay the price for Nikki's death, and courtesy of his mental act of transference, that someone was to be Senator Matthews.

"Not at all," she lied, "but my service didn't tell me how...tall...you were."

"You're sweet," he complimented, reaching out to her with his bony hand. "But I didn't catch your name."

"Sindy," she replied, staying out of his grasp, "Sindy Foster."

"Yes, that's right. I had forgotten. Well, Sindy Foster, which would you like to handle first—our business or our pleasure?"

"Business before pleasure, that's what my daddy used to always say," the blond intoned, sitting down next to him and placing her purse in her lap. With her legs crossed ever so tightly at the hips, her skirt rode up her generous thighs exposing everything to plain view. With her legs cocked that way, she looked to him as if she were naked from the waist down.

"I want to hire you on a long-term basis," he offered, eyeing her female parts lecherously. Even as he spoke, he felt his member stir in a way it hadn't for years.

"Sorry, old-timer," she lamented, chomping on her gum in an alley-cat sort of way. "I only do one-nighters, not weeklies."

"It's not for *me*, you bitch!" he yelped, raising his voice quite unexpectedly. "I have someone that I need thoroughly compromised. I want to hire you to seduce this man; get him hooked on drugs; do whatever it takes; just soften him up so that I can run him."

"Run him?"

"You know—handle him, make him more manageable, more susceptible to control."

"You want me to move *in* with this guy?" Sindy questioned, taken back by the suggestion. "Play house and all that?"

"Perhaps," he answered noncommittedly. "Like I said, whatever it takes to wear him down. Tame him."

"And how long am I supposed to *live* with this trick?" the bimbooker pressed, holding tightly to her purse.

"How many times must I repeat myself?" Whetstone snapped in an exasperated voice. "For however long it takes! At least a couple of months I would say."

"Do you have a picture of this guy?" she purred like a cat about to receive a dish of warm milk. "Is he ugly or grotesque somehow? I could never sleep with a fat slob or..."

"Or someone like me?" Whetstone interrupted candidly. "Yes, I have a picture of him, but no, unlike me, he's not grotesque."

"You must want this fella pretty bad to go to all this trouble," she reasoned, parting her legs enough for him to see what she had to offer. "How much is this job worth to you?"

Reacting angrily to her lewd proposition, Whetstone reached over and smacked her viciously across the face with the back of his hand. The force of the blow sent her reeling from her chair and onto the floor. Hovering over her like a madman, Whetstone seemed as if he were aching for an excuse to strike her again.

"What was *that* for?" she cried, touching her bruised mouth with her hand to see if he had drawn blood.

"To get your attention," he asserted callously as she got

back to her feet.

"Okay, already, you have it," Sindy yelped, furtively slipping her hand into her purse and grasping the hilt of her hidden blade. Its cold metal was reassuring to her fevered grip.

Moving unexpectedly fast for a man of his size and age, he rose to his full height before assaulting her again. This time he jabbed at her chin with an uppercut. But anticipating his move, she sidestepped out of it, deflecting the power of his fist with her arm. As she swung around behind him, she jockeyed for position, wielding the long knife in her hand like a pro.

"Like to play rough, eh?" she gasped, slashing at him with her blade and slicing into his arm in the process.

"Damn you!" he screamed, the blood dripping from his mangled appendage.

"Now listen you," she bellowed even as he pressed his free hand to the wound to stop the bleeding. "I've met all kinds of weirdos in my life, so your macho, tough-guy act doesn't impress me one little bit. If you want me to take this kid down, it'll cost you. Plenty."

"Here," he offered, tossing her an envelope stuffed full with a thick wad of bills. "This ought to cover your first month's expenses. The man's name and his summer address are on the back of the envelope. Also, his itinerary as best we currently know it. If this is to work, sweet cheeks, you must make contact with him immediately. I'll expect no less than weekly reports as to your progress."

Thumbing through the tall stack of bills, the blond addict declared, "This is an awful lot of cash." Then, as she read the name on the envelope, she asked, "Any relation to the Senator?"

"Yes, his grandson," Whetstone replied, tearing a swatch of cloth from his shirt and pressing it against the gash on his arm. "Actually, he has *two* grandsons—make sure you nab the right Matthews. I am told the Senator is very protective of the other boy—avoid *that* one at all costs."

Still wielding her knife with deadly intent, Sindy slipped the envelope into her clutch. "Now that we have our business out of the way," she observed keenly, "what say we get down to the more pleasurable portion of this meeting?" Even as she spoke, she hiked her miniskirt up high enough to reveal her sheer panties to his depraved and lascivious eyes.

"What do you have in mind?" he stuttered, the pain of his cut forgotten as the bulge in his pants lengthened.

"If you've got a pair of handcuffs around here or a length of stiff rope, I'm sure I can take care of that little problem of yours," she advised, grinning from pierced-ear to pierced-ear like a Cheshire cat. "From my experience, tall men like you have big…"

That's all the taunting he could take. Before she could even finish her sentence, he lunged for her again. And once more she fended him off easily, only this time with a vicious blow to the ribs. Groaning, he fell to the floor in pain. But in his own sadomasochistic way, he was enjoying himself immensely. As he lay there clutching at his side, she kicked him once in the gut just for good measure.

"Again," he begged. "Again."

"You're nuts!" she yelled, backing away from him in horror. "You're out of your fucking head! I'll call you in a week like you asked, but from now on you deliver my money by courier. I don't *ever* want to get this close to you again!"

And with that she turned and left.

That Night
Along the Frontier between Canada and the United States
Dark Eagle was running across the broken and uneven ground as fast as his powerful legs would carry him. A large hunting knife hung from a sheath at his belt and a bear-claw

choker gripped at his neck. Even though the Amerind had no time to stop and ask himself why, it seemed as if he had been running his whole life through. Only *this* time, he was being chased! And not by American robot sentries like the last time, but by a pair of mean-looking Canadian Mounties— the real McCoy, just like in the old days, only much less forgiving. Whereas the border robots weren't all that difficult to evade so long as one followed an irregular, zigzag pattern when trying to escape from them, the Mounties with their force guns and their genetically altered equines, almost always were. Bearing down upon their quarry at a gallop, and applying the most carefully of rehearsed cornering-and-capturing techniques, the red-coated Mounties did their level best to uphold the Royal Canadians' adage of always getting their man.

Dark Eagle had faced such pairs of horse-mounted coppers before, and though the Amerind was incredibly fleet-footed, he couldn't possibly hope to outrun them on their steeds. Instead of being swifter, he had to be smarter, more resourceful, more vicious. Dark Eagle knew this forest in every intricate detail, and if the Amerind was to survive this encounter he would have to turn that superior knowledge to his advantage. He knew, for instance, that the Elders had ordered garroting tripwires strung up all throughout these woods; all Dark Eagle had to do was drive his pursuers through one of these neck-severing traps and then he could safely escape. But this was easier said than done, even for a man of his considerable physical abilities. Not only was Dark Eagle uncommonly handsome, but beneath the skin of his lean, hairless body, beat the heart of a true warrior. He had flat, powerful hands; a pair of dark, piercing eyes; and a ponytail of jetblack hair drawn in close behind his head. If not for the fact that it was the twenty-fourth century instead of the seventeenth, it would have been easy to picture him roaming the plains of the American West before the arrival of the Euros.

Ordering his legs to deliver yet another burst of speed, Dark Eagle swerved and darted towards a familiar grove of trees, the pair of Mounties hot on his tail, their close-fitting, three-quarter length coats making them appear larger than life. Just ahead of him, stretched taut between two giant maples at a height of perhaps seven feet, was a microfilament of wire, a filament so thin it was invisible to the naked eye, yet a filament so tough, so keen-edged, it would slice through flesh like a razor if struck at any speed above a trot. For the record, the Royal Canadians were galloping towards him from opposite directions at better than 45 miles per hour. Though their genetically-improved equestrians were capable of moving at up to 60 miles an hour on open, dry pavement, here in the forest such speeds only invited broken limbs—sometimes the horse's, more often the rider's.

Seconds later, while Dark Eagle was still some fifty yards away from the nearest garroting line, he heard a metallic clicking sound cutting the silence of the woods. It could only mean one thing: even as the Mountie to his rear was straining to maintain control over his panting horse, he was cocking the spring-loaded mechanism of his force gun. Trembling with doubt for perhaps the first time in his life, the Amerind brave feverishly sketched a gruesome picture in his mind of what was bound to happen next. It was not a pretty thought. A force gun was more like a cannon than a gun: its barrel was short and its stock wide, and at this range its awesome 32mm shell would blow a two-inch hole clean through a man.

At the sound of the trigger being cocked so close up behind his ear, Dark Eagle ticked off the seconds until his death. It was not so much that he wished to die, or even that he secretly courted death, only that he did not fear it. Men of his steel *never* feared it; they faced it squarely.

Making up his mind that facing it was exactly what he had to do, he chose his moment. Pivoting hard to his left, and at a ninety degree angle away from his earlier direction of travel, Dark Eagle spun to face his attacker head-on. Even as he swung around to confront the man, he deftly popped his long blade from its sheath at his belt. In one fluid motion, he flung it with deadly accuracy towards the charging horse. Part of what these animals had gained in speed from their creators' genetic tinkering, they had lost in thickness of hide; their thin leather coat was their Achilles tendon, and Dark Eagle knew precisely where to strike. Before the Mountie could get off a shot from his force gun, the Amerind's knife had struck the bio-stallion in the neck, slicing its jugular vein in two. Rearing back on it haunches in pain, the blade protruding from its bloodied throat, the horse threw its muscle-bound rider to the dirt even as the steed itself thrashed about furiously in its death throes. Though the second rider was still bearing down upon him from the far side of the grove, now the odds were passably even.

Jerking his bone-handled knife from the horse's neck even as the unsaddled Mountie fumbled on the ground for his weapon, Dark Eagle rapidly closed the distance between the two of them. Flinging himself onto the scarlet-coated man like a wildcat taking down his prey, the Amerind pinned the officer to the earth, plunging his already crimson-colored blade into the constable's throat. As the point penetrated the Mountie's voice box, there was a sickening crack of twisted cartilage followed by a low, gurgling sound.

Keenly aware that there was no time for delay, Dark Eagle leapt the six feet to where the dead man's gun lay in the dirt. Without even pausing to catch his breath, he braced himself firmly against the nearest tree, took aim at the remaining Canadian, and carefully squeezed off a round from the already cocked weapon. Dark Eagle had never killed a man with such a gun before, and he was stunned by the result. Not only did he find himself practically knocked senseless by the recoil, when the blast from the force gun hit the big man in the chest, it blew an enormous hole through his jacket, perforating his sternum in an explosion of blood and guts. The man was dead even before he could be decapitated by the garroting wire hanging just inches ahead of him in the night.

Dark Eagle took no particular pride in what he had done, but in a world where survival of the fittest was the law of the land, few were fitter than he. And it was a good thing too, because with the odds stacked so heavily against the Amerind cause, they needed every break they could muster.

Eight
Rainstorm

The four of them were in the lead gcar of the caravan bouncing down the winding road in the direction of the river. Ziggy and fat-Jim were in the front seat loudly debating for the third time whether or not they were on the right highway, while Sam and his brother Lester sat behind them doing their best to ignore their quibbling friends. Lashed tenuously to the roof of the auto was an improvised carrying rack, and strapped precariously to *it* were two shiny aluminum canoes. With each turn and pothole in the road, the sleek vessels squeaked and groaned noisily against one another, and to the drivers of the other similarly equipped gcars in the procession behind them, the jiggling rooftop ensemble looked as if it might crash to the ground at any moment.

Despite last year's fiasco, Sam had high hopes of actually *completing* this year's competition. Unfortunately, he and his buddies were outfitted mainly in summer-weight clothes, clothes which were totally inadequate for contending with the freezing rain and blustery, overcast skies which greeted them this uncommonly cold June morning. Only Lester was wearing a decent pair of boots and even these he had borrowed at the last minute from his buddy Abe. Nevertheless, this canoe race would be the staff's last chance to blow off some steam before camp opened for the summer two days hence, and not even the nasty weather could dull their understandable pride in what they had accomplished in the two weeks since their training first began.

As Sam sat there in the gcar daydreaming, he imagined what opening day would be like. It would begin with the harsh beep-beep of a gcar-horn echoing eerily across the lake from the freshly-mown field on the opposite shore. The grating sound would be a signal that the first boys had been deposited on camp property, a signal that before the day was out, the newcomers would number in the hundreds. Some would be arriving by private coach and some in the classic comfort of their parents' gcar. The less fortunate ones—the ones who would be arriving in a cranky mood—would be those rolling in aboard one of the camp's poorly-ventilated school buses. The disposition of *those* Scouts could only be described as surly. After having survived the summer's heat back in the city, the long, un-airconditioned bus ride north would have proven to have been a disaster. It took only one gcar-sick kid to guarantee that the entire busload would arrive queasy, a phenomenon Sam had witnessed first hand once before and hoped never to see again.

Letting his mind wander still further, Sam was reassured

by his grandpa's prompt reply that he would look into the airchop incident, though honestly, how much could the man be expected to learn from what little Sam had sent him? Without an ID number to identify the aircraft, without a pilot or a logbook, without even so much as an accurate description of the whirlybird, how easy would it be for the Senator to track down the phantom craft? Well, the answer was obvious—he couldn't. Which only served to reinforce Sam's determination to do some sleuthing of his own. But before Sam could decide on a story he could use to convince Stovepipe to let him go into town and use an info-terminal, he was jolted back to the here and now by a bump in the uneven road.

Staring glumly out the window now at the gray landscape, his thoughts were disturbed even further by the racket of two pots clanging together just behind his head. The oversized gcar Stovepipe had entrusted to Ziggy for the weekend was filled to the ceiling with sleeping bags, canoe paddles, life preservers, cook kits, and a couple canisters of personal belongings. At every blemish in the pavement, the overloaded cargo-hold would surge with a tiresome clatter; with each new pothole they struck, the overburdened roof would creak ominously. And to make matters even worse, a particularly irksome rattle was emanating from a watertight green box Lester had lugged along with him on the trip.

Tired of listening to this irritating ratatat directly behind his ear, Sam finally said to his brother, "What's in that thing anyway?"

"Just some fishing gear," Lester lied, his answer plausible enough not to be challenged further.

"Count me out on the fishing," Ziggy interjected from behind the steering wheel. Despite his infectious exuberance for life, most everyone in camp agreed Ziggy was an uncommonly levelheaded fellow. Indeed, it was on the basis of his trustworthy reputation that Stovepipe had consented to lend his gcar to Ziggy for the weekend rather than to Lester; this despite the fact that Lester was three years older than Ziggy and had had his operator's license that much longer.

"Count me out too," fat-Jim parroted before resuming his running argument with Ziggy as to their present location.

"Land's-sakes," Sam announced to no one in particular. "Don't you think it's a little bit nuts for us to even be out here? I mean look at all this damn rain!"

"Perhaps," Lester countered in his scheming tone, "but if just for once you would think this one through like a man, little brother, you would see that there is one positive aspect to this bad weather after all."

"Oh yea, and what's that?" Sam questioned as politely as he could. Usually, Sam was the quiet, thoughtful one of the bunch, oftentimes having nothing whatsoever to say, but when he *did* speak, he was always direct and to the point. Though he probably would never have admitted it in public, Sam secretly wished his brother had stayed back in camp today with Abe, rather than coming along with him and the others on this canoe trip. Not only that, he wished Lester hadn't even joined the camp staff at the last minute like he did. Having his brother around often made Sam feel uncomfortable.

"Along with all of us guys," Lester retorted with a macho smirk smeared across his face, "there will also be a hundred cold and wet *Girl* Scouts out on the river today." Lester prided himself on being a rowdy, fast-talking fellow, and although he had a certain quickness of mind, little that came out of his filthy mouth was of lasting importance.

"I tell you, this is the right road," Ziggy scolded Jim for the umpteenth time. "Now give it a rest!" he ordered in his eminently practical tone. Insomuch as the gcar was Ziggy's responsibility until they returned it to Stovepipe in one piece, it should only have made good sense that whatever Ziggy said should be final. And with everyone else it was. That is, everyone else except fat-Jim.

Jim was the exception which proved the rule: he thrived so much on confrontation that no matter how often he lost a fight and no matter how badly he was put down by the others, he always set himself up for another fall. He was the pudgy, insecure one without which no group of boys was complete; the one at the very base of the pecking order; the one who became the butt of every practical joke; the one who was bound to become a social-worker, or worse yet, a lawyer, when he grew up.

"This cow isn't riding in *my* canoe," Ziggy decided, his dark eyes flashing angrily in Jim's direction. "We haven't even gotten out on the river yet and already he's in my face. Which of you two wants to sail with this tubbalard?"

Lester and Sam exchanged troubled looks in the back seat. To see them sitting there side by side, it was a wonder the two brothers were even related. Sam was a tall, good-looking young man with a lean body and a mop of unruly brown hair. Lester was a scrawny runt with a swipe of a moustache, a puddle of dark hair, and a pair of cat-like eyes.

"We'll flip for him," Lester volunteered, turning to see if that was okay with his brother. "You call it, Sam, heads or tails?"

"Heads," Sam answered even as Lester popped the coin into the air of the moving gcar.

"Damn!" Lester swore as he peeked at the results of the coin toss. "It's tails. Okay, big Jim, it looks like you're with me, but you sit in the stern."

"I *hate* the back," Jim complained. "You know that. I want to sit..."

"Either you sit in the back," Lester snapped irritably,

"or else you're not coming with me at all."

"Quiet down, you two," Ziggy ordered as he slowed the gcar to a crawl, "I think we're here."

Just ahead of them, at a place where the highway crossed the slowly winding river, the roadbed sloped gently down towards the water's edge. This was the launch site and it was jammed packed with dozens of vehicles off-loading hundreds of eager Scouts. Undeterred by the storm, these young men and women were venturing here today from towns and camps all across the midsection of the state, and to make the long journey worthwhile, each two or three-man team would be competing for ribbons and prizes to be awarded in a half-dozen different categories. Queuing up as they arrived at the check-in point, the captain of each rival entry registered his party with the parka-clad race officials and obtained a detailed map of the river along with his team's designated starting time. As each competitor's turn came, the canoeists dutifully tightened their rainslickers and set their silvery craft in the water to begin the arduous thirty-five kilometer trek.

Even as the boys' turn to launch approached, the pace of the drizzle quickened noticeably, and before the four young men from Na-Cha-Tan had even rounded the first bend, they were drenched to the skin and shivering uncontrollably. Silently cursing their misfortune, they paddled into the wind as the cold rain blasted their faces like slivers of glass. But determined not to let the horrid weather get the better of them, they stoically pushed on. And to keep their minds off the appalling conditions, they jabbered back and forth about inconsequential things, telling each other dirty jokes, and singing one raucous camp song after another until they were hoarse in the throat.

"What do you call a woman who has lost eighty percent of her intelligence?" Lester quipped obnoxiously between verses. He was sweating and his face was beet red from the effort of trying to cut the churning water with the full length of his paddle. Weight-wise, he and Jim were badly mismatched, and despite the ballast of their equipment in the center of the craft, Jim's bulk at the rear had raised the bow of the canoe, Lester and all, from the water. This made it all but impossible for Lester to do an effective job of paddling.

When no one immediately solved Lester's denigrating riddle, he delivered the punch line himself, "Widowed." And when his wisecrack was not promptly acknowledged by a round of uproarious laughter, he repeated himself, "Widowed! Don't you dullards get it? She lost eighty percent of her intelligence when she was *widowed*."

"Lester," Sam scolded, embarrassed by his brother's crudity, "no wonder there are no women in your life. With your lousy attitude, who would have you?"

Irritated by the rebuke, Lester dug his paddle into the river as far as it would go, splashing water in Sam's direction. But tossed by the crosswind, most of the spray flew right back in Lester's face, soaking him even worse than he already was. "You'll see," Lester bellowed with false modesty, kicking himself for being so stupid as to drench his own clothes. "Just watch," he boasted, "I'll pick up a real juicy one tonight at the dance."

"Yeah, we'll see," Sam mumbled, delighted that his brother's stunt had backfired.

"Speaking of women, check *these* babes out," Ziggy advised hoarsely, his dark Mediterranean eyes studying a couple canoe-loads of eager young Girl Scouts who were swiftly overtaking them.

Flirting enthusiastically with the mademoiselles as they flew past, the four Scouts found their well-intentioned come-ons totally snubbed. Judging by the girls' speed and determination, it was evident these women were Grade A serious contestants more concerned with winning the race than with securing attractive dates for this evening's mixer— a big mistake in the boys' minds, but true nevertheless. Disappointed at having been ignored despite their best efforts, the men from Na-Cha-Tan plodded dejectedly on. For them to win this competition had been ludicrous from the start, and given today's trying weather, now even finishing it seemed increasingly doubtful.

Though they had traveled no more than a mile and a half since first putting in, the four were getting colder minute-by-wet-minute, and Sam, for one, was beginning to seriously question just how much longer he would be able to hold out. Already his bare hands were wet and numb, and his body was shaking. And then, as if to add insult to injury, Mother Nature chose that precise moment to crank up the wind speed a notch further, depressing the wind chill factor another couple of degrees. This development only made their circumstances that much more dire.

When yet a second quartet of girls whizzed past them at top speed, their lacquered paddles slicing effortlessly through the water in perfect unison, it only served to remind Sam how out-classed they really were. Ready to throw in the towel after less than forty minutes of effort, he recommended they huddle their canoes under a bridge-crossing for a summit meeting. At least there the windbreak would offer them a few minutes respite from the drizzle.

"I'm afraid we're breaking some sort of world speed record for slowness," Sam pointed out to Ziggy as his buddy studied the map they had been given at the outset of the race. The bridge they were parked under was an easily identifiable landmark on the aerial plat.

"I'm cold, Ziggy," Sam admitted matter-of-factly, his teeth chattering. "Real cold."

"Me too," Ziggy concurred as Sam steadied their canoe

to prevent it from drifting back out into the rain.

Nodding their heads in agreement from across the few feet of water still separating them, Lester and Jim pulled their craft alongside. Only, as the aluminum skin of the two canoes made contact, they scraped annoyingly past one another like a fingernail on a chalkboard. Then, propelled by their remaining inertia, both canoes clanked noisily against the bridge abutment, making it sound as if they were being torn asunder.

Pointing to the map over the screech of metal brushing against concrete, Ziggy explained, "Even though it's several river-miles from this bridge back up to the launch site where our gcar is parked, it can't be more than a mile by foot along the highway." To illustrate his point, he held the wet parchment up for everyone to see, tracing the squiggly line of the river across the countryside with his finger. As he did so, he indicated several spots where the meandering ribbon of water met up with the road.

"Are you suggesting that we *walk* back?" fat-Jim cross-examined incredulously.

"No—I wouldn't *think* of forcing you to hike all that way," Lester teased mercilessly. "God forbid, you might burn off some of that blubber."

"Ignore him," Sam recommended, speaking in gentle tones to his overweight companion. "What's your plan, Ziggy?"

"Let me guess," Lester interrupted again before the squat Sicilian could say a word. "We leave the canoes here, walk back up to the gcar, then return with it to retrieve our stuff. Am I right? Or am I right?"

"Yep, Lester," Ziggy agreed, delighted to finally get a word in edgewise. "As per usual, you are right. If we do as I recommend, we'll be warm inside of an hour."

"I'm not walking that far," fat-Jim whined. "Besides, don't you think someone should stay here to keep an eye on our stuff."

"Suit yourself," Ziggy chided, "but none of us own anything worth stealing."

"Speak for yourself," Lester objected, nervously eyeing his green tackle box. It occurred to Sam that he hadn't let the watertight container out of his sight since before they had left camp. "Anyway, these boots of Abe's are killing me. They're too tight. I would never be able to walk that far without working up a blister."

"So *both* of you stay here then," Sam urged, eager to be rid of the two irritants for awhile.

Silently sulking at the thought of being stuck alone with Lester for an hour while Sam and Ziggy left to collect Stovepipe's gcar, Jim refused to even help his friends haul the two equipment-laden canoes from the water. This made Sam fume inside, but he kept his mouth shut. Eyeing fat-Jim with contempt and cursing the foul weather, a haggard-looking Sam hunkered down under the protection of the bridge for a moment, before marching off into the unrelenting downpour with Ziggy.

As Tonnelli had promised, it didn't take them long to retrieve the gcar and return with it to the bridge, but by the time they had gotten back, a horrendous argument had erupted between Jim and Lester. Though this development was not all that surprising considering that they had been at each other's throats since before shoving off, now, as the four of them manhandled the canoes back into place on top of Stovepipe's gcar, and as they stowed the equipment in the cargo-hold, the two really started getting into it. This made for a very tense situation, and distracted by the verbal sparring between his two wayward partners, Sam didn't notice that Lester's precious fishing box was deliberately left behind under the bridge while everything else was being loaded. Moreover, with his eyes constantly being matted shut by the unforgiving rain, Sam never saw the impression left behind in the mud by Lester's boots, an impression with a familiar cross-hatched pattern and a six-pointed star down the center. With the altercation on the verge of turning physical, Sam debated whether to intervene, but before he could act, a shout rang out from the lips of his friend.

"Land ho!" Ziggy bellowed, pointing upstream a few hundred yards.

All heads turned to see a motorboat approaching the shore with two canoes in tow. Huddled in each dugout were three very wet, very cold, Girl Scouts. In the last hour, with the rain having turned so severe, the patrol boat had been cruising the river rescuing those too chilled to go on. And with each mission of mercy, the captain was using his craft to haul the unlucky ones to the nearest road crossing where they could be left safely behind before being picked up later by gtruck.

Pulling the canoes alongside the riverbank underneath the bridge, the skipper of the motorized boat waited patiently while the girls off-loaded with their gear before speeding off in search of other misfortunes still stranded out on the river. In the downpour, no one paid any attention to the fact that the driver of the motorboat had grabbed Lester's tackle box from where it had been sitting under the bridge and placed it onboard with him.

As the ladies began making their way up the slippery embankment from the water's edge, Sam polled his buddies. "Shouldn't we invite them to come warm up with us in the gcar? They look pretty cold to me."

"That would of course be the polite thing to do," Lester recommended judiciously as the four men shut the vehicle's doors and made themselves comfortable, "but let's wait 'til the first one turns around so we can see what she looks like.

In cases like these, where a woman's looks are involved, one can never be too careful, you know."

When the leader of the cavalcade came into view, dragging her wet life jacket and her busted paddle behind her, it was an inauspicious start: regrettably, she had a face only a mother could love. "Let's get outta here!" fat-Jim urged, as if he himself were the catch of the century.

"Not so fast," Sam objected before Ziggy could start the engine. "The second one's okay." Rolling down his window without a moment's hesitation, Sam shouted, "Young lady! How would you and your friends like to come dry off with us in a nice warm gcar?"

Grinning a big "yes" at him, the pretty girl signaled her companions ahead, and with the ugly one leading the pack, the six windblown women piled into what, moments earlier, had been a spacious and roomy auto. "Thanks," the cute one nodded as the girls giggled and squeezed bashfully into the idling vehicle. "My name's Sara," she announced, flashing Sam a winning smile.

With the ten of them crammed in there like sardines, and with the heater running full tilt, it wasn't long before they began wrestling their soaking wet raincoats to the floor. As the windows fogged over and the interior began to take on the qualities of a cramped sauna, a pile of perspiration-clogged sweatshirts shortly followed the raincoats to the deck. Now, between the overwrought heater and the long-ago expired deodorants, the aroma inside the gcar was reminiscent of a towel hamper in a high school locker room immediately following the big game; only, it seemed as if a mildewing pair of dirty gym socks were buried in with everything else in that hamper.

At first, no one said a word. In fact, if someone hadn't unexpectedly passed gas at that moment, the tension in the gcar might never have been broken. But then, with the air cleared, so to speak, a round of nervous adolescent giggles echoed against the opaque glass and the way was paved for introductions. The white knights went first, followed by the damsels in distress.

To begin with, there was Ziggy—the dark, curly-haired fellow occupying the driver's seat; then, sitting next to him in the front, there was Sam—the tall, lanky one with the broad shoulders and the light-colored eyes; next, there was Lester—the shorter, devious-looking fellow sitting directly behind Sam; and finally, wedged in the far rear, there was Jim—the fat, insecure one.

Then, in no particular order, there was Cathy—the ugly one, Jana—the nondescript girl perched on Jim's lap, Judy—the darkhaired belle who had already caught Ziggy's attention, Beth—a big, bestial woman who had obviously grown up on a farm, Sindy—an aloof gal with blond hair and big breasts, and finally, Sara—the nice looking one who had caught Sam's eye the instant she came up the hill from the river. As it turned out, the girls themselves were from two different troops and had only just met when they happened to get stranded close to one another out on the river. As it also turned out, both Sindy and Sara were so new to their respective troops, they barely knew where their own canoe-mates grew up. Sindy, Jana, and Beth were from towns Sam had never heard of, while Judy, Sara, and Cathy were from Madison, the state capital.

Squirming uneasily in the cramped space once the introductions had been completed, there was little more that could be accomplished by sitting there any longer. Indeed, now that the circulation had finally returned to their toes, everyone was mighty uncomfortable, and the girls especially, were eager to get back to their campsite to change into some dry clothes. According to the rules of the weekend-long outing, the Boy Scouts were supposed to tough it out in canvas tents like "real" men, while the women were forced to endure the comforts of a nice dry cabin over at the riverside campground. Only, these boys had planned ahead. Pooling their resources beforehand, these fellows had rented a flat for the night so that, unlike the rest of the staff, they would be well-rested and freshly showered for the sock-hop this evening. After all, the canoe race wasn't about winning, it was about meeting girls!

As Ziggy set the gcar back on the road for the short drive towards the women's quarters, Sara whispered something in Sam's ear. Though he couldn't be certain, he thought he heard her say, "See you at the dance tonight." Unfortunately, he was too keyed up, not to mention embarrassed, to ask her to repeat herself. Thus, when moments later the gcar emptied, he wasn't sure whether to be hopeful about this evening's prospects, or apprehensive.

Nine
Sock Hop

Despite Sam's prodding to hurry up, he and his buddies arrived at the gymnasium behind schedule. Having been unable to get Sara out of his mind since they parted company only hours ago, he was worried that the mixer had already gotten underway without him, that the best looking girl in the place had already been asked to dance even before he had a chance to ask her himself. It was for this reason that he bounded across the school lawn from the parking lot to the door, grunting an audible sigh of relief when he heard the band still warming up inside.

As the four latecomers entered the old building at a dash, they could hear the emcee instructing the female participants to line up along the north wall of the gym and the Boy Scouts to congregate along the opposite wall. Rushing to the boys' side of the room along with all the others, Sam waited for the inevitable announcement.

"The first dance will be ladies' choice," the emcee's voice boomed over the microphone, filling the air with electric anticipation. "After that, it's all up to you fellas."

"I *knew* it," Sam grumbled to no one in particular. Icebreakers the world over have always started out the same way: girl picks boy. And why *is* that? Sam wondered, shifting nervously from one leg to the other. Perhaps it was because, despite all their macho talk, boys at his age were bashful (if not downright terrified) when it came to members of the opposite sex. If propagating the species had been left solely to the men, the human race would have died out long ago.

Suppressing an adolescent chuckle as the boys around him eagerly crossed their fingers hoping to improve their chances that the right girl would pick them, Sam decided not to, just to be different. Instead, he scanned the eyes of the young women standing across the way until he found precisely the set he was searching for. Intently focusing his steely gaze upon Sara's lovely face, Sam beamed widely in her direction, confident he could draw her attention to him by sheer willpower alone. So certain was he that Sara would walk up to him and ask him for that first dance, he discounted any other possible outcome. But then, at the very last second, just to be sure, he laced the first two fingers of his right hand together and held them high above his head where she would be sure to notice. From the other side of the room, Sara acknowledged his signal with a curtsy and a nod.

"All right now, gals—pick yaw podners," the emcee twanged as the drummer in the band reverently tapped out a funeral dirge in the background.

On cue, the females cautiously pawed their way forward,

seeking out their helpless prey cowering on the opposite wall. Unlike the other felines in the pack, Sara did not hesitate in the slightest; to the contrary, she pounced across the gym floor like an accomplished hunter on the prowl, never once taking her eyes off her intended quarry.

"I want you to be my squeeze for the evening," she asserted with disarming directness. Even as she spoke, she placed her strong hands in his.

"What?" he babbled incoherently. "I mean, I thought you would never ask," he began again, attempting to maintain his composure in the face of her unnerving boldness.

As the cack band blared out its first unintelligible notes, he timidly escorted her out onto the dance floor. Glancing about the dance hall as the couplings slowly proceeded, Sam caught a glimpse of Ziggy with his arm around the shoulder of Judy, one of the other girls they had rescued that afternoon; and in another direction he spied Lester strutting his stuff in front of the tall, lean girl he knew so far only as Sindy. From where he stood, Sam couldn't see where fat-Jim was, but knowing how self-conscious Jim was about his girth and how withdrawn he was around girls, Sam figured he was already snuggled up alone in a corner somewhere. Catching sight of Sam's faraway look, Sara tugged impatiently at his arm, drawing him back into her circle.

When the band inaugurated the event with a medley of fast dances—the sort where the cack'n rollers weren't actually expected to touch one another—the room started churning, and the delirious participants began gyrating furiously without any apparent purpose or any apparent sense of rhythm. Unable to talk over the maddening beat, Sam and Sara joined in, two-stepping wildly until the sweat was pouring down their cheeks. It was as if they were in a jungle taking part in some sort of primitive mating rite. Hidden from reality by the throng of pulsating teenagers, their skin glistening from the effort, they acted out the decidedly pagan ritual in which communication between the sexes had to take place without the benefit of words or of physical contact. In fact, thus far, only their hands had touched. And yet, a bond of friendship had already been forged between them.

At the first break in the music, she pulled him close and panted, "You move like a panther." When she growled and tugged playfully at his ear with her mouth, Sam thought he would die. He was completely out of his element and totally unprepared for her daring, audacious manner.

"Why don't we sit the next one out?" he suggested, certain his legs were about to cave in beneath him.

But before she could answer, the band changed its style and the tempo of a familiar slow-song began to serenade the crowd. It was the kind of tune where the couples were expected to pull close to one another and actually hold each other while they danced.

Trembling, Sam hesitantly put his arms about her in the classical slow-dance pose: left hand on right hand; right hand on left hip.

"Relax, Tiger," she whispered, sensing his reluctance to grip her firmly, "and hold me...tighter."

He did as she instructed, and as he drew her close, he could feel her heart pounding hard against his own throbbing chest. The comforting beat of the music and the disconcerting lyrics of the ballad swam across the gym, intoxicating him in a way no liquor ever could. Sam found their embrace to be most satisfying, and for the first time he took note of the color of her eyes, the fullness of her lips, and the firmness of her build. It didn't occur to him that the song might ever end, or that he would eventually have to let her go.

But finally it did end. And finally he *did* untangle himself from her powerful arms. It was too late to untangle his feelings, however: he was love struck.

"I need some air," he stammered, laboring to catch his breath. "Let's go outside for awhile where we can talk."

Pausing for a moment to judge whether his intentions were honorable or not, she replied with a smile, "Sure, lover boy, I'm game for most anything!"

Grabbing their windbreakers from the chairs where they had left them, the two budding sweethearts headed for the door. Spying them on their way out, Ziggy gave Sam the time-honored thumbs-up sign with one hand even as he continued caressing Judy's shoulder-length hair with the other. There was no sign of Lester or of Sindy.

Although there was still the occasional flash of lightning in the distance, the rain had stopped for the evening, leaving the night air fresh and cool. Finding it a welcome contrast to the hot and stuffy gymnasium they had just exited, the two of them sauntered leisurely down the sidewalk with no particular destination in mind.

Not far from the school they found a park-bench which, except for still being damp from the earlier downpour, seemed a good place to stop. Removing his jacket, Sam offered it as a seat cover to keep their bottoms dry, and Sara gladly accepted his generous move, curling her face up into a smile before sitting down.

Unsure exactly what to say or do next, Sam tilted his head backward and began staring blankly at the night sky. Between the tattered edges of the receding storm clouds he could make out bits and pieces of the Milky Way. The stars were glittering dots of light which beckoned to him from across the miles. Silently wondering whether he would ever have the opportunity to venture beyond the Earth's iron grip, he was reminded how disappointing mankind's adventure in space had been thus far. Despite some noteworthy successes at the outset, man's colonization of the heavens had been a total bust, accomplishing nothing more than making the moon a convenient dumping ground for the Earth's nuclear wastes. There had been no "final frontier" as space enthusiasts had hoped four hundred years ago at the dawn of the space age, no fruited plains ripe for cultivation, no safe havens to escape the tyrants of the home planet. The final frontier had turned out to be nothing more than a barren, impenetrable wall, and irony of ironies, the last outworld settler had left the Red Planet in the very year of Sam's birth.

Intruding in upon his thoughts, Sara asked, "Tiger, do you believe in God?"

"My given name is Samuel, and I would prefer it if you would either call me by my given name or else just by Sam," he replied, sidestepping the more difficult issue she had raised. "Besides," he added with a note of deep respect in his voice, "my great grandfather went by the nickname Tiger, so it wouldn't be fair to his memory if I absconded with his well-deserved moniker."

"Okay, Samuel," she relented. "Now quit stalling and answer my question! Do you believe in God or not?" she demanded, turning more authoritative as she put him to the test.

"Of course I do," he responded, answering her with what he hoped would be a safe reply. "Don't you?" Although her cross-examination had him completely off his guard, he thought with sudden pleasure that she was even prettier than he had first remembered.

Ignoring his trite answer for the moment, she countered with an even tougher proposition. "Why, pray tell, do you believe in God, Samuel? Tell me *why*."

"Well," he stammered, fidgeting uneasily as he tried to settle on the best way to extricate himself from this predicament. Except for what his grandfather had attempted to teach him over the years, Sam had never really given more than a cursory thought to matters of "why." To the contrary, he had spent most of his life concentrating all his energies on questions of "when" or "how," as in "When will dinner be ready?" or "How am I going to get to tonight's basketball game?" Now, here he was, suddenly face-to-face with this delightful, infuriating, inquisitive girl who was drilling him on subjects normally reserved for the likes of a rabbi or a priest, and he didn't know how to react. Much as when he had struggled to fend off Abe's probing questions about America, Sam again found himself in over his head. Just what kind of girl was this anyway? a confused Sam asked himself as he struggled with a reply.

"Tell me *why* you believe in God," she repeated impatiently.

"Well, Sara," he began tentatively. "Do you see that star up there?" he petitioned, pointing to the constellation known to astrologers as Orion. "That, my dear, is *proof* that God exists."

Satisfied that his answer had a mature sounding ring to it, Sam recklessly continued. "My existence, your existence, the existence of the entire human race, for that matter, is proof positive that God exists."

Confident that his explanation would put an end to the interrogation, Sam edged closer, intending to ask her for a kiss. Only she wasn't through with him yet—not by a long measure.

"You are wrong, Samuel. Or else terribly naive. The existence of that distant sun, the existence of the human race, the existence of you and of me, these are all things which can be easily explained in terms of the biological and physical laws we have already discovered, laws like the Durbin Paradox or the Gluon Attraction Postulate. There are no mysteries here."

Though he frowned doubtfully at her, he kept his

mouth shut. Sam was stumbling badly and he knew it. If only she could stand with him on the shores of Lake Na-Cha-Tan, he might be able to make her understand. Sam had always felt that nothing less than a God could have conjured up the camp he loved so dearly, and that if a mortal ever wished to gaze upon His countenance, all he need do was look out across the shimmering surface of the lake any moonlit night and He would be there. This, however, was not the answer she was looking for.

"No, my good-looking friend," Sara insisted stridently. "If all you have to offer me as proof of God's authenticity is *our* presence, then I cannot share in your belief of the Almighty. The Bible and all its stories are but a work of complete fiction, a collection of legends the Hebrews once told themselves at night around their campfires to keep the boogeyman away. Listen," she added calmly, "you are an intelligent guy—I know you can do better. Try again."

Samuel Matthews, grandson of Senator Nate Matthews, great grandson of Nathanial "Tiger" Matthews, nodded his head, grinned, and plunged into the murky waters once more. He had never been tested by a woman in quite this way; he found the novelty rather exciting.

"How can you conceivably hope to explain beauty or love or truth in terms of chemistry or physics?" he rebutted, expecting to gain the upper hand with this tact.

"How indeed?" Sara replied, thwarting him.

"How can you possibly account for honesty or fidelity or determination with respect to some obscure equation or some puzzling physical law? You can't!" he exclaimed, answering his own question before she got a chance to interrupt. Even in the midst of their debate, Sam was becoming absurdly conscious of little things about her: the way her hair seemed to hover and float gently each time she shook her head, the way the moistness of her lips shone in the moonlight.

"Maybe," she retorted aloofly, "but then again, maybe not. To begin with, acknowledging the existence of a human emotion like love, or a trait like honesty, does not prove or disprove anything at all about God. And in the second place, just because *I* cannot unscramble these traits in terms of a physical or a chemical law, does not mean that someone with the appropriate *schooling* cannot. Understanding much of this is a function of education, of training. Just consider the work that has already been done demonstrating how violence is a function of one's genes, and how—with the proper medication—that tendency can be suppressed. I am confident that the same sorts of relationships will one day be proven true for every emotion you can list."

"Huh?"

"The pattern of the tides, the shifting of the tectonic plates, the changing faces of the seasons—*all* these events were once thought to be controlled by a god of one sort or another. Nowadays, all these occurences are easily understood as being caused by some physical phenomenon; in the case of the tides, by the movements of the moon; in the case of the tectonic plates, by the rolling of the Earth's molten core."

"Did you say *easily* understood?" Sam countered in surprise. "Land's-sakes, woman, you must be kidding! It takes a Ph.D. in Chaos Theory to decipher the patterns in the tides. And what about free will? Is *everything* dictated by our genes?"

Even before she could open her mouth to answer, Sam reached out and touched her hand. He was tired of matching wits with her and wanted desperately to alter the flow of their conversation in a more pleasant direction. "How would you feel towards me if I said I loved you?" he probed gently, trusting she would respond favorably.

Without flinching, Sara shot back, "Are we talking

about love or merely about sex? Are you suggesting a trip down the aisle or just a one night stand?"

Stunned by her directness, Sam stumbled around once more, searching for the right words. "Well..." he mumbled confusedly, "I...don't actually know." Like a ship without a compass, he was absolutely lost at sea.

"Listen, bub," she challenged forthrightly. "If you can look me straight in the eye and promise that we will be married in the morning if only I will let you sleep with me tonight, then we can continue with this conversation. Otherwise, good night, and sleep tight." And with that, she got up from the bench and started to walk away with a determined step.

"Feisty broad," Sam mumbled grimly to himself, terrified by this wonderful-looking girl who had successfully cornered him in less than half an hour. He was in a fix unlike any he had ever been in before. Marriage was about the last thing he had on his mind today, and no matter how delightful this woman might have been in bed, he was not prepared to bargain away the rest of his youth in exchange for an evening of pleasure. Though it pained him no end to turn her away, Sam was much too honest a man to lie.

"Sara, I must confess: I genuinely *do* like you," he declared before she could get more than a few steps afield. "But under the conditions you have laid down for me, I don't see as if I have any other choice. I'm just not prepared to make that sort of a commitment to you. Alas, our conversation must truly be over."

Reluctantly drawing a deep breath as he plucked his windbreaker from the bench, Sam lumbered to his feet and offered to escort her back to the dance hall.

"Oh Sam, sweet loveable Sam," she cajoled. "Thank you. Thank you ever so much."

"What do you mean *thank you*?" he exploded, his heart

rate spiking along with his anger. "Listen, lady…"

"No, you listen!" she ordered abruptly. "I'm trying to thank you. I'm trying to thank you for respecting me enough to speak the truth—*and* for turning me down. Since you have refused me—and in a most gentlemanly manner, I might add—I must have you."

"Have me?" he burst out loud. "Confounded woman! Give me one reason why I should spend even another minute here with you. So you can probe and dissect me *further*? No, mam, I have had enough! Have a nice life," he concluded as he stomped away in the direction of the parking lot.

Not willing to give in that easily, Sara chased after him, her outstretched hands straining to reach him. Arresting his departure within two strides, she spun him around and kissed him full on the lips. Astonished by her aggressiveness, Sam pushed her away in horror. But undaunted by the snub, she came back for more. Her breath was hot against his face; her muscular body supple and lithe.

Sam spluttered, "I think…"

"Don't think. Don't talk. Don't leave. Just kiss me, you fool," she cooed, a hungry, animal-like growl surfacing from deep within her.

Sam gave her a tentative kiss. And then another. By the third meeting of their lips, their bodies were pressed firmly together, and their hands were conducting a preliminary exploration of each other's frame.

They broke, and Sam was about to say, "I love you," when she put her hand gently to his mouth and stopped him cold.

"Don't say it," she begged, her eyes melting his resolve.

"Can you read my mind?" he questioned, still unsure what to make of this girl.

"Only your body," she replied matter-of-factly, her hand brushing against his trousers, "and there I sense a certain newfound firmness about you. But, Romeo, let's not confuse love with lust," she whispered wantonly, licking his ear with her tongue.

Hearing her words and smelling her body's fragrance, Sam thought for an instant of having her in the back seat of Stovepipe's gcar, but before he could act on that impulse, a distressingly familiar voice softened his passion.

"Okay, you two, break it up!" Ziggy demanded, a false sternness in his tone.

Their lips still wet with desire, Sara and Sam gradually uncoupled, an audible sigh escaping from their quivering mouths.

"The dance is over, kids," Ziggy continued as Judy hung from his arm, a contented smile adorning her face. Behind them, the gymnasium could be seen gradually emptying. "It's time to go home."

"Leave us alone," Sara objected fiercely. "Tiger and I are just getting started."

"Tiger, eh?" Ziggy quipped, grinning at his friend. "You know, Sara, maybe you are right: Sam *is* such a dull sounding name. Well, Tiger, what'd'ya say? Shall we call it a night? It's late and we ought to get these ladies back home."

Reluctantly nodding his head in agreement, Sam laced his fingers with hers. Holding hands, the two young couples made their way through the slowly dispersing throng. They found a thoroughly dejected Jim waiting impatiently for them in the school parking lot.

"Have you seen my brother?" Sam asked, though he really couldn't have cared less about the answer.

"Yeah," fat-Jim creaked in a derisive tone, "he was with that Sindy, and the two of them left the dance a long time ago. He said to go ahead without him."

Shaking his head with disbelief before turning to Sara and Judy, Ziggy offered, "Need a ride back to your campsite?"

The girls giggled and answered, "Sure," in unison. Then Sara added playfully, "But no shenanigans."

"Miladies," Sam clamored, applying his most chivalrous tone, "you have nothing to fear, but fear itself. I will protect both your honor and your chastity from this fiendish rogue," he assured, motioning towards Ziggy as if the Sicilian were some sort of troublemaker.

Sara rolled her eyes and got into the gcar. "Home, James," she instructed in the manner of a lord to a servant.

"Your every wish is my command," Ziggy humbly replied as the five of them crawled into the vehicle for the short hop across town.

"I wish we didn't have to say 'so long'," Sam murmured, bravely pressing Sara's hand into his own. He was sullen because the chances of ever seeing her again seemed awfully slim. Trembling as he spoke, he added, "Please don't forget me too soon."

"How could a girl forget a swell guy like you?" she complimented as Ziggy pulled up at the campground. "Not a chance!"

His spirits soared as she spoke.

"I guarantee you, Sam: we will be together again before the summer is out! But first, you must tell me how to reach you. Heck, I don't even know your last name."

"Matthews."

"Like the Senator?"

"Yes, spelled the same way," he confessed, not wanting to scare her off by revealing that *the* Senator Matthews was his grandfather.

After exchanging addresses and kissing her good night, Sam walked back to the gcar, an airy bounce in his step. He was giddy, even buoyant. For the first time in his life, he had met a new and deliciously different species of female, one refreshingly unlike the dimwits he had known from

Farmington High, one worth pursuing further.

By *stars*, it was great to be alive! he thought, merrily kicking up his heels. Just great!

Ten
Sara

Leaning heavily on the gnarled wooden cane Flix had given him that desperately cold December morning just before he died, the senior Senator from the proud state of Missouri hobbled across the tiled floor of his luxurious chambers in the west wing of the Senate Office Building. With each step he took, a shallow metallic ping reverberated from deep within his cane, a ping which reminded him that a rifled gunbarrel ran down the entire length of its hollowed-out core. Hidden in a recess of the staff's curved handle was a single-action trigger, and should the occasion ever arise that that trigger had to be squeezed, a single, rather large calibre shell would promptly be expelled from its mouth at tremendous velocity.

Pulling off his flak jacket and hanging up his face mask, Senator Matthews sank into the nearest easy chair. Big city life was depressing at best. It was too hazardous nowadays for someone of his standing to go outside without a Stromberg vest strapped across his chest, and on two days out of five, a face mask was necessary as well on account of the bad and worsening air pollution. So it was with some relief that he could at last be at ease in the air-conditioned splendor of his own chambers.

Revisiting the conversation he had just concluded with President McIntyre over at the New White House and the firm rebuke he had given the Chief Executive for commuting Silas Whetstone's life sentence and setting the scoundrel free, Nate permitted a satisfied smile to crack his usually serious countenance. Alongside the steady decline in the power and the influence of the Presidency had come the ascendancy of the Imperial Senate. And as the oldest sitting Senator and as the longest-standing Chairman of the Military Oversight Committee, Matthews was perhaps one of the five most powerful men alive on the planet today, a station which permitted him a great deal of latitude. It was not so much that he abused his power as it was that he rarely relinquished it without first exacting a high price. Much to Nate's delight, President McIntyre had paid dearly for his cooperation today.

It wasn't long, however, before the gratified look on the Senator's face had metamorphosed into a scowl. His cancer kept him in a great deal of pain, and unfortunately, there was almost nothing the doctors could do about it. No algorithm presently existed to cure his vicious disease, and even the Acceleron treatments they had prescribed for him had failed to cure the inoperable, tissue-eating menace. He knew his days were numbered, yet strangely enough, this was not what was bothering him at the moment; for the present anyway, he was less troubled about the state of his own declining health than he was about what would become of the Matthews' fortune, the Matthews' name, and the Matthews' power once he was gone.

From the time the Matthews clan had first come to America from what was then Scotland, they had been a proud and patriotic bunch. Nate's grandfather had once traced their geneology back five hundred years to a Byron Matthewson, a pioneer who had settled in Illinois and who had fought for the North in the War Between the States. Along with several hundred others, Byron Matthewson's name had been inscribed on a monument standing in downtown Peoria, a shrine which commemorated the honored dead from that conflict. And with each succeeding generation, there had been at least one Congressman, or one Captain of Industry, or one War Hero to bear the name of Matthewson, later shortened to Matthews. With every generation, that is, until the present one.

Nate's father, Nathanial "Tiger" Matthews, had been the Governor of Missouri, and he himself had been that state's ranking U.S. Senator all these good many years, but now it seemed as if he was to be the last of the Matthews' scion. Considering the extent of the Matthews' fortune, it was a depressing thought indeed.

Franklin, Nate's only child by his first wife, had turned out to be a renegade. Running away from home without ever finishing high school and never bothering to gain a proper education, Franklin had been forever relegated to performing menial jobs for hand-to-mouth wages. And as if that wasn't depressing enough for someone of the Senator's ilk, Nate's second wife, Musette, had never been able to give him any children. This was thanks to a gunshot wound she had suffered years ago, a wound inflicted by Overlord Mao and one which had prevented her from ever carrying a baby to term. As for the *succeeding* generation, though Franklin had managed to find the time to sire two boys, the first seemed determined to be every bit as successful as his old man. Which left Samuel.

To Nate's way of thinking, Samuel was the last, best hope for the Matthews' line. He was a smart, good-looking fellow who not only had to regularly fend off a flock of girls, but who had also set for himself some very high lifetime goals. Despite his promise (or perhaps because of it), Sam was constantly in trouble at school, a circumstance which weighed heavily on Nate's mind. Though he put this down as being chiefly the result of his older brother's bad influence (not to mention his father's complete lack of attention), it disturbed Nate no end. The Senator was paranoid that unless he himself kept a careful watch over the boy—something he had failed to do with regard to his own son Franklin—Sam was bound to go wrong just as Lester had.

Despite his many time-consuming responsibilities as Senator, as well as Chairman of the powerful Military Oversight Committee, Nate had committed himself to taking the young man under his wing and showing him the way. Remembering his own difficulties at Sam's age, Nate had nurtured his grandson through both school and Scouts. And fearful that the boy would get into mischief if he stayed at home all summer long with nothing to do, Nate had convinced him to apply for a counselor's position at Camp Na-Cha-Tan. Much to his chagrin, however, after returning from his trip overseas, Lester had done likewise, reasoning that the experience would help prepare him for his upcoming stint at the Naval Academy this fall. But now, after what Director Harper had told him about Abe Levinson, the runaway Israeli agent masquerading as the camp's Rabbi, and after Officer Jenkins had helped him identify the shape on the sole of the boot Sam had sketched as a Mogen David, the mark of the Mossad, Nate was understandably worried. Inasmuch as the Senator himself had had countless encounters with scores of lowlifes over the years, he was not content to leave his favorite grandson unattended, especially not where Lester's negative influence would be so close at hand. That's where the girl had come in.

When he and Harper had first chatted about this mess the other day, the Director had assured him that someone topnotch had already been assigned to look in on Sam, and that that someone would report in with Nate following their first encounter. But not until yesterday, when that someone finally called him for an appointment, did the Senator realize that the *he* was in fact a *she*. Without thinking it necessary to consult with Nate as to his plans, Harper had contracted for the use of a fresh new operative enrolled in the apprentice program, a sharp young female who could make contact with, and keep an eye on his grandson without making it appear too obvious—a "cherry," to use the Director's words. Nate was furious over the development and had demanded an immediate consultation with the girl, a consultation he had now planned out carefully in his mind. She was expected at his office at any moment now, and if she was the right sort, he had every intention of buying her loyalty.

As he sat there fretting over whether Harper had picked the right person for the job, he closed his eyes, hoping to get in a short nap before she arrived. But before he could fall asleep, a self-assured knock came to his outer door.

"Yes, who is it?" he bellowed from the comfort of his chair, shaking himself awake.

"Director Harper sent me," Sara announced through the closed door.

"Please come in, won't you?" he yelled back without moving. Having never met the woman before, he wasn't quite sure what to expect; Harper had said only that she was rather plain.

As Sara ambled confidently into the room, Nate was immediately struck by how attractive she was. Nothing at all like Harper had led him to believe. Her sweater was tight and her skirt was short. Her legs were muscular and, to his old eyes, her buttocks were sculpted works of art. Like a woodsman or a Zealander, she had glowing red cheeks and a set of penetrating round eyes. Despite his many years and his worsening cancer, Nate still had a fond eye for the ladies, and for the briefest instant he imagined her standing naked before him. In his reverie, he found himself delighting over her washboard stomach and her firm, full breasts.

"My name is Sara Logan," she murmured, extending her hand to him in the classic gesture of goodwill. "You wanted to see me?"

The sound of her voice was enough to shock him back to the present, and his face reddened measurably as he realized that he had been mentally disrobing her.

"Why, yes," he stammered, feeling suddenly ashamed of his carnal urgings. Only it was too late; she had already picked up on them.

"Don't you think you're a mite old to be staring at me that way?" she started in on him in a combative tone.

"What way?" he retorted innocently, averting his eyes from her chest as if his mother had just scolded him for putting his hand in the cookie jar.

"Senator, don't treat me like a child—I'm a full-grown woman."

"Yes, I can see that," he jousted playfully.

"And I've seen that look before."

"My, but aren't you the feisty one," Nate snapped back, enjoying the spirit of this rugged young woman. "If you didn't want to be scrutinized that way, I dare say you might have dressed more conservatively."

"Indeed. Now come to the point, Senator, or else I will be on my way. Director Harper has me on a tight schedule this morning."

"Geez woman, Harper can go to blazes!" Nate interjected, the cleft in his chin reddening. "I want to know how your first meeting went with Sam. I understand you two met on a canoe race or something."

"Yes, Senator, that's correct. I must say, your grandson Sam is a fine fellow," she complimented sincerely, slumping into the nearest chair as if she had been on her feet for hours. "But I really do think that by asking me to babysit the lad, you are wasting not only my time, but the Agency's money as well."

"Perhaps, but since I control the Agency's purse strings, not you, how it spends its appropriations is really none of your concern, now is it?" Even as he spoke, Nate thought again of Flix's enigmatic black book tucked securely away in the wall safe behind his bar. Though the code book had been updated innumerable times since Nate first took possession of it, it was still the key to the entire underground military-complex Flix had set up before permanently retiring from public life.

"You didn't ask me here today for a lecture," she asserted testily, crossing and uncrossing her legs in an unnerving fashion.

"Oh, but I did," Nate contradicted, his eyes riveted on Sara's fidgeting limbs. "I am a very powerful man, but at the present time nothing means more to me than that boy. Though I imagine Director Harper has already briefed you adequately, let me make one thing perfectly clear: I mean for you to *babysit* Sam, not seduce him, and I mean for you to obey *my* orders, not Harper's."

"I'll do whatever my boss tells me to do," she retorted

defiantly, again repositioning her long legs in a provocative manner. Unlike the previous instance, however, this time she intentionally exposed a flash of her upper thigh as she uncoupled her knees. Though it was a childish ploy, it was the only thing she could think of to slow down the pace of the conversation sufficiently. There was at once a glaring contradiction in the directions the two men were giving her, and she needed a moment to sort things out. Director Harper's instructions had been quite specific: seduce Sam by whatever means possible, but otherwise keep your distance from Na-Cha-Tan. Now here was the boy's own grandfather telling her practically the opposite. It made for a perplexing dilemma: whose orders should she obey?

"I realize that officially you are on Harper's payroll, but for *this* assignment, I want you to be on mine." Even as he spoke, the Senator lumbered to his feet and hobbled over to his desk without the aid of his cane. Opening a side drawer, he extracted a plain leather belt and held it before him. Sewn into the body-side of the narrow waistband was a zipper. Undoing the zipper partway to expose the contents of the hidden pocket, a sleeve filled with gold coins fell into his hand.

"There are forty-eight in all, my girl; a hundred thousand new dollars worth if you'll have them."

"I guarantee you now have my undivided attention," Sara confirmed, warily eyeing the bullion-filled belt, "but I don't see how, short of being on camp staff myself, I can keep regular track of your grandson."

"I don't actually need you there 'round the clock—I already have someone in place for that. What I need is…"

"Who? Who do you have in place?"

"Sorry, but for the moment anyway, I can't tell you her name."

"*Her* name?!" Sara balked, an envious tinge coloring her

voice. "You hired another *woman* for this?"

"I'm surprised. You didn't strike me as the jealous type," Nate chuckled, an adolescent smirk filling his wrinkled face. As only he could know, Miss Loddy was hardly any competition for this fine specimen of a female.

"Well then, get on with your lecture," she harrumphed, her eyes still fixed on the gold-laden belt he was holding.

"America is coming apart at the seams," he croaked, zipping the hidden pocket of the belt shut and tossing her the heavy waistband. "Put it on," he instructed, "zipper side in."

Giving the Senator a look of, "How stupid do you think I am?" she nevertheless did as she was told.

Without missing a beat, Nate continued. "As a dear friend of mine once warned me—you would have liked him by the way—the wolf is finally at the door. Hawaii has finally broken free, our border with Canada is a powderkeg, and after three decades of civil war, Mao's son Ling is firmly back in control."

"Mao?"

"Sorry, my dear, but I'm afraid he's a bit before your time," Nate apologized. "What are you, all of twenty? I'm speaking of Overlord Mao Tsui. Thirty plus years ago, he died in my home town of Farmington, Missouri. Not too many people are aware of this anymore, but I was the one who finished him off."

"I never knew that," she admitted, making a mental note to check out his story with Director Harper the first chance she got. The more Nate talked, the more her respect for him grew. He wasn't just a broken down old man as the Director had led her to believe. He had served his country with distinction and had done so for four times as long as she had even been alive.

"As I was saying, America has been severely weakened, and if we eventually are forced to go to war with China…"

"*War*?" she interjected, coming to attention in her seat. "I've heard no talk of war!"

"I know, my sweet, and you may not for several years yet, but we narrowly avoided going toe-to-toe with Mao the last time around, and I suspect his son Ling has every intention of finishing what his father once started. In my business I *have* to look at all the possibilities," Nate elaborated. "As Chairman of the M.O.C., I am privy to developments few others even know about. Overlord Ling and I go back a good many years, and because of what I did to his father, Ling has it in for me. Inasmuch as Sam is my only heir—the only Matthews worth saving—Sam is the one Overlord Ling is most likely to go after. Now that Ling is no longer distracted by a power struggle back at home, and now that he has consolidated his control over the mainland, he is bound to make good on his promise to avenge Mao's death. That's where you come in—I may need you to run a special errand for me."

"Errand? What sort of errand?" she quizzed, fingering the money belt she had already tightened in place around her slim waist.

"I may need you to get Sam across the border."

"Which border?"

"Into Canada."

"That's impossible."

"For me, maybe, but not for you."

"Why should I chance it?"

"I just gave you a hundred thousand reasons," he retorted. "You work for me now, remember?"

"That'll cost you two hundred," she pointed out as she rose to leave. It was clear to her that for the very first time she had him just where she wanted him. "Will there be anything else?"

"As a matter of fact, yes," he answered, staring her

straight in the eye. "I need to know what your cover is."

"Director Harper has arranged for me to be the daughter of Ambassador Nussbaum. He lives on Lake Mendota in Madison."

"I've been to Nussbaum's estate; isn't that a bit too fashionable of an address for the smalltown girl image you are trying to cultivate?"

"The best we could do on such short notice," she admitted impatiently. "Was there something else on your mind, Senator?"

"No, that will be all," he stated in a tone which told her she was dismissed.

Eleven
Wimachtendienk, Wingolauchsik, Witahemui

The lore of the Amerind and the traditions of his culture were so deeply intertwined with the fabric of the camp program, and indeed with the soul of Scouting itself, that it would have been difficult, if not impossible, to imagine Na-Cha-Tan without them. From the Cub Scout mascot "Akela" to the spiritual leader of Boy Scouting "Allowat Sakima," the visual imagery of Scouting had always been entrusted to the Noble Savage. The Callout for the Order of the Arrow was an integral part of that rich Amerind heritage.

Every other Friday evening of the summer, the dance team members of the staff would gather to adorn their chests and their faces with grease paint, and to don their handmade Indian garb in preparation for conducting the ritual for the first rank of the Order.

The Order of the Arrow was an honor organization whose members were supposed to personify the Scouting ideals at their finest. First and foremost, they were to be excellent campers: young men who lived according to the precepts of the Scout Oath and Law, and who—like the Braves of a long-dead tribe of Algonquin Amerinds—readily accepted the obligation to unceasingly set a high example for others to follow.

The O.A. was a singular organization in many respects, not the least of which was that its new members were elected to be Called Out, not by a vote of its *existing* members, but by a secret ballot of qualified *non*members. And what made the Callout especially riveting for the participants was that those boys elected months ago in their hometown troops would not even know of their election until this very night.

Three levels, or ranks, could be bestowed upon members of the Order, each with its own particular induction ritual. The first level, referred to as the Ordeal, was a public ritual, whereas the other two ceremonies—the Brotherhood and the Vigil—were private affairs open only to existing O.A. members who attended under the threat of expulsion if they ever revealed the deeply secret nature of their proceedings. For the record, both Sam and Ziggy had attained the second level, that of the Brotherhood.

The Ordeal commenced with the solemn Friday night Callout. And like any elaborate Broadway production, a successful Callout required many hours of practice and planning beforehand. The ceremony itself was held in a large natural bowl buried deep within the virgin forest. Four hundred feet across at the rim and perhaps fifty feet deep at its center, the bowl, or depression, was anchored at one end by an immense stand of birch and collared all the

way around its circumference by the most statuesque collection of maples the Spirits could ever have provided.

As dusk slowly descended upon the land, a long procession of campers made their way silently along a trail which
meandered through the woods from the shore of the lake to
the lip of the Bowl. They were led by a fierce-looking Brave,
his arms folded sternly upon his chest. The path on which
they trod was marked every few feet with a burning smudge
pot, a churning cauldron which spewed the odor of kerosene into the night, but precious little in the way of illumi-
nation. As the boys shuffled quietly along the trail and into
the Bowl, their left shoulders bared in the centuries' old
tradition and the right hand of each Scout gripping the right
shoulder of the boy marching in front of him, only two
sounds disturbed the gathering darkness—the occasional
crackle from a smudge pot as a bug was incinerated in the
burning kero, and the slow, regular pounding of a giant
war-drum somewhere in the distance up ahead.

In the center of the Bowl, a triangular-shaped platform
supported an enormous unlit fire, a fire which—like the
raised platform beneath it—was erected in the shape of a
humongous triangle. The log-cabin style frame of the fire
stood in excess of nine feet tall and measured no less than
twelve feet long on each side.

The prismatoid skeleton of the fire was built from a
dozen or more massive birch logs, logs which had been
hand-carried into the O.A. Bowl from deep in the forest
where they had been felled. Although the largest base-log
ever used for a Callout fire measured over two feet in
diameter and demanded the efforts of no fewer than 26 men
to lug it into position, transporting these behemoths typically required no more than 15 sturdy shoulders.

The first and the largest log of any Callout fire rested on
the ground along its entire length. As for the second log,

one end of it rested on the ground while the other end was perched in a notch that had been chopped into the tip of the first. Completing the triangle, the third base-log rested in notches carved into the free ends of the first two. The balance of the fire's scaffolding was constructed according to the same scheme with each subsequent log notched in the fashion of a pioneer's cabin circa 1850. To complete the picture, the interior of the "cabin" was stuffed to overflowing with limbs, small logs, and dry kindling.

Now, as the awe-struck Scouts filed reverently into the Bowl village by village, and as they took their seats on the log-benches which encircled the Bowl's upper rim, the only sound that could be heard was the constant heavy pounding of a wooden mallet against the taut leather head of the Chief's war-drum. Except for the smudge pots placed every fifteen feet or so along the seating logs, the only source of light thus far was from the moon as it peered curiously over the tree tops to survey the proceedings getting under way down below.

Despite the advancing dusk, there was still enough daylight to observe the dingy-colored sand which filled the Bowl, only tonight it wasn't dingy. Tonight, the sand had been "painted" with figures and shapes paying homage to the Na-Cha-Tan tribe. Using the yellow of sawdust, the black of charcoal, the red of sweeping compound, and the white of flour, a twelve foot-long Thunderbird—its menacing beak agape—adorned the Bowl on one side of the central platform, while an ominous storm cloud of similar dimensions enriched a second side. A giant arrow ran from one end of the Bowl to the other, its shaft bisecting the fire platform through the middle.

As a cue that the Callout was about to begin, the war-drum sounded two closely-spaced beats. Even before the echo of the second thump had died away, a swift, barefooted

Brave burst into the Bowl from out of the woods. Clenched in his left hand was a graceful hunting bow, and gripped in his right, a gleaming arrow. And except for the grease paint which adorned his chest, only a loincloth sheathed his body. Without a word, the muscular lad sprinted two-thirds of the way around the circumference of the Bowl before pausing at the claw of the sand-painted Thunderbird to offer a respectful sign. Then, with a practiced hand, he nocked the arrow across the bowstring and thrust its chemically-treated tip into the burning kerosene of the nearest smudge pot.

Once the flames had danced their way up the shaft of the long, thin arrow, the athletic-looking Brave turned and aimed the burning missile towards the heavens. Stretching the bowstring taut, he paused momentarily to consider its flight path, then released the sparkling projectile into the night sky. Hissing madly at the moon as it sailed majestically up and over the first row of trees, the flaming barb landed just where he had intended it to—on a hillock in the woods just beyond the rim of the Bowl. Quietly and without fanfare, a small contingent of staffmen equipped with waterbuckets followed the sparkler's path back to Earth, and just to be sure of snuffing out any nascent danger of forest fire, they doused the ground around it with water. Then, as abruptly as he had arrived, the scantily-dressed Indian dashed rapidly from the Bowl, the hushed silence again broken only by two staccato beats of the ancient drum.

Like an apparition seemingly conjured up by the night air, the imposing figure of Allowat Sakima materialized at the entrance to the Bowl, his dignified headdress of eagle feathers adorning his shorn scalp. Bound together with leather thong, the headdress flowed regally down his back, the tail feather brushing lightly against the dust at his moccasin-clad feet. In the Medicine Man's hand was a fierce looking staff decorated with six bear claws and two owl feathers.

His deep voice booming across the assembly, Allowat Sakima proudly recited the legend of the Na-Cha-Tan. "Scarcely anyone still recalls the splendor of simpler times past," he began as he paced confidently back and forth across the Bowl next to the Thunderbird. "But coursing through the veins of a special few amongst us, the benevolent blood still flows, noble and exalted…"

His deliberate words matching the tempo of the drumbeat, Allowat Sakima took several minutes to recite the tale. But once the story was told, his stern voice grew subdued, "…and may the Infinite Spirit of all good Scouts bless our undertaking here tonight."

Reverently kneeling to the earth, the Medicine Man clutched a handful of sandy soil between his fingers and flung it towards the mammoth, unlit fire patiently awaiting his bidding at the center of the Bowl.

To the incredible bewilderment of the expectant Scouts, as the sprinkling of sand ricocheted off the birch-log frame, a flash of chemical light cracked the darkness. Then, as if by magic, the monstrous fire ignited with a whoosh to the ooh's and aah's of the astounded audience. Even those who had witnessed this wonder of modern pyrotechnics before could not fail to be moved upon seeing the spectacle again. The burst of flame shot skyward, and within minutes, the fire was burning furiously, flooding the Bowl with its reassuring light. Clearly visible now, the Thunderbird took on an animate quality.

With all eyes transfixed on the roaring inferno, few of the mesmerized Scouts observed the sudden appearance of the four fire-hoop dancers as they emerged noiselessly from their camouflaged underground pits near the fire platform. But once the loincloth-clad dancers had enflamed their kerosene-soaked hoops and had begun a display of their rigorously practiced art, the crowd's attention quickly switched from the blazing fire to the bold, sweat-glistened bodies of the hoop dancers.

Stepping into their hoops first with one leg, then with the other, then jumping through the flaming circles with both feet before adroitly flipping them over their heads like a jumprope, the robust fire-dancers performed seeming acts of magic with their burning hoops. Round and round they went, the searing fire melting the carefully applied grease paint on their exercise-hardened bodies. Though the exhibition lasted for only minutes, it totally hypnotized the gathering. No one wanted it ever to end, but as the covering on the flaming hoops was rapidly reduced to ash, the impressive display had to draw to a close.

No sooner had the fire-dancers sprinted from the Bowl, than five fierce-looking newcomers joined Allowat Sakima center stage to perform the final act before the Calling Out. The time-honored feather dance was less a dance than a step, its purpose less a telling of a story than the teaching of a lesson.

Their arms crossed proudly across their brawny chests, a single white feather clutched in each hand, the Braves' toe-heel gait kept pace with the methodic beating of the drum. Taking several toe-heel steps closer to the crackling fire before traveling the same number of paces back the way they had come, the warriors turned and circled, going one quarter of the way around the giant Bowl in a clockwise fashion.

With each solemn stride the Braves would arch their sinewy backs, extending first their left foot and then their right, in a long, exaggerated reach of each leg. And with each dignified step the Indians took, they set down first their toes, and then their heels, as they acted out the ancient rite. Arms crossed and head thrown back, it was a very graceful, very noble dance. Three more times they repeated the zig-zag pattern in unison: a few steps towards the blazing fire, several steps back, then one-quarter of the way around it. On the fourth and final approach to the giant triangular-shaped fire, the grease-painted natives unfolded their crossed arms for the first time and—to a pair of heavy drum beats—tossed their weighted feathers into the inferno as a symbolic offering to the Spirits.

Slowly and deliberately the cavalcade toe-heeled back away from the center of the Bowl, their arms once again crossed high upon their chests, the drum once again pounding out a proud cadence. Only *this* time, there was an almost imperceptible change of atmosphere, of tone, of purpose.

The drummer sounded two closely-spaced beats on his instrument. Obediently, the Braves marched in toe-heel fashion to form a single-file line along one side of the central platform. As the procession assembled, the silent warriors scanned the brilliantly-lit faces of the boys sitting around the perimeter of the Bowl, studying each set of wide eyes by the glow of the roaring fire. The moment of truth had arrived!

Hopeful boys, elected months ago by secret ballot, had only minutes more to wait. If they had been selected by their peers to become members of the Order, they would know shortly.

The parade of Indians continued their slow advance, their keen eyes penetrating the night, searching the illuminated crowd for the faces they had memorized over the course of the past week, the faces of the select group of Scouts due to be tapped-out at this evening's ceremony. To help the runners locate all the boys they were supposed to grab, spotters had positioned themselves at strategic locations around the Bowl.

For one last time the war-drummer struck two closely-spaced beats, and then it began. What was once a solemn undertaking careened off on a new tack, one that perhaps could best be described as mayhem, albeit *rehearsed* mayhem, but mayhem nonetheless.

Letting loose a terrific battle cry, the Indians dashed swiftly and abruptly into the tense audience, physically grabbing the prospective O.A. members from the ranks of the crowd. Startled by the primeval screech, the entire gathering gave an involuntary jump as the hooting Braves shattered the former serenity of the proceedings.

Each boy due to be inducted into the Order was pulled, sometimes dragged, from his seat by one of the warriors, and taken at a run down to the center of the Bowl where, with terror-filled eyes, he was thrust before Allowat Sakima for the tapping-in. Even over the loud crackling of the thundering fire, one could still hear the smack of the Medicine Man's palm as he firmly slapped the bared left shoulder of the inductee three times. Wimachtendienk. Wingolauchsik. Witahemui. Leaning reverently over the quivering Scout, the Medicine Man whispered a set of instructions in his ear before sending the lad to wait in line with the others. For that boy, his Ordeal had begun!

The day-long challenge of the Ordeal was part of a noble tradition which dated back seven centuries. Much like the tribal rites of an earlier epoch where a man underwent a wrenching physical trial, often receiving an irrevocable mark in the process as a sign of his courage and his enduring commitment to the tribe, *this* Ordeal was a test of a young boy's budding Manhood. It was designed to promote personal reflection through solitude—building a fire that night with just two matches but without any tools; sleeping under the stars without the benefit of a tent or even a luminabeam; enduring twenty-four hours of utter and total silence; and performing twelve hours of physically exhausting labor with only bread and water to sustain him.

When, by this hour tomorrow night, the Ordeal was concluded in a second, almost cult-like ritual, that boy would be one step closer to adulthood. By then he will have solemnly sworn to regard the ties of brotherhood as lasting, to seek to preserve a cheerful spirit even in the midst of irksome tasks and weighty responsibilities, and to endeavor to be unselfish in service and in devotion to the welfare of others. From that moment on, as custom had it, the initiate was no longer to be considered the same person, and reflecting his elevated status among the people, he was oftentimes given a new name to accompany his new responsibilities.

In the words of Allowat Sakima: He who serves his fellows is of all his fellows greatest!

Twelve
Dark Eagle

Even as the outcries of the Indians and the drumbeats of the Callout echoed faintly in the distance, Lester Matthews and Abe Levinson moved stealthily through the shadows in the direction of their rendezvous point in Little Grasshopper Valley. Little did they know they had company.

Inquisitive by nature, Sam had grown suspicious enough by now of Abe and of Lester to pay closer attention to their activities. Thus, when he spied the two of them slipping out of the Callout together before it was concluded, naturally he followed. What trail they were on and where they were headed was an open question, a question Sam intended to learn the answer to. At times, he wondered whether his suspicions weren't just the product of an overactive imagination, yet,

Sam couldn't possibly deny what he had seen.

To begin with, it had been too much of a coincidence that day when he and Ziggy had stumbled across the airchop lifting off from Little Grasshopper Valley. It was too big and too noisy for Abe and Lester not to have seen or heard the thing, which meant they had lied. No one lies unless they have something to hide. But Sam hadn't been sure of the connection until last week when, curious about this thing called Judaism, he had listened in on one of Rabbi Abe Levinson's sermons. It began in a strange foreign tongue, then continued on in English:

> Ba-ruch a-ta, A-do-nai E-lo-hei-nu,
> me-lech ha-o-lam, she-a-sa ni-sim
> la-a-vo-tei-nu ba-ya-mim ha-heim
> ba-ze-man ha-zeh.

> Praised be Thou, O Lord our God,
> Ruler of the world, who didst wondrous things
> for our fathers, in days of old at this season.

From what Sam could gather from Abe's sermon, these people, these Jews, believed in a much sterner, a much less forgiving God than his own, one to whom it wasn't possible to just say "I'm sorry" and be off the hook. No, the Hebrew God was much more demanding than that. If easy redemption was what one was after, by all means he shouldn't sign up to be a Jew. It seemed to Sam as if that fact alone might account for Judaism's durability down through the ages, although that strictness, that self-policing exactness, had undoubtedly had something to do with its inability to attract a mass following as Christianity had. Modern peoples preferred simple solutions over complex ones, and if Jesus Christ was willing to suffer for all their sins, why should they?

But the thing which had made the biggest impression on Sam, the thing which accounted for him being out here in the woods tonight following Abe and Lester in the dark, was the prayer shawl, the tallith, Abe had worn that day around his shoulders as he delivered his sermon. Easily seven feet long and woven from the finest silk Sam had ever laid eyes on, the tallith was fringed along the border in gold lace and had a series of pale blue markings embroidered on the foreground. And hanging about even with his chest on each front panel was a distinctive six-pointed star. There was no mistaking it at all. It was of precisely the same shape and precisely the same dimensions as had been on the bootprint he discovered. And that could only mean one thing! Abe had been there that day as he suspected. And probably Lester as well.

Now, as Lester and Abe made their way along the root-obstructed trail under the cover of night with Sam trailing them not far behind, they found the going a little trickier than it had been earlier in the day with the sun at their backs. The difficulty with a late night operation was finding one's way through the thick woods without tripping. Knowing this, Lester and Abe had slipped out of the Callout early, but if they were going to reach the intended meeting place on time and without being seen or caught, they would have to be extra cautious. After their close call with Sam and Ziggy two weeks ago, the two co-conspirators weren't taking any unnecessary chances tonight.

For one thing, with the last pilot having been apprehended by Canadian authorities and then summarily executed for high treason, there would be a new man in the cockpit this evening. Unlike his predecessor, this man would not be an intermediary; he would be one of the rebels himself, an Amerind from southern Alberta. All they knew about him so far was that his given name was Inok. But according to their contact, he answered only to Dark Eagle.

Though Abe and Lester had set out on the trail long

before the sun had descended fully below the horizon and though the nighttime sky was not yet entirely pitch-black, the floor of the forest was already dark. Unless one wished to turn an ankle or break a leg, traveling with a lit lumina-beam only made good sense. But afraid of arousing suspicions when they first snuck off into the woods, the two men had kept their lights dimmed, figuring they couldn't afford to ignite the beams until they were well away from the Bowl. By then, Lester and Abe had each tumbled to the ground more than once, and Sam himself was hopelessly lost. In the dark he hadn't gotten more than two hundred yards before he had twisted his ankle and fallen hard against a rock, opening a nasty gash on his forehead. Irritated at his own stupidity, but knowing he couldn't go on any further in this condition, Sam hobbled back to camp with the support of a downed limb as a crutch. He had to see Miss Loddy first thing for a shot of Acceleron; otherwise, his swollen ankle would never heal by morning, and he would have a lot of explaining to do.

Not realizing that Sam had been tailing them for a distance, Abe and Lester continued on their way. Even under the best of circumstances it was at least an hour's walk out to Little Grasshopper, only they didn't have that kind of time to spare. Thus, once they were far enough away from the Bowl to use their lumina-beams, they set off at a jog, their lights throwing queer shadows out in front of them. Not being in very good physical shape, Lester could hardly keep up with his Israeli counterpart.

Despite his cover as the camp's naturalist and its rabbi, in actuality, Abe was a hardened soldier. Orphaned when his parents were killed in the nuclear attack on Mecca, he had later been recruited by the Mossad to hunt down and kill the Shi'ites responsible for the calamity. The operation had gone off the wire, and along with several others, Abe had ended up in a Neo-Rontana torture camp.

For more than a century—ever since the assassination of Rontana himself—the Americans had controlled the Persian Gulf lands formerly ruled by the madman. When they finally withdrew their troops from the area about a dozen years back, they ceded control over the Gulf to their Israeli allies. Despite the occasional insurrection, it had turned out to be a sweet deal for both parties, what with the Americans being guaranteed a steady and sure supply of what little oil remained in the subterranean fields, and the Israelis being guaranteed the revenues necessary to maintain order in the zone. The only fly in the ointment was the Neo-Rontanians.

Though it proved to be only a matter of weeks before the Mossad was able to free Abe and his companions from the clutches of their Rontanian captors, it had unfortunately been sufficiently long for them to screw up Abe's mind. Though he returned to active duty with the Mossad after the mandatory rest and rehabilitation period, he would never again be the same. After his ordeal, he was more interested in retribution than in anything else. The Rontanians had brainwashed him into believing that the great Satan America was at the root of all his troubles. After all, it had been America who had killed Rontana, it had been America who had robbed Rontana's followers of their homeland, and it had been America who had stood idly by when his parents were killed. Therefore, since Abe's enemy was America, and since America's enemy was the Amerind rebels, it only logically followed that Abe's *ally* had to be the Amerind rebels. Somehow, given enough hallucinogenic drugs and enough electroshock therapy, it all made sense.

Abe had obtained Lester's name through the Network as being sympathetic to the cause, and when Lester arrived in Israel—ostensibly for a foreign exchange stint—Abe got himself assigned to the detail charged with safeguarding the newcomer. Together they hatched a plan for Lester to finagle a work visa out of his grandfather so that Abe might enter the States without suspicion. In a nutshell then, that is how Abe happened to be here tonight helping Lester set out flares so that the airchop could set down safely in the dark. Seven flares in all: three along each side of the valley and one in the middle. Then they waited.

Eventually it came. Beginning as a low hum from the east, there was surprisingly little noise for a machine its size. Not until the stubby-winged, rotor-driven craft had swung around to land, did the sound rise to an audible roar. But except for Abe and Lester, no one in Camp Na-Cha-Tan heard the muffled whine. By now the Callout was completed, and with the gathering dispersed, the participants had already retired to their tents for the night.

Hovering over the landing site, its floodlamps scanning the area for any unusual activity, the airchop's pulsing rotors kicked up a blizzard of sand and dust in their faces. Indeed, for a very long moment, it looked as if the stealthy-skinned warbird wasn't going to put down at all. Apparently, Harper's ongoing crackdown on the shipment of munitions north had had its desired effect, and the pilot wasn't taking anything for granted. Not until Lester gave the agreed upon all-clear signal, flashing his lumina-beam skyward three times, did Dark Eagle cut the flying machine's turbines and set the stubby-winged aircraft down on the wet soft ground.

Once the rotors had slowed appreciably, Lester and Abe cautiously approached the cockpit. Hidden in the woods about seventy-five meters away was a cache of weapons they had received in from another team earlier that day. Deposited in a shallow pit they had dug into the soft ground, was a footlocker full of megaflares, another filled with mini-Uzis, and yet another stuffed with manual firebombs.

The pilot who exited the airchop was an uncommonly handsome man. He had a head of long, jetblack hair drawn into a ponytail behind his neck, and the lean, hairless body so typical of an Amerind. His piercing round eyes were dark, his flat hands powerful, and his skin the color of ochre. A hunting knife hung from a sheath at his belt, and a pair of night-vision goggles dangled from his hand.

"You Dark Eagle?" Lester grunted apprehensively as Abe shifted uneasily behind him.

"Who wants to know?" Inok returned gruffly. After the last pilot on this run had been captured and killed, no one was above suspicion—and certainly not these two characters!

"My name is not important," Lester rejoined flippantly. "If you've got our money, we've got your stuff."

Moving more swiftly than a deer, Dark Eagle popped his blade from its sheath at his side and pressed it firmly under Lester's scrawny neck, drawing a trickle of blood in the process. "I do not like your tone," the Amerind clarified, his other hand locked squarely behind Lester's head so as to prevent him from budging. "Hand over the weapons and perhaps I will let you both live."

"Okay, buddy, relax," Lester petitioned, squirming breathlessly. "You have to believe me: I meant nothing by it. Now, if you have a motorized dolly onboard with you there, I'll have my friend here collect up all of your stuff and then you can be on your way," he suggested, stumbling backwards as Dark Eagle loosened his vise-like grip.

Motioning to a compartment door located just behind the pilot's seat, Dark Eagle undid the latch and retrieved the motorized dolly. Then, while he and Lester discussed the terms of their trade, Abe went into the woods to gather up the three footlockers of matériel.

"Here, this is for you," Dark Eagle asserted, pulling a

pouch stuffed full with small bills from his pocket and handing it across to Lester.

Taking a moment to count the wad under the glow of his lumina-beam, Lester began to shake his head in anger. "This isn't what I agreed to," he objected. "I told your people I wanted more. It was all explained in the coded message I left with the firing fuses under the bridge."

"This is as much as the Elders can afford right now," Dark Eagle declared cooly. Though he knew that this was a lie, the Amerind was contemptuous of this frail Euro with the pathetic-looking moustache.

"Unless the price is raised, I refuse to broker any more shipments," Lester remarked, digging in his heels. He thought of himself as a pretty sharp operator, and he couldn't help but think that he had now outmaneuvered his swarthy opponent. "I have expenses, you know."

"So do we," Dark Eagle reported, standing his ground. His temper was bristling just below the boiling point. "Anyhow, it makes no difference to me whatsoever—I am merely a courier and hardly in a position to negotiate fees with the likes of you."

"Listen, I know all about you, Inok."

"Dark Eagle," the muscular Amerind corrected.

"Whatever," Lester snapped impatiently. "Why can't you people have regular names like everyone else?"

By this time, Abe had returned with the three footlockers, one stacked on top of the next upon the bed of the mechanized dolly. The lid of the uppermost case had been forced open and the Israeli was holding a mini-Uzi in his right hand. Though it measured barely 14 inches in length, the automatic weapon was about as deadly a machine-gun as ever there had been built.

"We *people*?" Dark Eagle fumed, reaching for his hunting knife again.

"Heh you, not so fast," Abe warned, thrusting the Uzi out in the front of him, his fingers resting menacingly on the bolt. "My friend here has told you what it is we want, and that is to be paid more money. Just what do you intend to do about it?"

"I'll deliver your message to the Elders," Dark Eagle consented, warily eyeing the business end of the Uzi. The Amerind knew from experience that if Abe squeezed the trigger at this short of a range, he would not stand a chance. "Either the Chief's Council will agree to your demands or else they will not."

"You are nothing but a prairie-nigger," Lester spat out derisively. His brash use of the expletive was no doubt emboldened by seeing the gun Abe held in his capable hands.

Though the demeaning words had barely enough time to cross the distance separating the two men, Dark Eagle leapt at Lester, his nostrils flaring. Dropping his knife to the ground even as Abe fired a warning salvo into the night, Dark Eagle knocked Lester down and began pummeling him with his bare fists. Three times he smashed him in the face, but when Lester made no attempt to strike him back or to even defend himself, Dark Eagle reared back on his haunches and broke off the attack.

"If this coward is the best America has to offer," the Amerind declared as he got to his feet and brushed himself off, "then surely our cause will prevail." Even as he spoke, Dark Eagle sheathed his blade, grabbed the dolly and the Uzi from Abe, and—without saying another word—loaded them all into his airchop. Glaring at the two of them from inside the cockpit, he kicked on the rotors and was immediately airborne.

"That was a rather stupid move, wouldn't you agree?" Abe criticized as he shielded his eyes from the flying pebbles kicked up by the airchop's whirlwind.

"We'll see," Lester countered arrogantly. "In this business one has to take a few chances from time to time. Our friend Inok there has a seat on the Council's inner circle; I'm sure my message will get through."

"Listen," Abe interjected soberly, "I hope you are right, but in the meantime, we have got a long walk back to camp. If we don't want to be missed, we had better get a move on."

"But that's where you are wrong. Tonight, we won't *have* to walk back."

"Whatever do you mean?" Abe asked, his swarthy face twisted up into a question mark.

"I have a bit of a surprise for you this evening, my friend. My girl Sindy should be waiting for us with her gcar just up ahead on the logging road. With all the visitors coming up from the city for the Callout, I was able to sneak her into camp undetected this afternoon."

"You fool!" Abe exclaimed, seizing Lester by the shoulders and shaking him violently. "Why involve *her* in this thing for goodness-sake? Isn't it dangerous enough already?"

"Don't be silly; she doesn't know a thing."

"Yeah? So why risk her finding out? Why drag her all the way out here to pick us up?" he demanded, tightening his grip on Lester's scrawny frame.

"She promised me that if you were real nice, she'd do us both," Matthews suggested wantonly.

"*Do* us?" Abe exploded, shoving Lester away from him in revulsion.

"Drop the foreigner act, Abe. That not understanding English shtick may have fooled my little brother Sam, but I know better," Lester advised. "Yes, *do* us. Screw us. Capische?"

"Yes, I capische," Abe acknowledged as they continued on down the trail. "But one of these days your carelessness is going to land us both in trouble, real trouble."

"You worry too much, Abe. You'll see, it'll be fun."

"Thanks, but no thanks. Go ahead without me. I'll find my own way home."

"Suit yourself," Lester chided as the two of them arrived at Sindy's parked gcar. The lights were on inside, and in preparation for the upcoming festivities, she had already stripped to the waist.

"Doesn't the Hebe want any?" Sindy bayed, leaning her head out the open window and taunting the Israeli with her bare breasts as he receded into the woods.

"Guess not, sweet thing," Lester remarked, grabbing for her rock hard nipples through the open pane.

"His loss," she sniveled, disappointed by the setback. "Well, that just leaves more for us." Even as she spoke, Sindy extracted a sleeve of white powder from her handbag. "Here, try some," she encouraged, spilling half of it on herself, "I'm already flying. Wanna be my copilot?"

Thirteen
Après Moi Le Déluge

"Jenkins, you know him perhaps as well as anyone," Senator Nate Matthews said. The two of them were meeting behind closed doors in his chambers on the top floor of the Senate Office Building. It was Saturday morning. "Tell me as much as you can about the bastard."

"Well, sir, honestly, there's not much to tell," Officer Jenkins replied. He was a nice-looking young man with a strong chin. He was in full-dress uniform and by the deep creases ironed in his pants, Nate could tell he took being an officer seriously. He wore a sidearm, a double-action 9mm Ruger. There was a bead of sweat on his forehead where the strap from his face mask had rubbed against his skin, but with the severe thermal inversion today there was no leaving it at home; high humidity and a smog alert made for a nasty combination. "So far as I know, the one and only brave thing Director Harper has ever done in his whole life—the thing which launched him into the limelight and made him a national hero at a young age, the thing which helped get him where he is today—was to save the last of the Martian colonists when they abandoned the settlement in 2377."

"You don't trust him, do you?"

"Not in the least."

"Nor I," the Senator admitted, moving uneasily about the room with the aid of his cane.

"What's this all about anyway, sir?" Jenkins asked, twisting around in his chair so as to maintain eye contact with the old man. "First, all that stuff about the bootprint, now this."

"I have a problem. Actually, I have several. And I don't know who I can trust to help me solve them."

"How is it that a man in your position can have so many problems?" Though the question was naive, it was sincere. "Surely, there are dozens of competent people you can turn to besides me?"

"Advisors are a dime a dozen, Jenkins; only their obedience is a function of what you have on them. With you, however, it is different. You are a patriot."

"You flatter me, sir," Jenkins said, walking over to where Nate stood leaning against his bar. "How can I be of service?"

"You know of the airchop traffic?"

"Of course." It seemed such a silly question; after all, *he* had been the one responsible for tracking that mud down to its source, and the Senator knew it.

"And I told you about the letter I got from my grandson?"

"Yes, the other day when you called to set up this meeting." By now, there was a hint of impatience in his voice.

"Na-Cha-Tan is quite obviously the transfer point for some of the northbound arms traffic. I should like you to go there and investigate." The suggestion sounded as if it were an order. "Only on my payroll, mind you, not Harper's."

"You know very well I don't work for him—the Air Force pays my salary."

"Indeed."

"Anyhow, my sources tell me one of Harper's people has already been assigned to this case."

"I'm impressed! Your sources are correct, but she is a tenderfoot at best. Moreover, she's not actually on site; I can't actually be sure of what's happening round-the-clock."

"What would my cover be if I decided to do this for you?" Jenkins asked, crinkling his forehead into a frown.

"As good fortune would have it, a genuine Airchop Colonel takes his troop up there for two weeks about this time each summer. Perhaps you've heard of him? Colonel Robert McNamara Beck?"

"Colonel *G.A.* Beck?"

"Yeah. That's him. Colonel Beck's contingent leaves for Na-Cha-Tan tomorrow—Sunday. I should like you to go with him," Nate explained. "As his assistant Scoutmaster perhaps."

Jenkins nodded his head, then asked, "What about this Israeli Harper's so worked up over?"

"I should have figured that by now you two would have given this some thought, Jenkins. You tell me: what should we do?"

"So far as we know at Air Force Intelligence, he's broken no American laws, and although the Hebrews want him back, we presently have no extradition treaty with Israel. I can arrest him if you want, but as you know, he's traveling on a valid visa."

That comment hurt, and the pained look on Nate's face

showed it. "You don't have to remind me," Nate retorted
testily.

"No, I suppose not," Jenkins answered, regretting his
faux pas. "Will there be anything else?"

"Yes," Nate answered, swallowing hard. "Let's say,
hypothetically at least, that the public isn't fully aware of all
the military programs the U.S. is running."

"I should hope not," came the swift reply.

"Spoken like a true patriot."

"But sir, military matters should be left to the military,"
Jenkins correctly pointed out. "The public has no stomach
for such things. All *they* want is bread and circuses."

"Indeed. But now let's say, hypothetically again, that
the Congress itself isn't aware of all the military programs
this United States of America is involved in."

"I see," Jenkins replied more slowly than before. "Well,
that too makes some sense. After all, why should some
freshman congressman from Arkansas be privy to all that
you, the senior Senator from Missouri, knows? I can see
that." Though he granted the proposition, there was some
hesitancy in the soldier's voice.

"Indeed. But now let's say the President himself isn't
fully aware of all the military programs we're running?"

"I'd say someone was breaking the law." This answer
came without equivocation.

"Now you see my problem," Nate concluded, lowering
his head as if he were embarrassed.

Jenkins did not immediately answer.

"How long has this been going on?" he finally muttered.
"What sorts of programs are we talking about? What's so
damn important that it has to be kept secret from the
President?"

The Senator rattled them off. "Park Ranger salaries are
in fact training Green Berets, block grants for local police

departments are funding counterinsurgency strike forces, Coast Guard monies are paying for ramjets."

"Go on."

"Cancer algorithm research is paying to maintain stocks of the Ebola virus at the biowarfare lab in Fort Detrick, Maryland..."

"Enough already, damnit!" Officer Jenkins exploded, slamming his fist down on the countertop of Nate's luxurious bar. "We are no longer talking about a hypothetical situation! I know people who *work* on Biosafety Level Four at the U.S. Army Medical Research Institute of Infectious Diseases at Fort Detrick, for God's sake! This is for real! What I want to know is why?"

"I didn't start it," the Senator complained, trying to excuse himself.

"Who then?" Jenkins snapped.

"General Wenger."

"Who's he?"

"It doesn't matter, he's long dead, probably even before you were born, but he did teach me one very important lesson."

"What's that?"

"The Brazen Rule."

"Come again," Jenkins said.

"You know the Golden Rule, don't you?"

Jenkins answered. "Yes, do unto others as you would have them do unto you."

"Exactly. And the Brazen Rule is its more worldly sister: Do unto others *before* they can do it unto you. Repay kindness with kindness, but repay evil with justice."

"The ends justify the means?"

"Precisely."

"So, let me see if I have this straight," Jenkins barked in an accusatory tone, moving toward the opposite end of the bar. "To save the country, you prostituted its constitution?"

"How so?"

"The President is the Commander-in-Chief, not you."

"But he's a fool," Nate argued.

"You're missing the point, Senator. Either we abide by the constitution we swore to uphold or, we dispense with the whole idea of liberty altogether."

"But the underground military was supposed to give us the *edge* in time of crisis."

"Instead, you have wasted valuable resources on this venture," the younger man said. "Better to tell the public, nay the whole world, the true extent of our capabilities than to keep it a secret. If our enemies think we are weaker than we really are, that only invites attack; if our own *leaders* think we are weaker than we really are, that only invites unnecessary compromise. If this underground military of yours actually exists and if you are the keeper of its 'go' codes, I say go public with the damn thing, hand it over to the *Tribune* or to the *New York Times*. At the very least, do the honorable thing and give it to McIntyre. He's the President after all."

"I can't deny your logic, but what you ask is hard."

"Senator, with all due respect, I can't in good conscience leave here today to do your bidding in Wisconsin tomorrow without some sort of assurance that you will right this wrong."

"Okay, then *you* take the code book," Nate exclaimed, moving around to the back side of the bar where the wall safe was hidden.

"*Me*?! I don't want it," he objected. "For God's-sake, Senator, I'm not qualified to have possession of the damn thing!"

"Sure you are. You're the original patriot."

"I refuse."

"Okay, better yet: What say I keep the original book, but

you devise a single encryption key which we will then add to every existing code, a single encryption key known only to you and to me? If I die, or if my illness advances to the stage where I become incapacitated, or if I simply get too tired to carry on, it will be your responsibility to give the key to the President. That way, God forbid, even if the book were to be stolen or destroyed, it would be rendered useless without your key."

"All that does is make *me* a traitor."

"No, son, all that does is make you the most powerful man in America."

Seeing the old man's pleading eyes, Officer Jenkins nodded his assent. Like so many man before him who had been asked to walk the wall, he was proud to do his duty.

Cryptography was something Officer Jenkins knew a great deal about. The first step in encoding a message to make it undecipherable to others was for the sender to convert the message into a big number, a long string of digits. Next, the sender had to raise this large number to an exponent. Finally, the sender had to do some modular—that is, remainder—arithmetic. This particular methodology was applied because it did such a wonderful job of scrambling big numbers.

If, for instance, the message number were 3 and the exponent were 4, the coded number would be 81, that is, three to the fourth power. (In a real-life situation, the message number would be hundreds of digits long; when taken to an exponent, it would be that much larger.) Only then would the modular arithmetic come into play. To say that 81 equaled 1 modulo 10 was to say that when 81 was divided by 10, the division left a remainder of 1. The scrambled message that would be sent across the comm-lines or else the airwaves was only the remainder, the 1 in this case.

Without the exponent and the modulo, however, the

remainder was useless information to even the most determined of spies. Officer Jenkins knew that, without these, even a good hacker would need thousands of years on a good computer to break the code. That should be a thick enough cloak of security to protect the Senator's secrets.

Fourteen
TNT

Jack's Cue 'n Brew was a clean, well-lit place run by a wonderful, father-like proprietor known to the staff only as "Jack." His pub had a jukebox which was a comic throwback to another era; two pool-tables whose green-felt surfaces were scarred by years of abuse; plus a half-dozen dining-booths consisting of two benches covered in a cheap vinyl and a tabletop adorned with a worn-out tablecloth sporting a red and white checkerboard pattern. But that wasn't the half of it. Running along one wall—the wall a patron first faced when he crossed the threshold through the front door—was a timeless, twenty-two foot long bar. It was majestically framed on one side by a tarnished brass rail and on the other by a dozen "come on in 'n sit right down" style bar stools. Behind the bar, neatly spaced upon mirrored glass shelves, stood row upon row of half-filled whiskey bottles. To be served a chilled glass of tortan here was to take a step back into another age, an age where the patrons knew how to savor the singularity of this curious institution called a drinking hall. Here men gathered to imbibe and tell stories, to carouse and sing songs, to escape—if only for a moment—from their cranky wives and their dead-end jobs. Here, men could be men, and with so few places like this left in America, they were drawn here like moths to a light.

Standing guard behind the bar was an enormous wooden cash register, the likes of which hadn't been seen in the bigger cities for several hundred years, and whose value to a museum probably exceeded the price the entire rest of the establishment would have brought at auction. Only on special occasions would Jack use it to ring up a sale; otherwise, it just sat there idle, gathering dust the rest of the year. Today, however, was one of those special occasions because the resumption of the camping season at Na-Cha-Tan meant a doubling or a trebling of Jack's usual business. Though a handful of staffmen had already found an excuse to sneak out of camp and into his place over the past several days, not since camp got underway two weeks ago was everyone expected to be in attendance as they were tonight.

Looking like a bartender transported from out of the Old West, Jack proudly popped his suspenders with his thumbs and bid welcome to Stovepipe and his entourage with open arms. As the two men renewed their years' long acquaintance over a shot glass, the staff crowded in, chattering excitedly.

Variously described as R&R, B'n B, or TNT, a night out on the town meant a chance to release some of the pent-up frustration which inevitably accompanied keeping track of several hundred wild and energetic boys for two solid weeks at a time, twenty-four hours a day. Only, with the nearest town being some thirty miles away, and with so few of the staff being able to afford their own gcars, the Cue 'n Brew was the staff's usual watering hole. Jack's Pub, as it was so often called, was just a mile or so down the road from camp; a couple minutes by bus; or a third of an hour on foot.

"What's this B'n B stuff I keep hearing everyone talk about?" fat-Jim had asked Stovepipe on the short bus ride over there. As in years' past, the camp had leased several beat-up school buses for the summer, and while they weren't being used to drag Scouts to or from the camp, or else to cart them out to the river for a raft trip, the yellow monstrosities were the staff's means of getting around. As per usual, Stovepipe was at the wheel while fat-Jim sat behind him, pestering him with nonstop questions.

"Booze 'n Bimbookers," Stovepipe had translated boisterously as he guided the bus around the lake and out along the narrow camp road towards Jack's. Being the Director, it was his responsibility to see that everyone got there safely and returned home sober.

"I thought that was called TNT?" Lester had contradicted, his squeaky voice filtering forward from where he sat at the rear of the bus. As always, his manner was flippant.

Stovepipe shrugged his shoulders disapprovingly. "Dare I ask?"

"Tits 'n Tortan," Lester had spouted vulgarly as Stovepipe cringed. "Tits 'n Tortan."

But by then the busdriver had honked his horn to announce that they had arrived, and within half a minute everyone had piled into Jack's Pub.

Sitting at the bar, waiting to order dinner, Sam leaned over to Ziggy and remarked quietly under his breath, "You know, I heard the strangest noise the other night on the way home from the Bowl after the Callout. I know you're gonna think I'm crazy, but it sounded like an airchop," he whispered, nursing his still-tender ankle. "Just like that first day."

Up until this moment, Sam hadn't breathed a word to Ziggy about following Abe and Lester a short distance two nights ago, and with Lester sitting right there only three stools over, even now he had to be circumspect about how he addressed the issue. Yesterday after lunch, Sam had casually asked his brother about him and Abe heading off into the woods during the Callout. Lester's abrupt reply had been that he had stashed a bottle of tortan out behind the Bowl, but that it wasn't any of Sam's business and he had better not mention it to Stovepipe or else the two of them would end up in trouble. Sam had been content to let the matter drop, but he knew it was all a lie. As he had stumbled home that night, propped up by his makeshift cane, he had once again heard that same distinct whine of an airchop far away in the woods.

"You're dreaming," Ziggy responded in a teasing tone. "You are just having hallucinations because Beck arrived back in camp this morning with his troop."

Before Sam could admit to his friend that there was some truth in what he said, Stovepipe butted in on their conversation from the adjoining bar stool. "Let me just remind you fellas," he scolded. "I don't want a repeat of last year's war with Colonel Beck. There is to be no shenanigans, understood?"

Sam and Ziggy looked at each other, but when there was no answer from either of them, Stovepipe snapped, "Understood?"

"Shenanigans?" they replied innocently in unison. "From us? Whatever do you mean?"

"I mean, there is to be absolutely no GA this summer!" Stovepipe roared, his shrill voice carrying across the bar, turning several heads in the process. "And certainly not if it involves Beck!"

"Sure, boss," Sam and Ziggy parroted unconvincingly. "Whatever you say." Even as they spoke, they suppressed irreverent chuckles.

The initials GA stood for "goofing around" or "grand assault" or perhaps, "grab assing." The key to the game was playing a practical joke on someone or on a *group* of someones, and "getting away" with it—those initials again. Air Force Colonel Robert McNamara Beck was an ace at this sport, and his arrival at camp each summer chilled the hearts of every staffman who knew him. He had a well-deserved reputation as a GA artiste, and most every counselor held him somewhere between awe and fear. Indeed, this year Colonel Beck had arrived in camp prepared to do battle, a battle Stovepipe did not want to see get ignited. According to Stovepipe's snitches, Beck had come armed not only with a tough-looking assistant Scoutmaster, but also with a battalion-sized supply of GA style ammunition—red dye markers, rocket flares, M80's, thousands of feet of twine, miles of electrical tape, dozens of pairs of rubber gloves, and a host of other playthings. In last year's pièce de résistance, the messhall had been his target, a target which had easily fallen to the boldness of his prank.

Normally, the seating in the messhall was arranged to accommodate the two hundred or so resident campers efficiently at mealtime. There were two dozen rectangular tables, each bordered on their long sides by a bench and on their stubby sides by a folding chair. With wide aisles separating the rows, the twenty-four tables were grouped into three rows of eight tables each. Given the room's dimensions, any other configuration would result in chaos, slowing down the progress of the meal and interfering with the smooth operation of the camp program. And if there was anything Stovepipe insisted upon, it was an orderly camp program; when it came to his messhall, he was a stickler for detail. What Colonel Beck and his cronies did one day last summer was to spend the better part of a night altering the natural order of things.

Considering that the only light they had to work with that night was what little moonshine filtered through the trees surrounding the dining hall, it was a wonder they accomplished anything at all, but before morning of the next day broke, the GA'ers had rearranged and stacked all twenty-four tables plus twice that number of benches and chairs. Although it was a GA which rocked East Camp to the core and which personally angered Stovepipe, no one could deny that their handiwork reflected audacity and a measure of cunning. To this day, some people considered it brilliant.

To begin with, the perpetrators butted four tables end-on-end so that the line of flattops were perpendicular to the wall and flanked the left-hand side of the messhall's main entrance. Arranged thusly, the row of tables extended some thirty-five feet out into the center of the room. Next, the GA'ers repeated the same operation to the right of the doorway, positioning a second foursome of tables parallel to the first. And like the first set, this row also jutted straight out into the center of the room like a giant exclamation point.

Then—and this is where it must have gotten tricky—they carefully heaped another table on top of each of the eight initial ones, being careful to rest the legs of the second set squarely on the tops of the first. Finally, in what must have been a dangerous and physically demanding effort, they pyramided yet a *third* layer of eight tables upon the existing two. To accomplish this seemingly impossible feat, they had to stand tiptoe upon benches which wobbled with every breath, while at the same time hefting each heavy table up and over their heads, holding it aloft long enough to be certain that the legs of the upper tier had been securely seated on the surface of the table comprising the next lower story. All this in near total darkness! It was a precarious undertaking which threatened several times to collapse on them like a house of cards. When the job was completed, the stacks measured over eleven feet in height!

Being aligned on either side of the main doorway like a rampart, the precisely stacked piles of tables created the illusion of a grand hallway. And to reinforce that effect, the perpetrators used the forty-eight seating benches to form a roof, or a canopy, over the majestic archway. By placing the long benches so that they bridged the gap separating the top of the left stack of tables from the top of the right stack, Beck and his co-conspirators manufactured a high, flat, ceiling for their grand entranceway.

Yet, even after having done all of this, the GA'ers had so far only set the mood, the stage, so to speak, for their grand mischief. The thrust of the GA—framing the camp staff for the misdeed—was still to come. To successfully accomplish this goal, the crime scene had to appear as if a handful of disgruntled counselors had carried out the dirty deed to protest the lousy quality of the kitchen's culinary talents. Arranging the folding chairs in six neat rows at the opposite end of the "hallway" from the main entrance, they used a piece of tape and a slip of paper to personalize the back of each metal chair with the name of a staffman. Then came the decorations. Like so many streamers, five rolls of bunwad were unfurled and flung roofward to adorn the rafters of the cavernous messhall. Held down by masking tape, a sixth roll was put to literary use, spelling out the words CAMP FOOD STINKS on the floor in front of the first row of folding chairs. As a coup de grâce, they retrieved four full garbage cans from outside on the loading dock where they were standing ready to be picked up by the garbagemen in the morning, and placed two cans on either side of their banner as if to say: the food here tastes like garbage. Congratulating themselves on their courage and on their imagination, Beck's Marauders, as they came to be called, settled into their bunks for a short night's sleep, unsure what daybreak would bring.

Being in charge of the kitchen staff, fat-Jim was the first on the scene that next morning. He counted himself lucky in one respect: at least he had an alibi for his whereabouts the previous evening, otherwise he might have been accused of "discovering" his own treachery.

Swallowing hard as he contemplated the disapproving look on Stovepipe's face when he informed him what had happened, Jim first set the kitchen crew to work cracking eggs and mixing pancake batter, before trundling across the gravel parking lot to the Director's cabin. Knocking timidly on Stovepipe's door, he waited. But when there was no answer, he took to pounding on it with his fist.

As was occasionally the Director's prerogative, Stovepipe had intended to sleep through breakfast that morning. Considering that the previous night's drinking binge had ended only hours before, he was not amused to be awakened prematurely, and when the knocking on his door didn't let up, he opened one groggy eye to a digiclock which read 6:03 A.M. Though Stovepipe contemplated opening his mouth to yell at the rude intruder to leave him alone, he found the only sound he could utter was a groan. Hammered into submission by a thunderous headache which had erupted over his eyebrows like a volcano, he thought he would wretch if he even parted his lips to speak.

But outside on his porch, an impatient Jim began pounding on the door in earnest. He was worried that if he stayed away from the kitchen too long, his underlings would surely burn breakfast, and then he'd *really* be in hot water.

Within moments, he realized waking Stovepipe had been the bigger mistake.

"Who in the blazes is it?" the Director stammered from inside the cabin as he weakly lifted his head from the cot. "Leave me the hell alone!" he demanded, certain that a cerebral hemorrhage was but moments away. Covering his head with a pillow, Stovepipe curled up into the fetal position and prayed that death would come soon and that it would be painless.

Stretching out the word "little," Jim murmured through the closed door, "Boss, we have a leeetle problem up in the messhall."

"What kinda problem?" Stovepipe croaked, doing his best not to upchuck the several quarts of dark tortan-ale he had sucked down last evening.

"I think you'd best come see for yourself," Jim had replied, the perspiration running down his chubby face as he heard Stovepipe lumbering towards the door.

A cold washrag pressed to his clammy forehead like a bandage and a distressed grimace plastered across his ashen face, Stovepipe surveyed the situation through blood-shot eyes. It was obvious he wasn't happy. Deciding for the moment at least to leave the tables stacked just as Jim had found them, Stovepipe declared the messhall closed, ordering that breakfast be served out on the lawn instead. It was his considered opinion that by taking such a stringent step and intentionally causing breakfast to become a disaster, he could not only convince the staff just how disruptive such antics could be, he could leverage their guilt and count on peer pressure to force the criminals to come forward and admit what they had done. Much to Stovepipe's chagrin, however, his supposed lesson in humility backfired miserably.

Instead of being upset by having to eat breakfast outside, the entire Camp—staff and Scouts alike—*relished* the change of venue. Squatting on their haunches out in the parking lot or sitting on their butts under the shade of one of the magnificent pines nearby, they savored their pancakes and their eggs in a way they never had before. Drinking in the crisp morning air and sharing a few good laughs in the unstructured outdoor setting, everyone had a great time, commenting on how they couldn't wait to do it again. Of course, this only served to infuriate Stovepipe further, and right after breakfast he gathered the staff in the messhall for a stiff talking-to.

Though his head was still pounding from last night's binge, and though he couldn't speak above a whisper, Stovepipe recognized that if he didn't snuff out this sort of horseplay on the spot, the fires of shenanigans would burn quickly out of control. Ordering each man to take a seat in the chair bearing his name, Stovepipe quietly but firmly demanded that the perps fess-up immediately—or else. The silence which greeted him was deafening, and seeing as how no confessions were forthcoming, he made up his mind to clamp down hard on the entire staff. Trips to Jack's were cancelled and a 10 P.M. curfew was instituted until further notice.

Though his harsh penalties were met with groans and with protests of innocence, Stovepipe would not be swayed. This was unfortunate, because although he had no way of knowing it at the time, he was punishing his people for something they had not done wrong. The results, however, were quite predictable.

Instead of his measures having a settling influence on the staff as he had intended, pulling the noose tight only served to fuel a "go for broke" attitude among the most impulsive jokesters in the group. Figuring that Stovepipe couldn't penalize them any more severely than he already had, these characters—Sam and Ziggy included—were tempted to engage in a bout of horseplay they otherwise might not have, and before long the camp was swamped in one GA after another.

Like a highly contagious disease ripping through an unvaccinated population, Colonel Beck's messhall stunt ignited a rash of practical jokes which quickly infected both camps, temporarily disrupting the program on both sides of the lake. When, much later that summer, the Colonel was revealed as the instigator of this particular outbreak of GA "flu," several of the older counselors felt it was their duty to even the score at their first opportunity. And now that he had arrived back in camp with his troop in tow, that opportunity was once again at hand. Knowing this and knowing how inviting a target Beck made, Stovepipe wanted to put a stop to it even before it could get started. Though he shared some of the staff's resentment over having been "had" last summer, he was adamant that the epidemic not be spread again this year.

"I mean it!" Stovepipe said, repeating his admonition to Sam and Ziggy as the three of them sat with their elbows propped on the counter of Jack's bar. "Under no circumstances is there to be any GA this summer. Leave Colonel Beck alone! Do I make myself clear?"

But Sam and Ziggy just smiled. They had already made up their minds what they were going to do, and nothing he could say was apt to sway them.

"I'm hungry," fat-Jim whined from the opposite end of the bar, reminding them all just how long it had been since lunch. In the background the jukebox was blaring out the latest in cack music.

"Is food all you ever think about?" Ziggy cross-checked in a caustic tone.

"The only bad thing about being on camp staff..." Lester grumbled as he leaned forward across the bar so he would be sure of being heard.

"You mean, besides the low pay?" Jim interrupted in his usual snivel, reaching across the counter for a menu.

"Yes, I mean *besides* the low pay," Lester snapped back impatiently.

"What, then?" fat-Jim insisted as Sam and the others listened in.

"There aren't enough women around here," Lester replied, an evil smirk on his face.

Though Sam didn't say anything at the time, it seemed to him as if women and money were the only things his brother ever thought of anymore. All Lester wanted to talk about lately was how rich he was going to be and how many women he was going to bed.

"Sounds like you'll be stuck jacking yourself off just like last summer," fat-Jim taunted, knowing that he would get Lester's goad with that crack. "Or maybe you and Miss Loddy ought to get together," he giggled. "You two would make a lovely couple."

His eyes flashing red with anger, Lester looked as if he might strike Jim right there on the spot, but before the dispute could flare out of control, Ziggy tactfully stepped in. "Let's not get into it tonight, okay fellas? Stovepipe has already given us permission to leave camp next weekend to visit those girls we met on the canoe race, so there should be no need to resort to masturbation just yet."

"A lotta good that does *me*," Jim moaned, rapping the edge of his menu on the formica. "I didn't *meet* any girls on the canoe trip."

"So, while we are away visiting the honeys," Lester rebutted unsympathetically, "you will have all the privacy you need to do Miss Loddy or else to jack…"

Trying once again to sidetrack the elder Matthews, Ziggy broke in, "Those girls live only a couple of hours away, and though Stovepipe here is too cheap to lend us his gcar again for the weekend, my friend Sam tells me he has worked out all of the details."

"Well, I sure hope my little brother has worked out *something*," Lester remarked eagerly, thinking back to Sindy and the night before last. When Abe had refused to join in on the fun, that had just meant more of her for him.

"I know what you mean," Sam nodded. "I sure wouldn't mind seeing that Sara again." Thinking back to that first evening outside the school house, he had to admit she wasn't the only reason he had for making a trip to Madison. Yes, he wanted to see her, of course, but he also wanted to get his hands on an info-terminal connected to the Net. The terminal here at Jack's had proved inadequate for the job, and except for giving him the name of a reference text, *Jane's Encyclopedia of Aircraft*, he hadn't been able to call up anything more than rudimentary information on airchops. Though he had once thought highly of the idea of talking to Colonel Beck about what he had seen as Stovepipe had suggested, now that seemed rather ludicrous. Without having something specific to tell the man, without having something specific to *show* him, it would all be a big waste of time. What Sam really wanted was a way to access *Jane's Encyclopedia*, and that he could only do at the university computer in Madison.

"Heh, loverboy," Ziggy commented as the others hooted their agreement behind him, "you practically had your tongue down the poor girl's throat when I found you after the dance."

"Oh?" Sam contradicted defensively, coming back into the present. "And how 'bout my brother? He never even came *home* that night. By the way, where did you two go that evening anyway?"

"Not that it's any of your business, but are you insinuating that that pure young thing and I did something wrong?" Lester retorted, knowing that they had. "Sindy's just not that sort of girl."

Sam just rolled his eyes and smiled. Nodding his head knowingly as the friendly banter went back and forth, he contemplated what kept this group together. For all of their differences, these guys around him were very much alive. They each fervently believed that every single one of life's precious moments was to be savored and consumed with relish, that boredom was an ailment reserved strictly for others, that idle time was the province only of idiots. And like all men their age, they each pictured themselves as being indestructible.

"Are you guys gonna order something?" Stovepipe urged as Jack looked on. "Or are you just gonna stand there all night and argue?"

"I'll buy the first round," Lester offered, trying to appear as grown-up as possible. "Barkeep," he barked in an authoritative tone, "set us each up with a liter of the good stuff."

Eyeing Lester warily, Jack splashed five bottles of ice-cold tortan-ale down on the bar in front of them. Dependent as he was on the summertime upswing in his business, he couldn't afford to have more than a passing concern with whether his patrons were of drinking age or not.

As the evening crowd slowly filtered in, the noise level in the place steadily rose. And before long, the pub was vibrating with the harsh sounds of pool balls cracking against one another and with nickel-plated coins being tapped nervously on the counter. Unintelligible cack music trumpeted from the jukebox and raucous laughter erupted from the throng with startling regularity. Drink after drink was served up and just as quickly downed, and after several tortans, Sam began to feel light-headed.

Not having had much experience with alcohol, he was unprepared for its dilatory effects. Overwhelmed by the impression that the floor was moving slowly beneath him, he didn't have to touch his hand to his forehead to know it was awash in perspiration. Certain he was about to fall down faint, Sam reached out with one arm to steady himself. But instead of being comforted by the feel of a bar stool as he had expected, he was embarrassed to discover he had inadvertently placed his hand on the tender thigh of a shapely young woman sitting next to him. Apparently, she had taken Ziggy's seat when he left for the bathroom to relieve himself.

As Sam turned to apologize to the newcomer for his affront, he could not help but notice her breasts jiggling freely beneath the loose, provocative weave of her open-mesh sweater. In fact, so little of the fishnetting obstructed his view of her taut, white skin, she was for all practical purposes, naked from the waist up.

"How 'bout an ale, milady?" he stammered drunkenly, his eyes fixed on those sweet-looking orbs, his heart pounding hard inside his chest.

"Thanks, but how 'bout a kiss instead?" she countered wantonly, drawing her half-naked body closer to his. Her scent was that of an animal in heat.

Astonished by the fullness of her lips and by the lustiness of her welcoming nuzzle, Sam was at a loss for words. Even though the tortan had dulled some of his senses, nothing could block the erotic sensation as she worked her tongue across his cheek and into his mouth. Aroused by the feel of her erect nipples pressing desperately against his chest, Sam began to fondle her amateurishly.

"Heh there, good buddy," Ziggy shouted as he returned from the men's room, "sorry to interrupt you mid-grope, but I thought you told me you were hot on *Sara*?"

"I am," Sam muttered, fumbling for words, his face reddening.

"So, since when do you try to make it with every bimbooker who happens to slither your way?"

"She's a *bedder*?" Sam cross-examined with sudden disgust. "Damn!"

"Yep, old friend, she charges by the hour," Ziggy confirmed assuredly even as he carefully studied the woman's well-maintained physique for himself.

Cursing his stupidity, Sam pulled back from the prostitute in revulsion. His grandpa had taught him that such women were to be avoided at all costs, and he was irritated with himself for having been so easily duped.

Seeing that things weren't going to go her way, the disappointed working girl who had been enthusiastically working him into a lather only moments before, abruptly turned off her contrived passion. Glaring angrily at Ziggy for robbing her of a trick, the big breasted woman stomped indignantly from the bar, slamming the screen door shut behind her.

No longer supported by the bimbooker's firm embrace, Sam felt his knees beginning to buckle beneath the dead weight of his drunken body. Clutching awkwardly for a bar stool to help break his fall, he slid unceremoniously to the floor, striking it with a resounding thud. As he lay there on the linoleum dazed, his clothes sopping up spilled beer like a sponge, everyone around him began pointing at his crumbled form and laughing at his stunt.

His last thoughts were of a rickety old sailing ship being tossed unmercifully about by a ferocious storm. He imagined himself a seasick passenger onboard that swirling vessel. Dashing from his berth in haste, he realized he wasn't apt to make it topside in time to lean over the gunnels. Then everything went black.

Fifteen
Madison

"This should be a great weekend!" Sam exclaimed as the three of them strode energetically out of camp at five A.M. that next Friday morning. Although working with young Scouts every day, all summer long, was his job after all, Sam could not easily forget the intriguing girl he had met only weeks ago on the canoe race. And though he had done his darndest to put Sara out of his mind, ever since leaving her side, images of her kept intruding in upon his thoughts almost on a daily basis. Not that it necessarily interfered with his work as a counselor, but at times, it was distracting. He kept seeing her glowing red cheeks, her round, penetrating eyes, the swell of her firm, uplifted breasts. Over and over he replayed the same scene in his head, and it wasn't long before he found himself daydreaming about being with her again. Each time this happened, he had to remind himself why he was there at Na-Cha-Tan to begin with.

The camp's program was designed to provide boys an opportunity to grow not only as individuals—acquiring new personal skills and knowledge—but also as leaders and as fully participating citizens. And it was the camp staff's responsibility to see that this growth took place. Sometimes this was a difficult task because the members of the camp staff were themselves such a composite. They had diverse interests, dissimilar hobbies, distinct personalities, and different religions, yet they all shared a common creed: to help every camper reach the highest possible degree of Scouting know-how and to have fun doing it.

To be successful, a counselor at Na-Cha-Tan had to have the energy of a volcano, the understanding of a clergyman, the wisdom of a judge, the tenacity of a spider, the decisiveness of a general, the diplomacy of an ambassador, and the common sense of a parent. Not only did he have to possess the knowledge and the skills of a good outdoorsman, he also had to possess a love, and a deep and abiding appreciation for the wide variety of campers he would encounter over the course of a summer. Campers came in an agonizing assortment of sizes, shapes, and colors, some with the antics of a monkey, some with the stubbornness of a mule, and some with the mischievousness of a devil. And although the campers would often try a counselor's patience, a good staffman had to be able to see beyond that immediate annoyance to the unique individual beneath and help the boy smooth out his rough exterior so that he could mature. On top of that, a counselor had to frequently cope with the sometimes inconsiderate unit-leader who knew it all and enjoyed nothing better than putting a staffman on the spot and testing whether he could push the counselor's temper to the ignition point.

Staff members had to know how to spot signs of trouble: the tendency towards homesickness in the first-year camper, the hazing tradition prevalent in some troops, the lack of a well thought-out program in others, the untreated infection or the festering wound. And they had to know who to report to in case they actually uncovered trouble: the chaplain for the homesick boy, Stovepipe for the Scoutmaster who turned a deaf ear to hazing, the commissioner for the troop with a poorly-trained leader, the medic for some, the ranger for others. Some decisions the staffman could make for himself; others he had to refer higher up.

Though the counselors were there at camp to serve, and not to look upon their assignment as a personal vacation, unless there was a certain amount of release from the day-to-day drudgery, tensions would rise and performance would eventually suffer. And while the tomfoolery of GA relieved some of the pressure, and the occasional trip to Jack's some more of it, for the older fellows, a weekend off every once in a while was to be expected. It was on such an enterprise that Sam, Ziggy, and Lester were engaged today.

No sooner had Sam arrived back in camp following the canoe race, than a letter had been sitting there waiting for him. Would he come visit her in Madison, Sara had written, and when? Could he bring Ziggy along too? And how about Lester? Could they borrow Stovepipe's gcar again like they had for the canoe trip? If not, how would they get there? Though the arrangements had been practically impossible to make long distance, eventually Sam had prevailed, devising a scheme which could work. And now, if all went according to plan, the three of them would find their girls awaiting their arrival at the end of today's trail.

Unfortunately, Stovepipe had other plans for the weekend and couldn't lend them his gcar, so they had no choice but to hitchhike all the way to Madison, a hundred miles away. Although this was a considerable distance, after having been sequestered in camp for such a long time, the prospect of an extended trip did not faze them in the least. By leaving Na-Cha-Tan early in the morning, they hoped to arrive at their destination sometime late that afternoon, then have all day Saturday with the girls before returning to camp late Sunday evening. Stovepipe's only stipulation had been that they be alert and ready for counseling no later than eight A.M. Monday morning.

"Judy, here I come!" Ziggy boasted cheerfully as the animated trio rounded the south end of the lake. Having just crept above the horizon, the morning sun was already warming their backs.

Mindful of the fact that Sindy was not from Madison but would nevertheless have to meet them there, Lester remarked, "Here's to Sindy—may she be able to read a road map."

"Of course, Sara is the best-looking one of the litter," Sam taunted, "but I'll permit you two boys to dream if you must."

As they marched confidently down the road, their boisterous chatter rocking back and forth, they felt self-assured, even cocky. Their spirits were high. Having managed to pull off a three day holiday, and with dates no less, made them king of the hill in the eyes of the rest of the staff. Every other counselor in camp was jealous of their good fortune, and well they should be, Sam reasoned: they were indestructible! Seeming so today anyway, he reveled in his triumph.

After a while, though, the three grew somewhat less ebullient. In the last hour they had seen only two gcars, and both of those had zoomed by, completely ignoring their outstretched thumbs. Eventually, as the sun rose ever higher in the sky and as the day grew steadily warmer, they fell into a disconcerted silence; they could not possibly hoof the remaining ninety-four miles on foot.

Yet, even as their fears of not finding a ride began to mount, a badly-sparking blue gcar came alongside. Seeing their hopeful thumbs stretched roadward, the driver pulled off onto the shoulder just ahead of them. If Sam had taken the time to study the gcar more closely, he would have noticed that its tires were bald and its frame dangerously rusted, but such as it was, the gcar looked like a king's chariot to the three desperate men.

"Need a ride?" the pimpled driver yelled to them out of the half-opened window.

"This guy's a real genius," Lester ridiculed under his breath, his adolescent moustache a humid smear.

"Shush," Sam ordered. "Beggars can't be choosers; we need a ride."

"We'd love one," Lester yelled back to the kid, "especially if you're going in the direction of Madison."

By now the three of them had caught up with the idling blue "thing." All the windows were rolled down and the sound of the radio greeted them as they stood there breathlessly alongside the gcar. The long-haired motorist intoned in an absentminded sort of way, "Get in already, walkers of the road. How do? My name is Bob. I *live* in Madison."

"Thanks loads for stopping," Sam nodded appreciatively, jubilant over their stroke of good luck. "We were beginning to think we'd *never* see our girls!"

The tattered seats of the sedan groaned as they piled into it through the unlocked doors. A half-eaten sandwich of some duration decorated the floor of the front, while mounds of dirty laundry consumed most of the space in the back. A jagged crack perforated one side of the windshield.

"I'll take you where you want to go on one condition," the gypsy bargained before they could even get comfortable.

"Oh? And what is that?" Ziggy probed, afraid of being put back out on the hot asphalt.

The traveler set out his terms. "You have to guarantee me that you will one day repay my generous favor by picking up at least one hitchhiker yourself. But that is not all: You must also make *them* promise to carry on the same tradition to *their* riders. If the chain remains unbroken, no one will ever be forced to walk again. Do you swear it?"

The boys looked at each other quizzically before chuckling irreverently, "Yeah, sure!"

"Bless you my friends," the vagabond bubbled as his foot slammed the accelerator to the floor. "May peace and love follow you all the rest of your days. Now hold onto your hats, folks; next stop is Madison." As they roared off down the road, the blue demon sparking wildly, Bob shouted over the din, "By the way, loverboy, in what part of town does this bird live?"

Glancing at the little slip of paper stuffed in his shirt pocket, Sam answered with Sara's address up on Lake Mendota Drive.

"Rich bitch, eh?" Bob questioned with a devilish wink.

Sam looked at Ziggy for help, but his friend's voice was drowned out by the roar of the wind whipping through the gcar's open windows. Shrugging his shoulders, Sam grunted out an unintelligible reply. It was obvious that for the next hour or so, any further talk would be all but impossible.

Reduced to silence by the racket, Sam wrestled in solitude with his thoughts. Not being very well acquainted with the city of Madison, he had had no way of anticipating that the mere mention of a street name was enough for a road-gypsy like Bob to conclude something about status, about power, about wealth. It all seemed so incongruous and out of place. Though Sara had appeared common enough when they first met, for all Sam knew, he might be dangerously out of his league. Once again he was thankful for not having divulged to her that he too had come from a rich and powerful family.

Doing his best to keep his mind off this exciting, confusing woman for the moment, Sam allowed his thoughts to drift aimlessly with the cack music blaring from the radio. Chuckling to himself lightly as the wind twisted his hair hopelessly into knots, Sam thought again of last night's escapade. Though Stovepipe had made them swear that evening in Jack's not to aggravate Colonel Beck, Sam and Ziggy had been unable to resist the temptation. Ever since the messhall episode a year back, everyone had agreed the Beck caper was long overdue. That episode had spawned a disastrous three day-long GA war between him and the rest of the staff, a war from which he had emerged unscathed and from which they had emerged the clear losers. This year, though Colonel Beck had again come to camp prepared to do battle, he didn't actually think anyone had the guts to challenge the master. He was wrong.

Sam and Ziggy concocted and assembled a simple, yet rather ingenious device which they set up inside the Colonel's cabin while he and his assistant Scoutmaster were away last night at dinner. To begin with, the two culprits mounted a narrow shelf above the doorway and above each of the cabin's four windows. Next, they took six, two-quart tin cans, and up near the top of each one, just under the rim, they punched a small hole with an awl. The perpetrators then filled three of the six cans with water and three more with flour they had stolen from the messhall earlier in the day. On the improvised shelf they had mounted over the door, they carefully positioned two of the cans—one filled with water and one filled with flour. The other four buckets were placed in no particular order on the stubby shelves nailed in place above the windows.

A cord was secured to each can through the hole they had punched at the can's lip, then the lines were drawn taut and tied to a single main line which was itself connected to a teeter-totter mechanism they nailed to a table placed in the center of the room. Lines were similarly strung to the door handle and to each of the window latches before being fastened to the opposite side of that same teeter-totter. Now, if the door were to be swung open, or if a window were to be lifted to circumvent the booby-trapped door, the teeter-totter would rock, bringing down all of the buckets—presumably on someone's head. Air Force Colonel Robert McNamara Beck—the obnoxious, undisputed master of GA—was that intended someone.

The Colonel had already begun the evening angry over his troop having been bested in an intervillage competition of capture-the-flag, so when he returned to his dark hovel last night after a very long and frustrating day, he was looking forward to eight solid hours of uninterrupted sleep. Hastily flinging open his cabin door without even stopping to consider the possibilities, the Colonel unwittingly triggered Sam and Ziggy's nasty device, inundating himself with a cake-like mixture of flour and water, and pasting the interior of his hut with a combination of ingredients which would become steadily more mealy as they hardened. Infuriated at having been "gotten", Beck shoved Officer Jenkins aside and stomped down to Stovepipe's cabin sputtering and swearing. Pounding on the Director's door with his fist, his clothes still drenched in water and white flour, he demanded satisfaction. But he got none. Despite Stovepipe's stiff admonition to the staff against pulling off any GA's, he couldn't help but laugh at the comic sight Colonel Beck made standing there in his doorway. The man had it coming, and that's all there was to it.

Thinking back upon the success of their prank, Sam was sitting there now with a silly grin painted on his face when Bob's gcar threatened to suddenly skid off the roadway and onto the road's graveled shoulder. Jarred from his deliberations by the sound of pebbles smacking against the undercarriage of Bob's jalopy, Sam clutched his seat cushion and prayed for a straight section of pavement. To his constant fear and amazement, somehow their wild-eyed driver managed to negotiate the country backroads at breakneck speed, his long hair streaming out behind him in the wind like a tail. Glancing over his shoulder at his buddies in the back seat, Sam saw that they too were sitting there white-knuckled, hanging on for dear life. Only their occasional chirps of laughter helped to relieve the tension as they silently debated whether they would live out the day.

Sixteen
Wolf Lake

Despite the terrifying, edge-of-the-seat ride, they pulled up in front of Sara's house without incident less than two hours later. Lake Mendota Drive was like something out of a fairy tale. The sprawling brick homes and the expansive, well-manicured lawns which lined the wide boulevard paid witness to the aura of wealth which Bob had already planted in Sam's mind.

"Thanks for the ride," Ziggy remarked as the three of them tumbled out of the gcar and onto Sara's front drive, oohing and aahing at their surroundings.

"Don't forget the promise you made," Bob reminded them as he brushed his long hair out of his eyes with his fingers.

"We won't," Lester returned, a mischievous, evil smirk

plastered across his face. "And we certainly won't forget you."

Acknowledging the trio with a wave and a big dumb grin, Bob gunned his motor and peeled out of the driveway, his left arm dangling precariously out from the open window. Watching the road-gypsy speed out of sight, Sam felt lucky to still be alive, and at first, he didn't even notice Sara running up the hill from the lake to greet him. Yet, as soon as he got a glimpse of her lithe frame out of the corner of his eye, he forgot all about their eccentric driver.

She had been sunning herself at the water's edge, and her oil-soaked body glistened between the folds of her skimpy swimsuit. He had never seen her like this before, and up until this very moment, had only fantasized what she might look like with her street clothes off. Still, there was no possible way he could have been prepared for how superb her figure actually was. Like an athlete or perhaps a long distance runner, she was rock-hard muscular with a set of biceps and a pair of buttocks which had been sculpted by many hours of working out with weights. It took Sam's breath away.

However, it wasn't only her great looks which had caught him by surprise. Though Bob's smart-aleck comments regarding Sara's address had given him a hint that she probably came from money, not until he stood in her front yard did he begin to suspect the full extent of her family's wealth. He was flabbergasted. The Logan home was more like a manor than a house, more like an estate than a residence. It was built into the hillside in such a way that the front door was at street level where the four of them currently stood, while the patio where she had been sunning herself earlier was at the elevation of the lake, nearly three stories below. As a result of the slope, the secluded backside of the house had a spectacular view out upon the placid, blue-green waters of Lake Mendota. Moored at the

Logan's private dock was a pair of motorboats, an aluminum rowboat, and a two-man kayak. Because hydrocarbon
fuels were in such desperately short supply, owning a
motorboat, for instance, was a luxury afforded only by the
very upper crust, and yet, these people owned two!

Sam was astonished by how terrified this discovery
made him feel. The house plus the grounds around it were
simply marvelous, as were all the spacious homes neighboring it along the block. But what really clinched the Logan's
upper class status for Sam was the enormous *size* of the
place! Though Sam had also come from a prestigious and
well-regarded midwestern family, such outward trappings
of wealth were unfamiliar to him. He had seen pictures of
such homes, but never before had he stood in front of one.
It made him wonder whether Sara was in fact who she
pretended to be.

"Sam! You're here!" she welcomed even as Lester stammered enviously under his breath, "Damn, little brother,
you've hit pay dirt!"

"You're here at last!" she exclaimed, approaching him at
a run, her breasts threatening to jiggle their way out of her
bathing suit. "And hours earlier than I expected, you rascal.
I'm so happy!" she spouted, throwing her arms around him
and pressing her scantily clad body against his. Before he
knew what was happening, she was kissing him full on the
mouth and staining his clothes with splotches of sunoil
from her wet, oil-drenched body.

Though Sam was unprepared for such a forward, public
display of affection, he didn't hesitate in hungrily kissing
her back. It might have been a long, drawn out embrace if
not for Ziggy's interruption. Repeatedly clearing his throat,
he made it clear he was eager for them to be on their way.
When the two lovebirds finally broke, and Sam looked up,
Ziggy was frowning and Lester was pacing irritably back

and forth behind him.

"Well, my pretty," Sam said, staring into her eyes with deep affection, "we have got the rest of the day and all of tomorrow to enjoy each other's company, but I sense that my partners in crime here are impatient for us to pick up *their* consorts."

"Don't worry," Sara explained as she zealously grabbed for his hand, "all the plans have been made. Judy and Sindy will meet us at Judy's house, then I will drive the six of us up to a secluded lake just twenty minutes north of here. Figuring you would all be tired after your long trip, and that you wouldn't want to come all the way back here into town just to sleep, I made reservations at a motel near the lake just in case. That is, if that's okay with you?" Her eyes aglow, she squeezed his hand suggestively.

"You've hit the jackpot," Lester whispered lewdly into Sam's ear, his own mind churning.

"Motel?" Sam stammered, afraid he was going to faint. "I'm not sure…"

"Don't be bashful, my love," she oozed lecherously, her grin bewitching him.

"Yes, my love," Lester mocked defiantly, just out of earshot, "don't be bashful!"

Struggling to regain his composure before the color in his face gave him away, Sam confessed, "Your plan sounds just…great." By now, he had forgotten all about the university computer and *Jane's Encyclopedia of Aircraft.*

"Let's get going, then," Lester urged excitedly, "I'm sure you two are not the only ones around here who are hot to trot. But do we have to rent a motel room? I'm not sure I have enough credits on me to afford that."

"It's all taken care of," Sara giggled, "it's already been paid for."

Even as the boys stared at one another dumbfounded,

the bellow of an older voice rang out from the house. "Sara! Sara Logan! Come here please," her mother motioned to her from the front porch a hundred yards away. Had she been standing right there next to him, Sam might have guessed that this lady was too young to be Sara's mother. Instead, his heart sank as he feared the next hour would be spent with introductions, personal histories, explanations, excuses, and goodbyes.

"Okay, mom," Sara yelled back. But as she turned to run up to the house, her buns barely concealed by the lower half of her orange bathing suit, she whispered over her shoulder, "Stay here, I'll be right back."

Torn between doing what was right, and doing what he had been told, Sam opted to stay put and watch from across the lawn as Sara and her mother talked. It didn't look as if the two of them were having an argument, but when they disappeared into the house together, he wondered if perhaps some unforeseen problem hadn't suddenly developed. In fact, he was just about to go up to the house himself and smooth over whatever difficulty had arisen, when she returned to the front door dressed in street clothes and struggling with a heavy picnic basket.

"Here, let me help you with that," Sam yelled, running to meet her halfway. "Is everything copacetic with your mother?"

"Oh, yeah, I told her we'd be back sometime on Sunday."

"You *told* her?" Sam asked, a little taken back by her reply. "Just like that? Land's-sakes, I have never *told* my parents anything in my whole life!" he admitted, trying to imagine having an adult conversation with his father.

"But they have tried to tell *you* plenty," his older brother sneered, knowing what a loser Sam thought their father was.

Unsure what to make of Lester's snide comment, Sara just smiled and directed them to her gcar. "My mom trusts me implicitly, and so we get along just fine." Even as she spoke, her description of their relationship seemed just a little bit out of place to Sam, and for a moment he wondered whether that woman was actually Sara's mother or whether perhaps Sara had been adopted. For the second time now since arriving at her doorstep, Sam found himself questioning certain details about her identity. What little he knew of her background didn't seem to jive with her reality, and if he could find a diplomatic way to bring it up, he intended to ask her for an explanation.

As Sam contemplated what she had said and how she had acted, Sara drove them across town from her fashionable Lake Mendota address to a more middle-class neighborhood where they picked up Judy and Sindy. Though Lester didn't seem to notice or to care, to Sam it appeared as if Sindy had aged considerably since they first met just three weeks ago. No longer did her face have the look of a twenty-year old, and though the long-sleeve cotton shirt she was wearing hid the IV tracks on her arms, after his experience with a working girl at Jack's the other night, Sam wondered whether this blond-headed temptress with the big breasts and the husky voice wasn't in fact a bimbooker too. If so, what did she want with Lester? After all, he wasn't all that good-looking, and he certainly had no money to speak of.

Their destination was to be a secluded place in the middle of nowhere called Wolf Lake. Sitting next to Sara as she guided the gcar through the midday traffic, Sam studied her up close, noticing details he had never taken account of before. To begin with, he realized that she was probably older and more mature than he had first thought, and yet, her youthful body was firm and her posture erect. Her leg muscles, while well-developed, were not bulging like a steroid user's might be; still, she looked to him as if she could defend herself in a fight. He imagined that she knew karate or else jujitsu, and while she was not thin, her frame was clearly devoid of any unnecessary body fat.

Allowing his eyes to linger upon the firm profile of her breasts, he was embarrassed when she whispered to him, "Almost there, loverboy." It was as if she had been reading his mind.

At the outskirts of town, Sara turned north to follow a county road. Exiting it after ten minutes or so, she pulled off onto a dirt-covered spur which was marked with a brown state park sign. Before long, the side road spilled into a clearing in the woods, and that's where she stopped. Nestled in the forest before them, its incandescent beauty egging them on, was Wolf Lake. Framed by the peppered white bark of a stand of paper birch, Wolf Lake was more of a pond than a lake, but it was nevertheless singular in its beauty. Unlike the color of Na-Cha-Tan or even Muskrat Lake, its hue was a silky blue, a blue which bid them enter.

As fast as she could bring the gcar to a sputtering halt, Ziggy flung open the backdoor and bounded for the water, tearing his clothes off as he went. It had been a good many hours since his last shower, hours which had included a sweaty hike along a hot, dusty road and a long ride in an unairconditioned gcar, and like Sam and Lester, Ziggy was pungent. Figuring a dip in the lake could only improve matters, he scampered to the water buck-naked.

"How 'bout a skinny-dip before we snarf down the goodies in your mom's picnic basket?" he yelled, shouting over his shoulder as he tiptoed the last few yards across the stretch of pebbles separating the forest from the shore.

Seemingly possessed by this unfamiliar waterhole, the intrepid Sicilian entered the water with a diving splash, surfacing twenty yards further out with a hoot and a yell at the bracing temperature. The cool water tasted sweet and clean.

The others weren't quite so bold as Ziggy in their

nakedness. Not out of shame really, or even out of modesty, but more out of shyness. Sam, still in his undies, ran, rather than dove in, and Sara followed close behind. In the interval she had slipped behind a tree and was now sporting the bright orange, two-piece swimming suit she had greeted him in earlier.

Gasping pleasurably at the sight, Sam realized that on a well-proportioned body such as hers, hiding the erogenous zones behind a ribbon of cloth was infinitely more stimulating than stark nakedness could ever be. The mind and its powers of imagination were without a doubt the most erotic of all the sex organs, and he found his manhood stirring as a shot of testosterone raced through his system. Fortunately, his torso was already deep enough in the water to conceal the length of his arousal, but his eyes couldn't begin to hide his feelings. When she saw his hypnotized stare, she answered him with a look of, "Soon, very soon."

For Lester and Sindy, however, soon was now, and patience a dirty word. Side-by-side the two of them swam the hundred or so yards to the shallow, south end of the lake to continue what they had begun in the back seat of Sara's gcar on the short drive up here. Not knowing anything about the woman, Sindy's eagerness had surprised even the usually unflappable Sara.

As Lester and Sindy moved further afield, Judy—the most bashful of the trio—caught up with Ziggy, instantly engaging him in a laughing, splash-fest. Of the three sets of couples, these two came from the most similar of backgrounds which meant, of course, that they were the least compatible.

Searching the sandy lake bottom with his eyes open, Sam uncovered a cachet of clams. But knowing that the bivalves were only in season during the four months ending in "r", he passed over them, focusing instead on a giant crayfish half-buried in the silt just ahead of him.

Surfacing moments later with the eight-legged crusta-cean in one hand, he shouted to his friend, "Better put some bottoms on or else one of these guys will swim by and bite off your pecker." At which point he tossed the flailing arthropod in Ziggy's general direction.

Squealing with delight as Ziggy beat a hasty retreat for the shore and for his swim trunks, Judy chuckled and gave Sam the universal thumbs-up signal.

"This is the life," Sara sighed, crinkling the wet sand between her toes as she edged closer to where Sam lay, treading water.

"I hope I never grow old enough to forget this day," he agreed, smiling widely.

"I wonder how many others have ever had it this good," she moaned, playing her part to the hilt. "You know, for kids, we're pretty darn lucky."

"Damn lucky," he retorted, feasting his eyes on her perky breasts. Her nipples were pressed against the wet material of her swimsuit and no matter how hard he tried, he couldn't avert his gaze.

"Most of the world only *dreams* of living the way we do," she waxed philosophic.

"So true, but many of us tend to take it all for granted," he declared, thinking of her beautiful home up on Lake Mendota and how she couldn't possibly have any material concerns whatsoever. "I thank God…"

"Sam, we've been through this before: God has nothing at all to do with it!" she objected strenuously, flexing the muscles in her arm as she splashed herself with water. "People make their *own* luck. They tend to invoke God only when things don't go their way, or else when they cannot explain a phenomenon in purely rational or purely scien-tific terms."

As a faraway look erupted on her face, Sam stood there in the water, unsure what to make of this lovely, defiant, woman. Then, as quickly as her argumentative bout had come, it passed, and she turned more playful. "Kiss me, you fool," she toyed, thrusting herself at him.

Brushing her hair back with one hand even as he gently stroked her cheek with the back of the other, he stared longingly into her eyes. Pressing her wet body against his, she responded to his caresses by wrapping her arms about his waist. Purring like a kitten, she pulled him down into the shallow water on top of her.

Seventeen
Childhood's End

That night, as Sam slipped to the brink of unconscious-ness, he struggled to confront the confusing feelings he had for this fascinating, terrifying girl slumbering peacefully next to him on the bed. What with leaving Na-Cha-Tan at 5 A.M. that morning it had been a full day, and by the time they had arrived back at the motel that evening, there had been scant energy left to contemplate anything but sleep. Instead of engaging in any nighttime antics as they might have intended earlier in the day, everyone had settled comfortably into bed without so much as a good night kiss.

By two o'clock that afternoon the six of them had polished off Mrs. Logan's homemade sandwiches, and they were dressed again, ready to go out on the town.

"What are we going to do with the rest of the day?" Sindy had asked in that husky voice of hers, busily washing down the rest of the sandwich she had been munching on.

"How 'bout a movie tonight?" Judy had recommended, greedily eyeing her date even as he sucked down the last of the carbonated drink Sara's mother had sent along.

"That sounds great!" Sam had said. "I haven't been to a full-screen in years."

"Yes!" Ziggy concurred, smacking his lips with anticipation. "Real popcorn, not that hydrated stuff we get back at camp."

"It's agreed then," Sara murmured, signaling her approval. "And afterwards, we can stay the night at the motor lodge where I have made reservations."

"Wait a second," whined Judy. "By then, I'll need more than just popcorn to fill *my* tummy. I think these horny lugheads should buy us dinner *plus* a movie."

As the other two girls proceeded to nod their heads in agreement, Lester had winced uncomfortably. As per usual, he was pathetically short of cash. Looking to Sam and Ziggy for sympathy, he explained his situation as delicately as he could, and at Sindy's urging, they had all agreed to chip in to cover his shortfall. Later, after stopping for dinner at an inexpensive Italian restaurant Sara knew, and after taking in a full-screen for a mystery with a well-worn plot, they retired to the motel. Now, as Sam lay there in bed awake, listening to the rhythm of her breathing, he silently wrestled with his innermost fears.

What did being in love really mean? he asked himself, thinking that he was. What were the responsibilities? The burdens? How much money *did* it take to buy the good life? Where would it all come from? Could he face living life with a woman of independent means? How would he handle the confinement? For that matter, how would he handle the freedom?

Plagued by these questions, Sam lay there awake for hours, unable to sleep. When exhaustion finally did overcome him and his eyelids did finally close, it was a troubled and restless sleep. Much to his regret, the situation had not improved any by morning, and upon waking, he discovered that those very same questions were still foremost on his mind.

Saturday morning found them all desperately in need of a shower, and before anyone could make a move to stop them, Lester and Sindy had stripped to the skins and commandeered the bathroom. Pawing at one another as they stepped into the stall and drew the curtain shut behind them, the two shameless lovers reassured their stunned companions that by going first and bathing together they would be conserving not only the limited supply of hot water, but saving time as well. Unfortunately for everyone waiting patiently in the next room for their turn to wash up, it didn't turn out that way. Proceeding to lather themselves into a sexual frenzy with a bar of scented soap, the brazen duo was diverted by their vulgar foreplay from the ostensible purpose of taking a joint shower, conserving neither water, nor time. Even over the roar of the rushing spray, there was no denying the caterwauling of Sindy's amorous moans or Lester's passionate words. Indeed, the sounds of their lovemaking was so disconcerting to the other four, it wasn't long before they were left needing the cold showers they were forced to take.

While Lester and Sindy's open display of affection obviously unnerved both Ziggy and Judy, it clearly angered Sam. And it didn't take long for that anger to surface. Once all of the showers were behind them and the troop had gathered again in the bedroom for a summit meeting to decide on the day's program, the long-festering trouble between the two brothers erupted.

"It's a perfect day for a visit to the beach," Ziggy stated, propping the motel door open with the leg of a chair. A friendly ribbon of sunshine streamed in from outside, warming the room. Illuminated thusly, the tense lines in Ziggy's face revealed how agitated he was over Sindy and Lester's bathroom shenanigans.

"Beach?" Judy asked, looking forward to getting out of the confines of the small room. "What beach?"

"On Lake Michigan east of here," Ziggy explained, pointing vaguely out the door in that direction. "Beyond Kohler; at Sheboygan or thereabouts."

"That sounds good," Lester interjected, his tone clearly argumentative, "but I would much rather go back to Sara's house and try out her speedboat on Lake Mendota."

"No! That is strictly out!" Sara barked, noticeably irritated by the suggestion. "I do not want to go home even one minute early!" she insisted, knowing full well that her cover would be blown if she went back now. Ambassador Nussbaum's wife had been very adamant on that point; they were expecting representatives in from SKANDIA today and she could not change those plans for any reason. "Sorry," Sara added, softening her voice, "but that is out of the question."

"Lester, honey," Sindy cooed, patting her hand on the bed in a provocative manner, "I'd be content to stay right here in the room with you all day long." Her gesture was a clear invitation, and it ignited the explosives which had been smoldering since before the showering duet began.

"Listen, *honey*," Sara criticized as she shook her head disparagingly, "have you no shame? Using sex as a means of passing the time of day destroys the whole *beauty* of it all. If recreation is what you're after, then perhaps…"

"Get off your holier-than-thou pedestal, Lady Logan,"

Sindy snapped, knowing exactly what she had to do in order to separate Lester from the others. "I imagine you're a blooming virgin, and I wouldn't be surprised if you were actually *proud* of the fact. But what you need, Miss Lily White, is a good hard one. That is, if you wanna be a *real* woman...like me."

"Slut!" Sara yelled back, nearly in tears. "Whore! Bimbooker!"

"Heh, Sara, now you listen," Lester interrupted, stepping between the two women before there were fisticuffs. "Sindy is *my* girl. And how often we choose to do it—or where—is really none of your concern. So butt out!"

By now Sam had seen and heard enough. Intervening as much on Sara's behalf as on his own, Sam did what he could to extricate his girl from what was plainly a troubling confrontation for her. "Big brother," he began in a distressingly sarcastic tone, resting his left arm heavily on Lester's shoulder, "it appears to me that you have a severe case of Puzzled Penis. Although it is curable, it requires an IQ well above your own. You see, it isn't smart to let your Johnson rule your life. To cure yourself, all you have to do is keep your goddamned pants zipped!" he yelped, coming to within inches of his brother's face. "And your mouth as well! You're way off base on this one, Lester."

"Oh, am I?" Lester retorted defensively, shoving his younger brother roughly aside.

"Yeah, and while we're at it," Sam continued boldly, "you're way off base on something else too. Despite the fact that you wangled your way into an appointment to the Naval Academy this fall, you haven't the first *clue* what it means to be patriotic. I hear you and Abe talking; I hear what the two of you are saying about America and about our way of life. He's wrong about socialism being superior, and you're wrong to listen to him. This paternalistic system he is so proud of, this way of life which he has convinced you is so goldarned superior to our own, does not account for exceptional people like grandpa or President McIntyre. And any system which cannot account for individualists like them, or for other extraordinary men of guts and daring, is a system destined to fail. It will not survive. Eventually it must collapse of its own weight. And when it does, it will take scum like you and Abe down with it!"

Like a machine-gun spitting out a volley of deadly words, Sam did his level best to verbally shoot his brother down. And for a moment, it looked as if he had succeeded. Dumbfounded by the whole diatribe, Lester staggered backwards, wounded by the assault. But it wasn't long before he mounted a vicious counterattack.

Sitting down heavily on the bed next to Sindy, Lester cleared his throat to speak. "Sam, it pains me to learn that you are still that immature, still that emotional," the elder Matthews boy asserted, a note of pity creeping into his voice. "As for your mouthful of psycho-babble, you may find that not even your revered capitalism has the capacity to handle self-indulgent slobs such as yourself. Yet, even if it could, this money-grubbing, dog-eat-dog system of government you are so fond of, represents not economic freedom, but rather, economic *enslavement*. For God's-sakes, little brother, look at what we did to the poor prairie-niggers, to the chinks, to the wetbacks, to every newcomer who graced our shores and threatened the jobs of existing workers. Exactly when are you going to grow up, little brother, and see the world as it really is?"

Rising to his feet as if he were about to go bursting from the room, Lester forged ahead in a cocky tone, "Besides, since everything that came out of your stupid adolescent mouth was said in anger, I intend to ignore the whole of it."

Flexing the muscles of his right arm, Sam imagined his

clenched fist smashing its way into Lester's pointy chin, loosening a few teeth in the process. But before he could move to put that plan into action, Sara grabbed him, pinning his arms against his sides and stopping him in his tracks. Even as he struggled to free himself of Sara's grip, Sam was surprised to learn how much stronger she was than he.

Seeing his friend squirm to break free, Ziggy spoke up, hoping to head off a fight. "I guess we're all in agreement then," he interjected, "as I suggested, we should all spend the day together at the beach, right?"

"Wrong!" Lester corrected. "You four decide amongst yourselves what you want to do; Sin and I will spend the day right here."

"That suits me just fine," Sam retorted at wit's end, motioning to the others to follow him out the open door. "Let's get the hell outta here, before I hurt someone!" he snapped, leading Sara, Judy, and Ziggy from the room.

"Your brother's a first-class asshole, if you ask me," Ziggy mumbled angrily as the four of them piled into the gcar and Sara pointed it east towards Lake Michigan.

"I'm beginning to figure that out," Sam admitted, perturbed by the whole episode. "It's as if he *wants* to get himself into trouble. I tell you Ziggy, I just don't trust that girl. She seems much too eager to lead Lester around by the nose, and ever since he met her, he always seems to be going off half-cocked."

"Settle down, boys," Sara urged, the wind from the open window whipping through her hair. "Ziggy reminded me of a quiet little beach on the lake where we can all relax and allow the world and all of its problems to slip by unnoticed."

"That sounds nice," Sam offered, squeezing his eyes shut for an instant as if it would help him clear his head. "Where exactly are you taking us?"

"Kohler-Andrae," Sara replied, recalling the name of the state park on the water an hour's drive away.

"Is that anywhere near the university?" Sam asked, suddenly remembering *Jane's Encyclopedia.*

"Not even close. But if you need to visit the university for some reason, I can turn us around and we can go back into Madison first. Only let me warn you: on a Saturday morning in the middle of summer, most of the university offices are closed. Is it important?" Sara asked.

"Oh, no, it isn't all *that* important," Sam frowned, perturbed at having forgotten about it yesterday. "Anyway, I'd rather go see this beach of yours."

"And so we shall."

Still angry after his blow-up with Lester, Sam lamented, "To think that all my brother ever talks about anymore is sex and money, and then he has the *gall* to call America a money-grubbing nation. If the only productive thing we manage to accomplish in the course of our lives is breathing in and out day after day, then surely God has failed in his Creation. He never meant for mankind to merely exist; He meant for us to excel! He never meant for us to merely be alive; He meant for us to prosper!"

Pausing to look around at the others, Sam exclaimed, "Self-indulgent slob indeed!"

He got no argument from his friends because they shared the same "grab for all the gusto you can" outlook on life as he did. Though the four debated for a spell whether Lester could ever be convinced to alter his outlook on life, gradually, as they ticked off the remaining miles to the shore, their thoughts became less and less troubled, and their disposition more and more light-hearted.

Sara remarked on this phenomenon as she drove. "It is much like one of Newton's Laws—just as the force of gravity decreases with the inverse square of the distance separating two bodies, our happiness increases exponentially the closer we approach the object of our desire."

Ziggy and Judy exchanged confused glances, but Sam understood perfectly what she meant; he knew from previous conversations that she believed much of how the world worked could be expressed in terms of biological or else physical laws. And it really didn't matter whether it was true or whether it wasn't, only that she believed it to be so. For him, the genuinely scary part was that she was so much smarter than he, so much smarter than he would have liked to admit. It wasn't that he didn't appreciate a keen mind, only that he had never met a woman so eager to use it. He was still lost in thought when Ziggy exclaimed, "Boy, is the lake beautiful!"

When Sam looked up, he could see that they were driving along a low-grade gravel road which ran parallel to the beachfront. As they bumped along the graded strip, the surface got progressively more rutted until it finally thinned-out altogether.

"I reckon this is the place," Sara announced as she stopped the gcar in a tiny clearing hidden behind a massive sand dune.

Laughing merrily, everyone bounced out of the gcar and ran the thirty or so yards to the water's edge. Off came their sandfilled shoes, and into the waves they charged, still fully-clothed and splashing each other wildly. But the water was cold, and it wasn't long before they tired of this sport, retreating back to the beach and plopping their exhausted, dripping wet bodies down on the sun-baked sand. This far north, the waters of Lake Michigan didn't warm sufficiently for swimming until later in the season, and even then, it didn't remain that way for long.

Contented, Sam lay back full length on the beach and gazed skyward at the wisps of clouds which graced the heavens above him. Off to the right, near the horizon, a faint outline of the moon hovered, its slice of ivory against an otherwise blue sky reminding him how earthbound man-kind had truly become. Sam had always been sensitive to the fact that the colony on Mars had been deserted in the very year of his birth, that—except for the weekly shuttle trips to the moon to dump off spent nuclear wastes—man's adventure in space had all but ended. It made him wonder about the future prospects for *Homo sapiens* here on Earth.

For as long as Sam could remember, the world had been at war, and only because he had grown up in a serene location right smack in the center of the American heart-land, and only because of the efforts of his grandfather, had he been shielded from the worst of its effects. His home town of Farmington was surrounded by clean air, tall corn, humid summers, and the echoes of Mark Twain. Recently, however, as Sam had grown into manhood, and as he had faced the prospect of military service himself, the reality of all that fighting had begun to get the better of him.

Sam knew a little of his family's genealogy, enough at least to appreciate that his great-grandfather had been some kind of national hero back in the days of Rontana, and that even his grandfather had made a name for himself by somehow preventing the United States and China from going to war over Hawaii when that state first tried to secede from the Union. Only his father, it seemed, had done nothing of consequence to help America prosper. Even Lester, lowlife that he was, expected to join the military before long. With Grandpa Nate's connections, Lester had had no trouble being admit-ted to the class beginning this fall at the Naval Academy in Alameda. And then there was Sam. Though he had no wish to be like his father, a man who had drifted from one meaningless job to the next, he also felt no sense of duty to serve his country. If only the fighting would stop, perhaps the thought of military service wouldn't frighten him so.

"Do you think a time will ever come when the wars will end?" he ventured, still prone on his back in the sand. "When all the people will be at peace with one another?" The question was thrown out for anyone to answer.

"You mean like no more Hitlers or no more Rontanas?" Sara cross-examined in a disbelieving voice. "Don't be silly! My personal philosophy is that you can't uninvent things. You cannot uninvent the bow and arrow, you cannot uninvent the nuclear bomb, and you *certainly* cannot uninvent the way people behave."

"Hear, hear," Ziggy clamored, ever mindful of his own obligations to military service. "So long as there are people with strong needs, there will be others who are jealous of their prosperity. And so long as there are competing classes of people, there will still be wars. It's inevitable, Sam."

"That's so depressing," Judy commented with a sigh.

"Are you suggesting that if all these people with strong needs, as you put it, were to be eliminated, that the world would be *better* for it?" Sam questioned, wondering what his friend was driving at.

"In a sense, yes," Ziggy elaborated darkly. "Granted, the world would be a whole lot less interesting place to live, but at the same time, it would almost certainly be a whole lot more congenial place too. Eliminate the individualists and the quest for a lasting peace would no doubt be achieved."

Sara intejected, "Without the overachievers—the individualists as you call them—there would be no prosperity for *anyone*! If it wasn't for that zealous one or two percent of the population, we'd *all* still be living in caves!"

"Admittedly," Ziggy countered, "but at what price?"

"Do you think we are wrong to live the kind of life we do?" Sam probed, disturbed and confused by his buddy's meaning.

"Absolutely not!" Ziggy exclaimed. "The truth is, no matter *what* sort of life we choose, no matter *how* we decide to live it, someone or other is sure to condemn us for living it that way. Just look at your brother, for Chrissake!" Ziggy declared with some emphasis. "I believe that so long as there are no regrets, the life you live should be of no one else's concern but your own."

"Not even your parents'?" Sam questioned, thinking more of his grandfather than of his father.

"Especially not them," Sara recommended.

"Still, it has always been in my mind that eventually the wars would stop; that eventually mankind would concentrate his energies on something more useful than fighting," Sam idealized.

"Like what?" Sara murmured, snuggling up close to him as if to say, let's end this conversation and get on to something else more interesting.

"Oh, I don't know," Sam replied. "Space, perhaps."

"Space?!" Ziggy hooted. "Are you crazy?"

"Maybe," Sam admitted sheepishly.

"So, what's gonna keep everybody from killing each other back here on Earth long enough to let us venture back into space?"

"Democracy," Sam ventured. "The more democracies there are in the world, the fewer potential adversaries there will be for us, and the wider the zone of peace will be."

"Lekhaim!" Ziggy intoned raising his hand as if he were toasting Sam's words. "My friend," he asserted, "there is no one in this whole wide world I like better than you, but what you say sounds awfully farfetched to me. Why should a country's political system have anything at all to do with its willingness to go to war?"

"In a democracy," Sam explained, "it is a complicated business to persuade the people, the legislature, and all of the society's power bases that a war is really necessary. Consequently, in a dispute with *another* democracy, there will always be ample time to resolve the conflict without resort to arms. *And*, there will be virtually no risk of being the subject of a surprise attack."

"The ole live-and-let-live philosophy, eh?"

"Yes, live and let live," Sam murmured lethargically. As a yawn escaped his lips, he squeezed his eyes shut and grew quiet, letting his skin drink in the warm sunshine. He felt his wet clothes slowly tighten as they dried. He heard the irregular barking of the gull-birds overhead. He heard the gentle lapping of the waves against the shore. And then he heard nothing at all.

A millenium passed before he awoke. Seeing as how the others were still asleep, he silently slipped off his sand-caked pants and his wrinkled shirt before falling fast asleep once more. This time the afternoon sun baked his muscular legs and his brawny chest to a crisp. When eons later he awoke for a second time, a cool evening breeze had begun to sweep across the beach. One by one they all stirred.

Propping herself up on one elbow, Sara beamed at him hungrily, her eyes feasting on his bare chest. He touched her face with his hand, brushing a speck of sand from her cheek. Licking Sam's fingertips with her tongue, she nuzzled his palm like a kitten might her master's leg, sending his crazed mind into overdrive. Suddenly confused by the carnal emotions welling up inside of him, Sam pulled away. But no sooner had he done so, than he reached for her once again.

This girl was so alive, so strong; he was so frightened, so terrified. Perhaps nothing scared him more than forging any sort of permanent attachment with her. Until this very moment, he had always been a completely free spirit, devoid of any lasting ties, never having to contend with any restraints, never having had any limitations put upon his person. He had always been taught that sex without marriage was a sin, yet here he was contemplating intercourse while still fearful of the obligations which came with it. Though he didn't have much to go by, judging from the unhappiness of his own father in *his* marriage of convenience, any sort of lasting relationship seemed particularly uninviting. In the final analysis, however, Sam speculated as to which was ultimately more important—making a commitment to someone he loved or preserving his own freedom? He wondered whether it was possible to find some middle ground with this girl, whether lust and love were the same thing, whether sex before marriage was a sin greater than marriage without love.

As he stared into her delightful round eyes, Sam was sensible enough to recognize he had to address these questions of the heart before lurching any deeper into love with her. So far, he was only in love with the idea of *being* in love. But he knew that would have to change. If he was to be faithful to a single woman for the rest of his days, he would have to tame his live-each-day-to-the-fullest mentality, a task he did not relish and would rather not do.

Possessed by these deliberations, Sam's day descended slowly into night. By the time they arrived back at the motor-hotel, it was well past dark. There was a note from Lester on the nightstand, a message which said he was with Sindy and that he would find his own way back to camp.

Despite the late hour and despite the long day, this time sleep was not on Sara's mind when she slipped beneath the covers. He did his best to pacify her, but her needs were insatiable. Completely overwhelmed by the depth of her passion, once more he found himself out of his league, running to catch up. Afterwards, when he should have been exhausted, the energy of their lovemaking only served to whet his appetite further.

Sleep did not come quickly, and when the benefit of sleep did come, it was again a restless slumber. Over and over again, Sam was plagued by the same question—commitment or freedom?

Before he knew it, daybreak had arrived. Peeking through a narrow separation between the drapes, a thin sliver of morning shone directly into Sam's drawn face. Rolling to one side, he put his back to the sun and watched in quiet fascination as the bedsheet rose and fell with the tempo of her breathing. A mist came to his eye as he digested the sad truth: he just wasn't strong enough yet to be an equal partner with a woman as assertive as this one.

Realizing that their paths would probably never cross again, he did what he could to commit the gentle curves of her hips and the smooth firmness of her breasts to memory, to reserve a special place in his brain where their time together could never be erased. The uncomfortable truth was that after returning Ziggy and him to Na-Cha-Tan that afternoon, Sara would drive out of his camp—and out of his life—forever. Childhood had come to an end.

Eighteen
Abe

Though Lester and Sindy reveled in each other's arms, few relationships were less sincere or more contrived than theirs. Her interest in him extended only as far as the money Whetstone was paying her, and his interest in her was founded on nothing more than a pathetic insecurity in his own manhood. It was a rather simple proposition: she had been hired to corrupt him by any means possible, and he was content to bed any woman who paid him the time of day. Yet, for whatever reasons the two born losers were drawn together, they were each delighted to have a willing partner with whom to practice their less than adequate sexual techniques. After Sam and the others left for the beach that morning, the two of them stayed in bed to hone and polish their craft. Over and over again, for hour after hour, they worked at it until they both had been consumed by the effort. Finally, when every ounce of passion had been drained from their systems, they left the motel in search of further adventure.

Whereas Sam and Ziggy returned to camp the very next evening, officially Lester never did. Thanks to the efforts of his grandfather the Senator, Lester had already been guaranteed a commission at the Naval Academy beginning in August, so blowing off the last few weeks of summer camp to be with this girl didn't seem like such a bad idea under the circumstances. Stealing a gcar and robbing a foodmart along the way, Lester returned to Na-Cha-Tan only long enough to gather his things. When he and Sindy arrived back at his cabin, they found Abe sitting there white-faced on his bunk, his hands caked in dried blood. This development was most unexpected.

"What the hell happened to *you*?" Lester interrogated, grabbing Abe by the shoulders as Sindy stood guard at the door keeping a watch out for any curious passers-by.

"I killed a kid," Abe admitted, unsure whether pride or shame should be the correct emotion. In his hand he still held the blood-stained knife.

"You did what?!" Lester exploded, his own face becoming ashen over the revelation. "Where? How?"

Shaking, Abe proceeded to explain. A coded message had come in from the rebels over the radio early that morning, and with Lester out of camp visiting Sindy in Madison, Abe had taken it upon himself to follow it up. As per usual, the instructions had been delivered over the airwaves in Seussarian code. Named for a twentieth century madman, such ciphers were built around a series of tongue-twisting rhyming couplets, and when used properly, were practically impossible to crack without having the proper key. Abe was to receive another load of arms in from the south, bury them in the forest temporarily, and then wait until nightfall for Dark Eagle to land and retrieve the cache. Despite their earlier precautions, it had never occurred to Abe that a nosy camper would follow him out into the woods and sit there quietly watching while he met the airchop, paid the pilot, and stashed the weapons. Not until Abe was on the trail heading back towards camp did the Scout confront him, and then, without even thinking of the repercussions, Abe had let his Mossad training get the better of him. Slitting the boy's throat and leaving him for dead on the trail near Little Grasshopper Valley, Abe had then hightailed it back to camp unsure what his next move should be.

Lester was stunned by what the Israeli had told him, and as he stood there now studying Abe's drawn face, it was obvious the man had finally snapped.

"We have got to get you out of here," Lester pleaded urgently once Abe had finished his tale. "We have got to get you out of here, and we have got to move that kid's body off the trail before it is discovered. If we stash the corpse alongside the weapons, it will look as if Dark Eagle did it. The authorities will never suspect us. Quickly now," Lester ordered, grabbing Abe by the arm even as he sheathed the man's knife and shoved it in his belt. "And the code book too. Our gcar is just up the hill. We'll drive it out to where Sindy met us on the logging road the other night, and then we'll hoof it the rest of the way into Little Grasshopper. Hurry! We haven't much time. Once that boy is reported missing by his Scoutmaster, they'll start combing the camp for him. How long has it been?"

"Just a couple of hours," Abe stammered incoherently.

"Let's hope we're not already too late," Lester declared in a sinister voice, his dark eyes meeting Sindy's.

Though Lester already had it fixed clearly in his mind what he had to do, Abe was in too much of a daze to see what was coming. Somewhere between the hallucinogenic drugs and the electroshock therapy of his torture at the hands of the Neo-Rontanians, Abe had lost his ability to cope with stress; now, he was undergoing some form of personal meltdown. Sindy, however, understood Lester's intentions perfectly. Seeing his cold, blank stare, she knew what had to be done. They had no other alternative: if she and Lester were to get away clean, Abe would have to be eliminated.

By the time the three of them had arrived back at the airchop landing site, a swarm of big black horseflies had already formed a disgusting mat of larvae around the boy's blood-caked neck. Though Lester found himself wanting to wretch at the sight, he covered his mouth and dragged the dead boy's body over to where Abe had earlier deposited the footlockers filled with weapons. Knowing it was time for him to make his move, Lester wiped his prints clean from the hilt of Abe's knife and removed a mini-Uzi from one of the footlockers.

After handling the stiff, putrid-colored corpse, the cold steel of the gun felt good in his sweat drenched palms. While Sindy momentarily distracted the Israeli by undoing her blouse partway, Lester slapped a magazine of shells into the bolt.

"Time to go," Lester reported as he signaled Sindy to move away from Abe's side and button herself back up.

"What is the meaning of this?" Abe implored, his face whiter than before. He wore a look of disbelief.

"You should never have killed this kid," Lester lectured, pointing the fearsome weapon at the Israeli's middle. "That was a big mistake."

"You have got to believe me, Lester. I had no choice," Abe whimpered, a look of panic now filling his eyes. "The boy *saw* me, for Christ sake! He would've turned us all into Stovepipe. What would you have had me do?"

"Anything but this. Now you're *both* Dark Eagle's problem," Lester spat out, dispassionately squeezing off several rounds. "You may now consider our association officially ended."

Staggering forward to clutch at his assassin, Abe collapsed at Lester's feet, his own blood gushing out to fill the indentations his boots had made in the soft earth.

Cracking the knuckles of his right hand with an unconcerned air, Lester stared solemnly down at his handiwork. Then, he and Sindy slipped calmly away.

As the crimson pool puddled out of Abe's bullet-mangled body, the diamond-shaped cross-hatching his boots had left behind in the dust, slowly filled with blood. If not for that night's ferocious rainstorm, the telltale mark might yet have been discovered.

"He's ruthless as hell," Sindy pointed out, reciting the story of how Lester had gunned Abe down at the foot of Little Grasshopper Valley. The two of them were bunking in a sleazy roadside motel, and while he was out cold on the couch from the effects of the tortan she had been feeding him all night long, she was using this opportunity to sneak away and call Whetstone from the public comm out in the lobby. It had been several days since their last contact.

"Are you afraid of him?" Whetstone asked, speaking calmly into the comm from the dimly-lit bowels of his shabby apartment.

"Of course not!" she asserted bravely, snorting a shot of the white drug as she spoke. "I love it! Anyhow, you should know by now that I can take care of myself just fine. I give the velcroid what he wants. He doesn't suspect a thing."

"Good. Keep it that way."

"Am I done then? May I finally dump this guy and get on with my life?" she probed, her voice revealing the boredom she had developed with this project. Though the money was good, and though Lester could be an interesting companion when the spirit moved him, she had never spent this much time with any one man since escaping from her incestuous father at age 14 to begin bimbookering.

"Not by a long measure, my sweet," the grotesque looking man solicited from his darkened room. "Not by a long measure." Even though Whetstone had been out of jail for more than a month now, he still could not stand the direct light of day. Confined by this malady to his gloomy flat, he lived a shadowy, almost pathological existence, an existence which might make one question whether his ailment was real or whether it was psychosomatic.

"What more do you want from me?" she whined, eager to get back to her old life of two or three tricks per night.

"Keep him entertained anyway you can, only be sure you get him to the Academy before opening day. August 26. Stay with him, Sinful," Whetstone urged darkly. "Now that you have his trust and his confidence, we are almost home. But he is useless to us unless he is addicted. He must be completely manageable—putty in our hands."

"We?" she asked, sniffing the last of her white powder. "Since when did this project become a 'we'?"

"Haven't I told you about my partner?"

"Must'a slipped your mind."

"Overlord Ling has taken a personal interest in our doings. In fact, he has sent along something special for you two."

"Oh, yeah? What's that?" she intoned, her voice becoming more slurred as the drug took effect.

"There will be a vial of blue-devils in with your next payment. Feel free to take some for your own use if you please."

"Blue-devils, eh?" she verified, licking her lips at the prospect. "Okay Whetstone, you ugly cockroach, you have yourself a deal: I'll stay with him until the 26th and I'll get him to Alameda on time, but if he's to pass the Navy's drug test on admissions day, you had better send along some Delude as well."

"Most ingenious. I hadn't thought of that. You're quite right, of course. I'll see to it."

But Sindy did not answer.

Staggering across the motel lobby, her mind blurred by the full effects of the addictive chemical, she left the receiver dangling there off the hook as she tried to negotiate her way back to their room. Had she cared to stick around and listen to Whetstone's final words, however, she would have heard him snickering at her from the other end of the line.

The trap had been set!

Nineteen
Missing

When Sam and Ziggy strolled into camp late that Sunday evening after having spent the entire weekend on the road, the atmosphere in the messhall was unusually grave. The sun had set hours ago, and though it was late enough for some of the staff present to have already showered and donned their bed-clothes for the night, curiously, not a single one of them actually *was* in bed. Typically, if there was to be an after-hours staff meeting or a late night round of staff snacks, it was not only announced several days in advance, the gathering nearly always had a party-like air to it. Tonight, however, something was distinctly out of place. From the harried looks on everyone's faces, Sam could clearly tell something was amiss. There was no food or drink set out on the dining hall tables, and as was plainly evident from the maps spread open on the tables in their stead, the theme of this hurriedly called meeting was serious. Though not much was being said, from what little Sam could gather, the conclave had been assembled only minutes before they arrived.

Off to one side, there was a huddle between Stovepipe, Colonel Beck, and the Colonel's assistant Scoutmaster, Officer Jenkins. They seemed to be engaged in a heated discussion, and for an instant, Sam thought he and Ziggy were in trouble over the stunt they had pulled three nights ago. With all that had happened to him these past two days, Sam had nearly forgotten that the last thing he and Ziggy had done before leaving camp on Friday was to GA Beck's cabin. But when Stovepipe signaled him to come over and join them, Sam knew it was something else altogether.

Stovepipe's face was grim, and seeing it Sam couldn't help but be reminded of the lost bather's drill which had taken place earlier in the summer. It had been a frightening, yet instructive incident.

Normally, during free-swim each afternoon, the Scouts observe the "buddy" system while in the water. Each boy checks in at the waterfront with a friend and both lads place their name-tags on the "buddy-board" before entering the swimming area. Then, at six or seven minute intervals, when the lifeguard whistles "Buddies!", each pair of boys stops swimming and clasps their hands together over their heads, holding them there until the lifeguard is satisfied that the count on the board matches the count in the water. If they do, swim resumes; if they don't, panic ensues.

On this particular day, free-swim had ended and all the campers had exited the swim area, taking their buddy-tags with them. Only there was just one little problem: though no boys remained on the dock or on the waterfront, a buddy-tag still remained on the board! There are only two possible reasons for a buddy-tag to still be hanging there after a free-swim is over: either a boy has left the area and neglected to remove his tag according to the rules, or else an unseen boy is still out in the water. Under these circumstances, the waterfront Director has no choice but to assume the latter, and until a runner can be sent to that boy's village to account for his whereabouts, a lost bather's drill must be conducted.

Even before setting off the klaxon, the waterfront Director orders his staff into the water to begin a series of carefully orchestrated surface dives to search the lake bottom in the swimmer's area. The klaxon is fixed atop a seventy-five foot-tall pole, and its screaming tones can be heard across the entire camp and as far away as Jack's Pub. Because a drowning victim has at best four minutes in which to be found, and because the routine of making continuous surface dives is enormously exhausting, at the first sound of the klaxon every staffman in camp is expected to drop whatever he is doing and race at top speed to the waterfront to spell the earliest arrivals. Although this particular episode turned out to be a false alarm—the boy was found lounging on his bunk back in his village—that was the last time Sam had seen Stovepipe's face this glum.

"One of our campers, Cliff Norris of Mohawk village, did not make bed-check tonight, and he is presumed lost," Stovepipe began, his bloodshot eyes brooding over the dark possibilities. "According to his Scoutmaster," Stovepipe continued, nodding his head in Colonel Beck's direction, "the boy did not return this afternoon from a hike he left on after lunch, and for now anyway, we are assuming he is still on Camp property somewhere. Roads border the Na-Cha-Tan property on all sides, so if Cliff managed to leave the Reservation, presumably he would have reached a road—

and a comm—by now."

"How long since he was last seen?" someone in the crowd of worried onlookers asked.

"More than seven hours," his white-faced Scoutmaster replied. The usually cocky, Colonel Beck was withdrawn and his voice was choked with emotion.

"Have you called the police?" someone else asked.

"Until we have satisfied ourselves that every square inch of Na-Cha-Tan has been searched, we are not going to alert the Sheriff," Director Tovas continued, his back hunched over a table as if he were about to be sick.

"My God, Stovepipe," one of the men groaned, "Na-Cha-Tan is huge! We'll never be able to do it ourselves."

Stovepipe was adamant. "We can. And we will. I want every staffman back here in ten minutes dressed in his grubbies. As soon as everyone's back, I'll be handing out search party assignments. This is no drill, folks; this is the real thing! It's getting pretty damn cold out there, so dress appropriately. And don't forget to wear your boots. Now let's get a move on!"

The staff left the short meeting stunned. Hurrying to their cabins, they donned their rugged clothing—jeans, sweatshirts, boots, knives, ropes, mosquito repellant, hats, gloves, lumina-beams. The thought that a camper was lost kept going through their minds as they dressed. What if the boy were hurt? What if...?

Reassembling in the messhall less than a quarter of an hour later, they awaited further orders. Outside, the pitter-patter of rain could be heard falling against the shingled roof as a storm front moved in. Ominous bolts of lightning began to light up the night sky, and as an ill wind started to blow, the temperature began to drop.

"Men," Stovepipe declared, his slender face looking more gaunt than ever, "there is a boy out there somewhere, a boy who has had very little experience with forest animals or with wilderness survival. He is scared, cold, hungry, and in a few minutes, he will be wet as well. He doesn't have the tools or the skills to build a shelter, nor does he know much about first-aid. He may be hurt or he may be in the process of *getting* hurt. And don't forget, thanks to the people at Greenpeace, the forest has been restocked with black bears and with wolverines. Although we haven't had a serious mauling in just under a dozen years, we must be prepared for that possibility. Smaller animals can be vicious too—Wisconsin is the badger state after all. Even the stings of our swarming ground bees can be fatal if the kid is allergic. And there are other dangers. Need I remind you of the risk of falling through the bog surrounding Muskrat Lake? Now, I don't mean to scare any of you unnecessarily, but there is a whole host of things which might have gone wrong and we have to be prepared for any exigency," he explained carefully, his tinny voice sounding more hollow than ever. "I do know one thing, however, and that is this: if the boy is still on camp property, we are going to find him. Is that understood?"

Every head in the room nodded, "Yes."

"Then let's do it!" Stovepipe exclaimed, raising himself up to his full height of six feet three inches. "The West Camp staff will join up with us as soon as I can get a bus around to the other side of the lake. In the meantime, I have broken you down into eleven teams of six men each," he clarified, referring to some hastily-made notes sitting on the table in front of him. "The Captain of each group will carry a .22 and a whistle. Each team will also be issued a two-way radio, a medic kit, a signal gun, two flares, and four quarts of water."

Pointing to a map he had spread out before him, Stovepipe continued, "Making use of natural landmarks like logging roads, paths, and such, I have laid out twelve zones to be searched. Since there will only be eleven teams, I will have to ask for volunteers later to scout-out the twelfth zone if we don't find the boy first. I really hope that doesn't prove to be necessary because I would rather not send a team up there."

"The north-end?" someone asked, his voice barely a whisper.

"Yes, the north-end," Stovepipe replied, swallowing hard. Even as Director Tovas said the words, Sam remembered what *his* first trip through the swamp at the north end of Lake Na-Cha-Tan had been like. Tromping through the marsh one day two summers ago, he had first been attacked by a swarm of mosquitoes so thick he had sucked one down his throat so far he gagged. Later, after he had been up to his knees in a muddy concoction of water and sewage, he had come back onto firmer ground only to discover that a half-dozen slimy leeches had attached themselves to his calves above his boot line. Pulling the worms off one by one and watching his own blood ooze out from the gashes they had made in his leg was one of the sickest experiences he could ever recall, and he had no intention of ever visiting there again.

"Now listen up!" Stovepipe boomed as he completed his instructions. "Each scouting party is to check in with me on the radio according to the schedule I am handing out to the team Captains now. I will either be here in the messhall or else out patrolling the logging road in my gcar. Don't miss those check-ins under any circumstances! I don't want to have to send out a search party to find one of my own search parties. Now pay attention so I don't have to repeat myself. The group assignments are as follows..."

As Stovepipe read off the team designations, the counselors gathered around their respective Captains. One by one, each crew was given a zone to cover, then was briefed with specific instructions regarding the terrain they would be searching—details like the location of ditches, trails, ponds, fences, power-lines, plus any known hazards. Then, one by one, each contingent was issued its equipment and was sent off into the cold, rainy night to canvass hundreds of acres in search of a lost eleven year-old boy named Cliff.

The crew Sam was assigned to had the disagreeable task of walking the entire eleven miles of highway which ringed the camp property. This was neither a simple nor a pleasant job. To begin with, the terrain they would be hiking over was anything but flat. Moreover, if perchance the boy had been struck by a speeding gcar while walking along the road, they were liable to stumble across his mangled body in their course of their hike. Just the thought of it turned Sam's stomach.

To cover the most ground as quickly as possible, the Captain of Sam's team organized the six men into three pairs of two men each. The first pair would march along the left and right shoulders of the highway, the second pair would walk the grassy gullies twenty yards either side of the roadbed, and the third pair would slug their way through the brush either side of the roadway at a distance of perhaps forty yards. Every fifteen minutes or so, the pairs would rotate their assignments. This switching-off of assignments was necessary because traveling through the wet and treacherous underbrush was exceedingly slow for the outermost pair as compared with the ones walking the shoulder. Not only that, the outermost pair had to endure a terrific amount of physical torment as they repeatedly tripped and fell over legions of downed logs in the dark. It made for a rather brutal endeavor.

Sam's crew departed from the messhall on their search-and-recover mission a little after midnight. At the outset, their pace was rapid—nearly a jog. Not only did they feel a sense of urgency, but the cold rain threatened to chill them dangerously if they didn't keep on moving to stay warm. Somehow, despite the physical obstacles, the six of them managed to maintain that murderous pace for more than two hours. As they made their giant clockwise circuit around the camp by road, they heard the sounds of the other search parties canvassing the woods in the distance off to their right. There was the incessant whining of the camp's siren from atop the tower down by the waterfront; the report of whistles being blown every two minutes by the designated member of each group; the frenzied shouts of worried staffmen spread all throughout the forest; and the occasional screech of a bullhorn when their hoarse voices could no longer carry the sound of the lost boy's name across the black reaches of Na-Cha-Tan.

For Sam, the last mile was pure torture. It became a test of his will, a challenge to his manhood. Like his teammates, he had been soaked to the skin long ago and was now raw and shivering uncontrollably. Not only had the thermometer settled in at an unseasonably cold temperature, but whenever the wind gusted, tearing viciously at their wet clothes, the windchill dropped even lower. Like the freezing man in Jack London's legendary story "To Build a Fire," it would have been easy to quit walking, to just lay down on the roadside and die.

Sam's legs were bruised, and his feet weighed a thousand pounds each; every step was an effort. His mind was so numb he was afraid he might step on the boy's inert body and not even realize it. He was approaching delirium. Exhaustion. Exposure. And yet, something inside was propelling him onwards long after his body had told him to quit, to give it up. But what was it? It couldn't be God; after all there *was* no God—Sara had convinced him of that. It couldn't be loyalty or kinship; he'd never even *met* the lost Scout. It had to be something else altogether.

Stumbling over a root, Sam fell face down into the mud for perhaps the tenth time in the last mile. Once again, he dragged himself unsteadily to his feet. He was tired beyond comprehension. He hadn't slept in twenty hours or eaten in ten. He wasn't even certain there was any feeling left in his toes. Yet he trudged ahead. But why, damnit? Why? What was in it for *him*?

And then, as he brushed a branch aside so he could pass beneath it, the answer hit him. It was so obvious, without even meaning to, he said it under his breath, "Duty." That is what had kept him moving forward all this time—a sense of duty. The words of the Scout Oath rang out in his ears, "On my honor, I will do my best to do my *duty*..."

Here in the dark, here in the drizzle, those sacred words took on a meaning they never had before. As did the slogan of the Order of the Arrow.

"He who serves his fellows is of all his fellows greatest."

"I promise to keep myself physically strong, mentally awake, and morally straight."

"Even in the midst of irksome tasks and weighty responsibilities, I will seek to preserve a cheerful spirit."

It all made sense to him now. In that one revealing instant, all those years of Scouting suddenly took on a new significance. These were no longer mere words that his Scoutmaster had made him recite; now they had definition; now they represented a way of life!

He had been but a teenager when the weekend began, only now, as that last mile of highway rolled before him to a close, and as the gates of Na-Cha-Tan came back into sight, he had discovered within himself the determination required to see a mean job through to the end.

Sam was no longer a boy—he was a man.

Twenty
Goodbye

Two days later, as Sam stood in the firebowl behind the messhall staring out upon the lake for the last time, it didn't seem possible that the summer could have ended this way. That something which had begun with so much hope and so much anticipation could have ended with so much despair seemed almost beyond belief. The only thing Sam could do was to replay the final scenes over and over again in his mind.

By 3 A.M. on that long and miserable night, an air of desperation had settled in over the wet and tired staff as they dragged themselves into the messhall for yet a second time. Despite hours of looking, there was still no sign of the missing boy, and as the last of the eleven original teams returned to their point of origin empty-handed, Stovepipe made final preparations to dispatch a crew to the untamed pocket of land at the marshy, north end of the lake. Given the long list of potential hazards a crew might encounter up there, he had been reluctant to take this risky step, but at this point, the inevitable could be delayed no longer: *someone* had to search the swamp! Still, considering the tricky terrain, Stovepipe had thought it best not to simply draft people for the assignment, but rather to recruit only those willing to go on their own initiative.

When the question of volunteers came up, Sam was standing next to the roaring fireplace, hugging himself to get warm and stomping his feet to restart his circulation. Although later, as he stood ankle deep in the muck of the swamp wondering whether he had made the right decision, at the time, Sam had surprised even himself when he was among the first to raise his hand to enlist for the north-end search team.

The seven man crew had set out from the lakeshore just beyond the East Camp waterfront area on a compass bearing of 10 degrees—almost due north. Fanning out in a long line with between seventy-five and one hundred yards separating one man from the next, they cut a swath through the dense woods a third of a mile across. Even with their lumina-beams calibrated to their highest setting, between the lingering darkness and the thick foliage, it was impossible for any man to see either the fellow to his left or to his right; the light of their lanterns was just too puny to penetrate the distance.

To compensate for this awkward shortcoming, and to avoid anyone from becoming lost or hurt, Stovepipe had recommended they take some special precautions before setting out. Namely, each group member was given a number, and whenever the group leader should blow his whistle, they were to each sound-off in numerical order. On a double whistle the team was to move on once more, and on a triple whistle, they were to converge on the center man.

The area they searched was a spooky landscape untouched by civilization. It was a mammoth jungle of dead and rotting logs all submerged under six to ten inches of water, a jungle dotted by irregular patches of giant ferns and vast expanses of chest-high thorn bushes which tore at their flesh each time one of them made the mistake of brushing past one too closely. As they moved cautiously through the swamp, the searchers' lumina-beams threw eerie shadows at their feet even as their ears were bombarded with the sounds so common to a marsh—the chirping birds, the buzzing insects, the howling wolves, the burping frogs. With the smudged moonlight hanging ominously overhead, their minds were enveloped by fears of the scary things they *couldn't* hear—the poisonous snakes, the bloody leeches, the hairy wolf spiders, the black bears. And if that wasn't enough to put every single one of them ill at ease, adding to the melodrama was the unending drone of the falling rain and the occasional bolts of lightning which coursed jaggedly across the sky.

Drenched to the skin and fighting fatigue as much as the underbrush, the crew followed their northerly heading for a mile and a quarter before reaching drier land at the swamp's upper edge. Their voices hoarse from shouting Cliff's name over and over again, they then swung to an easterly bearing of 60 degrees on which they remained until they reached the northern spur of a logging road so ancient it was no longer on any map. Regrouping there, the team turned south again following the spur back towards the center of camp. The trip had taken a full two hours, and in all that time there had not been a single trace of the lost boy.

As Stovepipe bided his time, waiting impatiently along

the side of the road for Group 12 to emerge triumphantly from the woods, there was an audible crackle from his two-way radio as a bolt of lightning rocketed across the heavens. He was leaning against his gcar, his face long and drawn, the hood of his poncho drawn tight to keep the rain off of his head. After an interminable delay, he finally saw the glow of their lanterns in the distance. But as they approached, he could see their dejected faces. His heart sank.

Digesting the grim truth wasn't easy for a man in his position—all of Na-Cha-Tan had now been searched and the Scout whose name had been shouted time and time again for five solid hours had not been found. Outsiders would now have to be brought in to join the canvass. These outside authorities would no doubt demand that the camp be closed, if only as a temporary measure, and that the campers be sent home until a scapegoat could be found. In all likelihood, Stovepipe would be that sacrificial lamb. And to make matters worse, the local authorities were weak-kneed politicians; they were rather dependent upon and ever so conscious of the loggers' influence, loggers who had always been of the mind that a Boy Scout Camp was an unforgivable waste of prime timberland. This sort of adverse publicity might be all they needed to close Na-Cha-Tan down once and for all.

Playing out the terrible consequences in his mind, Stovepipe felt as if he had unwittingly let the camp down. The look in his eyes revealed the panic he could not voice; the tears on his face went unnoticed as they trickled down his rain-drenched cheek. Clicking on his radio, he relayed the bad news to the staffmen waiting anxiously in the messhall for some word. Even over the racket of the storm exploding around them, there was no mistaking the disappointed groans on the other end. Informing them that he would be bringing Team 12 in empty-handed, Stovepipe switched off the walky-talky and climbed glumly into his gcar. There was little more that could be said or done.

As Stovepipe guided his vehicle slowly, even deliberately, along the rutted logging road back towards the main part of camp, his headlamps aglow and his rain-wipers sweeping back and forth across the windshield in a hypnotic cadence, none of his seven passengers spoke above a whisper. They were cold and wet and spent. Heavy eye-lids drooped even as morning arrived on schedule. Had there been no storm, the orange sun would have breached the horizon by this time. Instead, courtesy of the thick overcast sky and the canopy of towering oaks, the forest floor was still pitchblack, and this morning's dawn seemed no brighter than last evening's midnight. Although no one needed any special inducement to fall asleep, the rhythmic beating of the wiper-blades put them all out. Even Stovepipe himself, as he guided the bouncing gcar along the mudcaked road, was lulled to the edge of slumber.

Then, without warning, something out of the ordinary suddenly grabbed at his consciousness, jerking him to attention. Acting out of instinct, the Director stomped on the brakes, rolling all of his sleeping passengers to the floor. Confused and dazed, they groggily began to complain about the abrupt stop.

"My God!" Stovepipe exclaimed, clearly stunned by what he saw.

"What in the world is going on?" Sam cried as he climbed off the floor and back into his seat.

"My God!" Stovepipe declared once again, slowly opening the gcar door and pointing. "Can it be?" he stammered, his shrunken hopes rising. There, standing in the middle of the logging road, drenched to the bone and waving his arms wildly, was a scrawny little Scout meeting the lost camper's description. Even though Stovepipe hadn't been driving fast, in his exhausted stupor he had nearly run the poor kid down.

"Cliff?" Stovepipe had asked tentatively, his voice cracking with emotion. "Is that you, Cliff?"

Bathed by the glow of the headlamps, the boy's shaking head had been as disappointingly clear as the terrified look on his face. As he stood there shivering in the pouring rain, the boy explained that, no he was not Cliff Norris, but rather another boy from his village. Evidently, despite Stovepipe's strict orders to the contrary, most of Cliff's troop had snuck out in the middle of the night to join in on the search. They had been to Little Grasshopper Valley, Cliff's favorite hideout. Two bodies had been found there.

Even as Stovepipe, Sam, and the others listened to the grisly story, a cathartic thunderclap roared through the forest reminding them all of just who was in charge. Though Sam had wanted to cry, he no longer had enough energy left to even form a tear. Too exhausted to comprehend anything beyond the sketchiest of details, it was not until now, two days later, as he lingered in the campfire bowl to say goodbye to his beloved Na-Cha-Tan that the full impact of what had occurred began to sink into his head.

The boy's throat had been cut and the corpse placed next to the bullet-riddled body of Abe Levinson. The prevailing theory among the staff was that the two of them had presumably been killed by the same psychopath. Why they would have been out in the forest together was open to interpretation, but the speculation was that Abe, in his role as the camp's naturalist, had taken Cliff on a nature hike to Muskrat Lake, and that in the course of that hike they had fallen across either an escaped convict or else a local gone wacky. No one needed to be reminded that some of the locals were little more than pathetic hillbillies, people with a blatant disregard for human life. Because Abe was a foreign national, Federal agents had taken an immediate interest in the case, sealing off the area and shutting down the camp until their investigation was complete—until the end of the summer anyway. Sam was devastated.

Along with the rest of the staff, he had been questioned and released, but all they had seemed to care about was Lester's whereabouts at the time of the murders, of which Sam knew nothing. Their questions had made Sam suspicious, especially those of a serious-minded fellow who had introduced himself as Director Harper. Apparently, he was already acquainted with Colonel Beck and with Officer Jenkins, and from the way he acted towards both men—especially Jenkins—he wasn't fond of either one. In any case, his questions had made Sam curious, so while he was busy packing his things, Sam had tried to eavesdrop on the Federal agents talking in the next room. The only word he was sure of was "airchop."

Upon hearing that magic word, Sam's mind vaulted back to that first day on the trail, to the blinding swirl of rocks and mud which had been flung up into his and Ziggy's face, to the engine sounds he had heard after the Callout two weeks ago, to the letter he had sent his grandfather, to the chat he had had with Stovepipe, to the botched efforts he had made to figure the mystery out for himself. "Airchop" was the one word which linked Lester to Abe.

Though he wasn't sure how he knew, Sam had suspected the truth all along. And though he had utterly no proof to substantiate his claims, Sam knew in his heart that his brother was somehow involved in Abe's death, and that one or both of them were somehow involved with the airchop landings he had heard and seen since first arriving in camp. And yet, it was all so very confusing. Why would anybody care to land an airchop in the backwoods of Na-Cha-Tan? And what kind of cargo was so incredibly important that an eleven year-old boy had to be murdered over it?

So many questions; so few answers.

Though the Federal agents—Harper in particular—had asked him repeatedly about Lester—his habits, his where-abouts, his associates—Sam wasn't about to tell these yokels a thing; he would talk to his grandfather about this when he got back home. After all, besides Stovepipe, the Senator was the only one he had confided in about the airchop sighting to begin with, the only one who was in a position to straighten this whole mess out for him.

That discussion, however, would have to wait now until they met up in St. Louis tomorrow afternoon. For the present, he was doing his best to sort out his feelings. Though Sam had never considered himself much of a poet, as he took one last painful look around the firebowl, he sat down with a pen and a piece of paper in hand and wrote an ode to summer:

> Tranquil now, the vacant campfire bowl,
> Where, many a night, raucous laughter would
>   thunder 'n roll.
> Where, attended by God, the blue waters brook no
>   wave,
> Where, left to contemplate the noon, He judges
>   each soul to save.
> Tranquil now, the hushed campfire bowl,
> Where, Time holds Her breath, pretending to freeze,
> Where, one lingers near faint, at the ecstasy of Her
>   breeze.
> Where, Solitude reveals all, if only they would
>   listen,
> Promising them no regrets which might serve to
>   cloud their vision.
> Tranquil now, the empty campfire bowl,
> Where the answers come hard to all but the chosen
>   few,
> Promising them no regrets when their journey is
>   through.

Part II

Part II

Twenty-one
Mark Twain

How one travels goes a long way towards defining the man. Riding alone on horseback across the open prairie defined the cowboy. Flying in formation strapped into the cockpit of a high-tech fighter defined the pilot. Rolling along in an expensive foreign-built roadster oblivious of the speed limit, defined the successful upstart. Standing alone at the helm of a smoke-belching paddlewheeler defined the riverboat captain.

And even though the days had long since passed when a riverboat captain outearned a United States President, these rough-hewn men still plied their trade along the dirty blue highways of America. Sam had never been on a riverboat before, and though the glamour had evaporated since the days of Mark Twain, after the summer camping season had ended so abruptly, this trip with his grandfather promised to be a big adventure for the younger Matthews. That he was named for Samuel Clemens, a legendary riverboat captain turned author, only made the experience that much more authentic. Besides, Sam loved being with his grandpa and he delighted in hearing all the stories the old codger had to tell.

As for Nate, he planned to use the overnight trip upriver to draw himself closer to his favorite grandson. Though the Senator had never been able to confide in Lester, with Sam it was different. And with times increasingly uncertain and with his health failing him, it was important that he try and shield the boy from what he expected was the worst yet to come.

Leaving the docks in East St. Louis early in the evening, they headed upstream towards Joliet onboard the sleek paddlewheeler. Inland trains were far too crowded for Nate's taste, far too noisy; gcars too cramped, too uncomfortable; suburbs too expensive, too public. But for pure relaxation, traveling by boat was eminently appealing in all respects. While admittedly slower than other modes of transportation in the late twenty-fourth century, a trip on the water still offered a man a measure of comfort and privacy which harkened back to an earlier and simpler era when getting there was still half the fun.

In listening to what his grandfather had to say, Sam soon discovered that, unlike most of the docks strung out along the banks of this muddy river, the one they were departing from was fairly new, having been reconstructed after the calamity of 2380. And like most of what they saw on the trip north, this landmark had a story to go along with it.

Every other year for the past four centuries, one charlatan after another had spooked the public with their predictions of how the New Madrid fault would give out any day. And every other year for the past four centuries the charlatans had been ignored. By the time the fault actually did give way, most people had given up worrying about it. But as luck would have it, the destruction was far worse than anything that had been advertised, and legions of nonbelievers perished in the tragedy. Of all the many ruins lying along the banks of the giant river, one of the most spectacular was the Gateway to the West, the St. Louis Arch. Nowadays, only the base remained standing, the rest having been toppled into the water by the quake. Though the Arch itself was never rebuilt, to this day the shattered remnants were still a huge tourist attraction, much like the sunken *U.S.S. Arizona* of Pearl Harbor fame had been for centuries.

So began Sam's trip upriver and back into time.

Studying his grandfather's face as they sauntered along the deck hunting for a place to sit, Sam couldn't remember the Senator ever looking so ancient. But not knowing anything about Nate's incurable cancer, he thought only that the venerable old man was tired and overworked.

"Why are we planning to stop in Peoria anyway?" Sam inquired as the boat got underway.

"The earliest mention of the Matthews can be traced back to that area," Nate answered, fumbling with his cane. In his prime, the Senator had been a tall man with gray eyes and light, almost blond hair. He had been muscular, but not rock hard solid. Seeing him hunched now over his walking stick, Sam realized that his grandfather was not well. "Indeed," the patriarch continued, "our family has a rich and colorful history in the Midwest dating back well over five hundred years. When you and I get to Peoria, I will show you a shrine, a statue actually, which has stood in the courthouse plaza since after the Civil War. That statue commemorates all the honored dead from Peoria and from the surrounding counties who perished in that war—including one of our own."

"Seriously, grandpa?" Sam asked in a disbelieving tone. "A Matthews fought in the War Between the States?"

"Actually, Sam, in those days we went by a different name—Matthewson. On that statue is the name of a distant ancestor of ours who enlisted in the 11th Cavalry under the command of a Major James Johnson, then died defending the Union. His name was Byron Matthewson."

"Do tell. What brought the Matthewsons to this area?"

"The history of the white man in the Illinois Country, and in Peoria in particular, dates back to the late 1600s with the arrival of that famous duo, Joliet and Marquette. Following closely upon their heels, French fur traders came to the area, establishing Fort Pimiteoui there as the southernmost point of the Canadian jurisdiction. The French of Peoria were mostly illiterate; but they were a carefree people, and they were able to adjust rapidly to the many changes of political fortune which swept the landscape. Except for the occasional Jesuit mission, the fort was occupied almost exclusively by Amerinds until the Illinois Country was surrendered to the English in the mid-1700s. By then, the fledgling settlement had a horsemill, and even a blacksmith. Though their lives were filled with adventure and perhaps even some romance, the old village had to eventually be abandoned because of repeated Amerind attacks during the American revolution.

"By that time, however, the French traders had founded a *new* village downstream, at the foot of the lake. Later anglisized to Old Peoria, this new site—Au Pied du Lac in French—featured a fort and about fifty buildings strung out along the banks of the Illinois River. The narrow streets of Old Peoria were lined with simple log houses. Most had fenced-in gardens out in front and larger, tilled fields behind. The inhabitants—of which Ian Matthewson was one—raised pigs, cattle, and chickens. There were stockyards, a wine-press, a windmill for grinding grain, a church with a large wooden cross, several stores, and a handful of places to trade with the local Amerinds. There were blacksmiths, wagon makers, carpenters, and shoemakers. Out of this new village on the riverfront at the south end of the lake, the modern metropolis of Peoria sprang."

"Is that why we're going to Peoria?" Sam questioned, a note of disappointment creeping into his tone. "To see all this *stuff*?"

"I brought you along on this trip so we could talk unobserved."

"You sound troubled, grandpa," Sam noted, shivering in the night air as they stood out on the open deck chatting.

"I am," Nate admitted, all his worries, all his doubts, seeming to converge on this one point in history. "War is coming, and if any of the Matthews are to survive the destruction, you must be the one to leave America and go on to Canada."

"You're scaring me, grandpa. What is all this talk about war? Times have never been more peaceful."

"Achetez aux canons, vendez aux clairons," Nate mumbled, the French of his salad days tumbling out unexpectedly. At times, old men tend to forget what thought was like when they were young—the quickness of the mental jump, the daring of the youthful intuition, the agility of the fresh insight. They become accustomed to the plodding varieties of reason, and because this is more than made up for by the accumulation of experience, they tend to think of themselves as being wiser than those who are their junior.

"What did you say?" Sam asked, screwing his face up into a question mark.

"I'll explain it to you soon enough, but for now you must understand this: America has lost her taste for war. And that only invites it," he sighed.

"Come again?"

"Deterrence fails without a credible deterrent," Nate explained in a professorial tone. "Despite my best efforts in the Senate, we have been unilaterally disarming for years, and at the rate President McIntyre is going, it won't be long before we will not even be able to defend our borders. The Mexicans are constantly probing our defenses from the south, and their clamor to reclaim Texas as rightfully theirs grows louder with each passing month. And as you are no doubt well aware, thanks to the impotence of our fleet in the aftermath of the Nolan assassination, we have already had to disgorge our islands in the Pacific."

"You mean the Hawaii Free State, don't you?"

"Yes, but that's not the worst of it, Sam. In the Caribbean, Cuban pirates constantly assault our trading ships, and in the northeast, Huron claims on upstate New York and on portions of Quebec threaten to carve a hole out of both America and Canada, a hole which could lead to hostilities between our two nations for the first time since the War of 1812. And in a separate dispute, a movement is afoot to cede Alaska to the Canucks in exchange for admitting their Atlantic provinces to statehood. Not only that, the Amerinds of Ontario and Manitoba are growing stronger by the day. Sam, my boy, the nation is in flux!"

"Grandpa, I know you are a Senator and all that, but how is it that you know so much, especially about military matters?"

"Geez, son, I'm only the Chairman of the Military Oversight Committee!" Nate exclaimed. "But more to your point: I guess it's in my blood. As I started to tell you earlier, our family has a long and proud heritage of service to our country. Besides Private Matthewson in the Civil War, a Matthews has served with distinction in every single American war of consequence—all three of the World Wars, the

Ukraine revolution, the Peruvian uprising, even the Siege of Johannesburg. But the proudest moment in our family's history by far was when my father, your great grandfather, helped stomp out that demon of all demons, Rontana."

"You mentioned this Rontana fellow once before; surely, there must be more you can tell me about this guy than what I have already learned in school," Sam urged, never ceasing to be amazed by what his grandpa had to say.

"Ali Salaam Rontana. That was his full name, though to this day, some historians claim that he was a she. One hit team after another was sent in to assassinate this maniac, but each one met with defeat. That is until Tiger and Flix..."

"Tiger and *who*?"

"My dad, code name Tiger, and his best buddy Felix Wenger, code name Flix."

"Would that be *General* Wenger?"

"One and the same. The two of them were the sole survivors of the raid, and just barely at that. They did the dirty deed, but for security reasons their names were never divulged to the public until much later. Despite the shroud of secrecy, they were unquestionably heroes. Years afterward, when I was a freshman Senator, Flix—God rest his soul—was my Chief of Staff, and in that position he taught me a great many things."

"I can't imagine anyone teaching you anything, Grandpa," Sam gently teased. "What sorta stuff did this Flix teach you?"

"Well," Nate answered, remembering back, "besides how to use a gun and how to defend myself, he also taught me about the Brazen Rule and about the Iroquois Great Law of Peace."

"Slow down, Grandpa, one lesson at a time. What is the Brazen Rule?"

"Well, you have heard by now of the Golden Rule, I suppose?"

"Yeah," Sam granted, "do unto others as you would have them do unto you."

"Yes. And that's fine for priests and for rabbis, but it's not so fine for running countries, which was the business Flix and I were in."

"Which brings us to the Brazen Rule."

"Yes. Repay kindness with kindness, but repay evil with justice," Nate expounded, recalling the many hard decisions he had had to make in his lifetime.

"Land's-sakes, that doesn't sound like a very forgiving philosophy to me."

"It isn't, Sam, but it is the most human of all canons. Tit-for-tat and nothing more. Do unto others as they have done unto you."

"Reward others with tenderness when they are nice to you, but punish them with brutality when they are not?" Sam cross-examined thoughtfully.

"Precisely."

"Okay, Grandpa, I'll be sure to remember that, now what about this Iroquois thing?"

The Senator explained. "Historians have long attributed the central tenets of our Constitution to the likes of Thomas Jefferson and Benjamin Franklin, but few people today realize that the League of the Iroquois greatly influenced the founders as well. The Great Law not only embraced the ideas of democracy and of federalism, it also guaranteed them freedom of religion. They even had a mechanism for impeaching their poor leaders and for amending their constitution."

"I have always been a great fan of the Amerinds," Sam asserted, reflecting back on his love for Scouting and for the Order of the Arrow, "and I have always had the greatest respect for their customs and for their traditions, but if this is true, how come we're not taught anything about it in school?"

"The nature of racism is to never give credit where credit is due."

"The Brazen Rule again?"

"Yes."

"Do you miss him?" Sam asked as Nate's eyes misted over.

"Flix? Yes, I do. But I have many momentos of our long association. This cane, for instance," he said, rapping it firmly against the planking. "My black book, for another. The two of us accomplished a great deal together. In the course of my first term, we tangled not only with Silas Whetstone, but also with Overlord Mao."

"But, grandpa," Sam countered as they strolled slowly along the rolling deck of the paddlewheeler, "all that happened such a long time ago. I thought you once told me that Overlord Mao had died and that Silas Whetstone had been sent to jail?"

"It's true, Sam, Mao *is* dead. In fact, I have it on good authority that he enjoyed a most hideous death," Nate reported, thinking back upon his own despicable role in that sordid affair. "And as far as Silas Whetstone is concerned, he *was* sent to jail, only now he's out. Unfortunately, our family's troubles with the Chinese did not die with Mao. I fear that they are *still* not over."

"I don't understand," Sam acknowledged haltingly. "What kinds of troubles are you talking about?"

"I don't have all the facts yet, but it seems to have something to do with your brother Lester. Then again, I may be getting a bit ahead of myself," the old man replied with a pause.

"Lester?" Sam interrupted pointedly. "What *about* Lester?" he asked, prepared to dive into a discussion concerning the airchop he had seen in Little Grasshopper Valley that day and his suspicions regarding the deaths at Na-Cha-Tan. Only Nate didn't give him the chance.

"Now, where was I? Oh, yes: A struggle of succession followed Mao's death, and China was plunged into civil war, a war which lasted for nearly three decades. Only recently, after enormous bloodshed and after years of ruthless plundering, has Mao's son Ling been able to consolidate his power base and assume his father's throne."

"So? Of what possible concern is this to me, to us?" Sam queried, breathing in the pleasant night air. In the background, the gentle chug-a-lug of the paddlewheel's steam engine could be heard murmuring softly. It was the sort of tranquil, rhythmic sound which could easily put a man to sleep if he let it.

"Damnit, boy, listen up!" Nate exploded in an uncharacteristic outburst. "During those frightful years, Ling was so busy battling rival chieftains for supremacy of the mainland, he had no time to bother with us Matthews, and though I had pretty much forgotten about him until recently, he had definitely not forgotten about me. A lot happened during those turbulent years. When your grandma Musette recovered from her gunshot wound, we were married, but Franklin—your dad—refused to accept her. Instead of coming back to D.C. with your grandma and I as we had originally planned, he ran away from home without ever completing high school."

"Land's-sakes! Do you mean to tell me that Dad never even finished high school?" Sam verified incredulously.

"Shush, Sam, you're not supposed to know that," Nate observed, afraid that in his haste he may have spoken out of turn. Despite the cool breeze which was beginning to roll in from across the wide river, the two of them lingered on the deck of the ship exchanging stories. "By the way, to put your mind at ease, after Lester and you were out of diapers, your father *did* finish up his degree in night school. In any event, by the time Ling could turn his attention back to us,

Frankie had grown up, gotten married, and settled at the Matthews' homestead in Farmington with you two boys. But it was not until late this spring when Lester returned home from his semester in Israel and asked to enroll at the Academy, that I got the first inkling that our troubles had begun all over again."

"What troubles, grandpa?" Sam cross-examined hastily. "Tell me please, *what* troubles?"

"I was never able to shield your brother like I did you," Nate answered, sidestepping Sam's question as he stared absentmindedly out across the black water. "Actually, I'm probably as much to blame as anyone else. He was so much like your father; I must not have been tough enough on him."

"So, if Lester was such a rotten egg, why did you pull so many strings to get him a commission?" Sam questioned, a jealous tinge in his voice.

"I thought the regimen of the military would do him some good," Nate confessed. "But only time will tell for sure."

"I wonder," Sam interjected, thinking back on how Lester had acted with Sindy that morning in the motel room, how all he seemed to care about anymore was sex and money. "Grandpa," Sam stammered, ready to spill his guts about the airchop and about the murders, "I have reason to believe Lester was involved in some bad stuff this summer."

"Geez, did he drag you into this too?" Nate cursed, suddenly worried that despite his best efforts to protect the boy, Sam had been sucked down into the abyss along with his brother. From talking with Miss Loddy and with Officer Jenkins yesterday, the Senator already knew about the killings and about Lester's suspicious disappearance. From those same conversations he had also learned how Director Harper had personally headed up the investigation, a curious development which had only served to make the Senator distrust the man even more than he already did. Though

Harper would no doubt deny it, the Director had probably tried to come up with something incriminating which he could use against Nate at some point in the future.

"Am I to understand then that you knew what Lester was up to all along?" Sam probed disbelievingly.

"The arms shipments? Yes, I was most definitely aware of them," Nate admitted after a long pause. But when he saw Sam's face go white, the Senator realized Sam had been in the dark on that particular point from the start.

"That explains the airchop I saw," Sam stammered. "Did Lester...*kill* that boy?"

"No, that's not our interpretation of the events," Nate declared, recalling the details of Jenkins' report. "But he may have murdered the Israeli."

"Abe?" Sam trembled weakly. "And yet, even after all of this, you have the...the...*audacity* to help him enlist in the Navy? As an officer, no less?" Sam verified, not sure what to make of his grandfather.

"It's ironic, I know, but exposing him would only hurt you. I haven't got long to live now, and I can't prevent his entrance to the Academy at this late date without either ruining my own career or else smearing the Matthews' name..."

"What did you say?" Sam cut in, his mind focusing on the first part of Nate's reply. "Are you telling me you're sick, grandpa?"

"No, son," Nate lied convincingly. "It's just a figure of speech; all old men say they haven't got long to live. Now don't interrupt me again until I'm finished. What I was trying to say was that smearing our family's good name just to bring Lester to justice isn't worth the price. Besides, Harper over at Internal Intelligence has no proof."

"Harper?" Sam interjected. "Did you say Harper? He's one of the guys who interrogated me at camp!"

"I know, Loddy told me. But there were no witnesses.

My only concern now is for your safety. If Lester has been compromised, they may come for you next."

"I'm old enough to take care of myself," Sam announced, struggling to digest this latest revelation.

"I know you think that, Sam, and I respect your self-confidence, but believe me when I say this: against the likes of *these* people, you won't be able to take care of yourself. That's why I—how do you put it?—pulled some strings. I got us some help."

"What kinda help?" Sam questioned, his voice uncertain. In the muddy light of the moon his grandfather's face had a quizzical look to it. For the first time Sam was alarmed.

"Please don't be angry with me," Nate begged, his timeworn hands outstretched, his tired eyes pleading.

"Land's-sakes, grandpa, how could I be angry with you?" Sam declared in a reassuring tone.

"My motives were pure—you have got to understand that."

"I do, I do, but what in the world are you talking about?"

"Well, to begin with, there was Miss Loddy."

"What about her?" Sam asked, reflecting back on the hard-of-hearing, relic of a nurse Na-Cha-Tan had hired for the summer.

"I asked her to get ahold of me if you got into any trouble."

"I'm flattered, but you needn't have bothered."

"I'm afraid that's not the least of it, Sam. Officer Jenkins was on my payroll as well."

Sam was flabbergasted; he didn't know what to say.

"Not only that, there's someone here I think you should meet," the Senator advised, signaling to an attractive woman who was leaning against the rail fifteen yards away.

When Sam turned his head to see who Nate was motioning to, the pain of recognition fell across his face. His jaw dropped.

"What is the meaning of this?" he asked, his voice cracking. "Sara? Is that you? What the hell are you doing here?" Sam demanded, his furious eyes darting from one co-conspirator to the other.

"Sit down, Agent Logan," Nate directed, offering Sara a deck-side chair without answering any of Sam's questions.

"*Agent* Logan? You mean to tell me it was all a *scam*!?" Sam grumbled fiercely. "The come-ons, the sex, the banter, was all a put-up job? I suppose the Lake Mendota address was a lie too? And the 'God is Dead' spiel as well? And that wasn't your mother on the front porch, was it? Good God, would someone please tell me what the hell is going on around here?" he gulped, a blank look on his face. "I want some answers, damnit!"

"Let me explain," Nate offered, holding out his hand to his grandson.

"Yes, do," Sam intoned flatly, refusing to sit. "I thought I could trust you, grandpa," he snapped. "And you," he barked bitterly, his outrage directed at Sara, "I thought I *loved* you."

"Don't be too hard on her, Sam. Her motives were pure. She was following orders—my orders."

"Orders?" Sam exploded, staring hard at the old man. "What orders?"

"I told her to keep an eye on you."

"Oh, is that right?" Sam shot back unsympathetically, casting an evil eye in Sara's direction even as his grandpa winced. "She was a goddamn babysitter?!" he screamed, edging nervously away from them. "Look up babysitter in the goddamned dictionary you two, and show me where it says beguile and seduce!"

"That's quite enough, Sam," Nate scolded even as Sara turned her head to avoid meeting his eyes. "Won't you please sit back down and let me explain?" he implored, rapping his cane against the deck for emphasis.

"I have heard enough," Sam responded, his arms crossed high on his chest. It was the pose of a feather dancer fresh from the Callout ceremony.

"No, you haven't," Nate returned firmly, getting to his feet and grabbing Sam by the elbow. "Sara has got to get you across the border."

"The *border*?!" Sam boomed without thinking.

"Shush," Nate warned, looking around to see if anyone else had heard his remark. "No one must know," he whispered.

"Must know what?"

"All I can tell you is what I have told you before: war is coming. Though I have increased America's readiness through every means at my disposal, it won't change the outcome. If any of the Matthews are to survive the conflagration, you must escape across the border and seek refuge in Canada. Now whether you like it or not, Sara is going to guide you across. All the preparations have been made, including the special identicard you will need once you get there."

"What about mom and dad? What about your precious Lester? What about *you*, for Chrissake?"

"Your father is an idiot, and Lester is nothing more than a common criminal. All that matters to me now is you."

"Why Canada of all places?" Sam asked, a look of resignation on his face.

"They speak English there for one thing; I have contacts there for another. I should still be able to visit with you from time to time if I have official business which brings me across, and of course we'll be able to talk on the comm. Now, the discussion is over, Sam. It's settled."

Twenty-two
Frontier

To say that the trip north had been long and boring would have been a gross understatement. The first leg from Chicago to MinnePaul had been by coal-burner and then on again to Butte where they had rented a jeep before attempting the drive to the border via Missoula and Kalispell. Where a hundred years before no one would even have thought twice about making the transit, in this century it was a high risk endeavor. Crossing the border without a certified passport was not only illegal, it was hazardous; if one was caught without the proper papers in hand, it meant being shot on sight. Not only were there the robot sentries on the American side, across the border there were the Royal Canadian Mounted Police with their force guns and their bio-stallions.

The two travelers would first pass into Glacier National Park, then they would proceed into what was once known as the Waterton-Glacier International Peace Park. After passing through Polebridge on the north fork of the Flathead River, they would park several miles south of the border before hiking east into the woods near Kintla Lake where Sara knew they could vault the fence safely. They would cross near Cameron Lake at the point where the Continental Divide separated British Columbia from Alberta. It would be a brutal hike at high altitudes across uncharted rocky terrain. If all went well, in six hours Sam would be in Canada; if not, they would both be dead.

Ever since yesterday when his grandfather had first left him in her custody, Sam hadn't spoken more than a dozen curt sentences to her. He had felt used, abused, and taken for granted. He resented the fact that his grandfather hadn't trusted him to take care of himself and that he had hired Sara to do it for him. And to make matters even worse, she hadn't told him the truth either! It had all been a lie, an act. She had befriended him, seduced him, taunted him, tested him. And now that it was just the two of them, he had no choice but to depend on her. And that rankled him no end.

"Are you going to hate me forever?" she began again as she unloaded their backpacks from the jeep. They had enough food and fresh water to last them for two days if necessary. If they encountered any sentries patrolling the area, they would hole up in an aged miner's cabin she knew of; if not, they would proceed directly across the frontier.

"Listen, Sara, I appreciate what you are doing for me, but don't confuse appreciation with forgiveness; I hate you for what you did to me."

"What exactly did I do wrong?" she countered, genuinely surprised by his vehemence. "I tried to watch out for you. I gave you my body, for Chrissake!"

"Bought and paid for by the Senator, I should imagine," Sam retorted, slinging the bulky knapsack onto his shoulder. After a summer of being out-of-doors all day long, his lean body and his long and muscular legs were tanned to a deep, rich brown. Even as they argued, she nodded approvingly.

"Bought and paid for? Don't be silly," she snapped indignantly as they set off into the woods on an old logging road, her rifle slung over her shoulder next to her backpack. "To the contrary, as you so eloquently pointed out onboard the riverboat the other night, your grandfather wanted me to babysit you, not seduce you. I gave you my body of my own free will."

"Hah! Free will?" Sam ridiculed, his unruly mop of brown hair buffeting as he shook his head back in disdain. "What do you know of free will? You're nothing more than a high-priced bimbooker."

Stung by his words, Sara slapped him hard across the face. "Look you—I'll admit that when this first began, I was nothing more than a hired hand. But that was only at the outset. After that weekend we spent together, everything changed. You have got to believe me, Sam," she pleaded, her brown eyes brimming with tears. "Getting you across the border is dangerous business; I'm not doing this only for the money! I very much want to see you safe on the other side."

Sulking, Sam did not reply.

"And as for your grandpa," she added emphatically, "don't you dare even *think* of holding a grudge against him. That old coot only wants what is best for you."

"He is a work of art, isn't he?" Sam conceded, smiling for perhaps the first time since they began their unlikely trek into the mountains.

"More like a fossil. He ought to be in a museum."

"You know…" But before he could finish his sentence,

she had cupped her hand over his mouth. "Shush," she ordered with military precision. "I heard something up ahead."

"I didn't," he whispered, perking up his ears. The forest seemed as still as ever; not even the wind was rustling through the hundred-foot pines.

"Stay here," she insisted, slipping her rifle from her shoulder even as she motioned for him to lay flat on the ground behind a massive log. Doing as he was told, Sam watched as she bolted silently ahead along the trail. For the first time since they met, it struck home that Agent Logan wasn't just a pretty distraction; she was also a trained killer.

As minutes passed without a sound, he began to worry that something terrible had happened. Suddenly conscious of the fact that he could never make it across the border on his own, he found himself feeling truly ashamed for having ridden her so hard. Maybe Nate knew what was best for him after all. But before he could make up his mind what to do next, the snap of a breaking branch cracked the silence a few yards away from where he lay. His heart pounding like a sledge hammer in his chest, Sam froze. Was it her or was it someone else?

Peeking around the log he had hidden himself against, he saw her laughing eyes and her bouncing hair. But just as he was about to issue a sigh of relief, he witnessed her stop alone the trail to wipe her blade clean on a bandanna she had stuffed in her trousers. The knife had been red with blood!

"Sam?" she whispered loudly, searching the ground for him with her eyes. "Where the hell have you gotten off to?"

Popping out of his hiding place, he promptly interrogated her. "What happened? What the *hell* happened? Did you kill someone?" he probed anxiously, gesturing towards her resheathed blade.

"Had to," she justified calmly. "He never would have let us pass."

"I thought you said there would only be *robot* sentries on the American side?"

"In my business, you must learn to expect the unexpected. His body is next to the trail about a hundred yards ahead, so if a mixture of blood and guts turns your stomach, I would avert my eyes when we get there."

"You mean to tell me you just killed a man in cold blood?" It was less a question than an accusation.

"There will be others," she said with some confidence. "The day is still young. Stay behind me and stay quiet. If we're lucky and if there's no more trouble, we will be at the cabin in a couple of hours. We can rest there before pushing through to the frontier."

Forced into obedience by her commands, Sam fell silent to study his surroundings. Trying to forget what had just transpired, he decided that there was perhaps no better month than August to be hiking in the high mountains of Glacier National Park. According to their maps, they were presently traversing an area referred to as Kintla Peak. Big, rugged, and primitive, Glacier National Park was perhaps the last of Nature's unspoiled domains, a region where Man and his civilization were reduced to insignificance by the wild grandeur of its millions of acres. It was a place for snowball fights in midsummer, for glacial solitude in any season, for fishing, for alpine flowers, and for camping along lonely and remote fir-fringed lakes. It was also a living textbook in geology, as pushing, grinding glaciers worked their magic to carve out lakes and streams from the bedrock. More than that, it was a dangerous place, a place where it was easy to get lost once off the trails, and where bears and cougars and hawks still held sway. No place for a tenderfoot to be out on his own. It was an unforgiving land where winter did not beat a full retreat until mid-June and where, as now, the dense forests were a blaze of colors set against a backdrop of snow-covered peaks.

Most of the park's hundreds of miles of trails penetrated into remote wilderness areas, and Sara was following one of these along the shores of an overgrown pond called Cameron Lake when she stopped in her tracks for yet a second time that day. Something about her demeanor told him that this was different from before. Peering over her shoulder, Sam saw what had brought her up short. A bear cub blocked the trail in front of them.

"What's the problem?" he whispered into her ear. "It's just a baby. We can easily shoo it away."

"Where there is a baby, there is a mama," she replied in a manner which suggested she knew what it was she was talking about. "If we accidentally get between the two of them, the mother will charge. They are very protective that way."

"Wonderful." The tone was sarcastic. "Where's the mama?"

"That's the dilemma. We may *already* be between them."

"Wonderful." There was that sarcasm again. "What do we do?"

"Back out of here as silently as we can…and wait." Even as she spoke, Sara motioned with her head back up the trail in the direction they had come.

"Wait?" he questioned in a loud whisper. "Wait for what?"

"Shush!" she ordered, slapping her first finger against her lips. "Yes, wait. Wait until the cub leaves, and then hope our smell hasn't attracted the mama in the meantime." Without leaving any room for further discussion, Sara began stepping backwards as quietly as possible, paying close attention to where she put her feet.

"What smell?" Sam cross-examined, following her lead.

Though he had once been taught the proper precautions to take when dealing with a bear as part of his training at Na-Cha-Tan, in the heat of the moment, his mind went blank.

"Bears have an acute sense of smell, and not only that, they are curious by nature," she explained, unslinging her backpack and dropping it noiselessly to the ground. Signaling for him to do the same, she added, "We're carrying food, remember? Bears are opportunistic feeders and they will investigate any new odors as a possible food source and take advantage of any easy meal which may be presented."

"Including us?" Sam verified, leaving his pack on the trail next to hers as they both retreated farther afield.

"It's been known to happen. That's why we are dropping our packs here and moving to a safe distance. If they don't approach within twenty minutes or so, we're probably okay."

It was an interminable wait during which they didn't say a word, but eventually the cub lumbered off into the woods.

"Can we go now?" Sam questioned, his legs cramped from crouching down on the ground for such a long time.

"Yes, but remember this: if a bear ever approaches you, don't provoke it. Do not throw rocks, or flash it in the eye with a lumina-beam, or challenge it in any way. The forest belongs to them; we're just passing through."

Nodding his head in understanding as they redonned their packs, Sam fell silent once more. From that point on for the rest of the trek, he didn't have much to say. Twice now she had saved his life, and he hadn't a clue how to repay her for doing so.

When at long last they finally reached the old miner's cabin without further incident, every muscle in Sam's untrained body ached. Flopping down onto the aged cot next to one another, the two of them quickly fell into an exhausted sleep. The fresh air, the altitude, and the miles had all worked their wonder. By the time they awoke hours later, they were horny and hungry. The first came first.

"When it gets dark, I am going to take you across the border," she explained, unbuttoning the top clasp of her tunic and unfurling her perky breasts before him. "But first, how 'bout one for old times' sake?"

"Here?" he stammered, glancing around. "*Now*? What if somebody comes?"

"The only somebodies who are sure to come are you. And me."

Sam grinned. "A man's work is never done."

"Don't think of it as work, darling," she asserted as she pushed him back onto the bed. "Think of it as making memories."

Twenty-three
Straight Hawk

The Council of Elders had been in closed-door session for more than two hours. The subject: to decide whether the time was yet ripe to lead their peoples into armed insurrection, or whether it would be more advisable to wait and build up their inventory of arms further. Though Dark Eagle himself was not a member of the Council, his father Tato was. Even so, the younger man had been invited up here to the town of Ochre River near Manitoba's Riding Mountain National Park not on the basis of his father's status, but rather on the basis of his own qualifications.

Of all the rebels, Dark Eagle was the one individual most in touch with their strategic situation; he knew precisely what their present stockpile of weapons was capable of and where they were lacking. Though the rebels had had little trouble acquiring sufficient guns and ammo, it took more than Uzis and manual firebombs to win a war; it took airchops (of which they had but two), plus tanks and missiles. Still, Dark Eagle was of the mind that it was time to move, and for two hours now he had sat quietly off to one side, while the Elders had debated the issue back and forth. Yet, not even once in all that time had he been asked to speak, and not being a patient man to begin with, he had finally run out of forbearance.

"You fools!" Dark Eagle suddenly exploded when yet another of the Elders stepped forward to counsel continued patience to the gathering. "You decrepit old fools! The longer we wait, the weaker we become!"

Tato stared hard at his only son. Astonished by the tirade, he wished he could silence his overzealous boy with just a word. But knowing that it wasn't his place, Tato said nothing. Only Straight Hawk, the eldest of the Elders, would address such an impertinent outburst. Silence fell over the group as they awaited the old man's reaction.

As was his way, Straight Hawk had no intention of rushing his reply. Squeezing his ancient eyes shut ever so slightly, the Chieftain cleared his throat to speak. His undiminished head of hair was white, and his weather-beaten face grim.

"Seven hundred years," Straight Hawk began. "We have waited seven hundred years for the return of our lands. You cannot seriously believe that one year more, or one year less, is apt to change the outcome?"

"Begging your pardon, Great One," Dark Eagle apologized as he rose to address the Council. "But the reason we have gone seven hundred years without our ancestral lands is because of cowardly leaders such as yourself. We must attack, and we must attack now!"

Glaring at them through a set of dark, piercing eyes, Dark Eagle took on a ferocious look. It was evident why he was held in such awe by many of the younger members of his tribe: Dark Eagle was a splendid-looking specimen of manhood.

"Cowardice is a subject of which you know little," Straight Hawk scolded calmly. "Only a Brave can know of cowardice."

"Am I not a Brave?" Dark Eagle screamed, his hand reaching for the hunting knife which hung at the ready from a sheath at his belt. "Have I not risked my life time and time again to carry arms to our brothers, to escape the redshirts?"

"I did not say that you were not *brave*," Straight Hawk countered sternly, "I said you were not a Brave. What is the difference you may ask? The difference is, you have not yet been tested in battle." Even as he spoke, the old man rose up to his full height and met Dark Eagle's steely gaze eye for eye.

"But I wish to be," Dark Eagle declared, drawing back a step. "All this talk is getting us nowhere. The time to strike is now!"

Not backing down, Straight Hawk advanced the same step Dark Eagle had just surrendered. "According to the Great Law, the time to strike is when the Elders say it is. Each tribe has a vote in this," he explained as he returned to his seat, "and each tribe is represented here at this table today. When last we voted, it was twenty-seven against six on the side of waiting. We have not yet taken a vote today, but I suspect if we did, the numbers would still be much the same. Would you have me override the Great Law of Peace just to satisfy your craving for blood?"

"Of course not," Dark Eagle admitted, dipping his head out of respect. Even as he did so, he stole a glance in his father's direction.

"The Iroquois Great Law has served us well these last

seven hundred years, and if we abide by its dictates, it will serve us well for the *next* seven hundred years," Straight Hawk justified. "But that is not why you are angry, and that is not why you were brought here today. What have you to tell us, Dark Eagle?"

"Recently, one of our conduits was murdered—shot in cold blood. I know this for a fact because I found his corpse when I flew into Wisconsin to retrieve the last batch of weapons. Next to him lay another body, one I didn't know, but judging by his size, the dead one was nothing more than a boy. That night it was dark and stormy so I didn't stay around long to investigate, but as near as I have been able to determine, our main contact—Matthews—has vanished without a trace. When the news broke, Federal agents moved in, and as a result, one of our key supply lines from the south has now been ruptured. This, plus the continuing crackdown by Director Harper, has made some of our other suppliers skittish. It is not only becoming increasingly difficult for us to obtain weapons, I have reason to believe there may be an infiltrator in among our ranks." As Dark Eagle spoke, he looked around the room with an incriminating stare, and with each animated turn of his head, his ponytail of jetblack hair lifted briefly off the skin of his suntanned neck.

"You are accusing one of us?" Straight Hawk probed with a broad sweep of his hand.

"No, Great One, but not all are who they seem."

"This is true always."

"Of course, you are right," Dark Eagle granted, lowering his eyes once more.

"We have a new supplier," Straight Hawk pointed out. "Elder Running Bear of the Kwakiuti tells us the yellow-skins can deliver force guns to us by freighter at the port of Vancouver. You need worry no further about adequate supplies, Dark Eagle. Return with your father Tato to make safe what Running Bear sends you. When the time for war comes, we will make the mountains of Alberta our stronghold. The mountains have fresh game; they have clean water and plenty of virgin timber. The mountains have everything we need to survive. When the time for war comes, we will strike at our enemies from there. Now, Dark Eagle, leave us. According to the Great Law, all of our votes must be conducted without an audience."

Consuming in a frenzied bout of wildness whatever little savings Lester had accumulated since graduating high school, he and Sindy wound their way cross-country in the gcar they had stolen three days prior. Lester had absolutely no perception of the repercussions his actions had caused back at camp, or of the shattered lives he had left behind in his wake. Nor did he care.

All that concerned him now was her and what she could do for him. He had known from the first time he held her naked body in his scrawny arms that she was a drug user, but he had callously shut his eyes to the danger, exchanging the risk of infection, of addiction, of destruction, for the prospect of sex on demand. It would never have occurred to him that she had been hired to do what she did, or that she didn't actually appreciate what he did for her in return. His own overgrown ego could never permit such doubts to creep in. And yet, as they made their sordid journey from the woods of Na-Cha-Tan to the streets of Alameda, he fell further and further under the influence of this despicable, wanton woman. Never a strong person to begin with, by the time they arrived at the coast, he was a hapless victim completely under her spell.

"Oh, Lester honey, why don't you try one of *these*?" Sindy cooed, offering him one of the shiny blue pills which had shown up in her last pay envelope. "They help me come so much harder," she lied convincingly.

On this, the last night before entering the Academy, the two of them had been popping pills and swigging tortan-ale for so many hours, the thought of one pill more or one pill less didn't seem to faze him much.

If only Lester Matthews had had more sense, he would have avoided this woman like the plague; if only Lester Matthews had had better judgment, he would have avoided her blue capsules as well. But after what she had already done to him this evening, Lester no longer had the strength to refuse her offer. And Sindy knew it. Surrender was in his eyes. She had been coaxing him down the slippery road towards blue-devil addiction for weeks. And now she had him where she wanted him—where Silas Whetstone and Overlord Ling wanted her to have him—under her thumb!

"Well, Sin, I don't know," he hesitated with the last, fleeting bits of resolve. Even someone as insecure as he was, couldn't help but be aware how perilous taking this drug could be. "What if they give me a blood test tomorrow at the Academy?"

"I'm way ahead of you stud," she proudly announced, pulling a second bottle of pills from her clutch. "See what I've got? Deludes!" She didn't have to explain to him that Deludes were masking agents specifically formulated to avoid a positive drug test.

"Good thinking, but those blue-devils are so...so..."

"Oh, Lester, don't be such a square! Such a *Boy* Scout!" she ridiculed with disdain, emphasizing the word boy as if it were something dirty. "*Real* men pop 'em all the time. They heighten one's sexual response, you know."

Uncrossing her legs provocatively, she spread them just far enough apart to gain his attention. "If you want to take *me*," she asserted, handing him the dangerous narcotic with one hand even as she stroked his upper thigh with the other, "you'll have to take *it*."

Her words had the tone of an order, an order he intended to obey no matter how stupid.

"Okay, sweet thighs," Lester relented, a lecherous grin spreading across his face, his eyes fixed on her parted legs. "If you think it'll help me do you better, then let me try one of those blue-devils already."

"Oh, honey," she bubbled excitedly, knowing that she had won, "I'm so proud of you! You'll see how right I am. I promise, our sex will be hotter than ever."

As his clammy hand closed around the gelatinous capsule, Sindy reveled in the sweet taste of victory: soon her assignment would be over, and she could go home. A blue-devil was such a powerful narcotic, ingesting as few as one or two hits ought to be sufficient to hook him. Once hooked and careening down the emotionally destructive path towards addiction, a blue-devil junkie would do most anything to feed his habit.

Though Sindy didn't know it at the time, she was about to become an accomplice to the single worst case of treason ever committed against the United States of America, a treason in which Lester would at least be partially responsible for bringing down his own country. When the moment was right, Overlord Ling intended to use Lester's chemical dependency as a lever to strike back at his old nemesis, Senator Nate Matthews. By threatening to withhold the drug Lester needed so badly, Overlord Ling would be able to compel him to do his dirty work, stealing certain sensitive military secrets from Nate's vault and delivering them to him. Only then would Ling's revenge for the death of his father be complete.

Handing him a beaker of tortan, Sindy looked on as Lester washed the blue-devil down his gullet, swallowing the pill along with what little was left of his self-esteem.

Twenty-four
Glück

Sam was not here in Canada of his own accord; still, after all the effort that had been expended to be certain he reached Alberta unharmed, he was determined to make the best of it. Though he was without a doubt a stranger in a strange land, Sam found Calgary to be a strikingly American city, especially for a country which claimed to loath America so. Like any other overgrown metropolis, the downtown was one steel-girdered high-rise after another; the suburbs ringing the fringe, one tree-lined boulevard after the next; and the no-man's land in between, an unending slum of dirt and crime. Like any number of cities its size back home, this one was gritty—noxious fumes hung heavy in the air, and slugs and bimbookers roamed freely along the streets.

Once Sam had checked in at the registrar's office and secured a room in the underground dormitory, he proceeded downtown to the provincial offices to apply for a driver's license. Although he didn't own a gcar and had no present intention of buying one, he still required an operator's license for the moped he hoped to purchase.

The provincial offices were housed in a classic, Roman-style building complete with marble columns, stone steps, and a granite facade. Surrounded on all sides by a legion of antiseptic-looking, glass and steel skyscrapers, the squat structure seemed out of place; yet like all of the buildings in the central business district, it sat upon a honeycomb of subterranean kiosks, underground malls, and cave-like apartment complexes. Due in part to Calgary's forbidding climate, over the centuries, much of its life had gone underground into the recesses of the earth. And who could blame them? Here, the seasons were marked by short, beastly hot summers; long, unbearable winters; and a year-round blanket of lung-choking smog. In fact, in some of the newer parts of the city as much as thirty stories of basement had been drilled into the bedrock, and something on the order of two million people called the Underneath their home. Unfortunately, Samuel Matthews was now one of them. After the open spaces of Farmington and after Na-Cha-Tan's unending acres of virgin forest, the confinement of his new quarters was disconcerting, even spooky.

The Underneath was a dark and dreary place replete with unseen sounds and unknown people, and it was at times like these that he longed most to be back home in Missouri. Reaching into the pocket of his trousers for a stick of gum, his fingers brushed against yet another brutal reminder of just how much his life had changed since he first set foot on Canadian soil.

Tucked in there between a few crumbled bills and a

tattered tissue was an unopened bottle of ascorbic acid he had been given by the nurse in the registrar's office. Also known as Vitamin C, ascorbic acid tablets were standard issue to all incoming freshmen to compensate for the stunning lack of sunlight which filtered down to the Underneath. As incredible as it might seem in this day and age, scurvy was once again the scourge of humanity, only now instead of mainly affecting sailors, it afflicted the big-city dweller. Determined to avoid this condition marked by its swollen and bleeding gums, Sam had already made up his mind that, no matter how foreign the practice, he would remember to take one pill each morning with breakfast. Still, everything about this place made him feel uneasy.

Even as he did his best to endure the twenty plus minute wait in line for the next clerk, he was haunted by his grandfather's final words to him as he and Sara had offloaded from the riverboat that day in Joliet. "Sam," he said with a tear in his eye, "if the Matthews line is to survive, if there is to be another generation of Matthews, you must leave the country. Go to the university in Calgary. I have it on the best of authority that there, at the School of Economics, they will teach you how to think. Not what to think, mind you, but *how* to think."

"May I help you?" The speaker who greeted him was an attractive, dark-eyed woman. Snapping out of his daydream, Sam was shocked to find that he had finally reached the front of the line.

"Good day, miss," he began, laying on his charming, midwestern twang. "I should like to apply for an operator's license."

"Two wheel or four wheel?" she asked crisply. Her sweater fit snugly, and Sam's attention was immediately riveted on the lofty swell of her bosom.

"Two wheel or four wheel?" she repeated, looking up

from her stack of forms to witness him giving her the once-over. Though his hands never left his pockets, it was as if he were mentally caressing her body. She blushed with embarrassment when his eyes met hers. "Sir?"

"Sam," he stammered self-consciously, "my name is Sam. What did you say? Oh, yes, two wheel. For a vespa. I mean, what is the fee?"

"You must be an American," she asserted, a tiny crinkle of a smile gracing her otherwise beautiful face.

"Yes, how did you know?" Sam questioned, smiling back. For an instant, a wave of panic swept over him as he wasn't able to put his fingers on the special identicard his grandfather had given him before leaving the States. Without it, Sam would have been considered an illegal alien and subject to immediate deportation. But there it was in his pocket, jammed between the bottle of vitamins and the material of his denim pants.

"Your accent gave you away," she answered matter-of-factly before turning businesslike again. "May I see your U.S. license?"

"Why, yes," he replied, pulling it from his pocket and placing it on the counter before her. As he did so, he couldn't help but notice how rosy and glowing her cheeks were, how clean and wonderful she smelled. She was a picture of health.

"Well, Mister Samuel Matthews," she noted as she stared at his license, "the fee will be…"

"Sam," he interrupted flirtatiously. "My name is Sam."

"Well, then, Sam, the fee will be fifty dollars, Canadian. You can pay the cashier over there," she explained, pointing to a window at the far end of the counter.

"It isn't fair," he pouted convincingly.

"What isn't fair? The fee?" she queried, surprised that the young man would find the modest charge exorbitant.

"No, the fee is fine," Sam answered calmly, studying the playful curve of her nose and the fullness of her lips.

"What then?" she quizzed in a perplexed tone, blushing again at his gaze.

"I have only just now arrived in Calgary, and I don't know my way around. I sure could use a savvy tour-guide to help me find my way," he revealed with a mischievous grin.

Chuckling, she waved him off. "Next?" she queried, speaking over his shoulder to the person standing in line behind him. "Who's next?"

Sam moved on with a satisfied look on his face: he had made his first contact in this puzzling new land.

The freshman mixer was held in the dormitory cafeteria. All the tables in the multipurpose room had been folded up and put away, and all the chairs had been placed facing each other along two opposite walls. In keeping with the early arrival of autumn, a fire roared in the fireplace, warming the room. The romantic crackling of timbers reminded him of Na-Cha-Tan, and for a moment he choked back a tear over the innocent world he had been forced to leave behind. It was at times like these that he missed Ziggy the most. They had barely had enough time to say goodbye and then he had been on the riverboat heading north with his grandfather. Only moments later, it seemed, he was here in Calgary at this dance.

Praying for any sign of friendliness, Sam studied the students' faces in the flickering glow of the fire, hoping to recognize someone—anyone—familiar. Sam was a naturally outgoing person, but these last several days had been tough on him. Americans were not universally held in the highest regard here in Canada, and the only friend he had been able to make so far was one Ravi Gurujal of Afghanistan, also an outsider. Ravi was two years Sam's senior, but because of the language barrier he had enrolled in a fresh-man literature course. That's where they first had met. Other-wise, the first week of college had been unremarkable.

Though Sam listened to the cack music for a quarter of an hour, it wasn't long before he decided this was going to be a wasted evening. While the other students were obvi-ously enjoying themselves dancing to the furiously pound-ing beat, Sam found himself standing alone in a corner sulking. Unlike the icebreaker in the gymnasium that week-end of the canoe race, tonight's emcee had made no attempt whatsoever to stir things up. Disappointed by the prospects, Sam began moving towards the door. That's when he saw her.

Like a figment conjured up out of a dream, there she was! Her lips glistening in the uncertain light, the girl was just as he remembered her—slim of waist and dark of eye. Only he didn't know her name. Unable to call out to her directly by name, Sam tried a different approach.

"Heh, you!" he bellowed, drawing nearer through the crowd. "Don't I know you?"

"No, I don't think so," she asserted. In her confusion, she glanced nervously to her left and then to her right to be sure he was actually speaking to her.

"Aren't you the driver's license lady?" he questioned, certain he had made her acquaintance before.

Pausing a moment to study his features, she smiled before speaking. "Yes, you're the American," the cute, brown-skinned girl declared, reaching out to shake his hand.

"Sam," he reminded her, "but I never learned yours."

"Nasha," she answered softly.

"Are you a freshman too?" he quizzed, thrilled to have someone friendly to talk to.

She giggled her answer. "Yes." Grinning bashfully, she asked, "Do Americans dance?"

Nodding, he invited her out onto the dance floor. With

the blaring cack music making conversation impossible, they joined right in with the others, doing their best to match the hand motions and the wild gyrations of the swirling mob around them. Intoxicated by the maddening tempo, it wasn't long before they had lost themselves in the revelry.

After twenty minutes of this wildness, however, Sam was exhausted. Parched by the effort, he dragged her to a counter where the chaperones were serving some sort of chilled concoction which tasted faintly reminiscent of a soft drink he was accustomed to back home.

"I need some fresh air," he advised, pushing her towards the door.

"I've heard that line before," she scoffed, feigning disinterest.

"Suit yourself," Sam barked abruptly as he started for the exit. Recalling how much trouble Sara had been at the start, he wasn't about to let *this* girl get the upper hand.

"Hold on, Sam," she begged, grabbing for his arm. "I didn't mean anything by it."

"It's a great line though, isn't it?" he teased right back, his bright eyes flashing.

"The American sense of humor," Nasha remarked as if the statement were some sort of universal truth.

"Come on now," he insisted, pointing her towards the door. "Outside we go."

Between the roaring fire and the body heat generated by hundreds of jostling students, the cafeteria had become superheated, and the outside air felt cold by comparison. Though it was in fact a fairly typical late summer night, as the sweat from their frenzied bout of dancing was chilled by a brisk crosswind, an involuntary shiver rolled over the both of them. Drawing closer as if for warmth, the two budding lovers marveled at the sparkling, star-lit sky.

"Nasha, eh?" he verified, trying to make conversation.

"What kind of a name is Nasha?"

She stiffened noticeably at the question, and he sensed that, without meaning to, he had unintentionally struck a raw nerve.

"You *are* brash, aren't you?" she criticized roughly.

"Well, I..." he stuttered, not sure how to extricate himself from whatever mess he had inadvertently stepped into.

"Are *all* Americans so brazen?" she asked pointedly even as she gripped his hand tightly.

"Well, I..." he tried again, his face drawn.

"I'm Aleutian," she admitted courageously. "There—now you know. Do you still want to be seen with me?"

"What are you *talking* about? I only just met you. Land's-sakes, woman, why should our date be over before it's even begun?" Sam cross-examined in an astonished tone. "Why in the world should I care whether you are an Aleutian?"

"You mean you *don't*?" Nasha probed hopefully.

"Of course not," Sam emphasized. "Your eyes and your...your...whatever, are what caught *my* attention," he replied, fumbling for words even as he stole another glance at her ample chest.

"I saw you staring at my sweater," she claimed, squeezing out a smile.

"Aleutian girls have two of them like everyone else, don't they?" he quizzed lecherously, still contemplating the mental picture he had painted of her breasts.

"Wouldn't *you* like to know?" she shot back with mock indignation.

"Yes, as a matter of fact I would, but first tell me this: what's the big deal about you being an Aleutian?" he inquired cautiously. "Are your people cursed or something?"

"In a manner of speaking," she replied. "In *my* country, the Amerinds are like the Negroids of *your* country—

second-class citizens. In fact, they call us prairie-niggers."

"I'm sorry to know that," Sam confessed sincerely. "I knew there were some disputes over Amerind claims to former tribal lands, but when I asked about your name, I wasn't making fun of it. Still, you have to admit, Nasha *is* a bit unusual."

"My brother and my father are the ones involved in those territorial disputes, not me. And as for my name, in my tribe, each newborn child is named for a star in the zodiac sign of their mother, the only exception being that no one is to take the name of another living member of the tribe. I would have been named Rigel if I had been born a boy," she pointed out. "And you, Sam, what are *you* named for?"

The tall, good-looking Missourian smiled and answered, "A riverboat captain."

"Did you once live on a river?" she inquired, finding herself drawn more and more to this man.

"Near one, actually. My grandfather was—still is, for that matter—a nut about the legend of Mark Twain, a riverboat captain who supposedly lived several hundred years ago and grew up not far from my hometown in Missouri. This Mark Twain was reputed to have been the pen name for an actual person, one Samuel Clemens. It is for him that I am named."

"Misery?" she challenged doubtfully. "You come from misery?"

Sam chuckled, "No, Nasha, not misery, Mizz-hurry."

"So, Sam of Mizz-hurry, what brings you to Alberta? America has a great many fine universities of her own."

"So it does," he confessed with a troubled look on his brow. "Well, briefly put, that same grandfather I told you about, the one who is so enamored with Mark Twain, insisted I come up here to avoid some troubles back at home. But listen, why don't we forget about me, I'd rather learn more about you."

"Well, Sam of Mizz-hurry, that will have to wait for another day," she advised, glancing at her timepiece. "I'm due home soon," she explained, edging towards the side-walk. "My father and my brother will have a fit if I am late, but I had a nice time tonight. Thank you."

"May I escort you home?" he probed, not ready to say goodnight.

"I think not," she politely rejected as she strolled in the direction of the tube-station. "We will meet again, however, of that I am sure."

Twenty-five
Algorithm

"While it is admittedly no exaggeration to say that the vast business of the calculus made possible most of the practical triumphs of post-medieval science, and while the calculus most assuredly stands out as one of the most ingenious creations of a bewildered human race doing their best to model the confusing world around them, I would argue that we scientists have chosen the wrong model with which to describe the universe. The differential equations of the calculus represent reality as a continuum which changes smoothly from place to place and from time to time. In today's class we will explore the question of whether reality is in fact continuous, or whether perhaps space and time are not as smooth as we have been led to believe. Perhaps space is broken down into discrete grid-points and time into discrete time-steps; perhaps it is only mankind's *models* of space and time which are continuous. If this is true, if reality is indeed *not* unbroken, then predictions become impossible, and small differences in the initial conditions may produce vast differences in the final outcome."

(Settling into his seat to begin taking notes, Sam considered the possibility that this class was not going to be as boring as he first had feared. He had specifically chosen a spot near the rear of the room so that if he should fall asleep, he wouldn't be noticed. But changing his mind now, he slipped down towards the front a dozen or more rows. Though the lecturer was a huge man, at least six and a quarter feet tall and nearly 300 pounds in girth, he seemed puny against the backdrop of the giant auditorium and the oversized stage on which he stood.)

"The illusion of continuity is deeply ingrained in our consciousness not only by the calculus of our scientists but also by our inability to perceive any such small or discrete units. In much the same way that the characters in a video seem to move when, in fact, the film is composed of discrete frames, or cells, time only *appears* to be continuous and unbroken. And to further complicate matters for most of us, none of our scientists are even *attempting* to perceive these tiny units of space and of time simply because their theories tell them that these miniscule units do not exist. Inasmuch as they prove their theories of physics using equations which begin by assuming reality is continuous, is it any wonder they conclude the very same thing? It is all circular reasoning and it proves nothing!

"I ask you then: What is an alternative theory? No answer? Consider this: instead of differential calculus, how about rules of order? As you will soon see, although the patterns formed by discrete units are all but impossible to describe with Newton's calculus, they are easy to express with an algorithm. What, you may ask, is an algorithm? It is merely another word for the term 'feedback rule'. An algorithm is a fixed procedure for converting input into output; for taking one body of information and turning it into another. A *recycling* algorithm is one whose *output* is fed back into it as the next cycle's *input*. By this method, feedback is the key to modeling reality."

(Twisting his head, Sam searched the auditorium to see if any of his residence-hall mates were among the hundreds seated there, but he saw no one familiar. He wondered whether he would *ever* make any friends here. As if living Underneath, as it was called, wasn't enough to make him homesick, he couldn't understand what Americans had done to deserve such disdain from the Canadians. It troubled him no end.)

"The power of a recycling algorithm is quickly apparent in the simulation of a physical process. By way of example, consider two planetoids, and consider a computer which simulates their paths as they orbit around their joint center of gravity in accordance with the laws of motion. The simulation takes their velocities and their positions at a given point in time, then computes those variables for the *next* point in time, and then feeds the new numbers back into the algorithm to generate yet *another* set of variables, and so on. In this way, one can describe a universe which proceeds tick by tick and dot by dot. It is a universe where complexity boils down to a handful of rules of order instead of untold numbers of differential equations.

"Rather than outputting variables, a recycling algorithm can also be employed to output shapes. Consider the patterns generated by nature. An algorithm can describe a leaf, for instance. Choose a random starting place somewhere on your sheet of paper, or on your computer screen. Then invent two rules—a heads rule and a tails rule. The rules tell you how to mark your paper from coin flip to coin flip. Upon throwing a heads, move two inches to the northeast; upon tossing a tails, move twenty-five percent closer to the paper's center. Now, start flipping the coin and marking points. Go ahead, I want you to do it for homework. If you throw away the first dozen or so points like a blackjack dealer burying the first card before a new deal, you will find your game producing not a random field of dots, but a shape, a shape which is revealed with greater and greater clarity as the game goes on. The act of writing down a set of rules to be reiterated captures certain global information about the shape. Historically, however, the problem has been how to *reverse* the process. That is, given a particular shape, how does one go about choosing a set of rules to *create* it?"

(As Sam listened to the big man speak, it occurred to him that perhaps this is what his grandfather had meant by instructing him to learn *how* to think, rather than *what* to think. It seemed to him as he listened to what his economics professor had to say, that there were more ways of looking at the world than he had previously imagined.)

"Over the past two hundred years, mainly through a process of trial and error, most biological shapes have succumbed to algorithmic re-creation—leaves, bones, ears, bronchial passages, and dendrites, to name a few. And thanks to these algorithms, biologists have been able to teach cells how to grow replacement parts, something which never could have been achieved by scientists caught in the cul-de-sac of differential equations. Unfortunately, there is no shortcut to discovering what shape a specific algorithm will lead to except to let the rule iterate and see what happens.

"Using differential equations and the calculus, it is

possible to predict the future state of a system without figuring out what states it will occupy between now and then. But in the case of recycling algorithms, you *must* go through all the intermediate steps to find out what the end product will be. In a real sense, therefore, there is no way to know the future except to watch it unfold. There is no way to know what the future holds any faster than 'running' the universe to *get* to that future. By now, you should all recognize this as Durbin's First Law."

(If only he knew Nasha's last name, or where she lived, he would call her, Sam thought as he sat there fidgeting in his seat. There was something about her which had piqued his interest. In their own way, each of them were both second-class citizens in this big, perplexing land.)

"And of very great importance to our discussion today is the fact that tiny changes in the rule being iterated may produce *enormous* differences in the end result. This is the underlying principle of Chaos Theory—that a small change in the initial conditions may be magnified via a series of cascading events to produce very great differences in the final outcome. A common expression of this phenomenon is, 'For want of a nail, the Kingdom was lost.'

"Now, let's see how this axiom impacts upon the world of finance. The idea that small events can have a *big* impact conflicts mightily with a fundamental tenet of traditional economics. Almost all economists believe that systems reach equilibrium over time, or at least, are always moving *towards* equilibrium. And on the basis of their calculus, these unenlightened analysts repeatedly mis-diagnose the future. Yet, in some instances, the feedback effect of a small disturbance to the system can lead to explosive results like a market crash or a financial panic."

(Would he ever see her again? Sam wondered, staring around the room hopefully. Nearly every freshman was

supposed to take this course, so she had to be here somewhere. Letting his eyes roam, he went from student to
student, searching for any hint of familiarity. Then, low and
behold, there she was, three rows over! Almost bolting from
his seat, Sam waved furtively in her direction. When Nasha
waved back, he rose from his chair and moved swiftly across
the auditorium for yet a second time this class period,
disturbing dozens of students along the way. Oblivious to
the complaints of everyone around him, there was a huge
smile painted across his face.)

"The traditional linear thinking of economists is that
small disturbances evoke small responses; that you can find
the tax rate which optimizes the economy's growth rate;
that you can find the market clearing price for a good; that
with a big enough computer you can solve for all the
unknowns in all of the equations and arrive at all of the
answers. But folks, what I am here to tell you today is that
it ain't that easy!

"It is only in our *models* of the economy that there are
equilibriums; in the *real* world, there are none! And why is
this so? Because economic activity is turbulent and uncertain. There is no way to know the future except to watch it
unfold. And there are no predictions.

"But it is also important to understand that this truism
extends *beyond* economics. Rolling streams, tectonic events,
weather patterns, and stock market prices all exhibit non-
linear tendencies. Even relations between nation-states can
be considered in this light. A small perturbation—the
bombing of a key communications link, for example—
might be all that is required to trigger a large and unpredictable consequence, including a world war."

(Even as the instructor mouthed the words, Sam's
thoughts turned to his grandfather. The Senator had spoken to him of war, and at the time, nothing had seemed

more farfetched. Now, here he was, listening to one of his first lectures of the season, and his professor was *also* speaking of war. Sam had debated the topic with Sara and with Ziggy, and even with himself. Perhaps war was more inevitable than he had originally thought; perhaps, he had better start paying closer attention to that risk and begin watching for those small perturbations which could set it off. Though he would be sure to ask his grandpa about it the next time they spoke on the comm, in the meantime, he couldn't take his eyes off the attractive Amerind girl sitting next to him. Whatever it was that the teacher had to say for the duration of the period, Sam didn't hear a single word. Without ever meaning to be, Sam was all of a sudden head over heels in love.)

Twenty-six
Smoker

Any man who has successfully traveled the difficult road to attain the rank of Eagle Scout considers himself one for life. Indeed, Samuel Matthews was such a man. And figuring that the best way for him to build a new circle of friends up here in Calgary was to seek out others who thought as he did, Sam began by contacting the provincial Scout office shortly after he arrived. Though he talked at some length with a Scout Executive, giving him his background and even volunteering his time to help out a local troop, Sam found his offer politely, yet firmly, rebuffed. Without the proper references, the official he spoke to was reluctant to have Sam in such close contact with the youth in his charge. The man did, however, suggest an interesting alternative.

It seemed that, some years back, Scouters of college age had formed a service fraternity called Beta Sigma, and that there was an active chapter right there on campus. The two Greek letters comprising the fraternity's name stood for the English letters B and S, as in Boy Scout, and as might be expected, given the juxtaposition of those two initials, their organization was the butt of more than the occasional off-colored joke. Even so, those who knew what the men of Beta Sigma stood for, and what they tried to accomplish, held them only in the highest of esteem.

Besides catering solely to former Boy Scouts, this fraternity was unique in at least one other respect. Unlike a conventional social frat, Beta Sigma members did not glom together in one corner of the Underneath ruling their dark and dank piece of the subterranean turf like a private fiefdom. These satraps, as the fraternities proudly called them, were off-limits to outsiders and dangerous to the uninvited. An unescorted woman, for instance, was as likely to be raped as she was to be made a virtual slave of her captors; a lone male could easily be tortured or killed if he accidentally strayed into the wrong territory. Granted, many of the Beta Sigmas lived near one another on the same level Underneath or else shared an off-campus flat, but these informal arrangements were a far cry from the notorious shenanigans so typical of other fraternal groups. Still, in keeping with the ancient Greek tradition, one did not merely sign up and join Beta Sigma—one pledged. And because of the special nature of its charter, pledging Beta Sigma was itself a unique experience. Whereas the driving force behind most of the fraternities on campus was to uphold a tankard of ale or else to put down a competing satrap, the goal of Beta Sigma was to uphold the Scout Oath and Law, to help other people at all times, as it were.

Despite having heard some pretty bizarre stories about

hazing rituals and about hell-week, Sam was not deterred from giving Beta Sigma a try. He naturally assumed that since Scouters were basically good, honest people, even a practice as arcane and outdated as pledging a fraternity could be nothing but good-natured fun. After all, he had done his share of GA's over the years and had even survived the rigors of an OA Callout, and few indoctrinations he knew of were more strenuous than the Ordeal. Just the same, he had decided not to attend the first meeting alone; though it took some convincing, his new friend Ravi had agreed to accompany him.

The gathering was held in an informal lounge located on the third sub-floor of the Student Center, and when the two of them arrived, they found the room jam-packed with people. It was an organizational meeting for prospective pledges called a "Smoker." From what Sam could gather, its name dated back to a time, hundreds of years ago, when—in a burning display of their prowess and their manhood—"real" men commonly lit up and smoked something called a cigar. Except for pictures Nate had once showed him of his namesake, Sam had never seen a cigar before, much less smoked one. But from what he understood, it was a cylindrical object manufactured from the leaves of the tobacco plant, a scruffy-looking herb whose cultivation had long since been banned. And although no one present at the gathering was actually *smoking* one of these green, phallic-symbols, the club historian wasted no time in passing around the Beta Sigma scrapbook complete with dozens of cracked and aging photographs from Smokers long ago. The yellowed snapshots clearly showed men of his age joyfully puffing away on these great, big cigars—stogies, as they were called. Seeing the pictures, Sam couldn't believe his eyes—the participants seemed to be actually *enjoying* themselves! Studying the indisputable evidence for himself, Sam wondered whether his grandpa was familiar with this practice. He must remember to ask him the next time they spoke.

"My people *still* do it," Ravi advised, reading Sam's mind, "but it's not good for you."

"Yes, so I'm told, but look at those smiles!" Sam countered, examining the disapproving face of the fellow who had just spoken to him. Ravi had dark eyes and swarthy skin, not dark enough to be a Negro, but far too shaded to be a Euro. "Despite the danger, smoking must have been pleasurable somehow," Sam concluded, passing the scrapbook on to the pledge sitting to his left.

Overhearing their conversation, one of the older members cruelly suggested, "Smoking was a curse the backward redskin put on us more advanced whites; a plague meant to repay the Euros for stealing their precious ancestral lands."

Even as Sam overheard the cursed words this man uttered, he could hardly believe his ears. No Scout he had ever met had expressed such disdain for the aboriginal tribes of North America. The term redskin, while having a certain historical accuracy—the Beothuk Indians of Newfoundland, for instance, smeared red ochre on their bodies—was considered a disparaging term by most. To hear it spoken now, out in open public like this, made Sam sick; he wasn't about to join a club filled with bigots. Yet even as he rose to leave, one of the other Actives intervened to put the intolerant dolt in his place.

"Norton, you are such a racist!" Laughlin exploded from a nearby chair, interrupting the first man's banter. "No wonder there's so much prejudice in this country against the Amerinds."

"Amerinds?" Norton shot back viciously. "Hah! Where I come from we call 'em redskins. Or prairie-niggers!"

"That'll be quite enough," the fraternity president counseled, banging his gavel and calling the meeting to order. "We are not here to discuss politics; we are here to discuss pledging. And if I hear any more derogatory talk out of you Norton, I'll ask for your resignation. Now, if there are no objections, I give you this semester's pledgemaster, Frank Rasmussen."

Frank was a tough-looking mountain of a man, aptly framed for his weekend duties in the Royal Canadian Mounted Police. It was a big man just like this one that Sara had killed that day in the forest, only that fellow had been an American.

"Welcome, pledges," Frank began in his gruff voice. "I am delighted to see so many new faces here tonight, but if you think Beta Sigma is some club for overweight Eagle Scouts, you have come to the wrong Smoker. Our pledge program is as tough as any on campus," he roared, his demeanor that of a drill sergeant. "And in case you have any doubts about who is in charge, *I* am! If after tonight you decide that you still wish to pledge Beta Sigma, for the next eight weeks you will do whatever I say, whenever I say it. And until I tell you differently, you will do whatever any Active tells you to do, unless of course you are told to harm another Active or another pledge. In *that* case, you will check with me first."

Pausing just long enough to let the color return to the faces of the prospective pledges, Big Frank went on, "If things get too tough for you, you may cease pledging at any time without disgrace, and in fact, we seek to eliminate unworthy candidates in just this way. Those who remain will be honed into a fine team. But understand this: even if you *do* stick it out the full eight weeks, that is still no guarantee that you will be accepted as a Brother. Acceptance as a Brother will be determined by a secret ballot of the Actives on Blackball Night just after the BeHolden Day break."

"You seem pretty cocksure for a big slug named Frank," Ravi boldly challenged without provocation.

"What's your name, boy?" the pledgemaster roared indignantly, pointing his finger at Sam's dark-skinned neighbor.

"My name is Ravi Gandu, sir. I don't take orders. And I don't go by 'boy'."

"You don't look Canadian to me, *boy*," Frank shot back, testing the younger man's resolve.

"I'm not," Ravi answered without elaboration.

"What makes you so special?"

"In my country, unless a man is part of the militia, he is not obliged to takes orders from *any* man."

"Well, we're not *in* your country, now are we? Whatever else you are, Ravi Fondue, one thing is for certain: you are a smart-ass. And I don't like smart-asses much. To be a pledge means to be a soldier, and in this man's army, I'm the boss. Now get down and give me ten!" Big Frank ordered, pointing to a spot on the floor in front of him where everyone would be sure to see.

"Yes, sir," the mouthy one replied as he obediently got down on the floor to pump off ten pushups. But as soon as he had finished, Ravi repeated his earlier challenge. "You seem pretty cocksure for a big slug named Frank."

"Pledge, you are to speak only when you are spoken to," Frank explained, again trying to put the foreigner in his place.

"Yes, sir," Ravi retorted with feigned meekness and a hearty salute.

"Okay, meatballs," Frank detailed, "our first pledge meeting will be tomorrow night. You are to be here at seven P.M. And bring a pillow case."

"A pillow case?!" Sam verified in a confused tone, looking crosswise at Ravi.

"Got gum in your ear?" Frank countered. "Yes, a pillow case. And it should be dyed purple."

"Purple?" one of the other pledges cross-examined.

"No, you're right," Frank agreed, "that's too manly for a bunch of lowlife pledges like yourselves. Let's make it pink," he decided to the groans of every newcomer. "Meeting adjourned."

Twenty-seven
Overlord

Though Sindy had only promised to remain with Lester until the Academy opened its doors to the incoming class at the end of August, once she arrived in California, it was hard to bring herself to leave. The Alameda Naval Base where he was stationed at was next to Berkeley and across the bay from Sanfran, and if ever there was a magnet for velcroids and lowlifes, this megalopolis was it.

The Sanfran metro area was a gritty urban center which ran for a hundred miles up the coast and forty miles inland; yet here, Sindy felt right at home. She loved mingling in with the crowds, browsing through the noisy bazaars with their scruffy specimens of humanity, strolling down the jam-packed streets with their noise and their mayhem, and visiting the congested marketplaces with their beggars and their pickpockets. Here, bimbooking was simple, and totally unregulated; here, drugs ran aplenty; here, the weather was cool and dry, and the scenery gorgeous.

Lost in this den of rot and decay, it had been easy for her to make up her mind to stay awhile longer and continue supplying Lester with the proper mix of blue-devils and Deludes to keep him going until break. Only now, as the long days of summer drew to a close, and as the chilly breezes of autumn began to nip at the hillsides, did she begin to get homesick for her old haunts and her old way of life. Indeed, she was just about to pull up stakes of her own accord, when the call from Whetstone had come in. The timing couldn't have been better—for either of them.

The first weeks at the Academy had gone well for Lester, and after midterms each Cadet was granted four days leave to prepare for the next quarter. Exhilarated at the prospect of having Sindy to himself for a long weekend, Lester had arranged passage for them onboard a military suborb headed into Lihue out of Oakland. Though the island of Kauai was everything Ensign Matthews had ever dreamed of, on their second evening together he realized that something was dreadfully out of place. From the moment he and Sindy had first climbed out of bed that morning, she had been recalcitrant and strangely aloof, and each time he had asked her for a blue-devil to help calm his jittery nerves, she had put him off as if getting a fix no longer mattered. It was not until after they had finished eating dinner that night, not until after the withdrawal pangs had really started getting the best of him, that it all came to a head.

"I've run out of capsules," she admitted dispassionately, looking him straight in the eye.

Lester was furious. "How am I supposed to get through the rest of our vacation without a hit?" he asked. "After all we have meant to one another, how can you do this to me?"

All of a sudden, his uniform didn't look so crisp as before, nor did his face look so young as it had. Clearly agitated, he looked as if he might begin crying right there in the restaurant.

Only then did she explain. "Now, Lester honey, you must understand: it isn't easy to get those blue-devils, nor are they cheap. Surely a man of your obvious intelligence would have figured out by now that I must be getting them from some one! And now, that someone wants to meet you."

"I thought you loved me," he said, his voice just a whisper.

"That someone is staying in the hotel just across the street." Even as she pointed to the opposite side of the boulevard, the sleeve on her lightweight cotton shirt fell away from her arm, exposing the track-marked flesh to the setting sun. "Not only can my friend supply you with all the pills you could ever want, he can help you advance your career as well."

"This sounds like a setup to me," Lester replied suspiciously, balking at her suggestion. But when an uncontrollable bout of the shakes rocked his body, and his stomach began doing barrel rolls, he quickly gave in to the first hints of withdrawal sickness. Clutching at his side, he gasped, "Okay, Sin, let's go meet your friend."

"Follow me," she ordered, helping him up from the table and leading him across the street, "Overlord Ling's suite is on the fifteenth floor."

It took only moments for the lift to bring them to the top floor, and only moments longer for them to navigate their way to the end of the corridor. Besides Lester and Sindy, there were three other people assembled in the well-appointed room. The first was a big mountain of a man introduced to them only as Chang. Though Chang just stood there immobile like a rock throughout the entire session, Lester never doubted the hulking man's ability to cause him pain if he chose to. Like a big gorilla, Chang had a sloping forehead, a pair of bulging arms, and a barrel-shaped chest.

The second fellow, who Lester never actually got a close look at because he stayed in a darkened corner of the room, was a tall, gaunt caricature of a man at least Stovepipe's height, only thinner. He had a tinny voice and an ugly sense of humor, and from the way Sindy spoke to him, Lester had the impression that, not only were they well acquainted, they were not on the best of terms.

The third man, the one who had called this meeting to begin with, was Overlord Ling. Lester had never actually met a Chinaman before, and he found this one particularly unusual. The Overlord had pointy ears and a flowing, fu-manchu moustache. His face was hardened by many years of war. Ling was the first of the three to speak.

"I do not believe I have ever had the pleasure of making the acquaintance of an officer in the U.S. Navy," the myste-rious Oriental said to the uniformed man. "Won't you please sit down, Ensign Matthews?"

"The pleasure is all mine," the Ensign replied, taking a chair. "Sindy here has not told me much about you, but she *has* said you can help me achieve greatness," Lester ex-plained, his hands trembling ever so slightly.

"And she is absolutely correct," the Overlord agreed with a twisted smile. "If greatness is what you seek, great-ness is what I can offer. If wealth is what you seek, I can offer that as well." The Chinaman was delighted to see the telltale twitch in the Naval officer's eye—it was an unmistakable sign of his blue-devil addiction.

Stepping back into the shadows where Whetstone was hunkered down into a chair, Ling whispered to the emaciated man. "This girl you dug up for us has done a good job; you may have her when we are through here today."

"I *do* seek wealth," Ensign Matthews boomed, drawing Ling's attention back to him. "But for the moment, I have a more pressing need which we must discuss." Even as Lester struggled to lay out his demands, his fluttering eye focused on the vial of blue capsules sitting on the shelf behind the Overlord.

"Well, Ensign," the Overlord bargained, winking at Sindy as he spoke, "I have needs too. Perhaps you possess something which can ease *my* pain, something which you would be willing to trade for these." Taking a step backwards, he turned and grasped the glass vessel filled with blue-devils. Against the dim lighting of the room the capsules appeared nearly black.

"Ensign," he taunted, holding the bottle tantalizingly close to Lester's face yet just out of his reach, "how many hours has it been since your last hit? Two? Three?"

Tears streaming down his cheek, Lester stammered, "Nearly four, sir." His hands were trembling wildly, and Sindy stepped forward to calm him.

"Perhaps, you are a much tougher man than I originally gave you credit for," the Overlord complimented. "Few Euros can go four hours without. I congratulate you. And you," he declared, looking across at Sindy, "I congratulate you as well. You have done a fine job with our boy here."

"You work for this bastard?" Lester screamed, ripping Sindy's arm away from his shoulder in disgust. "For God's-sake, Sin, look what you have done to me!"

She met his impassioned outburst with glazed, disinterested eyes.

"What do you want from me, Ling?" Lester exclaimed, jumping to his feet as if he were about to attack the Overlord with his bare hands. Even as he lumbered awkwardly across the room in the Overlord's direction, Sindy slid her slender hand into her purse, gripping the stock of her 9mm Smith & Wesson. If things got out of hand now, she would have no choice but to take Lester out.

"What do I want?" Ling calmly repeated. "Secrets."

"Secrets? What secrets?" Lester probed, edging ever closer to the Overlord. "I have no secrets!" he emphasized, his eyes twitching feverishly.

"I realize that *you* have no secrets," Overlord Ling pointed out in a condescending tone. "You, my friend, are just a bug, a pimple, a tool."

"Who then?"

"The Senator."

"My grandfather?"

"Yes, your grandfather," Ling elaborated, enjoying himself immensely. "Senator Nate Matthews, Chairman of the Military Oversight Committee."

"*That* is what this is all about?" Lester mumbled, dumbfounded by the whole scenario.

"Yes, that is what this is all about. Secrets. And revenge."

"Revenge for what?" Lester cross-examined, more confused than ever.

"All in good time, my boy, all in good time. For now, let's start with the secrets."

"But my grandpa is an old man," Lester objected, retracing his steps back to his chair. "What secrets can he possibly have which would be...of interest...to you?" As his body began crashing through the edges of a cold turkey withdrawal, Lester's speech was becoming more and more slurred.

"I know you are in pain," Overlord Ling jeered, rattling the bottle of blue-devils in front of the addicted man, "but if only you would be just a bit more cooperative, I would promise to ease your pain."

"What...do you...want...from me?" Lester mumbled

haltingly as he began to gag. By this time, his entire body was being racked by a series of dry heaves.

"Secrets," the Overlord repeated, his moustache twitching horribly. Yet even as Ling tried to explain what it was he was after, Lester met his gaze with a blank stare.

"I think he's gonna pass out," Sindy interjected, motioning for Ling to come over to where the Ensign was seated.

"Damnit, man!" the Overlord boomed, grabbing Lester by the shoulders and jerking him back to alertness. "I want the military code ciphers that are in your grandfather's safe."

"Are you…kidding?" Lester cross-examined, his voice growing steadily weaker as his energy reserves sputtered out. "You want me to…steal…the *ciphers*?"

"Yes," the Overlord replied matter-of-factly as if taking them would be a piece of cake.

"For God's-sake…I don't even know where he keeps them."

"You'll be told when the time comes."

"Give me a pill," Lester urged defiantly with his last ounce of strength.

"No."

"I need…one," Lester pleaded, falling out of his chair and onto the floor.

Lying there prone on the carpet, the Naval officer was a pitiful sight to behold. But not above begging, he tried once more. "Please…Sindy…someone…give me what I need. I'll do whatever you ask."

"I know you will," the Overlord declared triumphantly, opening the bottle and dropping one of the blue capsules into Lester's outstretched hand. "I know you will," he repeated, handing Sindy one as well.

Even as the long-delayed blue-devil took effect and Lester descended into unconsciousness, Overlord Ling, his brother Chang, and their guest Silas Whetstone, slipped into the adjoining room of the suite to map out their next move. Thinking that Sindy was out cold along with Lester, they had no reason to expect that she would be listening in on their conversation through the partly opened door. The subject was how to get their hands on the Senator's enigmatic code book.

"So far as we have been able to determine, he never keeps it on his person except during a national emergency or else a political crisis overseas," Ling pointed out, making himself comfortable in one of the overstuffed chairs. He could almost taste his imminent success.

"What sort of a political crisis are we talking about?" Whetstone questioned, moving towards the darkest corner of the chamber. From his own brief tenure as Chief Executive, he knew a term as broad as "political crisis" could cover a wide gamut of situations.

"Like a military alert or else a coup d'état overseas. A hot spot somewhere," Ling explained, signaling Chang to pull the drapes shut. It was obvious from the way Whetstone was squinting that the bright Hawaiian sunshine was bothering him a great deal. "Otherwise, he keeps it either in the wall safe behind the bar in his D.C. office or else at his home in Maine somewhere."

Knowing that the location of the secret code book was privileged information, Whetstone asked, "How did you learn of this?"

"Harper works for me," Ling calmly replied, checking the gaunt man's reaction to the news.

"*Jonathan* Harper?" Whetstone confirmed, leaning forward in his seat. "The Director of U.S. Internal Intelligence? He is a *mole*? I can't believe it," Whetstone gasped flabbergasted. "Again I have underestimated you, Ling."

"Convenient, eh?" the Chinaman declared, enjoying his moment of victory. "Nevertheless, I am of the opinion that if the Senator's office is broken into and the safe is blown, it will do us more harm than good. In that event, all I expect will happen is that the ciphers will be changed as soon as the break-in is discovered. On the other hand, if we can manufacture a crisis…"

"What, like an invasion or an insurrection?" Whetstone interrupted, his eyes animated.

"Yes, something like that," Ling agreed, stealing a furtive glance at his brother. "Under *those* circumstances, the Senator will pull the book from the safe of his own accord. Then, if we can arrange for Lester to be there when he does, our blue-devil junkie can knock the Senator out, copy the thing, then slip it back into the old man's hand before he even wakes up."

"Interesting idea," Whetstone nodded, "but it'll never work. The old man, as you put it, is far too cunning to be duped that easily."

"Perhaps Lester can spike the Senator's nightcap," Ling suggested. "He can visit his grandfather this coming Spring when he graduates from the Academy. We can give him a pocket copier to take in there with him."

"They're not that close, the Senator and him," Whetstone objected, shaking his head as if the plan were doomed to failure.

"True, but the Senator could hardly refuse to meet with the boy; after all, he got him his commission to begin with."

"And what about her?" Whetstone inquired, motioning towards the other room where Sindy was supposedly resting peacefully on the couch.

"What *about* her?" Ling countered harshly. "Now that Lester's hooked, we don't need her anymore. She's yours to do with as you please. You may kill her for all I care."

"Don't you think Matthews here will object if suddenly his girl turns up missing?"

"*That* blue head? I hardly think so," Ling verified in a surprised tone. "So long as he gets his dope, he's our puppet from here on out."

"Spring is a long ways off," Whetstone remarked, counting the remaining six months on his fingers. "Maybe we should send him to see the Senator *now*."

"As you correctly pointed out just moments ago, the two of them aren't that close. Grandpa Matthews will be suspicious unless the boy comes to visit him for a very good reason—graduation will have to do."

"But I thought you told me that the old man was sick?" Whetstone carped. "Cancer or something. What if he dies before then? If that happens, we'll *never* get our hands on that book."

"He'll make it a few more months," Ling reassured, twisting the long whiskers of his fu-manchu. "He has a very good reason to try anyway."

"Why is that?"

"He's teaching the other boy, the Mister Goody Two-Shoes, the one he spirited off to Canada, how to launder money."

"I don't follow," Whetstone admitted, shifting uneasily in his chair. "I realize that the Matthews are stinky rich, but laundering money doesn't seem like the Senator's style."

"Maybe I am overstating the case," Ling asserted, "but Director Harper has had a wiretap on his comm since before McIntyre sprung you from the penitentiary, and every time he and the boy talk, the subject is almost always money and where to move it to next."

"So, what kind of diversion will make Nate pull the code book from his safe on cue?"

"Consider this: we have been shipping arms to Running Bear and his clan of potlatchers for weeks now. Maybe we can leak it to Coastal Defense that a shipment of megaflares and force guns is coming through. That might be enough to scramble the jetchops out of McChord Air Force Base and..."

"And to activate the defense web," Whetstone interrupted, completing the Overlord's thought, "the Senator would need to give the proper password. Since all the codes are bound to be encrypted, and since there's no way he could have committed every single one of them to memory, he would have to pull the code book from his safe to be sure of giving the right one." A mean-spirited grin erupted on Whetstone's face as he saw what the Overlord intended.

"Exactly. All we have to do is time the emergency for when Ensign Matthews can be there with his poor dying grandfather."

"Splendid. I'll leave in the morning with Lester and the girl. I'll see to it that he's dropped back in Alameda, then I'll manufacture some reason why she should accompany me back to D.C."

"I'll send Chang along with you at least as far as the coast—just in case Matthews gives you any trouble."

"Fine. It's agreed then."

Twenty-eight
Hike

With the first quarter having drawn to a close and everyone needing a break from their studies, the drive from the city up to Lake Louise passed almost in silence. Arriving at Nasha's house shortly before daybreak, Sam and Ravi had picked the girls up early, hoping to arrive at the lake soon enough to spend the whole day on the trail. Glancing over his shoulder now at Nasha in the back seat, Sam had to admit she looked ravishing in the early morning sun. Far classier, he thought, than Ravi's uninspiring girlfriend Siona, but looks didn't seem to make any difference to him. Actually, since the night of the Smoker when both of them had agreed to pledge Beta Sigma, Sam and Ravi had become quite chummy, this despite the fact that Ravi was as old as his brother Lester.

Following the gently winding road ever higher into the mountains, it wasn't long before their nostrils were filled with the refreshing scent of pine. As the elevation rose and as they got further and further away from the industrialized megalopolis, the air became imperceptibly cooler and its taste steadily improved. Sam had grown up in the midst of the flat, American Midwest, and except for his trip through Glacier National Park with Sara, the sights and the smells of the mountains were utterly new to him. Still, it was an enjoyable newness. Residing Underneath as he did now, Sam always felt as if he were panting, as if he could never quite catch his breath. No nightmare he had ever imagined as a youth could have prepared him for the reality of living on level minus-eight. As a consequence, it shouldn't have come as a surprise to anyone that he was the first to fling open the door of Ravi's gcar and make a beeline for the shore.

The lake was as smooth as glass, its placid surface undisturbed by so much as a ripple. Bounded on three sides by a majestic ring of mountains, Louise was constantly replenished by the melt off an ancient glacier, a glacier which also lent her its cold blue color. Like a copper penny which had been oxidized by the elements, she was a sapphire against the azure sky.

For the first mile, the graveled trail was perfectly level as it ran along one side of the lake just feet from the shore. But when the egg-shaped loch narrowed at the far end, the path began to climb steeply into the mountains, initially crossing through a vast stretch of fir and pine before bursting out into an open meadow swimming in alpine flowers. The fall season was at its peak, and the autumn colors were explosive.

Being more accomplished hikers, Ravi and Siona drew farther and farther ahead, though the truth be known, the widening gap between the two couples wasn't completely unintentional. Sam had asked Ravi beforehand to give him and Nasha a little space; privacy was something the two of them had had precious little of so far in their relationship.

The higher they climbed into the mountains, the more pristine the landscape became. Sam knew from his map that at the trail's end, some five miles away, lay a tea-house where they could share a hardy lunch together, but in the meanwhile it seemed as if they were the only humans to have ever ventured out this far from civilization. Somewhere in the distance the rumble of a tiny avalanche caught their attention as a few hundred cubic yards of snow shifted downward, obediently obliging the inexorable laws of gravity. High overhead, a golden eagle soared on a rising column of warm air, achieving heights a climber could only dream of. Across the valley, a waterfall glistened in the morning sun, its torrent pounding down the wall of the opposite mountain from a snowfield high above. It was as if Nasha and Sam were the sole beneficiaries of a singularly refreshing dream, and for the first time in months, Sam felt the way he had so often felt at Na-Cha-Tan. He was once again at ease with the world. Everything was okay. It occurred to him that maybe he had been right about God all along; like Na-Cha-Tan, this place was divine.

"Isn't it delicious?" Nasha remarked, taking a deep swallow from the incomparable ocean of clean air they were wading through. "I just adore these mountains. My brother says the high country is our heritage."

"I can see why," Sam agreed. "They are uncommonly beautiful."

"I take it you are unfamiliar with this land."

"America has many such mountains, but where I grew up…"

"Mizz-hurry?" she panted, leaning on her walking stick

to catch her wind.

Sam laughed. "Yes, Mizz-hurry. Where I grew up it was quite flat, and except for the occasional earthquake, not much else…"

"Earthquake?" she cross-examined in a shocked tone.

"The epicenter of the New Madrid fault lies not far from where I was born. More than fifteen years ago, when the fault last slipped, it collapsed a famous American landmark into the river, a magnificent monument called the St. Louis Arch."

"I know little of such matters," she asserted innocently, cocking her head skyward to see if she could again spy the eagle Sam had pointed out to her earlier.

"I was only three at the time, so it really wasn't of any consequence to me," he said, lacing his fingers with hers. "You, however, *are* of great importance to me. I have never met such a wonderful…"

"Sam," she spouted hesitantly, "I like you too. But we come from such different circles! We can't possibly have a future together! You come from a powerful and wealthy American family; I, from a poor, unimportant Amerind tribe. There is no point…"

"No point?" he challenged emphatically. "Nasha, I am not going to pretend that this will be easy, nor am I going to suggest that we will lead some sort of a fairy tale existence filled with eternal bliss. All I *am* saying is this: I have never met a kinder, more gentle soul than yours. And if it turns out that we indeed *have* no future together, then so be it. But that's even more of a reason for us to make the most of our present."

With that, Sam swept her up into his arms and kissed her full on the lips. Never before had he felt so right about a girl.

Breaking loose of his hold, Nasha slapped him hard across the cheek, a furious glare in her eyes. Her palms cocked on her hips, she stared at him defiantly.

Stung by her response, Sam turned from her, and began walking on towards the tea-house alone.

"Sam, I'm sorry," she cried after him. "I have never been kissed before...I mean...you should have *asked*, damnit!"

Ignoring her pleas for forgiveness, he kept right on walking.

"Sam, stop!" she called, clearly on the verge of tears. "Please."

Without turning to face her, he came to a halt about twenty yards away from where she stood. Seeing that he was stopping to give her a second chance, she ran to him with arms outstretched, her heart in her mouth.

"I am terrified of love," she conceded, wrapping her arms around him and pressing her head against his back. "You are everything I want in a man, but this is going much, much too fast for me."

"Life is far too short for us to take things slowly," Sam objected. "I have no idea how long we will be together, so the sooner we get started, the better."

"Then you must meet my family," she advised, taking his hand and squeezing it tightly.

"Now who's rushing *who*?" he chuckled, afraid she might be serious.

"Where I come from," she explained, throwing off her fears and bounding merrily ahead of him on the trail, "you don't marry the woman, you marry the tribe."

"What?" he gasped, doing his best to catch up with her. "Did you say *marry*?"

But already she was out of sight around the next bend, enjoying herself famously. It couldn't be more apparent that these two were in love.

By the time their day had come to a close, the four hikers were tired and happy. Though their legs were sore from the climb and the skin on their faces red from the wind and the sun, their spirits were as elevated as the lofty mountains they had just conquered. Yet, after eleven miles of wending their way along the twisting and rocky trails, they had worked up a ravenous appetite, and in their present condition, surely nothing could be more satisfying than a megadose of carbohydrates. After considering the long list of possible candidates, a vote was taken and three of them agreed that nothing ranked higher on the satiation scale than a bread and cheese fondue. While the girls showered in the public bathhouse, the boys waited in line for a table. Having a few minutes on their hands, Sam took Ravi aside to alert him to the finer points of preparing such a feast. It was the one recipe his grandmother Musette had made him learn in exact detail.

"The cheese fondue," Sam began, his mouth watering. "This culinary delight begins with a half-pound of gruyère per person, a jigger full of kirsch, two ounces of a processed cheese, a clove of garlic, two loaves of a well-crusted French bread, plus two cups of a dry white wine."

"What in the world is kirsch?" Ravi interrupted, his eyebrows knotted together in a question mark.

"Let's see: kirsch is a colorless, unaged brandy distilled from cherries. Now do let me finish. After wiping the inside of the fondue pot with the clove to cure it, the garlic should be minced and put in the jigger along with the brandy, a dash of pepper, a pinch of salt, a teaspoon of baking soda, and a teaspoon of potato flour or else cornstarch. The wine should then be heated in the pot, and handfuls of the grated cheese should be stirred in until each morsel is entirely melted. Allowing several minutes for some of the wine to cook off, the bubbling cauldron is slowly stirred with a long-necked wooden spoon until the wondrous emulsion has had a chance to thicken. At which point, the jigger of ingredients is then added to the brew, causing it to rise."

"Sounds delicious!"

"It is. To consume, skewer bite-sized chunks of fresh, hard-crusted bread onto long, thin forks and dip them, one at a time, into the fondue. Serve with plenty of chilled, dry white wine. Among the rituals considered part of the meal is always stirring the pot in the same direction—clockwise in the northern hemisphere—and always buying each of the gourmands another glass of wine anytime someone loses his portion of bread in the pot."

Smacking their lips at the thought of what was yet to come, but knowing they still had quite a wait before being seated, it wasn't long before their conversation turned to the subject of Ravi's dissertation. Although Ravi had done much of his undergraduate work back in his native Afghanistan, with that country's continuing civil war, he had transferred to the Calgary Institute to complete work on his Master's degree. His thesis concerned a highly technical matter Sam knew little about. Nevertheless, he was curious to learn more.

"The science of game theory helps us to understand how people act," Ravi began, his swarthy skin glowing with the pride of knowing this subject well. "More importantly, it helps us to understand how they *react*."

"Game theory? Your dissertation is about *games*?!" Sam questioned, his face twisted into a disbelieving grin.

"Most decisions in business, in politics, in war, are a function of how you believe your opponent will respond in the *second* round to what you have done in the *first*. And knowing that there *will* be a response in the second round, affects what you will actually do in the *first* round. And so on to subsequent rounds. It is linkages and it is feedback. In a zero-sum game such as poker, the grand total of all the players' losses exactly offset the sum total of their gains; in a positive-sum game like free enterprise, the total of all the gains *exceeds* the total of all the losses; finally, in a negative-sum game such as war, the sum total of all the losses exceeds the sum total of all the gains."

"I guess I don't see the point of all this. There *is* a point, isn't there?" Sam complained, his empty stomach growling.

"Give me a minute," Ravi bargained. "The simplest and the earliest game is what we economists call the Prisoner's Dilemma. Consider this scenario: Two armed robbers are captured and jailed separately. They are each told that if neither confesses, each one will serve just one year in prison. If, on the other hand, only *one* confesses and if that confession helps to convict the other, the squealer will go free while the silent party will serve ten years. If *both* confess, however, *both* will get four year terms. I ask you," Ravi challenged, gloating a bit, "what will happen? Remember, the prisoners are jailed separately and cannot communicate with one another."

Scratching the stubble on his chin as he prepared his answer, Sam replied, "Let us call our prisoners Able and Baker. I would argue that no matter which strategy Baker chooses, Able gains by confessing. If Able confesses and Baker *doesn't*, Able goes free; if Able confesses and so does Baker, Able gets four years versus the ten he *would* have gotten if Baker had confessed while Able had kept silent."

"Precisely!" Ravi bubbled as the wait for a table gradually shortened. "And in fact, faced with these tradeoffs *both* prisoners will confess and *both* will end up going to jail for four years. This is what we call the Prisoner's Dilemma."

"Land's-sakes!" Sam exclaimed excitedly. "What in tarnation does this have to do with economics?"

"Well, consider the case of a producers' cartel, for instance. To control output, the cartel sets production ceilings for each member. So long as no one cheats on their quota, everyone cleans up. But the fly in the ointment is that a loan cheater will gain even *more* profit if he defects from the cartel and cuts his price. Of course, if he is successful in his defection, before long cheating becomes rampant."

"But what if Able and Baker could find a way to communicate?" Sam countered, keeping an eye out for the girls. Spying Nasha from across the parking lot, he motioned for her and Siona to come join them in line outside the fondue shop.

"If the prisoners could communicate," Ravi replied, "they would surely not confess."

"Or what if they made a binding commitment to one another beforehand?" Sam asked, shifting nervously from one sore foot to the other.

"Like what?"

"Oh, I don't know. What if Baker promised to kill Able if he confessed?" Sam postulated.

"If Able believed the threat was genuine, he would not confess. But in that instance," Ravi elaborated, "the rules of the Prisoner's Dilemma would no longer apply. Now we have a *new* game called Tit-for-Tat. This strategy begins in a cooperative or else a silent mode. That is, most players prefer to wait for an opponent's first move and then respond to it, rather than going first themselves. Once a player defects, however, his opponent echoes what his adversary did in the previous round. That is, people, businesses, even nations, respond in kind to how they have been treated in the past. If you were treated well by someone in the first round, you are apt to treat *them* well in the next round; if you have previously been treated poorly, you will subsequently treat *them* poorly. Given such a strategy you will switch your behavior as many times as your opponent does."

"That sounds an awful lot like something my grandfather once tried to explain to me," Sam remarked, silently nodding to Nasha as she and Siona joined them in line, "only *he* called it the Brazen Rule. Do unto others as they have done unto you."

"Was he an economist?" Ravi asked, pecking Siona lightly on the cheek. For perhaps the first time since they met, Sam saw in Siona what must have caught Ravi's attention long ago. Beneath her plain-jane exterior was a hearty, fun-loving Scottish girl. It had taken Sam awhile to learn to pronounce her name correctly, but now he thought he had it right: Shona.

"Is he an economist, you ask? No, a Senator," Sam admitted, taking Nasha's hand and drawing her near. After her shower she smelled delicious, and he was all of a sudden conscious of his own less than perfect aroma.

"If your grandpa is a Senator, he knows all about games. Countries play them. Corporations play them. Politicians, most assuredly, play them."

By now the girls had been drawn into the discussion and Nasha offered the following. "Okay, fellas, here is a game you two economists can play: Imagine that you and a group of your friends are dining at a fine restaurant with an unspoken agreement to divide the check evenly following the meal."

"You mean like us?" Ravi teased.

"No, you cheapskate, *not* like us," Nasha objected. "In the first place, we have agreed beforehand what it is we are ordering, and in the second place, we have agreed who among us is going to pay for it. Now hush your mouth and give me a chance to explain," she scolded, starting her narration over. "As I was saying: You and your friends are dining out at an expensive restaurant and you have agreed to divide the check evenly among all the members of your party. The question is: What should you order? A modest chicken entrée or the pricey lamb chops? The house wine or the Cabernet Sauvignon '83? If you are extravagant you could enjoy a superlative dinner at a bargain price."

"But if *everyone* in the party reasons the same way and if *everyone* splurges, the group will end up with a hefty bill to pay," Siona correctly pointed out.

"Exactly my point," Nasha interjected. "Why should others settle for pasta when someone else is having grilled pheasant at their expense?"

"So what should we call this game?" Ravi interrupted, wondering if he could somehow incorporate it into his dissertation.

"How 'bout calling it the Unscrupulous Diner's Dilemma?" Sam offered, half jokingly.

"Good name, "Nasha agreed. "But think about it: the Unscrupulous Diner's Dilemma, as you have so aptly named it, typifies a whole class of serious problems we face as a society today. Why should I work hard if I can easily collect welfare? Why should I conserve power if my neighbor doesn't? Why should I not make full use of free medic care when everyone else does?"

"Bright girl you've got there, Sam," Ravi acknowledged approvingly. "I am definitely beginning to see her point. This really *is* about cooperation, isn't it?"

"Absolutely," Nasha nodded, rendering an impertinent curtsy. "And promoting the common good. In the Unscrupulous Diner's Dilemma, the common good is achieved by minimizing the amount of the check. Individuals are said to cooperate if they choose a less expensive meal; they are said to defect if they spare no expense—for everybody else, that is. Each individual can choose to either contribute to the common good, or else they can shirk and hitch a 'free ride' on the sacrifices of all the others. When an individual realizes that the costs of cooperating exceed their share of the added benefits, they will rationally choose to defect and become a free rider. Because every person faces the same tradeoffs, all members of the group will eventually defect."

"My Lord," Ravi gasped as if a light had just come on inside his head, "it is the Prisoner's Dilemma in a new guise!"

"Wait a minute," Siona declared, raising her voice so she would be sure to be heard. "If the players know they will repeat the same game with the same group on *another* night, the situation changes."

"Correct," Nasha acknowledged. "Each individual must consider the repercussions of a decision to cooperate or to defect. A diner who goes out with a group just once is more likely to splurge at the expense of the others than one who goes out with the same group of friends repeatedly."

"And in a *large* group," Ravi interjected as Sam turned to speak with the maître d' of the fondue shop, "a player can reasonably expect that the effect of his action, good *or* bad, will be diluted. That is why, for groups beyond a certain size, cooperation becomes unsustainable."

"But the longer the players expect the game to continue, the more likely they are to cooperate," Siona noted as the hostess showed them to a table near the fireplace.

"Which reinforces the commonsense notion that cooperation is most likely to succeed with *small* groups, especially those which are engaged in lengthy interactions," Ravi summarized, sounding like the economics professor he hoped to become. "Like families, for instance."

"Thus," Nasha asserted, trying to sound professorial as well, "what have we learned from the Dilemma of the Unscrupulous Diner? First, that small groups are more likely to secure voluntary cooperation than large ones, and second, that the optimum size depends on how long the individuals expect to remain part of the same group."

"More and more, the Unscrupulous Diner's Dilemma is beginning to sound like Ravi's Tit-for-Tat scenario," Sam pointed out as he studied the menu. "A person will cooperate if at least some critical fraction of the group is also cooperating. Otherwise, he will defect and buy the pheasant under glass. You know, as I think about it, this idea Nasha has cooked up might also tell us something about the underlying dynamics of a mob or even a stock market panic."

"You have got to be kidding!" she intoned, not seeing the connection.

"Hear me out. Consider a demonstration to overthrow the government. Once the number of demonstrators reaches some critical number, *everyone* defects. That is, the rebels know that as the number of demonstrators rise, the risk to each individual protestor declines, even as the potential for the group's overall success increases. Likewise, in a financial panic," Sam continued vigorously, "the same phenomenon is at work. Once the number of panicked sellers reaches some critical mass, it explodes in an uncontrollable rout."

"My Lord," Ravi exclaimed, "you have just described Chaos Theory! Not only that, I think you two characters have just written my dissertation for me!"

"We'll send you a bill," Sam quipped, winking at Nasha over his water glass. "Though I must admit, there is still one thing which worries me," he remarked darkly. "The tearing down of a bull market or the collapsing of a civilization might take only a matter of hours or days; the building back up, however, might drag on forever. It took ten *years* for the markets to recover from the crash of 2345; it took a *millenium* to recover from the fall of the Roman Empire. How long will it take to rebuild things if it all happens to fall apart again now?"

"Listen, you unscrupulous diner, don't be so morbid," Siona complained. "Aren't we ready to order yet? I'm starving."

"You're right, of course," Sam nodded, tipping his hand in the direction of the waiter. "Where are my manners? Garçon! Garçon!"

Twenty-nine
Closure

From the moment the suborb lifted off from Lihue in the Hawaii Free State with the three of them counted among the six hundred passengers onboard, Sindy had made up her mind that at the first hint of trouble she would strike at Silas Whetstone with deadly intent. She had overheard Ling give Whetstone the okay to kill her, and she couldn't help but remember how the gaunt man had acted towards her in their first and only face-to-face confrontation. Moreover, she knew she could no longer count on Lester to intervene on her behalf. Drowning as he was in his own well of self-pity, Lester blamed her for his predicament—and with good reason. When Whetstone informed Lester that she would be returning to D.C. with him for a few days, the Ensign didn't raise so much as an objection. He just shrugged his shoulders and went back to whatever it was he was doing at the time; so long as he had a few weeks' supply of blue-devils in his pocket, her whereabouts were no longer of any concern to him whatsoever.

Though she had initially decided to bolt just as soon as they exited the terminal at National Airport, on the short hop over from Oakland to D.C. she changed her mind. By then it had become abundantly clear to her that if she was ever to be rid of this horrid man, she would have to take matters into her own hands. With that objective in mind, she had hatched a second, more confrontational plan of attack; unlike her first strategy, this one almost demanded that she accompany Whetstone at least as far as his flat.

When they finally arrived at his apartment two hours later, it was just as grim and just as dark as she had first remembered it. And as she expected, he started in on her almost as soon as the door closed shut behind them.

"Now that we no longer have the distraction of your young stud around," Whetstone leered, his cheeks seeming more hollow than ever, "perhaps you and I can finish what we started several months back when I first hired you."

"I think not," she replied, holding tight to her handbag. "You are not my type." Despite being a drug addict, and despite being an amoral alley cat, Sindy was nevertheless quite resourceful: as always, her clutch was packed with everything a girl in her business required to stay one step ahead of the unsavory characters she serviced.

"If you're not here to sleep with me, then why in the hell did you even bother to come up to my apartment?" he snarled indignantly, looking her over very closely. Out of the direct light of day, her blond hair and her big breasts made for a rather attractive combination, a fact that he couldn't put out of his mind.

"A suborb is a rather public place for a murder, wouldn't you agree?" she calmly answered, drawing her 9mm Smith & Wesson from her purse. Gripping the stock tightly with both hands, she snapped the full 15-shot clip firmly into place.

"Murder?" Whetstone taunted, cool as ever. "Hah! You talk tough, bimbooker, but I know what a girl like you *really* wants."

"I don't think you have a clue."

Folding his spindly legs beneath him as he sat down in his favorite armchair, the once-upon-a-time President laced his long, thin fingers together in his lap. "Tell me then, Sinful, what exactly are you after?"

"How do I get next to Jonathan Harper?" she probed, the gun aimed directly at Whetstone's belly.

"You can't. And even if you could, what would the likes of you want with a man like Director Harper?"

"I heard every word that you and that yellow-skinned bastard said back in Kauai," Sindy indicated in her husky voice.

"That's too bad," Whetstone grunted, rising slowly, almost leisurely, to his feet. "That means I can't let you leave this room alive."

"As if you ever really planned to. Hell, it was your intention to kill me all along," she countered, tightening her grip on the Smith & Wesson.

"True. But I was hoping that we could've had some fun together first," he jeered, grabbing for her with his arms outstretched.

"Stay away from me, you bastard!" she commanded, deftly moving to one side without ever taking her eyes off him.

Disregarding her instructions, the madman advanced once again. This time, there was a deranged grin splattered across his face.

"I mean it," she warned, hesitating to fire. "Stay away or else!"

"Or else what?" he yelled, lunging at her for a second time. In his heart he didn't believe she had what it took to kill a man. He was wrong.

"This!" she shrieked, jerking the trigger back twice at point blank range.

Though the two explosions were deafening, it seemed as if the pair of bullets passed right through the man without doing him any harm. When he kept on coming, she squeezed off yet another round. This time he tumbled to the floor, a gush of blood streaming from his perforated chest.

Breathing a sigh of relief that it was finally over, Sindy instinctively slipped on the pair of latex gloves she always carried with her in her purse, and began rifling through his apartment. Though she had high hopes of finding either some cash or else some drugs, she came up empty-handed on both scores. Disappointed, she moved next to the comm, encoding the number for information.

The robotic voice intoned, "Please state your party's name and exchange. Be sure to speak clearly, and for better service, always spell the last name first and the first name last."

Sindy did as she was told. "Senator Nate Matthews, M-A-T-T-H-E-W-S, N-A-T-E, District of Columbia."

"One moment please," the machine replied, and no more than an instant later, the Senator's number was displayed on the narrow LED strip running along the bottom edge of the comm. Quickly jotting down the eight digits on a scrap of paper, Sindy tore off her latex gloves and exited the apartment almost at a run. Darkness had already fallen over the city, and she was eager to be away from the horrible man she had just shot and back out on the streets where she belonged. Her heart pounding, she raced up a nearby alley to a public comm at the next corner. There, she could place the call unobserved. Despite the late hour, it went through almost immediately.

"I'm sorry, but the Senator isn't in just now," the night-operator explained though Sindy knew it was a lie. "May I take a message? Perhaps he can call you in the morning."

"Listen you, tell your boss that Silas Whetstone is on the line and that he must speak with the Senator right away," Sindy replied, doing her best to get around Nate's obstructionist secretary.

Despite her sensible precaution in using a public comm to make this call, it was doubtful Sindy understood the full magnitude of the mistake she was now making. While she had admittedly overheard Ling say that Director Harper had placed a tap on the Senator's line, she probably had no idea that a call could be traced backwards to its source or that a voice-print of the caller could be matched easily against any existing police records. Inasmuch as Sindy had several previous arrests for hooking, those errors in judgment were about to cost her.

"I *said* he's not in," the receptionist insisted in a menopausal tone.

"Tell him, you witch," Sindy repeated just as insistently. The comm fell silent, and as she stood in the booth waiting to see if her words would have the desired effect, Sindy imagined that the woman at the other end of the line had a huge bun of hair propped up upon the top of her head, something on the order of a hornet's nest in size. But even before she could complete this laughable picture in her mind, a new voice came on the line.

"Whetstone, you have got your nerve calling me after all these years," Nate boomed in a peeved tone before Sindy even had a chance to introduce herself.

"Senator, we need to talk," she declared emphatically.

"Who are you?" Nate implored, not recognizing the girl's voice.

"Senator, my name is Sindy Foster. I apologize for the

subterfuge, but for the right price, I believe I can save you a great deal of embarrassment. Perhaps even make you a hero!"

"Young lady, I'm much too old to play games," Nate stated simply, wishing his accursed cancer could be solved. "I thought this had something to do with Silas Whetstone? Who are you anyway?"

"All I can say to you at this point is, I can prove Director Harper is a traitor. That must be worth *something* to a man in your position."

Senator Nate Matthews did not become one of the country's most powerful men by being lazy or stupid. To the contrary, he had attained the lofty position of Chairman of the Military Oversight Committee by constantly keeping one step ahead of the opposition, never letting his guard down, and remaining eternally vigilant. Granted, as he had gotten older he had made the occasional blunder, but he had more than made up for those few by being endlessly suspicious. He hadn't trusted Harper to assign the right person to watch over Sam at Na-Cha-Tan, so he had bought Sara's loyalty himself; he hadn't trusted Sara to do an adequate job, so he had brought in Officer Jenkins as backup; and once Sam was safely across the border, he had asked Jenkins to assemble a team to keep tabs on Lester. This he had done. Only, given Officer Jenkins' considerable responsibilities, reading the surveillance team's reports was not of the highest priority. Thus, it wasn't until just earlier today that Jenkins had called the Senator with the news. Though he had no way of knowing the full extent of the conspiracy, Jenkins had just informed Nate that a man in uniform meeting Lester's description had flown out of Oakland onboard a military suborb and, along with a woman, had been to the fifteenth floor penthouse apartment of a downtown hotel in Lihue, an apartment leased on a long-term basis to the Chinese consulate. Clearly, something was afoot, but what? Maybe this girl he had hanging on the other end of the line could provide him with some answers.

"Do you know what you are saying?" Nate cross-checked, stunned by her allegation that she had proof Director Harper was a traitor.

"Yes, I do," Sindy claimed. "Can we meet or not?"

"Yes, by all means," Nate replied, tickled to have some dirt on Harper for a change, instead of it being the other way around. "Is the day after tomorrow satisfactory? At my office?"

"I'll be there."

Hanging up the receiver, Sindy turned to face the night. The humidity of summer had evaporated, and a chilly breeze was now sweeping in off the Potomac. Hailing a taxi, she was back to her old haunt within minutes. Although being a bimbooker wasn't a very glamorous trade, at least she had the advantage of being able to pick and choose her own hours and select her own clients.

In her absence, another girl had commandeered her usual spot on the street, but with a menacing wave of her Smith & Wesson, Sindy shooed the interloper away and reclaimed her piece of the sidewalk. As the night dragged on, she realized a great deal had changed in the four months since she had last been here. And with so many new faces out trying to score, Sindy went out of her way to be extra careful about whom she did business with that evening. Nonetheless, on her third trick of the night, she knew she had found herself a peck full of trouble.

"I understand that you have been looking for me," the trim, good-looking fellow began as she unbuttoned her blouse and loosened her bra. He was much more athletic than most of her johns, and she was impressed by his nice build.

"I have been looking for you all my life," she cooed, playing her part to the hilt.

"Is that so?" he asked, loosening his tie. Curiously, he

hadn't yet removed his suit coat. "Isn't your name Sindy?"

"Yes, but you can call me Sin if you please," she answered, her husky voice softer than usual. "Now let me unbuckle your drawers there, big fella," she mouthed lecherously, reaching for the bulge in his trousers.

"Do you know who I am?" he asked, even as she bent to unclasp his belt.

Rising to look him squarely in the eye, the bimbooker took a moment to study the hard lines in his face. Her mouth was just inches from his when she asked, "Have I done you before?"

Reacting furiously to her offhand remark, the mysterious man backhanded her viciously across the face. His knuckles left a deep, red welt on her cheek.

"Look," she yelped, jumping backward, "I do sex, not violence. Can't you men understand that?" she groused, yanking her pistol from her clutch for the second time tonight.

"It's too late for understanding, little lady. You are in way over your head," he mocked, pulling his own mammoth gun from the shoulder holster beneath his coat. It was a big cannon of a gun, a .357 Magnum, and it was now in the hands of an expert.

"Who *are* you?" she cried, suddenly afraid.

"I am Jonathan Harper, the Director of Internal Intelligence. I understand you have been spreading nasty rumors about me, that you believe I am some sort of a traitor."

Even before the color could drain from Sindy's face, he had pulled the trigger, hitting the desperate woman in her gun hand and sending the Smith & Wesson flying across the floor. She screamed out in pain.

"Now," he snarled, reaching down to pick up her gun, "we are gonna do this real nice and slow. Don't worry, my dear, that first bullet won't kill you. Nor will the second. Not even the third. But you *will* die before we're done here today, that I promise. Now tell me, little lady, to whom have you been talking?"

Even as he spoke, Jonathan Harper loosened his tie a notch further. The Director knew he was going to enjoy this. To begin with, he had been furious to learn that Officer Jenkins had just "happened" to be at Camp Na-Cha-Tan without his knowledge, and at the time of the two murders, no less. That Jenkins had been there at all, could only have meant one thing: he was there at the behest of Senator Matthews. And if that were true, the Senator must have been suspicious of him even before Sindy had called accusing him of treachery. Who else besides Jenkins would the Senator have told? Harper mused, rolling up his sleeves as if he meant to get to work. Agent Logan? President McIntyre? It was anybody's guess, but the way Harper figured it, the time was now at hand to begin cleaning up loose ends—beginning with one Sindy Foster.

Regrettably, the Senator had reached that age in life where scanning the obituaries for departed friends was as much a part of his daily routine as checking the business pages for stock quotes or the sports pages for baseball scores. Though he wouldn't have known her face if he had passed her on the street, her name was indelibly etched in his mind. And when he opened the paper to that page, there it was in big, bold, block-letters: Sindy Foster, age 21, drifter, address unknown. Found dead in the alley behind the Savoy Hotel from multiple gunshot wounds. According to Police Chief Andrews, the murder would be treated as a Class 5 homicide; considering the transient nature of the victim and her long list of priors, there would be no investigation. Readers were directed to contact J.H. at Internal Intelligence with any information as to next of kin or as to the circumstances surrounding her death.

Stunned by the news, Nate just sat there staring at the paper, a blank gaze permeating his old and drawn face. If there had been any doubt in his mind before regarding Sindy's story, it was now all but erased. Unfortunately, whatever evidence she might have had concerning Harper's guilt had died right along with her. If the Director was to be removed from office, it would now have to be by other means.

Letting his eyes drift further on down the page, Nate had the second shock of the morning. *This* face was unmistakable: Silas Whetstone, age 82, former U.S. President, impeached shortly after assuming office. Found dead in his own apartment from multiple gunshot wounds...

As perhaps no other man in America could, Senator Nate Matthews knew there had to be a connection between these two deaths and that Jonathan Harper was undoubtedly that link. The nefarious man had to be eliminated, but how?

When the comm rang moments later, the Senator had his answer.

Thirty
Revolt

Shivering in the cold, still air of a brisk November night, Sam did what he could to pinpoint where their plan to GA pledgemaster Frank Rasmussen had first gone astray. It had all seemed so orderly, so sensible, at the start, but now as he and the others trundled their way along the road back into town with tears still streaming from their watery eyes, Sam went carefully over the events of the past few hours, analyzing their mistakes.

Going all the way back to the night of the Smoker when he and Ravi had first decided to join Beta Sigma, Sam had figured that pledging could be nothing if not good-natured fun. Only it wasn't always so. Much as the Ordeal had been designed to prepare a Boy Scout to take the reins as a confident leader, pledging Beta Sigma was supposed to build character. Yet, to accomplish these most noble of ends, the Actives often found it necessary to apply some rather harsh methods.

For weeks already, they had been deliberately ordering the members of the pledge class around like a bunch of serfs, seeking to provoke this crop of would-be members in much the same way as they themselves had once been provoked as pledges. Escort so and so back to her dorm, get her kiss print on your pillow case, meet the President of the University, wear yellow shorts every Thursday no matter how low the temperature drops, run buck naked through level minus-six singing the national anthem, chant the pledge cheer one hundred times in a row, do fifty situps in the quad dressed only in your skivvies, recite the Greek alphabet on a match, do sixty pushups, do an airplane on the floor in the lunch room, and so on and so forth.

Yet, behind all of this ritualistic abuse there lay a deeper purpose. Though at times these intentionally demeaning antics seemed nonsensical, they were meant to draw the five pledges closer together against a common enemy, to test their resolve and meld them into a single cohesive unit. Hazing was intended to elicit a response, and as might be expected, tensions between pledge and Active had been mounting towards the point of ignition for days. It couldn't have been more obvious that as a direct outgrowth of this constant barrage of belittling taunts, something had to give sooner or later. It proved to be sooner. Earlier this evening, to be precise.

Sensing that the pledges had had enough harassment and were on the verge of mutiny, the Actives had chosen this, the final Friday night kegger before the BeHolden Day break, as the time to purposefully pile on the pressure and try to bring it all to a head. Years of experience had taught them that when the pledges joined hands together in a revolt, the Actives had succeeded in their goal of building the newcomers into a unified team. They also knew that the retaliatory venting nearly always played itself out the same way—in the form of a dump aimed exclusively at the initiates' pledgemaster. As Sam recalled it now, his pledge class had reached the breaking point just under two hours ago.

Like so many previous shindigs, tonight's kegger was held in a drab, oversized lounge located on level minus-two. Although the community room was spartan and Beta Sigma had to share it from time to time with some of the less respectable fraternities on campus, it was conveniently situated close enough to the surface to make it easily accessible by guests and members alike. That Beta Sigma could even hold such a function on university property was a testament to the high regard in which they were held and to their wholesome reputation.

Yet despite the favored setting, as the evening wore on, and as everyone got progressively more drunk, the Actives became steadily more belligerent. For their part, the pledges rewarded their rudeness by becoming ever more recalcitrant. The tug-of-war finally culminated with Ravi's refusal to get yet another beer for the polluted Active named Laughlin. When Brother Laughlin followed this up with a threat to blackball the disobedient pledge at the upcoming induction vote, the entire pledge class balked, threatening to quit unless Laughlin recanted, which he did not. With Ravi and Sam leading the way, the pledges marched promptly from the kegger en masse, ready to do battle. The intended target of their fury was pledgemaster Frank Rasmussen.

Being an upperclassman and a Mountie to boot, pledgemaster Rasmussen was one of the few members well-enough-off to live above ground. And having all been asked at one time or another to come to Big Frank's apartment to perform some menial housekeeping chore for him, the group of five pledges had no trouble whatsoever finding his place in the dark. Figuring that the kegger would break up soon, they hoped to snatch him in the parking lot outside his apartment or else on his way upstairs.

Now, as they laid in wait outside the man's flat, they each took turns stomping their feet to stay warm. Because their pledgemaster had always given them the impression of being a lone-wolf type, and because he had never brought a date with him to a fraternity function, it never occurred to the fivesome that he wouldn't be coming home to his apartment alone that night. Even if it *had* crossed their minds, it certainly hadn't occurred to them that there would be a good-looking girl hanging from his arm, a girl who they thought was far more attractive than appropriate for a rough-looking man such as Frank. Yet, instead of doing the polite thing and waiting until she went home for the night, they moved in on the pair right away, intending to do everything in their power to embarrass their pledgemaster in front of this sharp-looking woman. Looking back on it now, this sense of false bravado had to rank as their first big blunder of the evening.

Quarter-inch rope and duct tape in hand, the quintet of pledges bounded up the stairs of Frank's apartment building in pursuit of their quarry, bursting in upon the couple necking in his apartment. As soon as Frank saw their angry faces, he knew what was afoot; his blonde-headed date, however, did not have a clue.

Having heard tales of gruesome satrap wars, and unable to fathom what was going on around her, she thought a genuine kidnapping was in progress. In a sense she was correct, only being a foreign exchange student from SKANDIA and being completely unfamiliar with the pranks fraternity brothers often played on one another, she could not possibly know that this was a special type of abduction called a "dump." In this most ancient of all fraternity games, the object was to take by force, if necessary, either an Active or a pledge, tie them up, and dump them somewhere on the outskirts of the city without an identicard and without any cash or other means of getting back home. Understandably frightened by the sudden appearance of these five strange men in her boyfriend's apartment, men who were obviously intending to abscond with her companion in the middle of the night, this poor, confused girl acted out of instinct, mounting a devastating offensive against the interlopers.

Jumping onto the kitchen counter and flinging open the doors to Frank's pantry, this wild, beautiful woman snatched a brand new bag of white flour from the shelf and stood poised above them, her arms cocked back over her shoulders. Before any of the hapless pledges knew what had hit them, she then plunged the five-pound bag of flour down upon their heads, knocking Ravi to the floor and spewing a thin coating of powder throughout Frank's tiny flat. Then, before anyone could make a move to stop her, the tall SKANDIAN female unleashed a second barrage, chucking drinking glasses at them from the cabinet above the stove. One by one the expensive goblets crashed against the floor and against the walls, shattering into a million slivers of razor sharp glass and threatening to land them all in the hospital by the time she was finished.

Neither Frank nor his kidnappers could have anticipated such a fury, so before it could get any further out of hand and she had a chance to destroy his apartment entirely, Frank offered to surrender peaceably with just one stipulation: with it being so cold outside, he be permitted to retrieve his long overcoat from the closet in his bedroom. This act of compassion was the pledges' second big mistake of the evening.

Not only was Frank a weekend Guardsman with the Royal Canadian Mounted Police, he was partial to absconding with matériel from the QM—knives, manual firebombs, tear gas, ammo—whatever he could get his hands on. When he went to his closet to get his overcoat, Frank shrewdly grabbed a canister of tear gas as well. Shoving the cylindrical container up the sleeve of his coat where it couldn't be seen by his kidnappers, he meekly allowed himself to be escorted from the flat over the vehement protests of his companion. Explaining to her in his fractured SKANDIA that everything would be okay, Frank submissively tagged along as he and his five captors made their way outside and across the parking lot to Ravi's waiting gcar.

Intending to drop Big Frank off in the middle of a tilled-under cornfield a couple of miles past the edge of town, the pledges drove well beyond the farthest entrance to the Underneath before slowing down to stop. Even though pledgemaster Frank was well aware that he would have to walk all the way back to campus on his own, never once during the trip did he seem perturbed or upset by his predicament. In fact, he appeared unconcerned, sitting complacently, even docilely, between Sam and another pledge in the backseat of Ravi's auto. This alone should have made them suspicious, but not until they reached the drop-off point and slowed to shove him out onto the pavement did all hell break loose.

Pulling the canister of tear gas out from where it had been hidden up his sleeve, Frank burst open the seal and dropped the pressurized cylinder onto the front seat. Leaping from the gcar with a big grin plastered across his face, Frank slammed the door shut behind him, trapping the hapless pledges inside the vehicle along with the exploding flood of noxious fumes. Caught completely unaware by this sudden turn of events, the pledges fell blindly from the sedan and out onto the roadside coughing uncontrollably.

Seizing his moment of opportunity, Frank swallowed a deep breath of fresh air before plunging back into the now vacant gcar. Beside himself at having successfully turned the tables on his would-be abductors, he proceeded to drive off, leaving the shocked pledges abandoned several miles from the outskirts of the city.

Bested at their own game by their intended victim, the five would-be Actives couldn't help but burst out laughing. It was an uproarious, cathartic sort of laugh which signified, in a manner of speaking, that things couldn't be better.

Thinking about it now as he and the others lumbered along the road back towards town, their eyes still smarting from the tear gas, Sam realized that, although they had failed miserably in one sense of the word, they had been successful in another. Because the pledges had executed their revolt in concert like a team, the experience—while an embarrassment—was not a total loss. For better or for worse, the tension between Active and pledge, between lord and serf, between big brother and little kid, had been broken once and for all. Now the pledges knew that so long as they acted in unison, they could no longer be individually intimidated by the threat of being blackballed at the vote ten days hence. As in the tale of the three musketeers, a "one for all and all for one" mentality had finally drawn them together into a single cohesive unit.

Despite all the taunting and all the ridicule they had had to endure these past weeks, the pledges had ultimately found within themselves the backbone, the esprit de corps, to stand together as a team. And *this* was what the Actives wanted to see; *this* was what pledging was all about. Now Sam and the others were ready to assume their rightful places as full-fledged members of the fraternity.

Thirty-one
Sara Redux

The call Senator Nate Matthews received yesterday morning had been from Agent Logan. She too had seen the pair of obituaries in the paper and had likewise drawn the connection between them. All she had said to him before slamming down the receiver was, "Get the hell out of there! Your line is tapped! He'll be coming for you next!" Though the exchange couldn't have lasted more than three seconds, it was long enough.

Needing no introduction to recognize her voice, Nate had immediately decided she must be right. Already on the edge from what he had read in the paper, he grabbed for his knobby, pine cane and for his aged Luger, and bolted from his plush Senate chambers as quickly as a man in his condition could. Forsaking the privacy of the VIP elevator, he opted for the crowded public lift instead. Though he wasn't sure exactly why, a sixth sense told him not to ride down to the lobby alone, that he would be safer if he kept others around him.

In the few moments it took for him to descend the six floors to the ground level of the Senate Office Building, he made up his mind that his next stop would be his house in Maine, the house Flix had willed to him when he died. Although it was more secluded than his homestead in Farmington, in Nate's estimation, the beach house was a far better spot to hole up for a few days until he could sort things out.

No sooner had he exited the lift and crossed the lobby intending to have the desk clerk summon his limousine, than she had been there, loitering by the door, acting like a lost tourist.

"Where are you headed?" Sara had whispered to him discretely, her dark eyes scrutinizing each face in the crowd.

"To my place on the coast of Maine," he had returned just as quietly.

"Good," she had whispered back, "I'll look up its location in the Agency's files, and I'll meet you there tomorrow morning." Then they had turned and gone their separate ways.

Tomorrow was now today.

The aged house was more a manor than a house, more an oceanside estate than a mere home. It was situated on a secluded stretch of beach below Bar Harbor, a stretch of desolate sand and wave-splashed rocks. Mount Desert Island itself was a wind-swept pocket of land sweet with the smell of balsam fir, stiff sea breezes, and old money. The island was unique in many ways, not the least of which was that only in the protected waters surrounding Acadia National Park could the humpback whale still be found within sight of land.

Boulders dotted the shore below the house and a pine-tree windbreak swept along the northern edge of the property. On one side of the manor, the screened-in porch had a fabulous view of the bay; on the other side, its enormous picture window framed an equally stunning glimpse of Cadillac Mountain. The weather this morning was cool but not frigid, and a delicate fog hung over the bay. Normally, on a day as splendid as this one, Nate would be content to sit for hours enjoying the quiet solitude of the sea, only today he was agitated. Today, he had no time to marvel at the spray of the ocean as succeeding waves exploded through the underwater cave at Thunder Hole and up into the air; no time to watch for the telltale discharge from the spout of a giant cetacean frolicking in the bay; no time to enjoy a roadside lobster bake complete with a cup of melted butter and a luscious corn on the cob. Today, all he could do was sit and wait.

He had expected her to enter by the front door when she arrived, so when there was all of a sudden a noise at the back, he sprang to his feet and grabbed for his cane, checking to be sure it was loaded as he went. Long ago, even before it had come into his possession, the walking stick had been hollowed-out inside and a rifle barrel had been inserted in place of the wood the designer had so carefully removed. The trigger was concealed in the crook of the handle just millimeters from his expectant finger.

"You scared me nearly half to death," he complained through the door. Though he was relieved to see her, his face remained ashen. To Sara's trained eyes, Nate had aged considerably since the first time he had summoned her to his office months ago. It was obvious that his health was not good. The lines in his face were deeper, and the consumption he was suffering had begun to reveal itself in the pallor of his skin.

"I wanted to be sure I wasn't followed," Sara replied furtively, "so I parked down the road a mile or so and approached the house from the beachside."

The woman looked as stunning as ever, and it made him feel ten years younger just to see her glowing red cheeks and her penetrating round eyes, her muscular legs and her rugged, strong hands.

"Were you? Followed, that is?"

"No," she replied curtly, taking his question as a criticism of her abilities. "May I come in?"

"Yes, by all means. Excuse my manners, I don't often have lady guests. May I offer you something?" he asked as he led her into the front room. It was furnished with an eclectic mixture of old and new, country and modern; and it obviously lacked a woman's touch. Even as he spoke, Nate propped open the back door to let a dose of fresh ocean air in; though it was rather cold outside, it had been some months since his last visit here and the house was stuffy from being closed up for so long.

"A danish would be nice," she suggested, staring hungrily at a box of sweet rolls Nate had bought on the way into town and had sitting open on the coffee table.

"A sweet for the sweet," he flirted, ever the gentleman. "Now tell me, young lady, what exactly is on your mind? I gathered from your call that the 'he' in your message 'he'll be coming for you next' is our own Mister Jonathan Harper?" It was as much a question as it was a statement.

"Yes, but how did you know?" Sara quizzed between bites on the sweet roll she had selected from the assortment spread out before her.

"Well, Sindy said…"

"Sindy?!" she gasped, nearly dropping the pastry in her lap. "For Chrissake, you *knew* her?"

"Can't say as I ever met the woman, but she called me

the very night she and Whetstone died."

"She called *you*? That surprises me, Senator. Do you know who she is, I mean, was?"

"Haven't the slightest," he answered. "A drifter, I suppose."

"And then some. She was also your grandson's girlfriend."

"That's ridiculous!" Nate clamored, grabbing a danish for himself.

"Not only is it not ridiculous, it is absolutely true. At the very moment I was courting Sam on *your* instructions, this drifter as you call her, must have been compromising Lester on Whetstone's."

"Compromising? In what way? Geez, Sara, if you already knew so much about her, why the hell didn't you tell me this before?" he asked testily. "Certainly I have paid you enough."

"I wasn't aware of her true identity until just yesterday. When I saw the obituary and the reference to J.H. at Internal Intelligence, I pulled up her file. I'm not exactly sure what Whetstone's interest was with the Amerind rebels, but Lester was unquestionably involved."

"This I believe," Nate conceded as he swallowed the rest of his danish. "But who killed Whetstone?"

"Sindy, no doubt."

"And who killed her?"

"Director Harper, I should imagine."

"In that case, you are also at great risk. He is, after all, your boss, and if Sindy was correct about him being a traitor, he will have put my house under surveillance by now."

"I recognize the danger," Sara allowed, "but tell me this. If Director Harper is a mole, who has he sold himself out to?"

"Interesting question. Like yourself, I too have been searching for the answer. I think…"

"Who owns him?" she wondered out loud before he

could finish. "Johannesburg? SKANDIA? Britain?"

"China!" Nate exploded emphatically. "That's who owns him! Has to be! Follow me on this: Barely a week ago, a man fitting Lester's description was seen leaving Overlord Ling's apartment in Lihue. A woman was with him; probably this Sindy. I already know from a report Harper gave me earlier this past summer—and which was confirmed by an independent third party—that Whetstone had been to see Ling after he was released from prison. Clearly, those two are in cahoots. Ling, after all, is the U.S.'s chief adversary. It only makes good sense that *he* is the one who has been supporting the Amerinds despite our best efforts to starve them of arms. That would complete the connection between him and Whetstone. They both have a reason to hate me—Ling because I murdered his father, Whetstone because he was impeached and sent to prison on my testimony. That's how Lester must fit in with all this—not only have they involved him in the arms shipments, they plan on using him to somehow strike back at me!"

"Bravo! Bravo!" This was a new voice. "I can see the headlines now: Despite his dementia, Senator Matthews finally figures it all out!"

Sara and Nate spun to face the arrogant speaker head-on. It was Director Jonathan Harper. He was framed by the door Nate had left ajar in the back to air out the house; in his hand he held a mean-looking gun, the same gun he had already used to murder Sindy.

"I thought you weren't followed," Nate carped at Sara disapprovingly. She was standing halfway across the room from him, her arm resting on the back cushion of the sofa.

"Me too," Sara returned quietly, her mind racing.

"I'm afraid that since you both have figured this one out, you both must die," Harper explained, keeping the deadly .357 Magnum trained on his female subordinate. Being the younger and more experienced of his two antagonists, Sara was of far greater concern to Director Harper than Nate ever could be. Harper knew if she had learned anything at all from her combat training, she could be downright menacing in a fight.

"You have come an awfully long way just to commit murder," Nate commented, stalling for time. Even as he spoke, he began drifting towards the left so as to increase the distance between himself and Agent Logan. Flix had often taught him that by widening the angle between a gunman's two targets, one would increase the odds for survival.

"Couldn't be helped," Harper responded, twisting his head to see what the Senator was up to. "With all that has happened, I have no choice now but to leave the country."

In the instant it took for Harper to shift his eyes from Sara to Nate and back again, she acted, diving over the back of the couch and pressing herself flat against the floor. Without even stopping to think about Nate and his deadly cane, Harper sprayed the sofa with shells, emptying the clip in the process. By the time he had paused to reload, Nate had already raised his cane-rifle and was pointing it at the man's midriff.

"Now, listen, you son-of-a-bitch," the Senator declared, his jaw set and his eyes aflame, "I imagine you are asking yourself right about now whether I am a good enough shot to hit you at this distance and whether I will be able to kill you with the single bullet loaded in the chamber of this gun. And I'm telling you in no uncertain terms that I am—and I will. So please drop your gun and surrender yourself peaceably. And you damn well better pray that Agent Logan is unharmed or else…"

"Old man," Harper interrupted in a disparaging tone as he fumbled for his spare clip, "you don't have what it takes."

Steadying himself against what he knew would be a

fierce recoil, Nate said, "I had what it took long before you were even potty-trained."

Believing he still had the upper hand, Harper slammed the clip home. But before he could spin and fire, Nate had already pulled the trigger on his own weapon, blowing an enormous hole through his opponent's belly. The Director was dead before he hit the floor.

"Jesus!" Sara gasped, viewing the Senator's still smoking cane in horror as she got to her feet. "You killed Director Harper!"

"What did you expect me to do? Offer him a pastry? Now listen, young lady, you have got to get out of here. As of this moment, you are officially a fugitive. If they are not already, the Agency will be out looking for you soon. Even as we speak, Sam is moving some money around for me in Canada; I'll see to it that an account is set up for you at a branch of the Chamberlain Bank in the Hawaii Free State. You'll be safe there, and don't worry about this mess, Officer Jenkins will be by shortly. He'll help me clean things up. Now get going before it's too late."

Looking first at Harper's bloody corpse then at Nate's wrinkled face, she kissed the old man on the cheek and said, "Thanks."

As she turned to leave, she added, "Now don't forget to have your office swept for bugs. And have that tap removed from your comm as well."

Without answering, Nate nodded. That was the last he ever saw of her.

Thirty-two
Beholden Day

Although Nasha had once warned him that he could not marry the woman without first marrying the tribe, the full import of that statement wasn't apparent to him until the BeHolden Day break. Unlike most students who used this lull in the school year to be at home with their families, Sam had no family to be with here in Canada. Not only that, with the satraps a constant source of trouble, he was afraid of being left alone in an empty dormitory on level minus-eight over a long weekend. To him, living Underneath was creepy enough, but to be stuck there for days on end with no one else around, was downright terrifying. Therefore, when she invited him to her house for the holidays, he leapt at the chance.

BeHolden Day could count as its antecedents Thanks-giving, plus a host of English harvest festivals dating back a millenium. Due in part to its universality, the tradition had spread in time to a thousand cultures, the Amerinds being no exception. Whereas in the big cities the holiday had degenerated over the centuries into an orgy of engorge-ment, in the smaller towns and in the simpler families, it was a more genteel, more civilized affair, somewhat reminiscent of its twentieth century cousin. The oversized turkey was still there along with the sweet potatoes, the stuffing, the corn, the bread, the cauliflower, the pumpkin pie, plus all the accouterments—the applesauce, the soup, the cranberry sauce, the salad, and the wine. Sam had sat at a table like this many times before, and so he was caught a bit off-guard when he found himself the subject of a cool reception.

The truth be known, Canada was not a very open society here in the late twenty-fourth century, and Nasha's family lived in a tumble-down section of the sprawling megalopo-lis reserved for such outcasts. The Amerinds' second-class status made them at once suspicious of outsiders, and thus Sam began the evening with an immediate disadvantage.

Thinking about it now as he sat there quietly at the table pondering what to say next, Sam realized that life was much like a ring of concentric circles. The inner circle was oneself; the next one out, one's family; then came the tribe; then the neighboring tribe; and so on. The farther away from the center one got, the more foreign things became. People venturing in from the outer circles, like he was today, were considered the "other," and while it might be exciting to fall in love with an "other"—as Nasha had—it was hard to take an other from an outer circle and make him part of an inner one. Even so, with the exception of Inok, Nasha's older brother, Sam soon found himself being grudg-ingly accepted into her family clan.

Inok—or Dark Eagle as he preferred to be called—considered himself the family's self-appointed defender of Nasha's virginity, and he had confronted Sam regarding this very point upon their first meeting a month ago when Sam had dropped Nasha back at her house following their day-long hike to Lake Louise. Tonight, as the family's BeHolden Day celebration wore on, Sam realized it was still a live issue.

"I would like to make a toast to Nasha's guest," her father proposed, directing all eyes upon Sam. "To Mister Matthews, our visitor from south of the border, I bid you welcome!"

Her father was a handsome man, and looking at him now, Sam could see where Nasha got her slim waist, her full lips, and her healthy-colored cheeks. From what Sam understood, the old man was some sort of a tribal Elder, and the fact that he, Tato, was welcoming Sam into his home was an honor of the highest degree. Sam was about to accept Tato's welcome and say a few ingratiating words of his own, when Nasha's older brother spoke up.

"Father!" Dark Eagle protested as everyone held their goblet of wine following Tato's salute. "How can you welcome this...this *American*...into our home?" The way in which he squeezed out the word "American" suggested he did so with some disdain.

"Son!" Tato exploded angrily, meeting Inok's dark, piercing eyes with his own. "Where are your manners? A friend of Nasha's is a friend of ours!" As he spoke, the Elder tugged at his wine, signaling to everyone seated that the toast remained in force and that it was time to eat.

"America has not been a friend to Canada," Dark Eagle pointed out even as he served himself a helping of turkey and passed the plate on to his cousin at his left. Like his father, Dark Eagle was uncommonly handsome. Though Sam had found the man's ponytail a curiosity when he first met him, tonight he didn't even seem to notice it.

Under the weight of Dark Eagle's criticism, Sam lowered his head, wishing he could shrink himself small enough not to be noticed. He had understood upfront that he was an outsider, but he never expected so much resistance to his presence.

Seeing how dispirited Sam had become by her brother's cutting remarks, Nasha put her hands to her face and began to sob. The rest of the table grew quiet as father and son verbally squared off on a matter of some passion.

"My dearest son, America and Canada have always been amiable," Tato explained, filling his bowl with hot soup. "But even good friends sometimes have disagreements. As an adult, you must accept that."

"Father, you know very well my feelings on this. There will be war soon. And when it comes, I fear America and Canada will stand against one another."

"How can you say that?" the elder man inquired, knowing the women of the family were not usually present for such discussions.

Jumping into the fray with nothing to lose, Sam interjected, "Dark Eagle is correct, Tato. If there is war, Canada *will* stand against America. Even my grandfather believes it to be true."

Dark Eagle was as surprised to have Sam agree with him as Sam was to have spoken up at all. Nonetheless, the whole exchange had left Sam quite ill at ease, and he cleared his throat to leave.

"I shall not be responsible for a family fight on an occasion as important as BeHolden Day," he announced earnestly, pushing himself away from the table. "Thank you, sir, for your hospitality," he declared, tipping his hand towards Nasha's father, "but I really must be going now."

"Father!" Nasha shouted, throwing her napkin down on the plate in front of her. "If there is no room for Sam at this table, then there is no room for me either. I intend to leave *with* him," she threatened indignantly, scrambling to her feet and drawing herself closer to the man she loved.

Embarrassed by these developments, Dark Eagle stammered, "Look, Sam...all we want are our lands back...none of us want war with America..."

"Nor do I," Sam admitted, edging towards the door with Nasha at his side.

"I apologize for what I have said," Dark Eagle admitted, lowering his head and casting a forlorn look around the table. "Father is right, of course—a friend of Nasha's *is* a friend of ours. Can you forgive me?" he asked, reaching out his hand in a sign of goodwill.

Sam gladly took it.

"Please sit back down," Tato begged. "And fill your belly with food. It is, after all, BeHolden Day. And tell me more about this grandfather of yours—he sounds like a smart man to me."

"The Senator is a very smart man," Sam replied proudly as he dug in.

"Is this the same Senator Matthews who heads your Military Oversight Committee?" Tato quizzed, his ears perking up at the mention of so prominent a name.

"You know of him?" Sam replied, suddenly fearful that admitting he came from a leading American family would further distance him from this one.

"He is a most powerful and respected man," Tato indicated as the dinner moved on to dessert. "Perhaps he is aware of our plight."

"I couldn't say," Sam returned politely. "But I would be happy to ask him how the U.S. could be of service to your people if you wish. I talk to my grandfather two or three times a week." Even as he spoke, Sam flashed back to Lester and to the airchop and to the camper lying dead in Little

Grasshopper Valley. That whole incident had revolved around the plight of the Amerind and their struggle to obtain weapons to support their cause. Though only months had passed since that horrible incident, his days at Na-Cha-Tan seemed like ancient history to him now.

"Please do not bother him with such trifles," Tato urged abruptly, afraid that he might have spoken out of turn. "It would be premature. I will bring your offer before the Council of Elders when next they assemble."

"I met a Matthews once," Dark Eagle interjected, altering the course of their conversation. "Unlike yourself, however, he was a most disagreeable fellow. Money was his only interest." Even as Dark Eagle spoke, his father glared at him for broaching this delicate topic. Though both men were acquainted with the Lester Matthews who had been an intermediary of theirs for a short time, only Dark Eagle had the temerity to bring the subject up.

"I doubt if the man you met could be related to me," Sam noted without asking for his name. "I have only one brother, and so far as I know, he has never been to Canada."

"Nor I to America," Dark Eagle quickly asserted, doing his best to extricate himself from the corner he had unwittingly painted himself into. Without revealing that he had frequently crossed the border illegally to pick up footlockers filled with weapons, Dark Eagle could not possibly pursue whether or not there was in fact any connection between the two Matthews. Still, he was understandably suspicious that all of a sudden out of nowhere should come this good-looking man intent upon courting his sister. Not only did the Amerind not like coincidences, he couldn't help but remember the two lifeless bodies he had discovered that day when he set his airchop down in that grasshopper-filled valley in Wisconsin—the boy whose throat had been brutally slashed and the Israeli whose body had been riddled with bullets. It had been a gruesome sight—one Dark Eagle was not apt to soon forget. To this day, the only conclusion he had been able to draw from it was that Lester Matthews had been the one responsible for the two killings. Which still left open the question of what to make of Sam. What was *he* here for? To infiltrate the rebel organization? This American would bear close watching, of that there was no doubt. Unless he proved himself a friend, Dark Eagle had no choice but to assume he was an enemy.

Thirty-three
Geld

"I must say, it is highly irregular to conduct such business by comm," the staid, pencil-necked businessman explained in a holier-than-thou tone which couldn't help but rankle Sam.

Safely ensconced in his room on level minus-eight, Samuel Matthews couldn't hear the wind howling outside; nevertheless, he knew winter had come to Canada in all its firm vigor. And with the year-end fast approaching, he had no time left to waste with this obstructionist velcroid; Nate had made it patently clear that these transactions *had* to be completed before midnight on the thirty-first.

"With a new client it is always our custom to handle these matters face-to-face," Winchester Holt elaborated.

"Surely you must know we do not deal with the general public?" Though he spoke with feigned politeness, his meaning was clear.

"Land's-sakes, Mr. Holt!" Sam implored testily. "Why in the world was the comm invented if not to conduct one's financial affairs quickly and discreetly?"

"Quickly, yes. Discreetly, no," the arrogant investment banker replied. "If you wish to trade currencies with *us*, you will have to be physically present to establish the account. Will there be anything else?" the banker concluded snottily as he prepared to break the connection.

"Is that your final decision, Winchester?" Sam persisted, not willing to give in to this petty, provincially-minded man.

"Why you impertinent little bug! That is *Mister* Holt to you, and another thing..."

"Now don't hang up on me!" Sam interrupted, afraid that he had pushed the starched white-collar too far. "Mr. Holt, I think you fail to appreciate the volume of commissions which you would be giving up by refusing to open this account."

"...I'll hear no more of this," the man insisted even as his ears perked up at the sound of a certain word. "How *much* in the way of commissions?" he probed, salivating at the prospect.

"Ah, *now* I have your attention," Sam retorted much relieved. "Over the course of a year, I should imagine the commissions would amount to tens of thousands of Canadian dollars. However, the trading would have to be done in a numbered account. Plus, it would *have* to be done over the comm. You will execute a trade only if I give you the correct password, and all funds moving into and out of the account will be by wire transfer to or from any one of three offshore banks I designate at the time of the trade."

Impressed with his caller's sudden directness, yet unable to cope with a novel situation, the banker stammered, "This is all *highly* irregular. I will first have to clear this with one of the senior partners. If I may please have your name and your commcode, I will call you back just as soon as I obtain the necessary clearance to handle your account."

"No can do, Winchester," Sam replied, testing the man's resolve once again. "I will call you if and when I require your services, but I will not give you my commcode under any circumstances. As for my name, we will settle on an acceptable password and that is how we will know one another. If that is not satisfactory, then I will take my business elsewhere. But considering that I need to trade ten shilling contracts today, right now in fact, it would be a shame indeed if we could not come to some understanding even as we speak. If we reach an agreement, I am prepared to wire you ten thousand SKANDIA krona to open my account. What will it be? Yes or no?"

The strait-laced banker took a deep breath and coughed out a hoarse, "Yes."

"Good," Sam replied. "If you will give me your inter-bank number, I will wire you the funds so we can get started."

"901-87923-40A."

"Fine. The password we will use is 'Tiger' and the activity statements should be sent care of the Chamberlain Bank, Lockbox 1482, Reykjavik, Iceland. Do you have that down?"

"Tiger, did you say the *Chamberlain* Bank?"

"Yes, the Chamberlain," Sam grumbled, growing weary of Holt's tedious cross-examination. "Will that be satisfactory or not?"

"Of course," the banker admitted. "The people at the Chamberlain are among the finest in the business. I commend..."

"Let's get on with it, then," Sam demanded impatiently, knowing he still had to call Nate when he was done setting up this account.

"Quite right," the trader agreed. "So tell me, *Tiger*, what are your instructions?"

"I want you to buy me five U.S. dollar put contracts March one-tens at market and ten Aussie shilling calls April eight-sixties," Sam instructed, jotting down some notes as he spoke.

"You're *shorting* the dollar?" the investment banker quizzed in a disbelieving tone. "With the possible exception of world war, what conceivable reason would there be for the dollar to fall?" he argued strenuously. "And why go long the *shilling* of all things?" he questioned as if it were somehow dirty. "Australia is practically an underdeveloped country for goodness sake!" His tone was unmistakenly paternal.

"My good man," Sam declared in an equally aristocratic voice, "your counsel is much appreciated, but Tiger has given you an order, now please execute it."

Several Days Later

"Grandpa, I recognize that you have mentioned this to me before, but would you mind explaining to me again why stocks trade in eighths and in quarters while currencies trade in decimals? Buying and selling in eighths makes no sense to me whatsoever."

Now that the New Year had begun and they had started trading with regularity, Sam made a point of calling Nate every two or three days to review the progress of their account. Their discussions were always frank and far-reaching, and Nate never once hesitated to reveal deeply-held family secrets to Sam over the comm. As Sara had recommended to him in their final meeting, the Senator had had his office swept for bugs, only he hadn't counted on the remote listening device set up in a building across the street, a device which was still monitoring his calls despite Jonathan Harper's death.

"History, my boy, history," Nate replied, suppressing a foul sounding cough. "You must remember your history or else all of our lessons will have been for naught."

"So tell me again," Sam requested politely. "Why do we trade stocks and bonds in eighths?"

"The answer goes to the very birth of our great nation," the elder Matthews explained. "To begin with, the American colonies had very little cash money in circulation. England wouldn't furnish the colonies with coins nor would she allow them to print their own. With paper currency almost nonexistent, the colonists had no choice but to trade in Amerind wampum, beaver pelts, grain, musket balls, and whatever else they could get their hands on, including the occasional foreign coin.

"The principal coin used by the colonists was the Spanish milled dollar and its eight fractional parts. This silver coin which could be cut apart and used in its smaller segments, was also known as the pillar dollar or as a piece of eight. After being cut, its fractional parts were referred to as bits, each bit having a value of twelve and a half cents. These coins continued to be a popular and a sanctioned currency until the middle of the nineteenth century. Indeed, to this day, our modern quarter is still known as two bits."

"This is all very interesting, grandpa, but what does it have to do with my original question?"

"Patience, boy. Let me finish!" Nate demanded, expelling a rough sounding cough again. "Or is that woman friend of yours the only thing on your mind these days?"

Sam had told his grandfather of his love for Nasha, and though the old man approved, he wasn't above chiding Sam once in a while. "Now where was I? Oh, yes," Nate continued, picking up from where he had left off. "It is believed that as early as 1725, wheat, tobacco, and even slaves, were traded at auction at the foot of Wall Street. Although we are not certain exactly when the New York securities market actually began operating, by then the Spanish dollar and its fractional eighths were well established as the customary medium of exchange. It's been that way ever since."

"What about the term 'blue chip'?"

"The term 'blue chip' undoubtedly originated from the game of poker where the blue chips—in contrast to the red or the white—had the greatest money value."

"And 'bottom fishing'?"

"The elusive hunt for the big one."

"There seems to be a mysterious connection between water and money," Sam remarked thoughtfully.

"Whatever do you mean, son?"

"Think about it, Grandpa. When you are doing okay, you're solvent. When you're not, you're illiquid. Oddly enough, one of the ways to become illiquid is to have taken a bath; which is to say, to have been hosed or else soaked. Businesses go down the drain. They are said to have drowned in a sea of red ink. Financing dries up. Unless, of course, somebody floats them a loan. Crashes mark the end of a speculative bubble. I ask you: How did this all come about?"

"Splendid question, my boy," Nate answered. "Actually, the association of water with money is nothing new, probably dating back to the first commercial shipping ventures. In the 1800s, for instance, the big worry was watered stock, a phrase borrowed from unscrupulous cowboys who used to make sure their cattle took a good long drink of water before weighing in at market. When the term was first applied to investments, watered stock was bad; it *diluted* the interests of the other shareholders by making more claims against the same *pool* of assets. In short, we have been lost in the mists of metaphor for a good, long time."

"Well then, what about the words 'bull' and 'bear'? How do *they* fit in with all this?" Sam asked, absorbing Nate's words like a sponge.

"For that we have to go to the opposite coast."

"Huh?"

"California," the Senator expounded. "These labels for market direction originated not on Wall Street, but in the mining camps of nineteenth century California. After gold was discovered at Sutter's Mill, many adventurers sought fortune in a camp called Hangtown which, at the time, rivaled Sanfran in size. Among the diversions sought by the miners on a Sunday afternoon was the bullfight. This institution had been introduced to Spain by the Moors in the eleventh century, after which it was brought to Mexico by the Spanish, where it became part of the fiestas held regularly at the Spanish—and later, the Mexican—settlements in California. The Mexicans, however, added a wrinkle of their own by arranging fights between their Spanish bulls and the native grizzly bears which roamed the California coast. These contests were based on the observation that the Spanish longhorn cattle, which had been brought to Mexico in quantity beginning in the early 1500s, had run untamed for years where they often encountered the grizzly in the wild.

"The game which entertained the miners so, involved chaining a thousand-pound grizzly to a huge stake in the middle of an arena, then turning a bull loose to confront him. The fights were short but violent with the bull sometimes winning by impaling the bear and tossing him up over his shoulders. Most of the time, however, the bear won by meeting the charge between the horns and wrestling the fifteen-hundred pound bull to the ground, breaking the animal's neck in the process.

"Because the gold discoveries created a flood of trading in mining shares, both in Sanfran and in New York, the terms 'bull' and 'bear' worked their way into the investment jargon to describe opponents trying to set the market's direction. A bull was someone who expected the market to rise; a bear, someone who expected it to fall. Remember: money can't buy happiness, but it sure can calm the nerves."

"Gramps, you know your history, that's for certain, but are you sure you know what you're doing on this currency trading you've asked me to do for you?"

"Sam, in securities trading there is no such thing as certain. There is only maybe and probably," Nate lectured, pacing the room as he spoke to his grandson via the speaker-comm sitting on his desk. Outside the window, a blizzard was swirling through the streets of Washington.

"But we're risking *so* much money," Sam countered sincerely. "I must admit, the whole thing unnerves me."

"I appreciate your concern, Sam, but your fears are unfounded. I sent you away to attend college because I was certain war was coming to America. So far, I have been wrong. Even so, I am still sure enough of that eventuality to risk my entire fortune—*our* entire fortune—betting on the outcome."

"But, grandpa, if you *are* right, and if America *does* go to war, and if she *does* lose as you predict, you might not even be around to collect your winnings," Sam correctly pointed out.

"But *you*, my boy, will be," the Senator declared proudly.

"Me?" Sam questioned in a surprised tone staring at the comm as if it might jump up and bite him.

"Yes, you, Sam," Nate clarified. "You are my heir."

"What about your son—my dad?" Sam questioned, suddenly unsure what to make of his grandfather. "What about your *other* grandson—my brother Lester?"

"I have provided for your father," the old man reassured.

"And as for Lester, forget about him. He's a loser, a spend-thrift, and a scoundrel to boot. No, this money belongs to you. But to preserve it, you must do *precisely* as I instruct."

"Okay, grandpa, whatever you say," Sam relented. "But why have you selected the specific trades we have made. Our broker keeps questioning me as to what we are doing. And why."

"Tell him nothing!" Nate ordered in an unusually stern voice. "One of the oldest dictums on Wall Street is that the people who know won't say, and the people who say, don't know. But if *you* are to learn the key to successful trading, there is one rule which you must always remember."

"And that is?"

"Achetez aux canons, vendez aux clairons."

"Sorry, grandpa," Sam apologized, "I know you have said that to me before but I don't have the faintest idea what it means—I don't understand any French."

"You never studied!" Nate scolded. "Achetez aux can-ons, vendez aux clairons," he repeated. "It means literally, 'buy with the cannons, sell with the trumpets'. That is, buy on bad news, sell on good," Nate translated.

Trying to be sure he understood his grandfather's expla-nation correctly, Sam verified, "Buy into the low prices which accompany bad times, then sell into the high prices which accompany good?"

"Exactly, Sam! Now you're getting the idea," Nate congratulated. "If you remember nothing else I have said, remember that. Financial markets are driven largely by mass psychology, plus a stream of irrational trading deci-sions. What's more, every change in the market—whether it's a new trade, a political event, or a twitch in interest rates—precipitates *other* changes. These in turn bring about still more changes, until a flood of change is soon cascading back and forth throughout the system. Mathematicians have a term for phenomena marked by this sort of interwoven change…"

"Chaos!" Sam interrupted modestly.

"You know of it?"

"Isn't that why you sent me to school up here? To learn?"

"Quite right. And have they taught you Occam's Razor as well?" the elder Matthews checked.

Having committed it to memory, Sam detailed, "Occam's Razor: the simplest explanation is the best explanation. Named after the fourteenth century English philosopher, William of Occam, who first proposed it. Razor is used in the sense of shaving an argument down to its simplest terms."

"Splendid. Now back to Chaos," Nate redirected. "Thanks to the stunningly intricate ways in which the chemicals in our bodies continually push one another into various reactions, human physiology is Chaotic. So too is the Earth with its interdependent web of oceans, atmosphere, and forests. So too are the financial markets. Thus— as you most assuredly have already learned by now— prediction is all but impossible."

"But if it is impossible to predict the outcome, then aren't we merely gambling every time we choose to invest?"

"To the contrary: just because we cannot accurately predict tomorrow's weather doesn't mean it won't snow again next winter or be hot the following summer. By carefully observing the conditions which prevail just before a market goes up or down, we can improve the accuracy of our guesses sufficiently close to the point of certainty."

"I see now," Sam clamored. "Achetez aux canons, vendez aux clairons."

"Yes. And as it applies here, perhaps you should reason it this way: the currencies of the undamaged economies like Australia and SKANDIA will rise dramatically as the war draws to a close, while the currencies of the chief combatants, and most especially the loser..."

"The United States?" Sam interrupted tentatively, knowing how pessimistic Nate was regarding America's chances.

"...will fall," Nate finished. "Yes, by all means, short the dollar, the pound, the franc, the mark, and..."

"I know, I know," Sam interrupted again, this time in an exasperated voice. "And go long the Australian shilling and the SKANDIA krona."

"Yes, but that is not all."

"It isn't?"

"No!" Nate emphasized, coughing again. "There is yet one more very important thing which you must not forget."

"And that is?"

"On the very day that a truce is called, you are to close out all your short positions no matter what. Do not be influenced by our Mister Winchester Holt! A week later, you are to close out all your long positions as well. Again, no exceptions. If you do as I have recommended, your profits should be huge. And don't forget to place the proceeds of your trading into the three offshore accounts we have set up in Reykjavik, Singapore, and Johannesburg."

"None in Canada?" Sam asked, perplexed.

"Absolutely not!" Nate exploded, practically shouting into the comm. "The French Canadians are much too volatile. As sure as day follows night, trouble will come to Canada yet, and you may well be forced to leave there just as you had to leave here. I can only guess where you will end up in that event, but at least one of the three places should remain free and safe. Oh, and before I forget, be sure to transfer two hundred thousand to that account number I gave you in Lihue."

"Already done," Sam reported. "Who is that money for?"

"This I cannot tell you."

"And you, grandpa? Where will you be after the war?"

"A captain goes down with his ship," the Senator clarified bravely.

"What does *that* mean?" Sam asked, bracing for the worst.

"Sam, don't forget what I have said: sell on the truce. And remember, good men predict, but *great* men act."

Thirty-four
Chrissy

"Oh, Sam, I'm so proud of you," Nasha exclaimed, bubbling in admiration over his accomplishment. Just to hear her voice and feel the squeeze of her hand made Sam feel all warm inside. It had been a hard-fought battle of several weeks duration, but somehow he had managed to pull it off. Which is not to say that he had done it alone, only that he had skillfully spearheaded the drive to its successful conclusion. But how to adequately describe his achievement?

The members of Sam's fraternal organization were an oddball collection of former Boy Scouts who, despite being of college age, were still hellbent on pursuing the Scout Promise to help other people at all times. Although the campaign known as the Ugliest Student On Campus was by far their most visible service project of the year, Beta Sigma was active each and every day trying to carry out the terms of their solemn oath—Christmas at the Children's Home, Valentine's Day at the Hospice for the Advanced Aged, weekend cookouts at the Girl Scout Camp, cheerleading for the Blind Bowling League, and so on and so forth. In fact, the fraternity's goals were quite simple: to be of service to their country, their community, and their chapter. And it was with this third objective in mind that each service project they performed on behalf of someone else was followed promptly by a service project on behalf of themselves, namely, a party, a kegger, a dance, a laker, whatever came to mind at the time. Hard work rewarded by hard fun.

Simply put, the competition called the Ugliest Student On Campus—or USOC for short—was a charity drive wrapped up in delicious tomfoolery. Over the years it had evolved beyond the status of a mere annual ritual until it had become almost an obsession—an orgy in giving, really. Like Groundhog's Day or St. Patrick's Day, the spring fundraiser was an event everyone in the university had come to eagerly anticipate. It was timed to coincide with the vernal equinox, and in the weeks leading up to it, hours upon hours of behind-the-scenes planning had to take place.

To begin with, each satrap, plus each of the off-campus fraternity houses, was asked to put forth one or more of their own to compete in the contest. Knowing that glossy eight-by-tens were the photographic propaganda which fueled the student body's voting, each participating rival had to do his best to dress up in outrageous garb and to distort his features with cosmetics or clay or other camouflage. The finished product had to be the ugliest, the nastiest, the most repulsive, mug imaginable.

These disgusting faces were then plastered on every wall of the campus, paraded about the university on mammoth banners, and affixed to dozens of huge donation jars which were distributed throughout the Underneath and elsewhere. For the eight days leading up to spring-break, the voting went on round-the-clock as volunteers manned the donation jars at tables placed in strategic high-traffic locations all over the university. To heighten the suspense, the fraternity posted enormous bar charts reporting the daily tally of each candidate's vote plus the overall take from the effort.

With cold hard cash being the only recognized means for casting a vote endorsing one's favorite Ugly, the clanging of coins against glass became a familiar sound over the course of the one week campaign. At the climactic end of the project, the innards of the giant collection jars were disgorged and all of the proceeds were given over by the fraternity to help a needy child or else a destitute family from the community.

Several ingredients—all mixed in just the right proportions—were required if the USOC campaign was to be successful: the intended recipient had to be needy, but not pitiful; the spring weather had to be cool, but not cold or damp; the contestants had to be ugly, but not grotesque; the administration of the university had to be supportive, but not dictatorial; and finally, the rivalry between the satraps had to be intense, without crossing the line to vindictive.

As to point one, if the intended recipient of the students' largesse evoked their pity—or worse yet—suspended their disbelief as to the depth of that person's plight, the otherwise charitable students would be revolted by the very idea of helping them out financially. Indeed, they might refuse to give anything at all, demanding instead that the provincial government involve itself to save the destitute waif.

As this spring's Chairman of the USOC program, it was Sam's responsibility to discover that right "someone" around which to rally the hearts (and the pocketbooks) of 28,000 students. Under the watchful eye of Big Frank, last year's chairman, newly-activated fraternity brother Samuel Matthews began his search by making the customary calls to the churches and the halfway houses. The individual had to be someone of scant financial means and yet, it could not be an irresponsible someone who was the hapless victim of his own stupidity, especially where drugs or where alcohol was involved. There were plenty of needy folks in a community the size of Calgary and although these people undoubtedly shouldered a great deal of pain, most of them were either outcasts of one sort or another or else involved in straits so dire, the fraternity was powerless to deal with them. And as Frank correctly pointed out to Sam as they reviewed the list of possible candidates, no matter *how* troubled, a drunk or a blue-devil addict would not make a good prospect for a USOC challenge.

With the kickoff date rapidly approaching and just two weeks remaining before he had to make a final recommendation to the Beta Sigma Board, Sam's file was still filled with nothing but pathetic cases. Then, only days before the deadline, he got a call from the President of the university. They had met once when, as a pledge, Sam had been given the assignment to go interview him. The President's wife did volunteer work at the Amerind orphanage in Sarcee, and she knew of a wonderful child named Chrissy whose situation was stark in its seriousness. If only the fraternity would agree to take on this project, the President would see to it that the Alumni Association set aside an honorarium on their behalf, an amount large enough to cover at least a semester's worth of pizza and beer. As the President explained this little Amerind girl's dilemma to Sam, he realized that, honorarium or not, Chrissy had to be the focus of this year's USOC campaign. No one in his right mind could refuse an orphaned girl laser heart surgery!

Although the procedure was fairly common—and not even all that dangerous—it *was* enormously expensive. Whereas algorithms had existed for years to genetically regrow an adult heart, the same was not true for juveniles. And without kin to donate clean tissue to use as internal "scaffolding," the chances of hiring a surgical team were remote. Untainted body tissue was perennially in short supply, and either a patient had to arrive at the hospital with enough of their own on hand, or else with a very thick checkbook in their pocket. Chrissy had neither.

For an orphan with a small, but growing hole perforating her heart, affording this operation was simply out of the question. That is, until Samuel Matthews took hold of it. In this man's mind, there was simply no obstacle he could not overcome. And though he didn't know it at the time, nor did it enter into his decision in any way, by adopting the plight of this little girl as his own, Sam was propelling himself from the outer circle of Nasha's family to the inner. In the eyes of Tato, and most especially in the eyes of Dark Eagle, this one simple act of kindness made him one of them.

The second ingredient for a successful USOC—and the only one over which Sam had absolutely no control—was the weather. If it should prove to be too warm of a spring, the students would never come indoors long enough to care about voting. If, on the other hand, it proved to be too cold or too rainy, the undergrads would gather in their subterranean rooms to listen to the latest in cack music or to view a kickboxing match on their visicast sets. Either way, they would avoid the Student Center where the contestants would be showing themselves off as they vied for the title of Ugliest.

As for the competition itself, to be successful, the competitors' ugliness had to be unusual but not grotesque. A stage axe bloodily splitting open the head of a prop mask was grotesque; eyeballs dangling from a misshapen skull was grotesque; a slimy, four-foot tongue hanging haphazardly from a toothless mouth was grotesque. On the other hand, consider a reddened face bloated to the point of bursting: To one side it might be bordered by a cauliflower ear, and out in front there might be three stubble-haired chins plus a ski-jump shaped nose; the shnoz itself would be topped with an unsightly mole sporting a single hair. Now *that* was ugly!

There was a natural tension between what the Governing Board of the university regarded as appropriate behavior and what antics the contestants were willing to engage in to arouse sufficient fervor among the student body. More often than not, the fundraiser reached a frenzy which exceeded the limits imposed by the administration, though in this particular instance, because it was the President himself who had suggested Chrissy to begin with, the administration cut them a little slack.

The culminating event of the weeklong effort was the gala Jerkoff. The Jerkoff was a charity ball where, in one final effort to solicit donations, the dozen or so ugliest contenders would make their final appearances before the "polls" closed. Parading themselves in front of the usually intoxicated audience and intentionally making a jerk of themselves (hence one possible derivation for the dance's name), the event took on a life all its own as trophies were awarded to the dance partners competing in a dozen different categories, from the chubbiest to the slimmest, the tallest to the shortest, and the most pathetic to the most endearing. Between the cover charge, the cash bar, and the cash contributions, the Jerkoff was always a huge moneymaker.

Despite her failing health, the nine year-old Chrissy made an appearance at the Jerkoff, accompanied by a visicast camera crew. That night, when the interview was broadcast on the ten o'clock news, her feeble voice touched so many hearts, over the course of the next twenty-four hours, an immense surge of donations hit the collection jars from all across the community. It was a truly remarkable outpouring of generosity, and Sam was an instant hero. Not only had he recognized a girl in desperate need, he had engineered just enough hype to make the whole thing work.

"Oh, Sam," Nasha beamed as Ravi handed him the final tally of contributions, "we're all so proud of you! Even my father called to say what a wonderful job you have done."

The entire fraternity was seated around a large table in the Student Center. The tabulating had been going on most of the night. Literally tens of thousands of dollars worth of coins and bills had to be separated by denomination and counted. When, sometime after midnight, Sam began to get a picture of just how much money was spread out on the tables before him, he had called the President of the university and asked him to post a security guard outside the door; after all this effort, they couldn't afford to have a thief hold them up and steal Chrissy's money. Despite being plenty irritated over having been woken up in the middle of the night, the President had agreed Sam was right and a representative from the local bank was expected within the hour.

"Well, you know," Sam began modestly, choking back a yawn, "I really was only a catalyst. My contribution to this whole affair was actually quite minor."

"Sam, don't be a fool!" Nasha scolded. Even as she spoke, other heads in the room turned to nod their agreement. There was no denying his accomplishment. "That lovely little girl wouldn't have lived much longer without your help," Nasha emphasized, grabbing his arm and pulling him to a corner of the room out of everyone else's earshot. "You saved her life, and I love you for that."

"Come to think of it, maybe we *should* celebrate," he

replied, returning Nasha's nuzzle. Holding her there in his arms, Sam allowed his eyes to roam over the full length of her body. It was a pleasant view. Sam never tired of her clean and wonderful smell, her full, almost pouting lips, or the upward swell of her ample breasts. That he was in love, of that there was little doubt, but what to do about it was still a conundrum.

"I see that devilish twinkle in your eye," she remarked mischievously, blushing just a tad. "Just what kind of celebration did you have in mind?" she teased, pressing herself against him seductively.

"Well," Sam stammered hesitantly, "I have been so busy with the USOC campaign these past few weeks, we haven't had any time to ourselves. What I mean is…how 'bout some nookie?"

"You Americans are such a stitch!" she giggled, patting him playfully on the chest with the palm of her hand. "You have invented a hundred different ways to avoid saying the word sex! Nookie, the dirty deed, humping, screwing, boinking, porking, fooling around…"

"Okay, already!" Sam interrupted testily, looking nervously around to see if anyone else had heard her outburst. "What I mean is, we never have. Do you want to or not?"

Still teasing him mercilessly, she retorted, "I could never have sex with any man who spoke so openly and so abruptly about something as delicate and private as making love."

"Boy, this courting stuff is hard work," Sam complained, his hopes crushed. "Well, if you won't jump my shorts, then at least you will be kind enough to point me in the direction of the nearest monastery."

"Are monks allowed to have lovers?"

"Probably, but surely none as attractive as you," he flattered, caressing her face with the back of his hand. "I imagine most of *their* women have moustaches," he chuckled, "or beards. So what's it gonna be? Sex or sequestering? Cuddling or cloistering? Humping or hermiting?"

"Well, if you insist, I suppose I could fit you in. If you get my meaning."

Too stunned for words, Sam just stood there flabbergasted. But before he could even stammer out a reply, she quickly added, "Maybe it is about time for you to go see my father. I don't think he would be happy if I lost my flower to anyone but my husband."

And with that, she rapped him gently on the chin, snapping his gaping jaw shut.

Thirty-five
Love and Hate

Spring in all its splendor had finally come to the Rockies, and with it had come thoughts of love. Sam was infatuated with this girl, and there was no sense in denying his feelings for her any longer. With Sara it had been all lust and intimidation; with Nasha it was all hearth and home. That she was a virgin, of that he had scant doubt—if nothing else, Dark Eagle would certainly have seen to that—but having once had a taste of sex with Sara, Sam couldn't help but wonder what it would be like to roll around in bed with Nasha. Though he wasn't apt to admit it, such thoughts were on his mind every waking minute now; only with Nasha, sex meant marriage. And marriage meant confronting her father.

It wasn't as if Sam were *afraid* of the man, only that Tato had given him the impression of being hard-as-nails. And if that wasn't bad enough, Dark Eagle had always viewed Sam with some suspicion, a puzzling state of affairs Sam could never quite comprehend, yet nevertheless did his best to ignore. Thus, it was with some trepidation that he pressed his finger to their doorbell that day late in April.

"Oh, it's you," Dark Eagle remarked with cool detachment, opening the door just a crack. Though he strongly approved of what Sam had accomplished as chairman of the USOC campaign, it would not be in his nature to admit as much to Sam's face.

"May I come in?" Sam asked, meeting Dark Eagle's gaze without flinching. "I'm here to see your father. I need to speak with him. Alone."

"Don't keep him too long," Dark Eagle replied, not yet stepping aside to let him enter, "we have a lengthy trip ahead of us."

"Where are you two off to?" Sam inquired politely. His question was intended more as a friendly overture than to gather any actual information, but the Amerind took it the wrong way.

"Our destination is none of your concern." The answer was abrupt.

"Don't be so gruff," Tato demanded as he arrived on the scene. "And let the boy in for goodness sake! Mister Matthews is obviously here for a reason."

Even as Dark Eagle disappeared upstairs, Tato led Sam into the front room and showed him to a chair. Although Sam had come to ask for his daughter's hand in marriage, and although he had rehearsed this speech a hundred times on the way over here, he didn't know where to begin. Though he couldn't just blurt it right out, once he and Tato got past the pleasantries, the serious business of negotiating began.

"I would like to marry Nasha," Sam stammered, a bead

of sweat bubbling up on his forehead.

"Surely you cannot be serious?" the Elder replied, trying to show as much surprise as he could. He had been expecting this for weeks already.

"But I am serious," Sam insisted, doing his best to keep up his courage.

"Contrary to *your* upbringing, young Matthews," Tato advised sternly, "in *our* world, marriage is not a creature of the state. Nor is it merely a product of frivolous lust," he added, looking cross-eyed at Sam with an accusatory glance. "All of *our* marriages are common-law understandings with money changing hands ahead of time. Among the tribesmen, nuptials are agreements between the man's parents and the woman's parents. There is a fee which must be paid for the wife, and considering Nasha's fine looks and her sharp mind, she should bring me a good price."

Striking a serious face, Nasha's father shook his head, "Sorry, Sam, I like you, I really do, but I cannot consent to your offer of marriage without first striking a bargain with your kin."

"But, sir," Sam argued, disappointed by this turn of events, "you know very well that such a deal is impossible. With the border being sealed on account of the poor relations between our two countries, I cannot even reach my folks by comm, much less arrange for them to travel up here to meet with you. And as for money, yes, I have some, but with college expenses being what they are, I haven't much to spare."

Seeing Sam's desperation, Tato laughed, "Sam, I say again, I like you, I always have, but marriages have to be arranged! It is our tradition! If you are to be one of us, you cannot begin by violating centuries of custom. Money and gifts *must* be exchanged beforehand."

"With all due respect," Sam challenged defiantly, "will

Nasha become an outcast if we should happen to marry *without* such an agreement? Will she be shunned?"

"You *are* determined, aren't you?" Tato asked, a tiny smile creeping across his otherwise leathery face.

"Quite," Sam replied firmly.

"How much money have you?" Tato probed in obvious reference to Sam's earlier offer of payment.

"Is two thousand enough?" Sam offered hopefully, shifting uncomfortably in his seat.

"No."

"Three thousand?" Sam murmured, raising the bid. "I have little more than that." Though he knew he had the resources to go much higher, Sam somehow sensed it wasn't the money Tato was after, but the commitment. Tato had to be sure Sam was serious.

"So be it," the old man relented. "It is Nasha who must share your bed, not I. If she wants to marry a man as poor as you, I shall not stand in her way," he concluded thoughtfully before adding, "but you will have to be inducted into the tribe first—blood ritual and all."

Gulping hard, Sam looked aghast. He didn't know what to say.

Having had his moment of fun at Sam's expense, Tato chuckled. But only an instant later he turned all serious again. "You are circumcised, aren't you? I mean, all our tribesmen are."

Tato laughed again, even harder than before, only this time it made Sam smile. He had finally crossed the divide from the outside to the inside. There was no looking back for him now.

Days Later

When the news of their deaths had reached him in China six months ago, Overlord Ling had been devastated by the setback. Not only had the demise of Silas Whetstone, Sindy Foster, and Jonathan Harper thrown an enormous monkey wrench into his plans, their murders had compelled him to make a precipitous change in his agenda. Without Whetstone to control Sindy, and without Sindy to control Lester, Ling had suddenly been forced to devise an entirely new strategy for manipulating the soon-to-be Lieutenant Lester Matthews. Though Ling was fully confident that Lester *could* be handled, instead of being able to employ sex and drugs to control him as he had originally contemplated, now Ling would have to use a totally different approach. If the Overlord's objectives were to be realized, he would now have to resort to something more substantial, something more painful, something more enduring. Nothing less than spite would do.

Knowing from his many years of experience how no therapy had a more permanent effect on a man than hatred, Overlord Ling had scheduled a second meeting with Lester in Lihue this past winter. Applying his malicious tonic with great success, Ling revealed to Lester that all of the considerable Matthews family fortune was to be given over to his younger brother Sam and none to him. And to back up his story, Ling had even played a tape for him, a tape of a conversation between Nate and Sam where the Senator had told Sam to put his older brother out of his mind. "He's a loser, a spendthrift, a scoundrel," Nate had said of Lester. "Forget about him; this money belongs to you."

Hearing that recording was all that had been necessary to bring Lester around. Even Sindy, had she still been alive, could not have done a better job on the boy than Ling himself had done. And to drive the point home, Ling had even promised to help Lester get his share of the family fortune if only he would cooperate.

After learning of his grandfather's intentions, all Lester

wanted now was revenge; revenge against the Senator for cutting him out of his will; revenge against Sam for being the recipient of Nate's largesse; revenge against his country for making him serve a master he didn't respect. Given his new state of mind, Lester was easily swayed to Ling's point of view, and it wasn't long before they both had agreed that the only way for Lester to even the score was for him to steal his grandfather's black book and deliver its parcel of secrets to Overlord Ling. The Chinaman made it perfectly clear that, although the American military had grown weak and lazy over the past generation, they were still a formidable power, and if he was to defeat them in the Pacific, he would need every advantage he could muster. Above all else, Ling needed the access codes in that book!

From the very start, the number of people who were aware that Nate's code book even existed could be counted on one hand, and with the thumb and the forefinger of that one hand having already been lopped off when Whetstone and Harper were murdered, Ling was no longer content to act merely as a supplier of guns to the Amerind cause. To the contrary, he now intended to become an active participant in the struggle. With the Americans having been so successful at arresting most of the flow of arms north across the border, Ling had become the Amerinds most reliable conduit, and now, by intentionally refusing to deliver them any more weapons unless they began putting them to good use, Ling hastened the inevitable. It all came to a head at the April meeting of the Council of Elders. Once again, it was held in their lodge outside Ochre River, Manitoba, and once again, Tato and Dark Eagle were in attendance.

"I do not think we can trust the yellow-skin any more than we can trust the white man," Fast Elk asserted, his knees stiff from sitting cross-legged on the floor for so long. He had been one of the Chieftains who, up until now, had been counseling the others not to move too quickly in declaring their independence from Canada.

"To this you get no argument," Running Bear interjected, "but the yellow-skin never took our lands from us as the Euros did. Not only that, the yellow-skin *has* provided us with all the guns and explosives we will need to win our freedom."

"But now he refuses to supply us with more unless we go to war," Tato countered, his son at his side. "Doesn't that make you the least bit suspicious?"

"I say we *go* to war," Running Bear of the Kwakiuti tribe exclaimed. He had been the one responsible for establishing the link with the Chinese in the first place.

"I say he has reasons he is not telling us," Fast Elk maintained, distrustful of Overlord Ling and his motives.

"The Great Law tells us that the enemy of our enemy is our friend," Running Bear paraphrased, trying to snatch the moral high ground before Straight Hawk interceded as he most assuredly would before long.

"But it also says that those who make friends swiftly cannot be trusted," Tato countered, equally adept at quoting the Iroquois Great Law of Peace.

"The yellow-skin lives far away from us across the ocean; of what possible harm can he be to our people?" Running Bear questioned, not willing to let any other Chief have the last word.

"Overlord Ling wishes to rule the world," Fast Elk correctly pointed out. "If America falls, he may simply become our *new* enslaver."

"I say we go to war," Running Bear exclaimed, repeating his earlier demand.

"It has been many months since last we took a vote on this matter," Straight Hawk advised in his eminently practical tone. While the other Chieftains had debated one another for the past half hour, he had sat quietly listening, his weather-beaten face like stone, his undiminished head of white hair unmoving. "If the vote is unanimous, or nearly so, then we will join with our Huron brothers and we will claim upstate New York for them and the Dakotas and Manitoba for ourselves. How say you?"

As the hands went up one by one, Dark Eagle noted with some satisfaction that Straight Hawk hadn't asked him to leave the room like the last time. When the vote was counted, Straight Hawk declared, "It is unanimous. Thirty-three to none. The seven hundred year wait is over."

Turning to Dark Eagle, the eldest of the Elders murmured ominously, "Now you will learn what it means to be a Brave."

Thirty-six
Negative-Sum Game

The old man was dying; Sam knew that for certain now. He could tell by the hesitation in the Senator's speech, by the cough in his throat, by the way his mind wandered when they spoke. And Sam was angry with himself that there wasn't a darn thing he could do to prevent this from happening. With the borders closed, and times as they were, he couldn't even be there at his grandfather's side when it counted the most. The best he could do was to contact the Academy and ask Lester to look in on the old guy—and even that wasn't much of a gesture. Indeed, as Sam stood there beside his desk waiting for the call to go through, it rankled him no end to have to ask his brother for a favor. He had tried first to track down their father, but that effort had ended in failure; Franklin Matthews never stayed in one place long, and as of last night, his comm was still out of service. Having no one else to turn to on such short notice, Sam's next call had been to the military operator: lowlife or not, Lester was still his brother.

When at long last Lester answered the comm, his tone was unexpectedly caustic. "Well, little brother, what's it been? Six months? Eight?"

"Try nine," Sam replied cooly, ready to spar with the older boy to get his way if necessary.

"Okay, nine. So what's the big deal? Why call me all of a sudden now?" It was very hard for Lester to cover up the anger he felt towards Sam. Ever since Overlord Ling had permitted him to hear the tape of that conversation between his brother and Nate, Lester's heart had been consumed with hatred.

"Grandpa is sick," Sam answered, his eyes sweeping the musty walls of his compact apartment with disdain. He wondered what sort of accommodations Lester had at the Academy; what sort of accommodations he and Nasha would be able to find once they were husband and wife. As far as Sam was concerned, getting married and moving out of this underground dungeon he was stuck in couldn't happen soon enough.

"So?" Lester blurted, interrupting Sam's thoughts. "Why should I care if the old fart is sick?"

"Because I can't come visit him and I thought one of us should."

"I see," Lester retorted, his heart pumping faster as a plan began to take shape in his mind. All of a sudden everything was coming together in a way no one had anticipated. This call might just be the opening Overlord Ling was looking for. Lester couldn't wait to tell him; the Chinaman would be delighted! In the first place, if this worked, he wouldn't have to manufacture a crisis at all. And of even greater importance, this way he certainly wouldn't have to worry about trying to time the crisis to coincide perfectly with Lester's visit. Thanks in large measure to the Amerind uprising, a crisis was *already* brewing and now, not only did Lester have a good excuse to visit his grandfather right away, his grandfather had a compelling reason to open his safe and remove the code book of his own accord.

Despite his exhilaration, Lester didn't let anything get in the way of his continuing grudge match with Sam. "So, like a coward, you ran off to Canada with your tail tucked between your legs, and now, when times suddenly get tough, I have to do all your dirty work for you? Is that it?"

"Coward?" Sam snapped indignantly. "Whatever do you mean?"

"I mean by running away, you avoided doing any time in the military."

"Land's-sakes, Lester! Grandpa *told* me to leave. I had no choice!"

"We all have choices, damnit! And I'm calling you a coward," Lester rebutted.

"Well, what about *you*?" Sam returned fiercely. "I wouldn't call supplying arms to the rebels all that patriotic."

"How did you know about *that*?" Lester stammered, breaking into a cold sweat. He couldn't imagine that Sam had actually seen him do anything at all, but this accusation had come at him totally out of left field.

"What do *you* care how I know? Is it true?"

"Absolutely," Lester replied, regaining his footing.

"And what about Abe?" Sam cross-examined. "Did you kill him?"

"Had to."

"And the little boy?"

"No, that wasn't me—Abe did him."

"They closed camp, you know," Sam snapped in an unforgiving tone.

"I had heard that." The voice was uncaring.

"Talk about a coward! You just disappeared! I suppose you ran off with that Sindy."

"For awhile anyway," Lester admitted, taking stock of their short time together. After leaving Kauai he never saw or heard from the girl again, and after the way she had treated him, he didn't much care *what* had happened to her. All he cared about now was ensuring that a vial of blue-devils and a packet of Deludes kept arriving like clockwork at his doorstep every Saturday morning.

"Well, by running, you got away with murder. And thanks to Grandpa, you never were brought up on charges. The least you could do is visit the old man before he dies."

"I think you're right, Sam," he relented after putting up a mock fight. "I'll agree to do it on one condition."

"Name it."

"You don't tell him I'm coming; I want it to be a surprise."

"Agreed. But make it soon; I don't think he can last much longer." And then without waiting for a reply, Sam broke the connection.

Feeling as down in the dumps as he did, about the last person Sam wanted to hear from today was Winchester Holt. Yet, when Sam spoke with his account executive at the Chamberlain Bank in Reykjavik shortly after hanging up with Lester, the representative relayed the message that Mr. Holt had called the bank wanting desperately to speak with him. Guarding Sam's anonymity as agreed, the Chamberlain had simply told the man they would ask Tiger to return the call the next time they heard from him.

Now, as Sam held the comm in his hand, it was Holt's strident voice he heard at the other end of the line. Applying the same arrogant tone Sam had always found to be so dreadfully condescending, the investment banker started in on him as if he meant to deliver a lecture.

"Tiger, it is just as I feared. Thus far, your aggressive currency positions have netted you nothing but huge unrealized losses. I must warn you: if you are unable to come up with additional equity by noon tomorrow central time, my margin department will insist that I sell you out."

When Sam didn't answer, Holt probed, "Do you understand what I am saying to you?" His tone was triumphant, as if he had won an important battle.

"I understand you perfectly, Mr. Holt, so you had best understand me with equal clarity. If your margin department should dare sell me out without my express permission, you will have a massive lawsuit on your hands," Sam threatened, his voice resolute.

"But, Tiger, the Amerind uprisings have spooked the markets. Instead of falling as you had hoped, the dollar has actually been *rising* the past few days," the panicked broker summarized. "Pardon the expression, but you are losing your butt! Not only on this trade, but on all your other shorts as well."

"Patience, my good man, patience," Sam counseled, remembering Nate's words not to be influenced by this fellow. "Although I am confident resolution is close at hand, to ease your mind regarding the adequacy of the equity in my account, I am encoding instructions to wire you more money even as we speak. And rather than retreat from my positions, I fully intend to increase them further."

"Further?! That is absolutely out of the question!" the pencil-necked banker yelped. "Your exposure is already HUGE! You are practically at exchange limits now."

"Yes, Winchester, I am aware of that," Sam retorted calmly. "Even so, I sense that we are but days away from war; things will change rapidly then."

"I sense it too," Holt admitted, "but you stand to lose *millions* if you are wrong about its outcome. What sort of man can stand that kind of loss?"

"If you have a weak stomach, I can always place my trades elsewhere. I have other brokers you know," Sam lied, hoping to bluff the man into submission.

"That won't be necessary, Tiger, I only wanted to be certain..."

"Actually," Sam replied with a hint of haughtiness in his voice, "where securities trading is concerned, there is no such thing as certain. There is only maybe and probably. Now, if you don't mind, would you please buy me three U.S. dollar puts June nine-twenties at 18?"

"Will that be day or GTC?"

"Make it Good 'Til Cancelled," Sam answered. "And thank you for your concern, Winchester. We will talk again soon, of that I am sure."

News of the Amerind Nation's bold plan to carve a homeland for themselves out of the belly of Canada and the shoulders of the United States found Nate on the floor of his Senate chambers throwing up. He was in excruciating pain, yet short of drugging him into indifference, there was little the doctors could do to ease his suffering. They had said it would get like this and finally it had.

Recognizing that he didn't have long to live now and that assisted suicide was the only sensible option left open to him, Nate planned out his final moves. Rather than blowing his brains out as some in his circumstances might have been tempted to do, he intended to finish it the accepted way, the honorable way. After spending a lifetime avoiding scandal, he wasn't about to sully his name this close to the end.

Pulling himself to his knees, Nate struggled across the floor to his comm. He had three calls to make—one to a medic-van to come pick him up so that he might be taken to the Bethesda Suicide Ward, one to President McIntyre, and one to Officer Jenkins.

After successfully completing the first, the Senator hobbled to his wall safe using his cane as a crutch. Spinning the tumblers on the dial, he extracted the enigmatic black book from its vault and placed it in the breast pocket of his coat. Even as he struggled through these, his final acts, he heard a faint, scratching sound at the door behind him, only with his condition steadily deteriorating, he paid it scant attention. Nate would keep the folio on his person until the last possible minute, then call the President and turn it over to him for safekeeping. Jenkins already had the encryption key they had added to every single code, and it would be up to him to deliver it to McIntyre personally. Now that the nation was on the brink of war, it mustn't be allowed to fall into the wrong hands.

When the old man turned to face the room once more, Lester was there, in full-dress uniform, and grinning like a Cheshire cat. Though Nate should have been suspicious of his very presence, he was much too weak even to think. He had no way of knowing Lester's reasons for being here, though if he had, he surely would have sent the nefarious boy packing.

After Sam's call had reached Lester at the Academy early this morning, he used the number he had been given to contact Overlord Ling. They both agreed this was precisely the sort of excuse they had been looking for as a pretext for him to visit Nate and steal the Senator's code book. Though they couldn't possibly have known of the precautions Officer Jenkins and Nate had taken to safeguard the sanctity of the codes if he died, by the time Lester had arrived on the scene, Nate had already done most of his work for him; now all Lester had to do was finish the job.

Farther gone than even the Senator himself had suspected, Nate crashed to the floor without even saying a single word. His own mind preoccupied with thoughts of revenge, Lester made no attempt to speak to his grandfather nor to comfort him in his final moments.

As Nate blinked in and out of consciousness on the short road to death, Lester rifled through the old man's pockets, easily finding the book he was looking for. Pulling out the tiny microcamera Ling had given him, Lester copied what he needed, then returned the slender pamphlet to the pocket where he had found it.

Neither Officer Jenkins nor President McIntyre was ever called that day, and Lester withdrew from the Senator's chambers only moments ahead of the medics arriving from the suicide ward. He had no time to lose: his battle group was preparing to set sail for the East China Sea the very next morning, and he still had an important delivery to make before leaving. Only then, would he receive his final instructions.

Thirty-seven
Nuit

From the day Tato consented to allow Sam and Nasha to be married, less than a month elapsed before they concluded their common-law nuptials at a small gathering of her family and their closest fiends. Under normal circumstances, it might not have been so rushed, but there had been a call to arms, a call Tato and Dark Eagle could not very well ignore. In its own way, therefore, this gathering was a bittersweet moment, on the one hand joyous because of Nasha's wedding, and on the other hand somber because Dark Eagle and Tato were leaving in the morning to join the ranks of the rebellion. Yet, even before the ceremony could get underway, Sam had to first take his place as a member of the tribe, undergoing a blood initiation and accepting a

tribal name as his own forever. Much to Sam's relief, the
blood ritual proved to be more symbolic than painful; more
ceremonial than gory.

With Dark Eagle, Nasha, and the others looking on,
Tato positioned himself directly in front of Sam with his left
arm extended out before him. Stoically pricking his own
thumb with a pin until he drew blood, the Chieftain turned
to Sam and pricked Sam's thumb as well. Then, without
ever once saying a single word, he pressed the two bloodied
thumbs together, intermingling their bodily fluids in a rite
as old as mankind himself. When it was over, and Tato had
given Sam his Amerind name—Nuit—it was time for the
marriage to commence.

Facing each other from opposite sides of the compact
dining room, the two young lovers exchanged their vows of
commitment, immortalizing their understanding with a
mutual pledge of fidelity. The table which stood between
them was covered with the finest tablecloth in the house,
and it was illuminated by six homemade candles. They each
held a goblet of tortan as they conducted their version of the
age-old ritual. From an anthology of American poets Sam
had found in the city library, each had selected a verse they
thought appropriate to the occasion.

Sam's vows, taken from the pages of Walt Whitman,
were spoken first:

> I give you my hand.
> I give you my love more precious than money.
> I give you myself before preaching or law.
> Will you give me your self?
> Will you come travel with me?
> Shall we stick by each other as long as we live?

Then it was Nasha's turn as she recited the cherished
words from E.B. Stevens and his "Song of Tomorrow":

I have but three treasures to give;
Guard and keep them well:
  Love, hotter than a prairie fire.
  Courage, mightier than a fearless warrior.
  Devotion, more steadfast than the mountains.
Never sick, never old, never dead.
Dare to move the world:
It is but yours to conquer!

When the ceremony was concluded, it was time for Nuit to learn some of the tribe's most treasured customs. Even though Sam's mind was focused more on his upcoming wedding night than on what Tato was trying to tell him, he was immediately struck by how important the selection of names was to the members of her tribe. According to a longstanding practice, each newborn child was to be named for a star in the zodiac sign of their mother. Nasha had been so named as had been Tato before her. If their firstborn was a girl, her name was to be Carina; if a boy, Rigel.

When at long last the interminable lecture was finally over, Nasha and Nuit were permitted to leave. But before they could begin their weekend-long honeymoon in the Canadian Rockies, Sam had to first move his meager belongings from his tiny flat in the Underneath to a modest place they had found for themselves on the edge of the sprawling city. Sam's sense of exhilaration at finally being able to get out of his subterranean cave for good was so overwhelming, so profound, he almost forgot what was expected of him once they reached their hotel room in Banff.

Though it was an elegant, almost castle-like hotel un-like any he or she had ever seen or been in before, her attention was riveted more on her new husband than on the ornate hallways or the lavish appointments. As they rode the glass-walled lift up to the third floor and strolled down the richly-carpeted hall towards their suite, she hung contentedly on his arm, drinking in his countenance as if this were the very first time she had ever laid eyes on the man.

But instead of returning her longing gaze, Sam slumped into the nearest chair as soon as they entered the confines of their private room. He was exhausted. It had been a long day, a day which had begun with their wedding ceremony and had then gone on without break through, first, the move from his flat, and then, the two hour drive up into the mountains. Though it was a long distance for them to travel, they had chosen this remote location because it was near the hiking trails and the mountain peaks each of them held so dear. Nevertheless, as soon as he sat down, he found himself on the edge of sleep.

"I thought you *wanted* me?" she carped, pouting like a spoiled, dejected child in the face of Sam's tired eyes.

"Of course I want you," he answered unconvincingly from his seat. His eyes were drooping and this morning's shave was beginning to show the result of ten hours' lack of attention. "If I didn't want you, why in the world would I have asked your father for your hand?"

"Certainly you must want more than just my hand. What I meant was, I thought you wanted to *have* me," Nasha suggested, wantonly unbuttoning her blouse and exposing her young, firm breasts to his increasingly eager eyes.

"Now I see what you are after," Nuit granted, grinning from ear to ear as he moved to the edge of his seat. "I have been thinking about this moment since the first day we met," he admitted bashfully, recalling how he had ogled her melon-like orbs that day at the driver's license counter.

"I know you have, Sam," she answered, dropping her chemise to the floor at her feet and cupping a breast in each hand, "and I appreciate you patience. But now it's time—time to take off your trousers and do me proper. On the bed, buddy, we have babies to make."

"Babies?!" he yelped nervously, jumping to his feet, a terrified look plastered across his face. "Can't we just have sex? I'm not so sure I'm ready to be a father yet," he added, backing himself trembling into a corner.

"Wives become mothers and husbands become fathers," she pointed out as if it should have been obvious. "This is the cycle of life and this is how it should be," she cooed, pulling him towards her and sucking on his earlobe as if it were a chunk of steaming hot lobster dipped in melted butter. "You are a good man, Samuel Matthews, and the only way to immortalize that goodness is for you to pass it on to the next generation. Now hurry up and do me proper so we can go and have some dinner. I'm starving."

Even as she spoke, she grabbed his buttocks firmly with one hand, and began stroking his manhood through the fabric of his trousers with the other.

"A husband's work is never done," he moaned as her genital caresses stiffened his resolve considerably. This was not the first time he had been intimate with a woman, and for an instant, he was worried that the expectant glimmer in his eye would reveal that fact to his new wife. Fortunately, however, if she saw his look, she didn't flinch, and he promptly got down to the job at hand.

Beginning with her temples, Sam worked his way methodically down the length of her firm, lithe body, pausing at the fullness of her lips, at the roundness of her breasts, at the flatness of her tummy, to enjoy what they each had to offer. By the time he had arrived at his final destination, she was fully aroused. Marveling over every square inch of her flawless skin along the way, he let his hungry tongue explore every nook, every crevice, every indentation of her perfectly formed shape. As the two of them slowly, deliciously, seduced each other, time stood still for a very long, drawn-out moment, and it wasn't long before her rock-hard nipples were pressed snugly against his heaving chest as they pumped each other towards climax in perfect unison. Sitting astride him like a cowgirl riding an unruly bull, she drove him deeper and deeper into her private parts until he could enter no further. So relentless was her passion, that even after he was done, and even after he had filled her full with the nectar of the Gods, she kept on bearing down on his member for more, cresting three times in rapid succession. When at long last she was finally satiated, she rolled off of him exhausted, a soft, warm glow reddening her tender cheeks, a contented look spreading across her pretty face. No more than an instant later, she had fallen fast asleep.

When the two of them stirred a half hour afterwards, they were ravenous and eager to explore the palace-like hotel they were spending the weekend in. Showering quickly, they donned their fancy clothes and raced down the stairs to the lobby to see about having a nice meal in the main dining room. Fortunately, it was late and the crowds had thinned out. The maitre d' seated them immediately.

Nasha was a simple girl from a simple background and she couldn't help but be awed by the grandeur of the banquet hall. The floor was slate marble and the high, plastered ceilings were supported by thick granite columns. Large, oversized oil paintings depicting western themes adorned the walls every few yards, and ornate chandeliers made from cut glass illuminated the serving area. Not only were the dining room tables solid oak and covered with the finest in linens, genuine silver utensils dressed the place settings and delicate, thin-stemmed glasses stood at the ready. Looking at the prices on the menu, she gasped audibly.

"How can we possibly afford this?" she croaked, afraid that her betrothed had overdone things just to impress her. "My God, Sam, one entree here costs what I make each week at the driver's license bureau! This is too much!" she exclaimed, pushing herself from the table. "Let's get out of here before we embarrass ourselves."

"Sit down!" he commanded with some force. "Everything is okay. Trust me on this."

"I trust you implicitly, but how can we possibly afford to eat in this place?" she interrogated, the timid sweep of her hand encompassing with one motion not only the majestic mountains just outside the door, but also the plush surroundings not inches from her fingertips.

"We can't," Nuit admitted, "but my grandpa left me a few bucks when he died and I didn't spend it all buying you." Up to this juncture, Sam had never revealed much of anything to her regarding the true extent of his wealth, and not wanting to mar the innocence of their relationship with money just yet, he was still hesitant to do so.

"You miss him, don't you?" Nasha asked, knowing how close Sam and the Senator had once been, and how highly Sam had always thought of his grandfather.

"Yes, the old guy taught me a lot."

"You've always been reluctant to talk much about him. Why is that?"

Stammering, Sam thought through his answer, picking each word carefully. "Well, Nasha, it's a complicated story, but it boils down to this: We talked often, the Senator and I, and somewhere along the line he told me what was afoot. With the Chinese supplying arms to support the Amerind uprising, that particular arrangement put me in an awkward position vis-à-vis you."

"How so? I don't understand what you mean," she confirmed making up her mind on what entree to order for dinner.

"Nate was the one responsible for Overlord Mao's death some thirty years ago."

"That would be Overlord Ling's father, wouldn't it?" she verified, her stomach growling from lack of food. "What of it?"

"Because of what my grandpa did to Overlord Ling's father, he and the Overlord were mortal enemies. My dilemma was that since the Amerind Elders had chosen to accept the Chinese as their *allies*, that would, by extension, make Nate their *enemy*. You know how the old saying goes: the enemy of my enemy is my friend. Since Dark Eagle already mistrusted me, I thought it best if I didn't make too much of Nate being my grandfather. I figured you and I would never be permitted to get together if your brother knew Nate and Ling hated each other so." Even as Sam spoke, he lowered his eyes in doubt.

"But my brother *did* know," she replied with some confidence. "He knew who you were and he certainly knew who your brother was."

"My *brother*?" Sam groaned, unsure how well-informed Nasha actually was on the subject. "What does Lester have to do with this?"

"I thought you knew," Nasha remarked in a surprised tone. "Lester was running arms to the Elders."

"I figured as much, but how did *you* find out?"

"Dark Eagle told me."

"How did *he* find out?"

"He dealt with your brother directly on at least one occasion."

"Did Dark Eagle think I was involved?" Sam snapped, a tinge of anger creeping into his voice. "Land's-sakes, did *you*?"

"No," she replied firmly. "He was of the opinion that you were *not* involved. But that made you all the *more* suspicious. Because of your close relationship with Senator Matthews and because of *his* connections to the American military, Tato and Dark Eagle reasoned you might not be Lester's brother at all, but rather a spy sent here to undermine the movement."

"That's preposterous," Sam blurted, glancing nervously

around the restaurant to see whether his outburst had disturbed any of the other patrons. "If you knew about all of this, why the hell didn't you tell me so before?"

"For the same reason you never told me about the girl you were in love with before you met me," she explained matter-of-factly.

"Whaat?" Sam stammered, caught off-guard by her insight.

"Nuit, I'm a woman, I could see it in your eyes."

"But that's ancient history. Whatever I once felt for her is gone now. The only one I love is you," he exclaimed, extending his hands across the table to her.

"I realize that and I love you too, only I had to be sure."

"She means nothing to me now," he insisted.

"I believe you. Are you ready to order yet?"

"Yes, I think I'll have the 'roo," Sam replied, contemplating the vast herds of leaping marsupials which roamed the giant farms of the Australian Outback.

"Red meat is no good for your heart, you know," she intoned, playing the role of overprotective wife.

"Nor is late night sex," he rebutted, "but I plan on having that as well."

"If you insist," she countered, "but it's your turn to be on top, big fella."

Sam was about to toss another taunt her way when the overdue waiter approached the table at a trot. "Hello, my name is Marvin," he began. "I will be your server tonight. May I suggest the house special?" he petitioned with all the pomp and circumstance a man of his station could muster.

Looking at Sam, Nasha giggled like a teenager.

Answering her with a grin of his own, Nuit suddenly realized that their life together would be perfect.

Thirty-eight
Holocaust

Two Months Later

The assault on the garrison north of Winnipeg began after eleven P.M. on a hot and muggy August night. This particular target had been singled out for tonight's raid for the simple reason that all four western provinces drew their ordnance from just this one depot; knock it out and it would be only that much harder for the Canadians to put down the rebellion.

Their faces and hands blackened with charcoal, the strike team made their way cautiously through the forest watching for any signs of the enemy. They were armed to the teeth with megalflares, nitro-projectiles, and dozens of manual firebombs. Creeping silently along the ground from

the base of one immense tree to the next, Running Bear of
the Kwakiuti led the way. This was *his* mission, and he was
confident that if only they could get in close enough, they
would be able to pull this off. From the satellite images the
Chinese had given him last week of the area, they had
developed a rough idea of the compound's layout. Arming
themselves accordingly, Dark Eagle plus three others in the
raiding party were each carrying precisely the right weapon
for the job, the one piece of hardware they could count on
to level the place—a manual firebomb.

Circular at the top like a conventional grenade, the hull
of a manual firebomb was covered with a sheet of plastic. At
the base was a handle five inches long, a handle which
enabled the thrower to hurl the explosive farther and with
greater accuracy than an ordinary grenade. The trick was in
the accuracy and the timing; for once the plastic shield was
removed and the casing of steel-like adhesive exposed to
the air, the bomb itself would adhere instantly to any
surface it contacted. The thrower had only fifteen seconds
from the removal of the plastic covering until the explosion
of the firebomb, so he had to move with dispatch.

Though each step of the operation had been carefully
laid-out beforehand, the attack was an ill-fated venture
from the start. Not only was the Amerind strike force sorely
outnumbered—a fact they knew in advance—there was an
undetected outer ring of security they hadn't bargained on.

As Dark Eagle had been quick to point out to Running
Bear when this mission was first being planned, their team's
principal weaknesses were twofold: one, they were on foot,
and two, without horses or motorized vehicles to support
their effort, they had to carry all of the explosives with them
on their backs. This meant the expeditionary force was by
necessity slow-moving, and when they unexpectedly encountered that outermost ring of Mounties and bio-stallions,

the results were predictable.

To begin with, burdened by their heavy knapsacks, there was little chance for them to outrun the angry horse-men. But it was far worse than that. Since they were operating in an unfamiliar forest at night, there were no garroting wires to chase the attacking Mounties into, nor any safe havens to escape to. Although Dark Eagle had faced such horse-mounted patrols before, it had always been alone, never as part of a group; given the current circum-stances, this was a recipe for slaughter!

Dropping his explosive laden backpack to the ground at the first hint of trouble and yelling to his comrades to do the same, Dark Eagle sprinted across the rough and broken ground ahead of the advancing Mounties, silently pressing himself against the base of a mammoth pine. Hugging the forest floor for dear life, he prayed that, rather than trying to do battle with this squad of heathens on their own turf, the others—his father included—would have enough sense to do as he had done, and drop to the ground. But somehow, amidst the sounds of trampling hooves and bloodcurdling shrieks, he knew a massacre was afoot.

With the air around him on the verge of exploding from the concussion of force guns expelling their deadly shells, and with the ominous glow of lumina-beams passing only inches from his face, Dark Eagle froze like a rock, becoming part of the landscape. To come out of hiding just to be cut down himself, made no sense at all. Better to survive and live to fight another day than to die in a vain attempt to overcome unbeatable odds. Plus, if a second strike force was ever to be assembled to clean up this botched job, someone from *this* contingent had to make it back alive—the Elders had to be warned of the bio-stallions the recon-naissance team had missed.

Though it took nearly an hour, eventually the horrible

screams died away. Even so, for a long time afterwards, Dark Eagle didn't budge, afraid of even drawing a breath. In due time, however, the Mounties moved on, snickering to themselves over how easily they had won the brief skirmish and how seemingly stupid the Amerind invaders were to have attempted this stunt on foot. Listening to their smug laughs, Dark Eagle couldn't help but agree with their assessment of the raid, yet he didn't dare vacate his spot until morning; not only had he lost his bearings in the dark, he wasn't about to leave the strike zone without first knowing what had become of his father.

The dew was thick upon the ground and the mosquitoes thick upon the air when the sun first began to peek above the horizon. Exhausted by a night without sleep, Dark Eagle unfolded his cramped and numb legs and got unsteadily to his feet. Picking up his knapsack from where he had dumped it on the ground during the battle last night, he didn't have to go far before he stumbled over what was left of his father. It was a gruesome sight. Tato's shoulder and left arm were missing. Nothing less than a force gun could do such damage; Tato would have bled to death in a matter of minutes.

Dark Eagle was a warrior, pure and simple, but of all the world's natural disasters, of all the world's possible calamities, nothing could have prepared him for this. Fires, tornadoes, earthquakes, even train wrecks, all paled next to the experience of seeing one's own father lying dead on the ground in a crimson pool of blood. Dark Eagle began to cry.

Kneeling as he was over Tato, his head in his hands, the young Brave did not hear the approach of the Mounties as they combed the woods looking for survivors. By the time he had reacted to their presence, it was already too late.

"Halt!" a brusque voice ordered him from behind. "Don't move, injun, or you're one dead prairie-nigger."

Though Dark Eagle did precisely as he was told, he rapidly calculated the odds for success, dismissing them almost as quickly. Resistance was futile.

"Get up real slow now," the Mountie ordered, cocking his force gun as he spoke.

Rising to his feet ever so deliberately, his arms raised up in the air in the classical pose of surrender, Dark Eagle turned to face his rival, his steely gaze as cold as a mountain glacier. The war had only just begun and already he was prisoner of it!

"WORLD PLUNGES INTO WAR!" the headline screamed at Sam as he sat before the breakfast table reading the paper and picking at his cereal. Instead of being elated by Nasha's news that she was with child, he was depressed. It was finally happening just the way Nate had warned it would.

For centuries, the Canadians and their American neighbors to the south had prided themselves for peaceably sharing the world's longest unguarded border, for generously dividing the immense resources of five great freshwater lakes, for accepting each other's currencies and products without trepidation, and for allowing their citizens to cross freely from one nation to the other without passport or visa. Oh, along the way there had always been a certain amount of friendly rivalry between the two countries, which—because the more industrious Americans enjoyed a higher standard of living, while the more socially conscious Canadians enjoyed cleaner air—had bordered at times on resentment, but as a rule, they had gotten along famously for generations. As a consequence, the swift transformation from bosom buddy to mortal enemy, from ally to hated neighbor, from trading partner to villain, was shocking to even the most vocal of antagonists. And to make matters worse, the issue on which their friendship foundered was not only quite minor in some respects, it also predated the formation of either great nation.

Ten thousand years after traversing the Bering Straits to North America from the west, the nomadic aborigines who first inhabited the New World were subjugated and imprisoned by the Euro interlopers who emigrated there from the east. These pale-faced newcomers were armed with powerful weapons and even more powerful ideas, ideas like private property and manifest destiny, ideas like monotheism and nationhood. Those Amerinds who weren't summarily slaughtered by the Euros' guns or by their diseases were promptly sentenced to spend eternity living on any number of desolate reservations the Euros had been kind enough to set aside for them. Only now, after a seven hundred year-long wait, the native peoples of North America wanted it all back; they wanted their ancestral lands returned, and they wanted a homeland free of their white masters.

In contradiction of the current political realities, the Amerinds of the United States and the Amerinds of Canada joined hands across that great, unguarded border and demanded that a nation of their own be carved out of the midridge of the New World. Huron claims on upstate New York and on portions of Quebec, coupled with Amerind claims to Manitoba and to both the Dakotas, threatened to rip the continent asunder.

Although the American Congress was initially receptive to the idea of an autonomous zone for the aborigines, the ruling French Canadians were appalled by the very thought. Even as the U.S. did essentially nothing to dissuade the Amerind rebels from seeking statehood, the Canadians brutally suppressed their movement back at home. Naturally, the U.S. and its neighbor to the north ended up on opposite sides of the explosive issue.

The test of wills soon catapulted into a war of words

which quickly degenerated into an anxious scramble to arms. Lines were drawn as positions hardened; gruesome acts of terrorism were committed by both sides. Now that the disenfranchised Amerinds had openly forged a security agreement with the Chinese and with other key elements opposing the United States, the backdrop was complete for a ferocious struggle.

Though the value of what Lester had stolen from his grandfather as he lay there dying was rendered partially worthless by the encryption key Nate and Officer Jenkins had added to each code, the book itself was filled with strategically important names and places—installations to be targeted, facilities to be bombed, people to be assassinated. Armed with these priceless secrets, the Chinese met the American threat in the Pacific even as Mexico and her allies pushed north into California and into Texas; the Canadians swept south across the Great Plains states while the Brazilians and others decimated the east coast. No one came to Lady Liberty's aid, and what wasn't destroyed by her enemies in the first round, was consumed by the flames of the civil war which followed shortly thereafter.

Not since the 1860s had a war been waged on American soil, and in the intervening five hundred years precious little thought had been given as to how to protect the American populace against such an eventuality. The people and the infrastructure were unprepared to receive the body-blow which was unleashed against them.

Tanks poured off ships; paratroopers dropped from the skies; biotoxins rained down upon the cities; and guided missiles were flung into the heartland.

The concrete melted. The fields burned. The children bled. The rivers boiled. The forests shuddered. The nation buckled.

Though it would take two years before it was over, what

was once the United States of America was transformed from a land of milk and honey into a desert of deformed scrub brush, and its billion and a half citizens ended up either dead or else scattered to the wind like Samuel Matthews. Never in the history of mankind had there ever been a holocaust to match this one.

Thirty-nine
Autumn

October 2401
A Year after The Great War

Far from the inflection point of the titanic struggle, Sam had submerged himself in his studies, doing the best he could to remain oblivious to the inexorable truth. Though he had tried to deny it on more than one occasion, there was no escaping the fact that by the conclusion of the war, he was the last American. It wasn't so much that there had been no other survivors, only that the few who remained alive no longer identified themselves with that particular nationality.

Even though he had made steady progress towards winning his Ph.D. in the interim, it wasn't an easy life. With Tato dead and Dark Eagle having been detained in a concentration camp until just recently, Nuit had ended up as head of the household, responsible for Nasha, her mother Tona, her sister, and her two younger brothers. Yet, in spite of the hardships and the pain, no single man alive could have been happier to be married than he was.

As luck would have it, Nasha hadn't "caught" that first time as she and Sam originally thought. Perhaps her body wasn't ready to play host to a child yet, or perhaps the strain and anger over the loss of her father had upset her system; in any event, she miscarried shortly after hostilities erupted. Though the delay in getting pregnant weighed heavily on Nasha's mind, for Sam it had been a relief of sorts. Not only did the setback give them plenty of excuses to continue practicing making babies until they got it right (something the two newlyweds pursued with relentless zeal), Sam found sharpening his skills as a lover to be a rather pleasant alternative to the prospect of immediate parenthood. In fact, the war had been over for more than a year when she brought him the good news for a second time.

Though Nasha had been making use of a uterine stabilizer to avoid a second miscarriage, they had made the decision early on not to tamper with Mother Nature by preselecting their newborn's characteristics as was the right and privilege of every married couple their age. Ever since the Human Genome Project was completed four centuries ago, trait-altering prescriptions had been available to allow prospective parents to choose in advance a wide range of physical attributes for their offspring. Indeed, at one time, Designer Genes were all the rage, what with the bright pink vials for popular female traits and the navy-blue vials for highly-prized male traits. Each contained a soft gel laced with a strand of laboratory-engineered DNA capable of replacing a specific physical trait with something more to the liking of the parents. Just prior to ovulation, the woman was to insert the gel high into her vaginal tract, and then, over the ensuing thirty-six hours, the hopeful users were to engage in frequent lovemaking. If the label directions were followed assiduously, the odds were excellent that the preferred gene would "take" while the undesirable one would be sloughed off. Yet, even if the parents blew it and somehow failed to dislodge the offending gene, they could always just simply abort the distasteful fetus, buy another vial, and try again.

Despite the latitude these drugs offered, Nuit and Nasha had judiciously avoided them and for two very good reasons. To begin with, tribal custom deeply frowned upon genetic tampering, and after her father had given his life to further the Amerind cause, Nasha was unwilling to risk sullying the memory of his name by committing such an indiscretion. Of nearly equal importance, however, were the legal constraints imposed by the province of Alberta. According to statute, only legally married couples could be issued a DNA prescription, and in the eyes of the law, Sam and Nasha were never legally married. They had entered into a common-law contract, a contract which was not recorded on the rolls of the district. Thus (though others in their circumstance had done so and gotten away with it), technically they were forbidden from walking into a pharmacy and purchasing a vial of Designer Genes.

It was late autumn now and she was in her fourth month. With her pregnancy now having advanced beyond the danger point of again losing her baby, they had agreed to make a daily walk part of their regular routine. This evening, as they rounded the second loop of their humble, working-class neighborhood, Nasha asked the question which had been vexing her since before they were man and wife.

"Tell me about her," she intoned, her words cutting through the crisp night air like a knife. Except for the sound of her voice, the air was still, the snow on the distant mountains having muffled the noises of the much closer city.

"Who?" Nuit asked absentmindedly, his thoughts a million miles away.

"You know very well who. I don't know the woman's name."

"Must we do this?" he pleaded, not wanting to tell her about his short-lived affair with Agent Logan.

"Not if you can't handle it," she snapped sternly, her face filled with the pain of not knowing.

"It's not so much that," Sam replied, kicking a loose stone across the sidewalk with the toe of his boot, "it's just that I would rather leave the past in the past."

"Suit yourself," Nasha grumbled, a pout on her otherwise pretty face. Between the glow of motherhood in her cheeks, and the cool, fall temperatures painting her nose red, she broadcast a beauty few women could match.

"Okay, already," Sam relented. "She and I spent a couple of nights together, but it meant nothing. My grandfather hired her to be my bodyguard, and then again later, to sneak me across the border into Canada."

"I always wondered how you managed that," she admitted, squeezing his hand as she spoke. "Even in those days, it was mighty difficult."

"Yes," he nodded, his thoughts drifting back to memories of that crossing, to their confrontation with the bear cub, to Sara's dispassionate elimination of the borderguard, to their feverish, almost hungry, interlude that night in the cabin.

Seeing his distant look, Nasha labored to read his mind. "So you thought she was in love with you, but she really wasn't."

"I guess that's right. I was an impressionable young man at the time, and I suppose she overwhelmed me with her female charms. I had never been with a woman before.

Nevertheless, I have never heard from her since. I suppose she's dead now, just like all the rest. It's over."

"Do you still think of her?" Nasha asked as they rounded the next block. Except for the window dressings and the lawn ornaments, every house looked the same. It was as if a giant house-making machine had stamped out one carbon copy after the next. Times were tough and uniqueness was a luxury few could afford. Even so, Nasha and Sam managed. Not only were they happy, they were contented and at peace with one another. "Do you still think of her?" she repeated softly.

"Not often," he replied resolutely. "Was I *your* first?" he cross-examined, turning the tables adroitly.

"What a silly question," she retorted, reddening noticeably. "You know that you were. My first and my only," she added proudly.

"Well, then, the matter is closed," he said, his voice firm.

Nodding her head in agreement even as she snuggled closer to the man she loved, Nasha remarked, "It's too bad about Ravi."

"You mean his banishment?"

"Yes. I liked him."

"Ever since the war ended, this entire country seems to have gone a little mad," Sam commented sadly, thinking back to the demise of his own homeland, to the strange loneliness he sometimes felt now that he was the last of his kind. "These Purist-Opportunity Laws the legislature has passed are obscene. All they do is discriminate against the non-Euros. As far as I'm concerned, Canada is definitely headed in the wrong direction." Pausing for a moment to pick his next words gingerly, he added, "Sometimes I wonder whether we shouldn't be looking for a new place to live."

"You mean leave Alberta?" she yelped, pulling back from him with a horrified look on her face. "How *could* I?

My family lives here, for God's-sake. These are my roots!"
The use of an expletive was so out of character for her, Sam
dared not go on.

"We could *all* leave," Nuit whispered, trembling as he
spoke.

"I won't hear of it," she howled, the tears beginning to flow.

"Don't cry!" he begged, lost as what to do. "I don't know
what I was thinking. Please, Nasha, don't cry. Everything
will be okay. I promise."

Rubbing her hand reassuringly, he quickly changed the
subject. "Now that Ravi's gone, what will become of Siona?"

"I understand she recently bought a suit and will be
moving south shortly."

"A *suit*?" Sam exclaimed flabbergasted.

"You know," Nasha indicated, wiping the tears from her
eyes, "a radiation suit. She's moving south with a group
that's going to try farming someplace called the San Joaquin
Valley. They say the entire region is polluted, that's why
they need the suits."

"That's crazy! It'll be a thousand years before people'll
be able to live in California again. Land's-sakes, why is she
doing it?"

"Without Ravi, she feels her life is over," Nasha related,
wishing she could have done something to console her
friend and keep her from leaving.

"Her life *will* be over if she tries that stunt."

"What would you do if you lost *me*?" Nasha quizzed as
they rounded the final block of their evening stroll. The
electric street lamps had come on and there was a faint halo
around each as the nighttime dew rolled in.

"How could I ever lose you?" Nuit asked, screwing his
face into a frown.

"You never thought you'd lose your grandfather. Or the
United States, for that matter. The unexpected *can* happen,"

she pointed out, reminding him of the hard lessons he had learned: how unpredictable life could be, how CHAOS had a hand in all events big and small. Despite the fact that the slowly unfolding drama of war had multiplied his net worth manyfold, it had been a shallow bliss, and trying to reconcile the loss of so many of his family members and loved ones with the events that had exploded around him had not been an easy task.

To begin with, on the eve of the Great War, there had been the loss of his grandfather to that incurable disease; then, a few months later, came the news of the death of his brother Lester when the Lieutenant's frigate was sunk in the East China Sea; then, when the defenses protecting America's heartland were breached, his good friend Ziggy; and finally, even before the Amerind rebellion could be squashed, Tato. When the peace treaty was finally signed, Sam had unwound his currency positions and moved the proceeds offshore just as Nate had instructed him to do, but there was no great joy in being a multimillionaire in a world gone berserk. To avoid drawing attention to himself or to his great wealth, Sam had insisted the two of them live quite plainly, with him teaching part-time at the university and she working at the driver's license bureau buried in the center of the city. Everything around him was topsy-turvy, and he was grateful for having had the good fortune of finding this fine girl.

Focusing again on the here and the now, Sam answered her as honestly as he could. "I don't know *what* I'd do without you. I suppose it would all depend on the circumstances: how old I was at the time, how old our daughter was."

"How do you know it's going to be a little girl?" Nasha asked, a quizzical look on her face.

"Just a feeling," he smiled back. "Somehow, the name Carina sounds more fitting to me than the name Rigel," he explained, thinking back to the lecture Tato had given them on their wedding day. The Elder had been quite specific in his instructions regarding the selection of their children's names, and Nuit and Nasha intended to honor his wishes.

"Well, listen up, bub. You can't raise a child without a mother, especially not a daughter."

"I'll be the judge of that," Sam insisted as they arrived back at the door of their simple bungalow. "All I can say for certain is this: daughter or no daughter, I just can't see myself setting up housekeeping with anyone else but you. Isn't that what true love is all about?"

Forty
Cleansing

Three Years Later

America, the Great Satan, had been defeated, but at what cost? Even now, four years after the conclusion of hostilities, the rebuilding of Canada had barely begun. Millions were still homeless, millions more hungry. But who was to blame for this outrage? Who should be held culpable for the terrible destruction? The suffering?

It was a sad truth of post-industrial life that when times got desperate and people became miserable, their leaders searched for a suitable scapegoat. Hitler found the Jews; Rontana, the Euros. In the summer of 2404, the French-speaking purists of Canada found the Amerinds. They decreed that Canada's genetic stock should be cleansed, made more white, more Euro. And like every purge of the last millennium, this one began in the government controlled media. For months now, the newspapers and the visicasts had been full of invective. Charge and countercharge. Ugly denunciations. Racial slurs. False accusations.

And as with every case of racial hatred, there was no use trying to figure out what "they" had done wrong because typically "they" had done *nothing* wrong; their only crime was that of being. Nevertheless, once a nation's opinion leaders were able to convince their impoverished subjects to think in terms of good and bad races, good and bad genes, their program of persecution became all that much easier. And so long as it was not your own tribe which was the target of the ostracization, officially sanctioned genocide could actually be rather amusing. Not only did it keep the people from focusing on just how miserable they truly were, it was a great way for the hungry and the unemployed to pass the time. Unfortunately for Sam and Nasha, this was the mood of the nation when they were sucked down into the morass.

Given the tenor of the times, retaining her clerking job in the provincial offices was itself an accomplishment which an Amerind like Nasha could be proud of. Though it was a menial post, it was still a position sensitive enough to warrant a background check, complete with a set of geneprints and a recent photograph. Unashamed of her heritage, Nasha had no hesitation disclosing her genetic stock to the authorities or wearing the lavender identicard which signified by the capital "A" plastered across its face that she was of Amerind, not Euro, stock. Regrettably, once her particulars were etched into the government computer's silicon memory, she—and the thousands of others like her—became easy prey for the fanatics when the purge erupted.

In the beginning, common people like Nasha and Sam

simply did not understand what the controversy was all about, nor how they should prepare for it. Had Sam been wiser or less naive, he might have reacted sooner; had he been more worldly or more in touch with the mood of the country, he might have located a place of safety where the three of them could have fled before the terror struck. Instead, he was so engrossed in his studies and in his teaching, so swept up in loving his wife and his new daughter Carina, that by the time he awoke to the danger, it was already too late.

The terrible nightmare began early in the morning of a searing-hot summer's day. It was the seventh consecutive day with a predicted high exceeding ninety-five degrees, itself an unusual circumstance for Calgary. In keeping with their daily routine, Sam, Nasha, and Carina departed just after sun-up from their unairconditioned flat at the edge of the sprawling metropolis and headed downtown. Though they didn't earn much, between her job and his summer teaching position, they kept themselves in groceries.

Protesting yet another trip into town, Sam's rundown gcar groaned and creaked as they listened off and on to the radio for the early morning news. According to the broadcast, last night in the Amerind ghetto-district—a war zone sandwiched between the gleaming downtown and the unending suburban ring—there had again been sporadic gang-related trouble. Though Sam was eager to learn the details, between concentrating on the rush hour traffic and watching Nasha feed Carina next to him in the front seat of the gcar, he wasn't able to pay much attention to the newscast. Not until after he had deposited Carina with her grandmother Tona for the day and dropped Nasha at the provincial offices where she worked, did he have a chance to turn the radio up louder.

Listening more intently now as he drove on into the

university, his eyes grew wide with disbelief. According to the commentator, there had been a severe bout of street fighting during the night and at least several reported instances of vandalism on the fringe between the Amerind ghetto and the innermost ring of suburbia. Apparently, a gang of drunken Amerind teenagers had hit the streets enraged over an incident the *previous* night in which a Mountie had purportedly shot and killed one of their peers over a trifling.

The temperature and the humidity were clearly getting to everyone, Sam reasoned, his own body already drenched in a pool of sweat as yet another unbearable day of blazing heat took hold. The angry young men prowling the streets were like loose molecules in a very unstable social fluid, a fluid which was clearly on the verge of igniting. It was the meltdown phase of Chaos in action, the phase where tiny perturbations exploded into devastating results. What had his economics professor once told him? For want of a nail, the Kingdom was lost.

As he approached the university, Sam realized that roadblocks had been established at two major intersections and that there were swarms of police sporting military-style helmets and brandishing automatic weapons. Some had force guns and others were sitting astride massive bio-stallions. Sam had never seen so many Mounties together at one time, but not making the connection between the newscast and the police presence, he wondered whether perhaps an important foreign dignitary wasn't expected on campus. Not wishing to get involved, Sam went straight-away to his office and began reviewing the thick pad of notes he had made for his upcoming morning lecture.

Sam's first class was abuzz with news of a confrontation which had occurred on the grounds of the university within the hour. His students related that a mob of hoodlum prairie-niggers had stormed a police barricade, killing two officers and injuring a dozen more in the process. The troopers had responded by cracking a few skulls with their billy-clubs and arresting scores of protestors. There were even unconfirmed reports of deaths among the demonstrators. One piece of gossip had it that a rowdy bunch of Euros had dragged an Amerind girl down into a satrap where she had been raped and murdered.

Sam settled the students down as best he could, but by the lunchbreak, the university was pandemonium. There were stories of bloody face-offs throughout the city and rumors of riots and looting in the financial district where Nasha worked. Alarmed by these developments, Sam tried to call her office on the public comm, but the line was dead and he couldn't get through. Apparently, the violence had spread to the Underneath where the trunk lines were buried, and all the comm-links had been cut. Distraught at not being able to reach his wife, Sam did what he could to suppress his mounting fear, going dutifully to teach his afternoon class. From a roster of seventy-five, only three students showed up for class, and what they reported made him gasp for air.

The Prime Minister had been shot and the assassin was alleged to be a Huron. Fearing an uprising, the Deputy Minister had declared an immediate state of emergency. Ordering the arrest of all Amerinds in the district, especially those in sensitive government posts, the Deputy Minister had issued an edict that the miscreants be held until he discovered the full extent of the conspiracy.

Stunned by this horrible turn of events, Sam prayed that Nasha's job was too inconsequential, that Nasha herself was too unimportant, for busy authorities to even bother with her. Still, not wanting to leave anything to chance, Sam acted. Promptly dismissing class, he raced down the hall at top speed determined to rescue his Nasha from this nightmare before it was too late.

Outside the lecture hall, he was engulfed by a mob of frantic students. The heavy, humid air made him nauseous, and for a moment, Sam was lost as to what to do. Unable to get to his gcar, unable to raise Nasha on the comm, unable to flag a taxi or even board a bus, Sam did the next best thing he could think of: he began making his way on foot along the twenty plus blocks to the provincial offices where they had first met.

Due to the crush of the throng, it was slow going, and with the constant wail of sirens blaring in the distance, he grew more and more panicked with each block. The closer he drew to the marble-columned edifice, the more often he was passed by paddy wagons filled with bloodied prisoners. It was unnerving.

The granite steps leading up to the courthouse were thick with uniformed guards, and it was obvious from the commotion outside that no one was being permitted to enter or leave the palatial building without prior clearance. Just as he was about to cross the street to inquire as to the whereabouts of his wife, Sam was suddenly approached from behind by a Mountie perched atop a sleek-coated bio-stallion.

"You there!" the officer yelled, his force gun held out in front of him like a cattle prod.

The voice was strangely familiar and when Sam turned to face the speaker, the large man briefly raised his visor as if to say it was okay.

Sam was at once elated and depressed. Elated because Big Frank wouldn't dare arrest a fellow fraternity brother; depressed because Frank knew Sam was married to an Amerind. For a moment, Sam's heart sank as he feared the worst; then his former pledgemaster spoke.

"Get the hell away from here, Sam! If I can find her and

save her, I will; if I can't, then she's done for and at least I will have saved you. Now git!"

Without saying so much as a thank you, Sam did as he was told, melting into the crowd with just one thing in mind—reaching his baby daughter before the police could fan out and arrest every Amerind in the land. As his pace quickened, he thanked God that Carina had been birthed at home and that he and Nasha had had a common-law marriage—maybe, just maybe, the authorities wouldn't know about the baby!

Praying that the lunacy unfolding around him in the usually tranquil downtown hadn't yet exploded out into the megalopolis' tentacle-like suburbs where Carina was staying with her grandmother, Sam dropped his satchel of books to the ground and loosened his tie. Accelerating his stride first to a trot and then to a run, he sprinted one city block after the next, oblivious to the mind-crushing heat which rose up to meet him from the concrete. It was imperative now that he get to Carina before the tidal wave of hysteria sweeping over the entire country drowned his daughter along with his wife.

"Nuit, that is the third time you have asked me the same question in the past ten minutes," Dark Eagle scolded, addressing Sam by his tribal name. They had both arrived at grandma Tona's house within a half hour of one another and were each anxiously awaiting word of Nasha's whereabouts. So many of their friends and associates had been rounded up already, both men were in a state of shock. Rumors in the Amerind community were that the authorities had already started shipping the prisoners to gene-extinction camps on the North Slope. These horrible places were little more than torture chambers dotting the frozen tundra above the Arctic Circle.

"Well, if it's the third time I've asked you the same question in the past ten minutes, then why won't you give me a straight answer?" Sam snapped, clearly on edge. His shirt was stained under the arms and around his collar with dark, grimy splotches of sweat. Though dusk was fast approaching, it was still beastly hot outside.

"Nuit, I don't know *when* we will hear...or even *if*," Dark Eagle replied somberly. "All I can tell you for sure is this: anyone who is able, is leaving the city as quickly as possible."

"Leaving?!" Sam quizzed confusedly. "Land's-sakes, Brother, where are they *going*? Where will they hide?" His voice became shrill as a note of desperation crept into it. "First America, now Canada," Sam croaked. "Is there no safe place in this whole goddamned world? How can this be happening?"

"Damnit, Nuit, get ahold of yourself!" Dark Eagle ordered, his dark eyes fierce with passion. "It *is* happening. People *are* dying. Even as we speak. Still, we must save as many of our tribesmen as we can."

"I can't leave her like this," Sam pleaded at the verge of tears, his mind flashing back over the few short years they had had together, the joys and the sorrows, the triumphs and the failures. "She's my wife!"

"She's my sister," Dark Eagle murmured matter-of-factly.

"Then you of all people must see how I feel," Sam insisted, his guts churning inside.

"I do," the Brave answered, "I do. But Nasha will die *twice* if you do not save her baby."

"Twice?!" Sam exploded with fury. "For Chrissake, Dark Eagle, she hasn't even died *once* yet!"

Pressing his hands to his eyes, Sam collapsed sobbing in the nearest chair. Nasha's mother Tona came to him from the other room where she had been tending to the baby and wrapped her fragile arms around his quivering shoulders. It was perhaps the first time she and he had ever made physical contact. It made him feel good.

Dark Eagle lowered his eyes and shook his head sadly. He spoke in a slow and even voice. "No one will survive the gene-extinction camps, Sam. And if we are still here when they come looking for us, *we* will die too."

"Where shall we go?" Sam questioned, grateful for the old lady's comforting arm. "My homeland is *already* a cinder."

"I know a man—Running Bear of the Kwakiuti—I should be able to arrange passage with him so that you, the baby, and my mother can reach the coast by coal-burner," Dark Eagle explained with unexpected directness. "Not only did you keep watch over my family while Tato and I went off to war, thanks to you, that little girl with the damaged heart was saved. Chrissy was one of us, remember? Now, it's high time the tribe repaid your generosity by returning the favor."

"And you?" Sam asked with deep concern. "What about you? What about the rest of the family?"

"I can no longer worry about myself," Dark Eagle replied stoically, his jetblack hair seeming darker than ever. To hear him speak and to watch him move, Sam imagined that if his tribe survived this latest upheaval, he would someday take Tato's place on the Council of Elders. "When faced with genocide, the word 'I' loses all meaning. Today there is only we."

"What does *that* mean?" Sam probed anxiously. It sounded to him like some sort of final farewell. "Have you forgotten? The rebellion was put down! The war is over!"

"I shall fight again," Dark Eagle boomed defiantly. "I have fought before; I will fight again."

"Fight?" Sam asked, shaking his head in disbelief as he got to his feet. "You? *Alone*?"

"No, not me alone," Dark Eagle replied. "There will be

others—thousands of men and women are gathering along the river north of Banff. Straight Hawk was right: we will make the mountains our stronghold. The mountains have fresh game, clean water, and plenty of timber; everything we need to survive. We will strike at our enemies from there. We will fight until the last one bleeds his last drop of blood."

"Why can't I join you?" Sam offered, somehow feeling responsible for Dark Eagle's plight.

"Thank you, brother Nuit, but this is not your fight. We don't want you."

"I see," Sam declared sadly, resigning himself to leaving what was left of his adopted family behind. "Will the three of us be safe once we reach the coast?"

"No!" Dark Eagle roared, his black eyes fierce again. "You must not stay in Canada! This whole country is about ready to tear itself apart," he advised darkly. "When you get to Vancouver, go directly to the harbor and buy yourself passage on a freighter bound for the Hawaii Free State. Sneak on board if you have to, but take Tona and take Carina and get as far away from here as fast as you possibly can."

Epilogue

The coastline had long ago faded from view and all that remained now were the warm waters of the Pacific surrounding him on all sides as far as the eye could see. Staring dejectedly out across the placid sea, his eyes brimming with tears, Sam lingered there on the freighter's sun-drenched deck. He was drinking from the cork-topped water bottle he had been given yesterday when the three of them had first come onboard. His brow was creased in thought as he struggled to comprehend where a story with such a sad ending could have begun.

Had running away been the right thing to do? Or would Nasha have wanted him to stay and fight alongside Dark Eagle and the others? Unfortunately, Nuit could never know the answer to that question.

Had profiting from the war been worth the price? Or should he have used some of his considerable resources to aid in the Amerinds' cause? Sam would never know the answer to that one either.

Would the wars never end? What about the wanton killing? The persecution? Was a lasting peace impossible? Was it beyond mankind's capacity, just as Ziggy had contended that day out on the beach? Or was there a chance?

Though the questions kept on coming and coming, the answers continued to elude him. Sam couldn't get over how his life had been torn apart, and as he stood there contemplating the cork stopper in his hand, he wondered whether he would ever again find a land of safe refuge, a place he could call home.

In his pocket was a scrap of paper. On it he had written an eleven digit alphanumeric code. Though it had been years since his grandfather had instructed him to set up a no-name, numbered account at the Lihue branch of the Chamberlain Bank, Sam had not forgotten. Perhaps he could trace the account number through the bank back to its rightful owner. Perhaps the owner was a distant cousin or a family ally he could turn to in this brave new world he was headed for. At the very least, the bank ought to be able to direct him to a place the three of them could stay until he found them permanent lodging. It would be a start anyway.

Even as he leaned out over the rail of the ship tossing tiny pebbles into the sea and downing the last of his ration of distilled water, Sam remembered standing in the camp-fire bowl that day feeling the same sense of loss, the same sense of hurt, of emptiness. Few men could endure such pain; fewer still the sadness, the sorrow.

First, the Fates had taken Na-Cha-Tan from him, then, in rapid succession, Sara and Nate and Ziggy; now they had taken Nasha from him as well. It was like paradise lost; all he had left to hold onto now was Carina. Not since he had been forced to say goodbye to his beloved camp had he ever hurt so badly. And again he found himself struggling to put his feelings down on paper, to achieve closure as it were, to pick up the pieces from his old life and go on to his new. He wrote:

> Like ripples on a pond, most memories melt swiftly away.
> Others linger like a footprint in wet snow, their fleeting essence hardened by the night, yet dissolved again by the stern light of day.
> The best few remain resolute, like a mountain, their mark steadfast against the crushing erosion of time.
> My memory of you, sweet Nasha, shall always be granite.

Folding his missive ever so deliberately, he slid it carefully down into the neck of the empty flask. Jamming the cork tightly into place behind it, he tossed the tiny vessel into the waves beneath him.

For a long while, he watched it bob up and down in the water. Then the bottle disappeared from view.

Tona approached with Carina in hand. Though the little girl had been walking for some time now, today her steps were uncertain as she negotiated her way across the rolling deck of the ship. Sam took his daughter and held her against his chest. She grabbed playfully at the whiskers of his unshaven face and stuck her fat little fingers into his mouth. Waiting for him to bite down gently, she pulled her fingers away at the very last moment. He smiled.

Though the last American had lost everything else in his life that mattered, he had not lost hope. Sam knew that so long as he was alive, the spirit that was America could not die; that so long as he kept her memory alive, there was still a chance for the future.